LOVE AT SECOND SIGHT

LOVE AT SECOND SIGHT

SZ.LAIBA

sz.laiba

To all the lovely girls that had a 'him.'
This book is for you.

<u>**Trigger Warnings**</u>
Emotional/physical child abuse
Trauma
Mild racism
Mental health
Panic attack

Playlist

Ya Adheeman | Ahmed Bukhatir | 4:00

Taweel Al Shawq | Ahmed Bukhatir | 6:06

The Way of the Tears | Muhammad Al Muquit | 4:25

Wedding | Muhammad Al Muquit | 2:58

The Beauty of Existence | Muhammad Al Muquit, Hamoud Al Qahtani | 4:20

Mustafa Jaan E Rehmat | Atif Aslam | 5:07

الله يعلم | Abdulaziz Alrashed | 1:06

أشتكي لله مني | Mansour Alkulaifi | 2:50

ACT 1

I

There was so much I liked about you.
Your smile.
Your voice.
The way you spoke.
Everything about you.

2

"I am indeed near. I listen to the prayer of every suppliant when he
calls on Me."
- Surah Al—Baqarah [2:186]

The best place to be during any time of any season is in a cafe. It's always warm and cozy here and it's typically quiet— especially in the mornings. There's always something being freshly made, hence the amazing smell. I used to come here a lot during my breaks or to finish work when I was in university, from when it opened to when it closed.

The cafe's filled with floor-to-ceiling windows and during daytime hours, on sunny days, the floors and walls are flooded with rays of sunlight.

I felt I could melt at that sight.

However, today, nothing at all in this cafe could make me happy once I heard those two words: *public speaking.*

"You want me to speak in front of hundreds of people? Are you in your senses?"

Ever since I released this book a couple of weeks ago, I haven't been able to have a single day of peace.

In front of me sits Elena, my astounding Italian editor, who also happens to be my manager, and one of my closest friends. She wants to discuss promotions. She wants me to speak in front of an audience. I, of all people, am probably the worst to ask for such an act. I can't speak without stumbling over words or without my legs trembling violently, as if they're going to buckle beneath me at any moment.

"Oh, come on, Huma. Don't you think you're being a little dramatic?" Elena asks.

"No. In fact, I think you being in charge of me should mean that you should also be the one to promote my book," I suggest. "That way more people would notice you, and we could get over this dumb book promotion."

She shakes her head disapprovingly as I lift my coffee mug off the table and take a sip. I watch as she pulls out a file labeled *promotions* from her minimalistic tote bag. She opens it up and examines the pages.

This book. The whole idea of it sounded good to me until I published it.

And don't get me wrong, I'm proud of myself to have the privilege of getting my book released at the ripe age of 24– especially as a hijabi– but parts of me think about the overall motive of the book. The thought process and where it came from.

Elena knows why I wrote this book. Elena knows the purpose of this book. Deep down, I sometimes regret it. Deep down, this book was quite a vulnerable move for me to make. I never thought in a million years that I would go as far as to write a book about some guy from high school.

She sighs and switches her gaze to me.

"Fine then. We can discuss book talks later. Right now, *you* need to focus on signing copies for your readers. You can go live if you'd like on any of your platforms and answer a couple of questions while signing books for your readers. How's that?"

I set the mug down and adjust myself on the couch, "I guess I could do that."

A bright smile forms on Elena's face, "Great! That's all you'll have to do today."

Great. I'm going to take a nap when I get home.

"Oh, and one more thing," she stops me. "You should choose which influencers you want to give the book to. It would help promotions a lot. Plus, you get a lot of reviews and feedback."

"Are we supposed to make a list now?"

Elena looks at the time, "It's only 3. We could spend an hour or two on the list and call these people to see if they're up to it."

I nod my head.

After creating a catalog of people and calling them up, we have six confirmed at the moment, and another twelve yet to be confirmed. Elena said she could add to the list later tonight, and I told her I could text her a couple of people whenever I thought of someone new.

"Okay, last thing," Elena exhales.

"There's more?!"

"Just one more thing."

She opens up the *promotions* file again, but this time pulls out an entire paper. She glides her eyes over it and before placing it in front of me. I take it into my hands gently, careful not to crease the edges.

It's a detailed document about how to prepare for an event and the expectations and terms I must follow in order to maintain a well-executed reputation.

I notice her face drop to a more serious expression as I place the sheet back down on the table.

"What is this?"

"I know you don't like public speaking, but this is an amazing opportunity to promote—"

I don't let her finish and shoot up from the couch.

"Oh God no. I'm gonna embarrass myself," I grab my bag, ready to leave.

Whenever Elena mentions something that requires talking in front of an audience, I panic. In most cases like this one, I would have left, but I'm trying to fix that. I've realized that maybe running away from my problems isn't the best thing to do. Eventually I'll have to face my problems one on one.

But I can start that tomorrow. *Yup.* Tomorrow sounds like a good plan!

"Huma, please, listen to me. You only have to say a couple of very, very brief things about your book. That is all. From then on, I'll take over like you want me to," she explains, maintaining a calm tone. "It's a great opportunity to get your book out there and let people know you're willing to talk about it."

"But I don't want to talk about it," I reply, quickly.

She aligns the papers and stacks them over each other, gently placing them back into their respective places.

Elena is quite admired for her character. She's always calm and composed in these types of situations. Not to mention how well she fits her personality. The way she dresses professionally and always appears so put-together.

Hiring her is one of the best things I've ever done.

But right now, I'm too nervous to give in to her charms.

She stands up and grips my shoulders with enough force that I could wiggle out of her hold if I wanted to.

But I don't.

"Just give it some thought, Huma. It's in a couple of weeks and, again, would be a great opportunity for you."

I smile vigorously, and give her a quick hug.

"Well, I think I should head out then. I'll text you tomorrow or later tonight about tomorrow's schedule. Sound good?"

"Yes."

"Great."

She leaves.

I don't.

I freeze in place at the thought that I may have to talk about my book in front of strangers. People that may be seeing me for the first time.

First impressions.

I can't do first impressions.

I'll disappoint everyone.

3

I unlock the door to my home feeling hungry and tired. I haven't eaten anything since this morning, other than the cup of coffee I had at the cafe.

I step inside and take off my shoes.

"Finally, you're home."

I set my bag down and see Aaliyah in the kitchen warming up something that appears to be leftovers in the microwave. This is my best friend. My whole entire family and I love her. And we also happen to live together. The decision was very hard for my parents to make when I asked them if I could move out. However, after quite a bit convincing, they gave in.

"Yep. Here I am," I exhale.

She looks at me with an arched brow.

"What?"

"Why do you look like that?" She asks.

I roll my eyes, "Okay, I might be tired, but that was offensive."

She laughs, "You want leftovers?"

With a quick nod, I head into the bathroom.

...

I direct my steps towards my room after taking a relaxing shower and talking to Ami for a nice hour. I throw on a baggy hoodie to cover up my hair while I set up my phone for the live. I get a couple of pens and move the boxes of books closer to me as I press the live button.

To my surprise, people start rolling in fast.

I smile and wave, "Hi guys."

Comments start flooding in with excited greetings as I take out one of the books from the boxes and place it on my lap.

Being in front of a camera and knowing people are watching me is much different than standing and speaking in-person in front of people I can see. I'm much more confident when I'm alone, rather than having strangers stare into my soul as I speak.

Another bonus: I don't have to stand.

I sign the first copy with ease and place it in a separate, empty box.

I look up at the screen and read.

"What is 'Splintered Heart' about?" I clear my throat. "It's about a girl falling in love with her guy best friend from high school. There are scenes of *our— their* relationship. How they met, how they got to know each other, and the effect that had on the main character after she graduated."

I feel out of breath. Not because of how much I spoke, but because of *him.* He makes me so angry. I hope wherever he is, he doesn't remember. Everything I said in my book is only the truth. The way he made me feel. The way I cried when he left. The way I never forgot him.

My story has a sad ending. Not every story is going to be happy, but God— writing the book was damaging. There were countless nights of just trying to understand where everything went wrong. Of course, the whole idea of being friends was wrong, but I never thought it could get as bad as it did. Trying to understand the severity of things and how I couldn't throw all the blame on him was crazy. I just hoped that he was okay. That after what he went through in high school only made his future better. It was relieving for me, too. Letting parts of him go. I just never thought that something as simple as being friends could be so painful.

I wish I never met him.

I read another question out loud.

"I got the inspiration from someone I met in high school," I smile.

What a great way to promote, huh?

Soon, the signed-books are piling up into the box and the first box is almost finished.

I sigh.

"I think I might call it a night, guys. I'll try my best to do another live soon, though. Bye!" I wave at the camera before shutting it off.

I force myself up onto my feet and head into the kitchen to retrieve my leftovers that are now cold.

"You were in there for a long time," Aaliyah says from the couch as I throw the haleem into the microwave to be reheated.

"I was?" I ask, almost as if I'm questioning myself.

I check the time and, sure enough, it's ten.

I join Aaliyah on the couch after squeezing a little too much lemon into my food.

"How was work?" I ask.

She takes a second to reply, "It was good. A couple of people came in to buy your book."

Aaliyah works at a bookstore. She's the manager, actually, thanks to her dad who gave the store to her and decided to retire soon after. Lucky for her, a majority of aspiring and prevailing authors strive in an attempt to get their book into her store. And Aaliyah, being the sweetheart she can be sometimes, decided to place my book into her store before I could even ask.

I nod my head slowly.

The TV's playing *Spider-Man: Far From Home.*

"You should've told me you wanted to watch Spider-Man. I would've brought some popcorn on my way home from the cafe," I grin.

She returns the look, "How was the meeting with Elena anyway?"

I play back everything, shivering at the parts where she asked me to do anything else other than sitting and listening to her speak.

"She wants me to talk about my book in front of people—"

"Oh my God, that's amazing! Please tell me you said that you'd do it," she interrupts.

I press my lips together, looking away.

What am I meant to tell her? *'I told Elena I don't wanna do it because I suck at speaking in english?'* She'll slap me. That wouldn't be a good enough excuse.

I unpause the movie and try to watch without looking back at her. Unfortunately, Aaliyah grabs the remote and pauses it again.

I stand up.

"You know what— I'm feeling quite tired today. I should probably head to bed—"

Aaliyah pulls me down by my arm, pinching my side.

"Okay, ow!"

"No. You don't get to feel hurt. Now you're gonna meet up with Elena tomorrow, and you're gonna tell her that you'll do it."

I click my tongue, rolling my eyes at the same girl who can barely complete everyday tasks without complaining.

"No! I'm not going to embarrass myself!"

She slaps her forehead, "Huma, you're not gonna die! I'll make sure of it!" she says.

I've known Aaliyah since grade one. Our moms met and became

friends almost instantly, which led to us being introduced to each other.

We had our ups and downs, and quite a lot at that. Throughout elementary school, we had fights where we literally wouldn't talk at all. We didn't get that close until high school. By then, we talked every single day. We were inseparable.

And now, here we are.

She was also one of the first people I told about Elias.

Her face lights up all of a sudden and it scares me.

"Are you scared Elias is gonna be there? When you're speaking? Are you scared he might be there watching you?"

My eyes go wide wondering how she possibly thought about such an outcome. I mean, sure, it was entirely possible...but how? If Elias showed up, I don't think I would have the ability to speak. He would be listening to me talk about a book about him. A book about him and I. Just us two. What if he remembered? What if he put all the pieces together and realized who I was? Or what if he didn't? What if, after everything I wrote in the book, he couldn't even hark back to it? I think that would be worse. That would mean he didn't think I was memorable enough to keep in his brain while I let him rip into my heart like an idiot.

Everytime I try to get over him, he's there again in a matter of seconds. He never leaves my foolish heart for too long. If I'm happy, he's still at the back of my mind. If I'm sad, he's right there— one of my top thoughts.

And whenever I think deeply about it, I think about what I would say to him if I could go back in time. To tell the truth, I still don't know what to say. I'm not sure my heart could take rejection if I had told him how much I liked him. But I don't know if this is the state to be in either. I tried focusing on myself, tried everything there is to try. The girls and guys make it look so easy. Some of them are used to this. Used to breakups. But I don't know if I could ever get over what he did to me.

I had other crushes from time to time after he left, but they were nothing like him.

He talked to me *first*. He was polite and nice to me. *He was Muslim.*

The first time I saw him was probably the moment I developed a crush on him. I got a good look at him. He was several inches taller than me, maybe 5"9, maybe 5"10. His hair parted in the middle, messy with random curls and waves. I told Aaliyah. I told her and didn't want to stop telling her. I just wanted to keep talking about him. I looked forward to math every single day after that and I hate that subject with my life to this day.

I snap out of my thoughts.

"Why the hell would Elias be there?" I ask.

She raises an eyebrow at me, "I know you're thinking about him. I know you so badly want him to be there."

I rub my eyes, getting up from the couch and walking slowly to my room. "I'm going to sleep a little early today."

"You still like him a lot— I know it!" She calls after me.

"Good night to you too, Aaliyah!"

I step over the piles of boxes of books and plant face first into my bed.

I won't think about him. I'm not wasting my time thinking about someone who probably doesn't even remember my face, let alone my name.

No.

I won't think about him.

4

"Indeed, Allah will not change the condition of a people until they change what is in themselves."
- Surah Al—Ra'd [13:11]

A couple of days later

I hold my breath as I wait for the makeup artist to come. I woke up awfully early today because I was so anxious about this stupid public promotion thing. The more I think about it, the more I regret agreeing with Elena. I try to repeat her words in my head.

Just a couple of things, and then I get off the stage. Just enough to convince the audience that my story's worth producing as a movie.

I hear footsteps coming to the room.

Through the mirror, a hijabi not too much older than me smiles. She wears a blue-grey, collared shirt tucked into high waisted loose jeans. She could probably pull off a trash bag if she wanted to.

I begin silently panicking again as I remember I have to be on stage in a couple of hours. Even in school, when we did group pre-sentations, I would do all the research work and read the slide with the least amount of information just so I would not have to speak too much. Individual presentations...don't even get me started. They were worse than terrible. Legs shaking, tripping over words, nervous laughter– anything that could result in my embarrassment– I did.

"You're Huma, right?"

"Yes," I smile back at her.

"Great! So, what look are we going for today?"

Elena and Aaliyah both told me to do whatever I want, but what help was that? I stare at myself in the mirror.

Considering I wouldn't be up there for too long, I don't want to be too fancy.

"Could we go casual…?"

"Sure!"

She gets started on me right away. She begins with a thin layer of foundation and moves along with blush. My mind starts to wander, trying to remember if there is anything I'm forgetting when I recall what I'm supposed to be wearing.

And then I realize I forgot my clothes at home. With a hopeful yet nervous laugh, I open my mouth. "Did Elena tell you what I'm supposed to wear?" I ask.

"She told me to let you pick an outfit," she replies, applying the third coat of mascara onto my lashes.

In these past few days, I've tried to convince myself it's all worth it. I called my parents and told them everything, and they said they would be there. So, if I don't do it for myself or the book, I might as well do it for my parents.

Story writing— whether it be published or not— has always been like therapy for me. I've tried to write in diaries, but unfortunately it didn't go as well as I planned. I think every girl goes through a stage where she keeps a diary with her. But for me, after a while, I forgot about the diary as a whole.

Now I sit here with an opportunity of a lifetime.

"Do you have anything in mind? On what you might want to wear?"

I scan my brain for the outfits I have at home since I'm at my last resort of choices. I'm going to wear a suit. The question is which one and where exactly I'm going to find one because all my clothes are at home and I doubt I have enough time to go home and get to Galaxy Entertainment on time.

She brushes my nose and cheeks with what appears to be a rosy-pink shade of blush.

"So, do you have any outfits in mind?"

"Yes. I was planning to wear a suit, but I would have to get it from home," I laugh, hoping she realizes I'm totally not in a frenzy at the moment.

"Oh, you don't have to do that. I also do wardrobe sometimes, so I have a couple of outfits if you'd like to see them."

"Oh my God. Thank you, that would be great!"

...

I end up choosing an elegant lilac shade for my suit and, let me tell you, the colour is to die for. The hue of lilac purple looks absolutely stunning. I pair the suit with a simple white under shirt that I tuck into the pants and a white hijab. I thought of going with a similar purple shade for my hijab, but balancing the white really put it together.

The makeup artist who I just found out is named Suja, decided she wanted to replace the black winged eyeliner with white eyeliner, which I was all for.

By the time we're finished completely, I have about twenty-five minutes before I have to get on stage. I thank Suja for all her help and quickly leave to head to Galaxy Entertainment.

I call Elena while I drive over to the office building.

"How much longer?" She asks.

My eyes dart to the GPS and then back to the road ahead.

"Five minutes— I'm almost there," I reply.

While I drive, I make an effort to recall if I'm forgetting any-thing. I have my phone, wallet, keys, my white heels, which I would switch into before leaving the car, and my...oh my God. When I stop at the intersection, I bolt my neck to look at the passenger seat, searching my bag for my script.

Oh God, oh God. I actually forgot it.

I forgot my script.

Now, this isn't totally terrible since I spent all of this week rehearsing and memorizing the paper, but I know the second I step onto the stage, I'm going to forget everything.

"Huma, are you still there?"

I snap out of it, registering that Elena is still on call and take a deep breath.

"Elena," I press my lips together.

"Mhm?"

I don't know whether I should tell her or not. I'm also unsure if my life will be on the line if I *do* tell her because she doesn't need anymore stress on her plate.

I take a deep breath before responding, "I'll be there in two minutes."

"Okay, hon, I'll see you inside then."

She ends the call while I search for a parking spot.

"Alright," I exhale. *"I just have to talk a little bit about my book. A very summarized version of it— that is it. Even if I forget everything, it's okay because I wrote the book."*

Except I don't remember anything. The stress has already made its grand entrance and now I'm spiraling in a crowded parking lot.

I park my car not too far from the building since I'm in a rush and do not plan on tripping on my way there.

I knock on the back door that has *'Staff Only'* plastered on it just as Elena throws the door open a little too fast, almost hitting me smack-dab in the face.

"Elena!"

"Oh sorry! But, oh my God, you look absolutely gorgeous. Your parents are going to love this!"

I smile at her as she leads me towards the dressing room. I don't need to change, but the staff need to help me set up my mic which places me in an awkward position as I stand there, waiting for instructions on what to do next.

The tension from earlier, from this week and from when Elena first introduced this event to me is slowly creeping back in a huge wave. The little moment of panic in the car was apparently only a warm-up because right now I can feel the intensity under my skin while they adjust the mic onto my blazer.

Elena comes into the room and begins explaining what to expect when I step onto the stage.

"There's going to be a lot of people in the crowd, but don't be overwhelmed. You have to remember they invited *you* to hear about your story. They want to hear this and what you have to say. Your story caught their eye because it's interesting and they liked it."

I continuously nod my head as I notice the copy of my book in her hands.

I wrote this book and these people wanted to hear me talk about it.

She hands me the book and leads me to the stage stairs after the staff adjusted the mic on me.

My heart is pounding. It's racing so hard in my chest I can't think straight. I begin walking up the steps closer to the stage. With every step, my heart beat increased.

In'Sha'Allah everything will go well.

That's all I can repeat in my head.

I wait for the hostess to say my name while I recite my speech...but

I cannot bring myself to focus. My hands are getting sweaty, making it harder to grip onto the book and I hate every second of it.

"Huma," I hear.

I turn around to see Aaliyah standing beside Elena.

"Breathe," she says.

I nod my head and give her a thumbs up. I take a breath. Another one. And one last one as I hear my name being called out loud.

I hear clapping, and, before I know it, I'm standing up on the stage.

Bismillah.

5

I'm awoken at the dead of night by the screaming of my phone. Buzzing. Shaking. Beeping. I try to ignore it, but whoever the hell is calling me at this unholy hour wants me to pick up desperately.

I turn over, annoyed and pick up the phone.

"Hello?"

It's Elena.

"Is everything okay, Elena?" I ask.

The last time Elena called me at this time, it was to tell me someone bought my book. That was the very first purchase for my book and I practically woke up the entire complex with the way I screamed.

"I need you to meet me at the cafe in the morning— I have great news!"

I smile a little, closing my eyes. "Oh? What is this *'great news'?*"

"You'll see tomorrow," Elena replies, ending the call before I can spit out another word.

I place my phone on the dresser and cover my face with my hands, excitement taking over.

Imagine the possibilities.

There are so many things in my mind, but I push everything aside for this book. Then a dreadful thought hits me; *What if Elias found my book?*

Surely not. He couldn't have. He basically disappeared after high school. I need to stop imagining him in my head. Him and I would never happen even with the unrealistic possibility that we would ever see each other again.

But why was he so comforting, and yet so annoying at the same time? The memories of him make me want to cry, but they also make me want to remember him forever. I want to forget him. I still wish I hadn't met him, but why was it that if I saw him again, I'd want to talk to him? Minus the hurt and pain— just the happy parts. Just the parts that had my heart smiling from the inside.

As I'm about to doze off, I hear the Adhan on my phone go off.

It's Fajr.

I get out of bed to pray, returning to my warm mattress after I'm done. I zone out, letting myself drown in the endless void that is my mind.

...

I'm up a little later than I should've been, excited to hear what Elena had in store to tell me. I say bye to Aaliyah as I rush through the door and to the cafe.

Elena's eyes instantly meet mine and she waves me over. I seat myself in my usual seat, setting my bag down and ordering a coffee when the barista comes over.

"You look happy," Elena comments.

My smile only grows, "I hope whatever you have to tell me is just as exciting as you made it seem over the phone."

Her signature bag is with her again, teasing me with what she might pull out this time.

But, just as expected, the *promotions* folder is looking me straight in the eye. "Okay...are you ready for this?!"

I have never seen Elena this excited so what she has to say is probably better news than my first book being purchased. I feel my leg shaking from the tension.

"So, I was answering a bunch of emails— you know, companies wanting to have your book in their store— but then I crossed over this industry. They're called *Galaxy Entertainment* and they have some of the most hit movies in the world. Their actors and actresses are well known too, and they wanted you to speak out about your book in front of them to discuss a possible movie for your book."

I sit there, stunned. Speechless.

"You're kidding..."

At this point, my leg is shaking violently, to say the least, and I'm sweating profusely. My heart feels like it might burst out of my chest and fall right into my hands and I simply cannot breathe. All the oxygen is sucked up by a single breath I take. I just look at Elena, who's smiling wide.

I feel like my body is slowly freezing bit by bit because when I try to stand, I nearly fall back down. I pull Elena into the tightest hug possible.

"Oh my God, you're actually kidding. My brain can't process this, Elena," I gasp for air.

She laughs lightly, watching me talk my nonsense.

"I love you! This wouldn't have happened if it weren't for you and your amazing editing and motivation skills."

"I'm just doing my job, darling. Don't thank me."

"But I have to. You are literally the best." I go in for another hug.

After the excitement and joy is partially over to the point where

I can finally sit down without bursting into tears, we discuss the rest of the work left to do.

"Okay. Now that we've got the most important thing off to the side, we need to discuss how this will be arranged."

"Okay..."

"I know you may hate me for this but I must ask," there's a dramatic pause before she continues. "Have you thought the public speaking through? You wanna give it a shot?"

I sigh.

With happiness there comes a price to pay. This specific price, I could not afford. And from everything from a book signing to going live, this was what I had to do. Speak in front of people. In front of strangers.

"Is there no other option at all?" I ask.

She closes the file.

"There really isn't, Huma. This is the chance for you to show off your story for how amazing it is," she starts. "Plus, the audience aren't strangers. They're actors, actresses, and directors. All these people. All you need to do is be confident."

Here we go again.

"If I do this, if I say a couple of sentences about my story, I'll be fine?"

She nods her head slowly, "Precisely."

I let out a deep breath, trying to contain the rising panic inside me. This was just a small price to pay for something life-changing. I could finally show off to all of the aunties who talked behind my back about how majoring in English would result in me becoming a failure. If you love and admire the subject, then the conversation with others should not be about how this subject will make you a failure. Every subject is a subject because it holds some type of importance. They wouldn't exist if that weren't true. I wish I could explain that to people who like to undermine others for not taking "as complicated of a major as them."

Those people need serious help if they believe that.

I force myself to look at Elena. "Okay, I'll do it."

She smiles softly and I see her relax a little.

I didn't know I stressed her out this much.

"If this works out, you could direct your very own movie. You would have famous actors and actresses as the cast and you would be able to pick. Isn't that exciting?"

I nod my head, yawning. The sleep was finally catching up to me.

"Okay. Now I'll give you an outline of your week quickly."

I groan.

"It's very quick, I promise," she says. "You meet up with me on Monday and show me the paragraph you wrote. If it's good, go home and sleep some more."

I snort.

"If not, we'll work on it here. Tuesday is our usual live. Wednesday, relax. I want you to mentally prepare yourself for the next day because Thursday is the presentation day. I have a friend who offered to do your makeup."

She starts to pack up her things slowly, and I copy.

"Wardrobe...wear what you want, but try to keep it professional. Wear a suit. You could easily pull off a suit," she winks.

"Women look better in suits, anyways," I add, and she grins.

"Friday is yet to be determined what you'll be doing since it entirely depends on whether they want to follow up with the movie deal or not. I say if I don't call or message— just relax."

That is a lot.

"Okay. Now, if you don't mind, I need to go sleep in my bed."

She stands up with me.

"I'll message you the rest of the details. Go to sleep. Sleep all day if you want. Just know that I want a detailed— at least one page—

paragraph about your book and why and what motivated you to write it. Let's say by Monday morning."

I stretch, mentally noting this new assignment and walk out after promising I'd get it done.

This wasn't much compared to the amount of stress I had when I was writing. A lot of tears, and a lot of anxiety on whether the book would get published or not.

I hope he's proud of me.

I remember waiting outside of the math room after the third-period bell rang. And, sure enough, he was there. He was hole-punching worksheets a couple of feet away from me.

He saw me, looked over, and just held my gaze. It was like a staring contest...Who was going to look away first?

Him.

I laughed a little to myself when he looked away. He looked back at me, the most adorable eye-smile accompanying his sweet face now. He had dimples that further complimented his face. I leaned against the door and watched as he went back to doing what he did. Even though he had only given me a subtle smile just now, I instantly knew when he smiled, he could make any girl swoon for him.

I sigh as I throw open the door to my apartment and crash onto my couch, not even making it to my bed.

God, how I wish I could see him again.

6

The second I step onto the stage, I'm standing in front of a handful of very important-looking people. They all look extremely intimidating, but I know I have to pull through. I can't let their professionalism and my anxiety get in the way of this occasion.

The clapping faded away.

I start with a simple introduction the same way I've been rehearsing.

"Hi everyone..."

After a quick preview of myself, I start to explain the inspiration behind my book and I talk about him. I take a breath. I know I can go on and on about him and how he made me feel. How the way he talked and everything about him was just so...*perfectly imperfect.*

"To my surprise, he was in grade twelve and I didn't realize that until it was too late."

That was a lie.

I knew he was in grade twelve by the third time I met him.

"He had this charm about him. I don't think there was anything I didn't like about him and I make that very clear in the book,"

I laugh nervously and the audience tunes in. "I'm sure there are a couple of people here today who also..."

Somebody in the audience catches my attention. A handsome stranger who I just have to stop and look at, but it isn't his beauty I'm stuck on; it's how familiar he looks. He's dressed in a white suit, and the focused and collected way he's looking at me makes me question...*Who is he?*

Focus, Huma.

I finish up briefly after my miniature heart attack and say good-bye to the crowd.

As I step down the stairs, I try to put a name to his face.

Aaliyah appears in front of me, "Huma, you did amazing!"

I beam and hug her.

"Where did Elena go?" I ask.

"She went out to talk with everyone. She's supposed to further market the book to the audience— mainly directors and such," she replies. "Do you want anything? The backstage people gave me a bunch of snacks, so I have extras."

I nod, "If you could bring water too that would be great."

She leaves.

I sit down on a random seat and close my eyes for a long minute. The room is partially dark with a very minimal amount of light coming from the dressing room and stage. I'm starting to collect myself again, the tension from my body finally coming to ease after the mess of not knowing what to wear, forgetting my script, and then having to go on stage.

While I wasn't up there for that long, it was how much I over-whelmed myself that made me feel exhausted.

I feel like my body is on autopilot by how much I'm sweating. I take off my blazer, leaving me with a white long sleeve.

I hear approaching footsteps.

"Please tell me you brought water— I feel like I'm in a sauna," I say, exhaling.

"Yes, actually. I did bring water."

It's a man's voice.

I open my eyes and look at the familiar and friendly face now smiling at me curiously.

Holy crap...

He breaks the seal of the bottle and hands it to me, "You did really well on stage."

I take it from his hands and take a small sip, suddenly not thirsty anymore.

Who is this guy?

"Oh wait— I almost forgot something," he leaves, returning with a bouquet of flowers...? Or are those plants?

I sit up straight and close the bottle, setting it to the side.

"You can't really see the colours in the darkness, but these are—"

"Lavenders," I interrupt. "The same colour as my suit."

The corners of his mouth lift up, exposing two, quite prominent, dimples.

Oh my God. No. It couldn't be.

He chuckles, "I mostly got them for the smell. Little did I know it would match you so nicely."

I thought the worst that could happen on stage was that I would trip. I thought the worst that could happen was I would start speaking about topics completely unrelated to the book. I thought the worst that could happen was I would stutter and trip over my words to the point where it was hard to understand what I was trying to say. But no. The worst that could happen was the man of my dreams would be sitting in the crowd like Aaliyah mentioned last week. The worst that could happen was *he*, the man who was the inspiration for my book, would be watching and listening to me recall all of our memories together.

No. It's not him. It can't be.

7

"Here, Huma. I got you some Doritos and water," Aaliyah hands me the snack, and I immediately rip it open.

He left after complimenting my book and mentioning how he loved the way I was so passionate when I spoke about it.

I'm still stressing over whether that was him or not. I don't know why, but it scares me. I don't want him to read my book, let alone act or direct it. If he is who I think he is, if it is Elias, then I don't know what I'll do. I might as well burn the book and fall off the face of the earth.

After the whole event is officially over, I say my goodbyes to Elena and my parents and head out with Aaliyah.

"What did you think about everything?" I ask, relaxing against the passenger seat of my car.

She grins at me, "Everyone was really nice...especially that one guy that you were talking to backstage."

Here we go...

"What guy?"

I know exactly which guy, but if I want to keep Aaliyah talking without me having to explain myself, this is what I have to do. Plus, I would much rather hear her go on and on about something I don't want to talk about just so I don't have to explain myself.

"Look at your lap," Aaliyah says. "Who gave you those flowers?"

My cheeks turn red. Luckily she can't see them because of how dark it is outside, or she would've said something. And yes, maybe I shouldn't have taken those flowers considering this guy might be Elias, but I can't just throw them away.

That would've been so rude.

Not going to lie, I'm starting to feel overwhelmed again. He was so important to me in high school and had a great impact on me and now here he is. Just standing there in front of me with his cute dimple-smile.

I felt tears stinging my eyes.

Why did he decide to show up now?

There's this weird sensation in my heart that I haven't felt for anyone, but him. The sensation when he was around, when he talked to me, when he smiled at me— I just can't believe I was so stupid to think something like *us* could even work. He didn't even see me like that. He probably treated me the same way he treated every girl. So respectful, so sweet. But I feel as if our connection was truly wholesome. Feelings aside, there was something so genuine and innocent about how we cared for each other.

Even when I wrote this book, I thought about what it would've been like if he stuck around after he graduated. What if he tried to see me? I wouldn't have started to date him, obviously, but in the back of my mind I thought maybe if he could just wait for me. Maybe if he could just be a little patient and stick around.

But that didn't happen.

I let my hopes up too soon, and now my heart has this crack in it that just constantly reminds me he was the one who hurt and ruined me. Granted, this was high school, and if I was being honest, most high school relationships don't go past grade twelve. But the way I felt for him— I wouldn't know how to describe it. He was so polite, so gentle when he spoke. He had a soft voice, just like the guy I met today. He was the one to talk to me first as well. If he hadn't spoken, I wouldn't have either. I didn't just talk out of the blue, especially with people I didn't know.

And even with all of this information, I know what happened then was bad. Even if both of our intentions were genuine, it doesn't make our bond any more halal.

"You know exactly who I'm talking about. The guy that came backstage to talk to you. I saw him give you the flowers, so don't you try and play dumb with me," she says.

I swallow hard.

"Aaliyah, he was just being polite. That's all this was."

"Oh no, that's not what I'm getting at, Huma. I'm talking about the fact that the guy you were talking to was Elias."

I try to act surprised, but just because he reminded both of us of Elias, it does not mean it was him. He's just another guy. I don't know him, and neither does Aaliyah. I know she expects a reaction, but unfortunately I myself was trying to understand who that was, and for some reason I didn't really want to know.

"Be realistic. That's not Elias," I sigh.

8

I hop out of the shower and quickly throw on my clothes before heading to the kitchen. I ate so many snacks at the auditorium, but I was still hungry.

Unfortunately, I couldn't stay long to talk to Ami and Abu after the whole speech because the staff was in such a rush to wrap up the conference. I thought of calling them earlier, but didn't want to disturb them. They must be tired, so it's better if I just called in the morning to see how they are and ask them what they thought of the whole thing.

Better yet— I'll go see them.

It's been a month since I've stayed home, and since Elena mentioned we might not have to meet tomorrow, depending on what the entertainment decided.

The cafe isn't far from my parents house either so even if I did strike the movie deal, I can drive over with ease.

I turn to Aaliyah, who's now in the kitchen searching for something to eat.

"Do you want to go to Ami's house tomorrow?" I ask.

This would be a great way for me to calm my nerves. With everything going on, I think a trip to my parent's house would be refreshing. Plus, I needed Ami's cooking to keep me going anyway.

"Mm, sure," she replies.

The doorbell rings, and Aaliyah and I both give each other suspicious looks. It's very rare for anyone to come to our doorstep so this is quite odd. I throw on a hijab quickly and peek through the peephole, but I can't see anything there.

I open the door and see a gift basket filled with various fruits. On the handle is a small letter. I pick up the basket and bring it inside, placing it down on the kitchen counter.

"Who gave it?"

Aaliyah locks the door while I open up the mini letter.

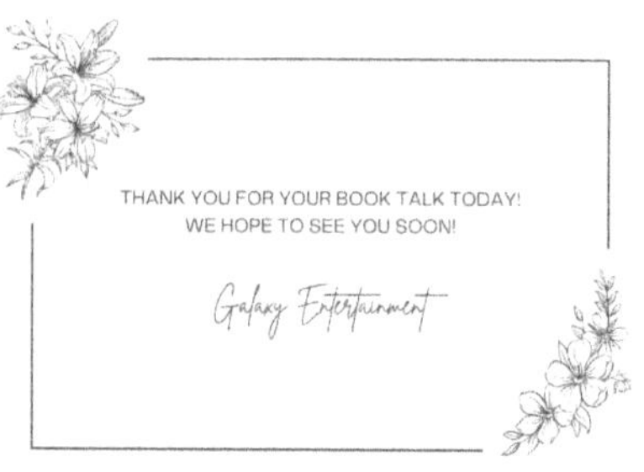

"Oh, it's from the entertainment," I smile.

"Awe, that's sweet of them. Now could we please eat something? My stomach is begging for food."

I could bring this to my parents' place tomorrow for all of us to share. Plus, I am not in the mood to down a bunch of fruits right now.

I turn on my heels, "How about we order some pizza?"

Aaliyah grins at me, grabbing her phone.

As I wait, I decide to head to my bedroom to attempt to clear up the boxes. This past week, I've been sleeping on the couch in the living room because of how messy my room has gotten and because of how stressful it's been. Now that I'm finally tired of the mess, it's time I clear it up. I fold the empty boxes and place them to the side.

They may come to my use later.

As for the almost empty boxes, I take the remaining books and stack them on my work table.

I make space on the floor and decide to package some signed copies and send them on their way to help pass some time. Aaliyah comes into my room and sits down with me.

"Do you want some help?" she questions.

"Sure," I place all the stationery between us and show her the addresses we have to send them to.

This wasn't the first time Aaliyah has helped me with something book-related. She's one of the only friends that has stuck around for a long time. She was also the only person besides my parents who knew about this book when I started writing. I told her everything about Elias whenever I saw him and just wouldn't and couldn't stop talking about him. But Aaliyah also knew how to listen. She didn't try to change the topic, she would just listen and would get all excited with me. I love this stupid girl with all my heart.

"Are you gonna tell Elena you saw Elias?"

I love her with all my heart most of the time...

"Aaliyah— for the last time— it wasn't Elias!"

She raises her eyebrows at me, "You know it was."

"Do you want me to write it down for you? It wasn't him. And besides, even if it was, I don't care."

She laughs, "Oh, please! That defensive mood would argue otherwise. There's a difference between not believing it was him and not wanting to believe it was him."

To my luck, our pizza arrives with a knock on the door, and I practically sprint to the door. I place the box onto the floor of my bedroom, throwing it open. Half veggie and half cheese.

Personally, I'm fine with both, but Aaliyah was the one that insisted on the cheese. No problem for me. I get the best of both worlds.

"You just got lucky, Huma. Don't worry, we have yet to finish our discussion," she narrows her eyes.

I stick my tongue out at her.

After we finish up, we pack a couple more of the books before sitting outside in the living room. We end the night watching a movie while we try to cram a couple of outfits into two bags for tomorrow's trip to my parents.

9

"So endure patiently, with a beautiful patience"
- Surah Al-Ma'arij [70:5]

A week has passed, and there's still no answer from Galaxy Entertainment. Elena and Aaliyah told me to stay strong, but I had let my guard down at this point. Elena only scheduled two meetings for this week. One on Wednesday which is today, and one on Thursday. I'm afraid she wants to tell me they scratched the movie deal or something, but the news she gives me when I finally sit down across from her is much more subtle.

"I contacted the entertainment company, and they said they're still discussing it," she says.

Patience is what I lack in this whole ordeal. If I could just convince myself to wait and be serene, maybe this wouldn't be so hard. Even so, I'm quite literally on the verge of a meltdown.

"I know we're already halfway through the week, but a popular bookstore in New York emailed and asked if you could come in and host a book signing if you're up for it," she suggests.

"Wha...?"

Her expression relaxes, as she shows me the email on her laptop,

"Look. They even booked us a hotel and asked if we could come tomorrow at three for a book signing."

As much as I don't want to admit it, this cheered me up a bit. I look at Elena, who is still smiling big, and I can't help but return the look. Maybe this movie deal isn't worth my time. Maybe I would have a second chance eventually, but this just isn't that time.

"Okay. Let's do it," I say, with a new sense of determination.

"One more thing," she takes a sip of the green tea in front of her. "We're gonna go by car—"

"Isn't that like eight hours?!"

She presses her lips together, "Probably ten with traffic."

Ten hours on the road. I don't think I could survive. I can already feel how congested I'm going to be from here. Shudders ride up my back as the thought crosses my mind.

"Where is it located?"

"Manhattan. It's the biggest bookstore in all of New York, and we'll be staying in a fancy hotel with a rooftop"

My jaw nearly drops. If I'm thinking about the same hotel, I've already seen photos, and the interior and exterior are to die for, but it is so expensive. It's over three-hundred a night, and I have never been more grateful that it wasn't any of my worries this time.

"Who's going?" I ask.

"Me, you, a driver, and we can bring Aaliyah as well."

That doesn't sound too bad.

"Okay fine, but I'm bringing my suitcase."

Elena laughs, "Sure."

The next couple of hours I spent packing for the trip. I told Aaliyah who was beyond excited, and immediately rushed to pack her things. I'm bringing my tote bag, my purse and a small carry-on luggage. Elena said the bookstore people wanted us there before three p.m when we called a while ago. They wanted us to stay for a minimum of two hours for the signing, so the goal was to arrive at two p.m., settle down, hijab and make-up, and then head to the bookstore.

Right now, it's seven in the evening, and Elena is scheduled to come pick up Aaliyah and I in an hour. We're supposed to be ready by the time she arrives, and she made it extremely clear by threatening my life that if we aren't ready, she would be beyond upset.

"Huma, do you have an extra hairbrush?" Aaliyah pops into my bedroom.

"Yeah, wait," I quickly grab the brush from my bathroom and give it to her. "Here."

"Thanks," she turns on her heels, but comes to a halt. "By the way, Elena keeps messaging you. She said she might come a little earlier, but we'll still leave at 7:30."

"Okay."

I make a quick mental note to eat something before we leave. I have a lot of snacks in my bag, but they're for the trip and strictly only the trip, so I have to be wise with the amount of snacks I eat now. I end up deciding to call Elena and see if we could make a pit stop to get take-out. I had already showered— in fact— as soon as I got home from our meeting, I jumped into the shower so my hair had time to dry.

In the kitchen, I see Aaliyah making us kabab sandwiches. "Do you know if Elena is gonna come inside and eat with us?"

The doorbell rings just as the words spill from her mouth.

"Good question."

I throw my hood on, and to my amusement, it's Elena. She's holding white roses as I let her in and turns around to hand them to me. "Oh, these are for me?" I smile, giving her a hug, as I take them into my hand. "Thank you. They're gorgeous."

She returns the smile. "Well, you did just get invited to go all the way to NYC to do a book talk."

I give her a look that says *it wasn't all me*, and *without her, I would be nowhere.*

"Did I mention you were invited?"

I take the flowers into the kitchen to put them away.

"Oh my God, you're finally here," Aaliyah gives her a side hug. "I'm just making us some sandwiches."

I place the roses into a tall glass I recently bought at the corner store and set them on the window sill. They look beautiful.

I take my sandwich from the counter and join the others on the couch.

"You two are fully packed, right?" Elena asks, taking a bite of the food

"Yeah, I just have to double-check my things and then we can leave," I reply. "Also, could we make a pit stop later in the ride to eat or no?"

"Yeah, we can, but I pack a lot of snacks and food because we're only making one stop for a big lunch. Otherwise, I brought boxes of snacks just in case we end up getting really hungry. We'll most likely have to make a couple of stops, but only for the gas station or if one of us has to use the restroom, and then we can get more snacks."

We talked for a bit before I made sure I had everything with me for the twentieth time.

I throw my tote bag over my shoulder and place my purse inside. I push the little button on my carry-on to pull up its handle and drag it into the living room. There, I see Aaliyah and Elena relaxing on the couch.

This whole thing is surreal to me. As much as I've been trying to digest what's happening, I somehow stay in this formidable shock where I'm in a frenzy trying to understand how much importance the upcoming event holds.

"Yeah, we're completely ready. It's 7:15, so if you could come a couple minutes before 7:30, that would just mean we hit the road a little earlier. Even if it makes no difference, every minute counts," Elena says into the phone, speaking to the driver.

I sit down with Aaliyah.

"Aren't you excited, Huma?" She turns her body to me.

The corners of my mouth rise, "Of course I am! They want me all the way in New York!"

She laughs, amused with my response as Elena walks over to us.

"Alright my lovelies, the driver is here and ready to take us on our adventure," she picks up all five— yes— *five* of her bags and opens the door.

"Elena, here, let me help you with those," I offer, and she rolls her eyes.

"I got this, hon. You're underestimating me."

Aaliyah locks up, and we make our way down the elevator outside where a minivan is waiting for our arrival.

A driver steps out and takes our bags, setting most of them in the trunk. The van is an eight-seater Toyota Sienna, which is way more room than we need, but I'm not complaining. We are going to be on the road for over eight hours, and I'm going to need room if I want to sleep and be comfortable, hence why I'm wearing sweats.

Both Aaliyah and I sit at the very back and Elena sits in the middle of the car to fit the dozens of bags she has.

Once we hit the road, I check my social media to let my readers know about the book signing tomorrow even though I've been posting that since I've found out and so has the bookstore.

I yawn, the sleep deprivation creeping back into me. I should take the time to sleep, but I have a couple of reasons to stay awake. One, it's hard to sleep knowing I was going to a very important event that is going to do great wonders for me in the near future. Two, I could not miss some of the sights this trip would bring from Toronto to New York, and three, I'm afraid if I fall asleep, something bad would happen. The last point isn't some bad omen of some sort, it's actually just me and my overthinking.

I know even if I tried, I wouldn't be able to sleep, so there was no point in doing so.

"Huma," Elena calls out my name. I lean forward in my seat in response. "You should continuously document your story just so people don't forget. I know the bookstore has been, but maybe give snippets of what you're doing."

"Okay," I reply, pulling my phone out to take pictures around me that could indicate I'm finally off to Manhattan, New York

...

For a while, I answer any curious questions about the book from the question box I put up. It keeps me busy for an hour or so before I turn off my screen to connect with my surroundings a bit and maybe even catch a nap.

Unfortunately, my curiosity wins when my phone starts buzzing like it's going to explode right on my lap. I pick it up and notice a message.

And then I see a name pop up.

More specifically, Elias' name. I press my lips tightly against each other and stare at his name. I stare as if I stared long enough, it would dissipate in front of my eyes. Thankfully, it isn't his account. It was a response with his name in it.

User3648: You should totally cast Elias Lee as the love interest if you make a movie

I ignore it, pretending it hasn't caught me off guard and proceed to answer other questions. I'm not ready to talk about him, nor do I think I will ever be.

book_loverr: What time does the book signing start and where can I buy a ticket?

I press the mic button to record a response, "Okay, so the book signing, I believe, will start at three and as for tickets— there are none. It's more like a first come, first serve situation, so try to come early, but no worries if you can't. I'm sure we will have more opportunities for book signings more often."

Elena tunes in, "I just double-checked for you hon, the book signing will start at 3:15. Maybe later, depending on how long the setup takes and when we arrive."

"Thank you," I pat Elena's shoulder. "So if you didn't hear that, the book signing, as of right now, starts at 3:15, but might differ depending on when we arrive and how long setting up the book-store will take."

After another fifteen minutes, I decide to stop answering any more questions or statements. Mainly because of how much that comment threw me off. Yes, it was a single comment, but I'm already creating scenarios that he may have already read the book and he knows exactly who I am. Even though I hope he never puts two and two together, it would hurt if he didn't remember anything from high school. The memories I had cherished and, at some points wish I had forgotten, never left my mind and never will. The truth is, I never want to forget, I just need someone to numb the pain a little. I think that's the problem with Elias. He didn't realize every interaction, every time we talked, everytime he smiled that he may have been pulling at my heartstrings.

I rest against my tote bag.

Maybe I'm just easily hurt. Maybe I'm the one with the flaws, and he's the perfect one. The one that only talked to me out of sympathy. Maybe that's it.

Elias never cared about me the way I cared for him. No. He didn't even give me a second thought romantically. We were best friends, but it was nothing beyond that. That's it. And here I was, a 24-year-old who had given in to his charm and written a whole story about him.

Wow.

When I started writing this story, I thought it could be a story just for me, and then I had the stupid idea of publishing it. To my surprise, people loved it. Even with all this, I feel stupid. I feel like this whole plan, this whole idea, is the dumbest thing I have ever done.

"Huma, are you okay?" Aaliyah asks.

I nod my head and smile, "Just a little tired. I might sleep for a bit."

Elena turns around and settles a hand on mine, "If you're nervous, there's no need to be. You'll be sitting the whole time, so don't think about it too much. Plus, you can always tell us if you're feeling uncomfortable."

I give her hand a squeeze, "Thanks."

If only it was the same with Elias. If only he was the one sitting next to me right now. I wish I could tell him everything. I wish I could confess to him, just to see what he says. Just so I can get this terrible feeling off my chest.

I wish he had never talked to me.

I O

"The present world is only an illusory pleasure."
- Surah Al-Imran [3:185]

So I lied. I eventually fell asleep, but I needed that nap after everything that happened. I fell asleep for two hours, according to Aaliyah and Elena. And now we have around seven hours left. The sun is still shining, but it's getting ready to go down in less than an hour.

I pull my feet up to the seat to get comfortable and look over at Aaliyah. She's calmly scrolling through her phone, cuddled up in the blanket I brought from home. Elena, however, was on the phone speaking quietly with someone from the bookstore. Meanwhile, I'm trying to listen in, but it's no use. Nothing she's saying makes sense, and I can barely hear the person on the other end.

The phone call reminds me of my own parents, who are aware of the road trip, but are not very fond of letting me go anywhere with just girls. Unfortunately, in our cruel society, we had to be afraid of every person, especially men, that passed us. You don't know what they're capable of— you don't know their intentions either.

I can't blame my parents for their overprotectiveness.

If I ever have kids, especially girls, they would be under my supervision and I would make sure they were safe in all circumstances.

I move towards Aaliyah, and she shifts a little to welcome my sudden arrival to her, "Have you finally woken up fully, or are you still charging?" She asks with a grin.

I laugh, "I think I'm on auto-pilot right now, but we're definitely getting there."

She switches her phone off and in the almost darkness of the car, I know exactly what she's about to say.

"We should read scary stories."

I grin. Aaliyah gets scared easily like me, but since there is more than one person, anything scary we talk about could easily be made fun of. Just as long as nothing scary actually happens to us— we'll be fine. And anyway, we have *Ayatul Kursi*

"Imagine you turn around right now, and you just see a face peering through the window," I say, lowering my voice as if there's someone really there, and she turns to look outside. I laugh, but I know that thought spooked me too.

"Do you think people are more scary or the paranormal?" I ask.

She narrows her eyes, "Hm. People, for sure."

I smile, curious to know her explanation. "Why do you say that?"

She raises her eyebrows, "You disagree?"

The answer is yes. I do disagree. While people doing inhumane things is scary, it's scarier when you don't know what's doing those inhumane things. With people, you know the weaknesses of both guys and girls, but what are you going to do when you can't exactly pinpoint that?

We don't really know every paranormal creature out there, and some people even tend to think stuff like that is fake. Me, not so much.

Jinns and witches are all a part of this world.

"Come on, Aaliyah, the word *creature* is freaky itself," I argue.

"That's true, but isn't it creepier for a human to act *insane*?" she asks.

Before I can say anything else, my phone buzzes. It's a notification from a random account. I typically avoid answering random DM's from people I don't know, but this one, like the previous response, has Elias' name on it.

It's a link.

God, why couldn't this guy leave me alone.

"What is it?" Elena asks. "It's not those spam comments, right?"

I look at her and laugh nervously, "No, no. It's all good."

They both give me a concerned look, and Elena asks the driver if she can turn the back car light on.

I press my lips together.

"What is it?" Aaliyah asks. "Did something happen?"

I shake my head, "No, no. It's none of that. It's just—"

I stop myself.

This is so stupid. How does it all spiral back to him?

I sigh and turn my phone towards them.

"It's a link...?" Aaliyah looks at the phone and then at me, confused.

I motion towards the screen, "Look closer. His name is right there."

She looks back at it and Elena places a hand on my arm.

This isn't about being dramatic. It's about the annoyance of seeing his name over and over with an unconfirmed and possibly failed movie deal.

"Elias? How...?" Aaliyah tenses up. "Huma, that's not him. You know I was joking when I said all that."

"People are sending me photos after photos and requests after requests to cast him. They think—" I start to tear up. "They think he fits the description in my story perfectly."

"It's not him," Aaliyah repeats.

I unlock my phone and search for his name. His name is the first to show up with the blue tick at the end of his username. I click on it and show them. I find a random photo that shows him wearing the black necklace from all those years ago.

Tears start to fall down my face. And now it finally comes to my realization that the reason why I didn't see it on him when we met a while ago behind the stage was because of how dark it was.

That really is him...

"I don't wanna do this anymore. I'm sure another author can take my place for the book signing. I can't afford to have him ruin my life any longer," I pull my sleeve to the palm of my hand and rub my tears away. "This book was a dumb idea!"

Elena switches my phone off, "This book was anything but dumb. You did amazing, and you'll continue to do amazing, hon. Just because some stupid guy is getting to your head, doesn't mean you should give him the time of day. He isn't worth it. If he cared, he would reach out personally and want to talk to you."

Elena is right, but he was the sweetest boy in high school. His entire demeanor towards me made my heart brighten. That is so hard to find nowadays and it starts to dawn on me how rare he was when I met him. He knew his boundaries, and he acknowledged mine too. He made sure I was comfortable with him around me.

Little did he know, when he made me comfortable, he also made my heart drop to my stomach. While I was so mesmerized by him, he pierced through my heart and made me feel blissful, but now I question why it feels so dull. Why did the same feeling that hyped me up, that made me feel like I was on top of the world, make me feel so weak? Is he the one to tarnish this feeling? It appears he might've not been as rare as I thought he was.

"I had a fear this would happen," Elena sighs.

"What?" I divert my attention to her, lost in whatever I was feeling right now.

"I just—"

"Wait," my eyes sharpen as I try my hardest to form a sentence. "Did you know about him this whole time?"

She looks at me shamefaced and nods.

I swallow hard, hurt that someone I trusted could keep something like that from me, "You knew I liked him, Elena...why would you keep something like that from me?"

Aaliyah steps in. "Woah, Huma, you were extremely vulnerable back then about him. Elena was trying to protect you."

I scoff, "Protecting? I think it's up to me whether I want to know that information, or not."

Elena gives me a pained expression and I start to feel bad about what I just said. I never act like this with Elena or Aaliyah, but all of this is news to me and I wish she had told me the second she had found out.

"Sorry, Huma. I didn't know you wanted to know that," Elena mutters, looking away.

Now I feel even worse, but it truly isn't Elena's decision to make on whether I get to know that knowledge or not. It surprises me that I never pinpointed who Elias was from the get-go even though he is pretty well known.

"I just wish you had told me," I reply, hugging my knees.

It's ironic that I can't even leave the car, and now we would be sitting in awkward silence for the next couple of hours.

I I

"My Lord has always been kind to me."
- Surah Maryam [19:47]

The light from the outside shines through the car window, creating a gorgeous glow. I've been up since last night and haven't been able to sleep. The only one who slept out of the three of us was Aaliyah.

I still feel bad. I want to apologize, but I'm waiting for us to pull over for a bathroom break.

Lucky for me, we're just about to.

"Anybody need to use the restroom?" the driver asks.

"I do," I say.

It's about to be prayer time anyway, so I should probably get ready for that as well.

I shake Aaliyah to wake her up, "Let's go. It's Fajr."

She nods her head, and I basically drag her out. I quickly use the bathroom and take a water bottle to rinse my mouth, face, arms, and feet before praying.

As I'm finishing up, Elena sits beside me on the prayer mat. Elena isn't Muslim, but she has always been interested in the whole idea of it. She grew up in a household that didn't follow any religion, so seeing her even have a bit of an interest in Islam made my heart brighter.

"I'm sorry," she says. "It wasn't my call to make, so I'm sorry."

My breath stops. I'm not surprised she came to apologize again, but remembering why she's apologizing takes something away from me. I don't know what. I don't know why or how, but I feel drained.

I know who Elias is now, and thinking back, it would have been better if I didn't know. I want to see if he's okay, though. After all these years of silence, I want to know that he's okay, and I think I got my answer the night I met him at the book conference.

He's better now.

The happiest I've ever seen him.

I turn to Elena and pull her into my embrace. She's trying to protect me and I get that. Sometimes you can love someone so much that you never want to see them get hurt. The more I think about it, the more I realize that I would've done the same. Even though it should've been up to me, I get why she thought hiding it from me was better.

"It's okay, I get it."

When I pull away, she's smiling with a great amount of relief plastered on her face. "Oh, thank God you're not mad anymore. I was worried you weren't planning to forgive me anytime soon."

The corners of my mouth rose, "I was always going to forgive you. I just needed time to digest it."

Aaliyah appears, amused by our conversation.

"Finally, you two made up," she stands on the prayer mat, and I stand up to make room for her. Once we're back on the road, we've only got twenty minutes left till we arrive at the hotel. I hadn't even realized until now that we've almost been driving for over nine hours, until Elena blurted it out.

It's now almost six o'clock in the morning which is much later than the expected time for our arrival, but we also had to count the bathroom and prayer breaks we had made, which was pretty much half the trip.

"We're almost there, Hon. Only ten minutes left, and then we all can sleep on a proper bed and eat a proper breakfast," Elena sighs against the seat.

She's, without a doubt, the most tired out of all of us since she's the one in charge of everything involving this event.

I pat her head, "You're doing great, Elena."

She laughs and reaches for a bag of food, ruffling through it. We ate so many snacks on this road trip, starting with four bags of snacks, and now we're down to half of that.

"Hold on a little longer, Elena. My mom packed us some home-made food for when we get to the hotel," I reply.

"Oh, thank God for your mom." Aaliyah says, and we all laugh.

Ami didn't want us eating junk food the whole trip, so she packed us a huge meal and even gave me her cooler so the food wouldn't go bad. Ami and Abu said they wouldn't be able to come to my book signing because this is the same day of Abu's appointment and it's important he didn't miss this one.

Abu doesn't have any issues, but he tends to miss his appointments because he's convinced he can never get sick.

Love the spirit, but no. I'm not about to have Abu miss another appointment.

Abu insisted on coming and was annoyed when neither Ami or I would take his side, so he's probably all grumpy at home.

As we finally reach the hotel, there are people with cameras standing at the entrance. They're snapping photos before we can even leave the car, while the hotel security instructs us to stay inside until they can clear up this swarm of people.

"Who are these people here for?" I ask Elena, while I investigate outside for any celebrity or someone who looks like they could be one.

"I'm trying to find out," Elena says as a car pulls up behind us.

A fancy, black car.

"I guess we're about to see for ourselves."

Aaliyah practically squeezes me into the corner of my seat to get a better look outside. "Who is it?"

"Maybe if you move off my lap, I can get a better view," I shoot her a look.

She ignores me as her eyes go wide.

Elena has almost the same expression.

Whereas I, not being able to look out the window, try to twist myself to look at the back window of the car, and that's when I'm able to identify the mysterious person getting out of the black vehicle.

He has on a white t-shirt with newsprints all over it and black cargo pants to match.

"Well, his fashion has enhanced," I comment as I sit back. I receive a look from both Elena and Aaliyah. "What? Have you seen him in high school?"

To my surprise, they burst out laughing, and when Elias is finally in the building, the crowd of people slowly clear off and we're allowed in.

Three workers come out and help us with our bags, taking them inside.

Personally, I don't like strangers touching my stuff, even if it is to help me out. Especially considering everything in my bags are personal belongings, but I don't stop the worker from taking my bags.

Not being the best at communicating, I hide behind Elena so he won't ask me for my tote bag as well. I don't know why I did it. In fact, he looks scared of me while I basically continue to kill him with my eyes.

"Huma, let's go inside," Aaliyah grabs my arm gently and ushers me in.

The interior of the hotel looks absolutely gorgeous, not that I didn't know before. Seeing it in-person made me want to come here all the time.

We're led to our rooms by the employees.

Right beside our hotel room, there are two very large, well-built bodyguards. They look scary as hell with their strict, intimidating faces, and while we arrive at our door, they step forward and look at us.

"What are you all doing here?" one of them asks.

"We're, um— you know, this is actually—" I'm interrupted.

"This is our room," Elena shows them the key and then one of them smiles. Yes, one of them smile. Not a crazy *'get the hell out of here, or I'll beat the crap out of you'* look— nope. He smiles.

The funny part is that he was smiling at me.

"Are you the author of 'Splintered Heart'?" he asks curiously.

Elena shoves me forward, so I stand in front of him.

I'll definitely get her back for doing that.

I slowly, but surely, nod my head and turn a light shade of pink.

This had to be the most embarrassing interaction ever.

"Well, I loved it. I think the whole idea of your story was amazing, and I have to admit, I cried a couple of times."

My jaw drops.

Not because he doesn't look like the type to cry, but because it surprises me how excited he looks. This man was just about to throw us out of the building for wanting to settle into our room, and now he looks like the sweetest giant.

He takes off his *Men In Black* sunglasses as a small smile appears on my face, "Do you mind if I come by later and have you sign my book?"

I laugh nervously. He isn't making me uncomfortable— I just happen to suck at speaking if you can't tell by now.

I swallow manually, "Sure, of course!"

The other tall guy puts a hand on his shoulder, "We need to get back to work, Michael. You can do this later."

He nods his head and turns back to me. "As you heard, I need to get back to my job, but you should join the book club we have. It's on Fridays at 9 a.m. by the cafe in Toronto."

I widen my smile, "Yeah, for sure. I'll see if I can make it."

His face softens, "Anyways, I'll let you get settled in and comfortable. Can't wait for your book signing!"

I laugh as he gets back into position with the other bodyguard. He gives me a small wave and I return the gesture.

I spin to where Elena and Aaliyah were standing just a couple seconds ago and realize the door to the hotel is open. I walk in and lock the door behind me.

Aaliyah is knocked out on the bed, and Elena is sitting up, talking on the phone as usual.

She ends the call and sighs while I take my hijab off and lay beside Aaliyah.

"Come, get some sleep," I say.

"No, I have to call—"

"Get some sleep, Elena. You need it more than us, and as much as I appreciate you, you need a break just like we do. So, come and sleep."

She smiles and lies down next to me. We quickly doze off.

...

12

"Indeed, what Allah has for you is best for you, if you only knew."
- Surah An-Nahl [16:95]

I wake up to a knock at the door.

Quickly checking the time, I see it's twelve.

Aaliyah and Elena are still out-cold, so I quietly get up and throw on my hijab before heading to the door.

I open it and see a whole tray of food.

"Order for Ms.Tariq. We have the whole breakfast menu for you," the man says. I look at him utterly confused, switching my gaze from his to the tray. "Not including any haram food, of course."

"No, I think you've got the wrong Tariq. I didn't order this," I reply, waving my hands around like a lunatic.

A soft smile accompanies his face as he pulls out a small card from in between the food. He hands it over to me and I look down at it.

Well, that seems strange. How did they know I was here? It could be possible they had seen it online about my book signing, but it doesn't make sense how they knew where I was staying. I shifted uncomfortably. I don't think any of the staff from the entertainment saw me, so this was odd to say the least. I wanted to wake Elena up and ask her what the hell was going on, but she needed all the sleep she was getting and I should probably deal with this on my own.

"Are you sure this is for me?" I ask.

He nods his head with a gentle laugh, "We got a call downstairs from someone wanting the whole breakfast menu. He said he wanted to make a good impression on you, so yes. I believe this is for you."

I hesitate for a moment and he catches it.

"I'm sorry ma'am, but if you want to make sure, I could ask next door. They were the ones to order it for you after all."

I almost drop the card from my hand, my eyes dilating.

Was it him?

Elias had entered this hotel, had he not? The two bodyguards were probably his, unless there was another huge celebrity that happened to be staying right beside me. But then again, was Elias even under Galaxy Entertainment?

Snapping back into reality, I give the polite man a quick smile and bring the tray inside. I shut the door and immediately pull out my phone from my pocket.

If I want to find out more about Galaxy Entertainment and Elias, I might as well search it up. Before I check what entertainment he works under, I check to confirm this is the same Elias. The sweet Elias from high school.

Name: *Elias Lee.*
Age: *25 years old.*
Place of Birth: *Scarborough, ON*

That is definitely him. Beside all of this, there was a photo of him showing his dimple-smile. It's a refreshing thing to see after all this uncertainty. The picture reminds me of his graduation photo I saw in our school's yearbook.

Back then, I wasn't even looking for his photo until I reached the graduates section. When I found him, I looked at it for a long while, realizing I probably would never see him again. It definitely hurt knowing he wouldn't talk to me anymore. It hurt to think I wouldn't be sneaking snacks into his backpack anymore.

Oftentimes, I wish I could go back and relive those moments just because of the way they made me feel. When I spoke to him, when I saw him, and when I thought of him, I felt as if I had won in life. I want to say I fell in love, and for a while, I believed that. That's why I was so pained, so heartbroken by his lack of interest in me. Then I grew, then I matured and realized that I was in love with wanting to be in a relationship.

This is not to say I wasn't attracted to him. I mean, there was a reason why I was tied to him, and I'm still figuring it out.

When he left, when I was forced to get over him, I couldn't like anyone else. I would have hallway crushes from now and then, but I never *liked* them. They were just crushes— no more than that.

What I want to know is how he manages to make me miss him so much.

I keep scrolling to find his record label and, eventually, it's right in front of my eyes.

Record Label: *Galaxy Entertainment*

No. No, I am not about to fall down this rabbit-hole again. I get rid of the tab on my phone and slip my phone back into my pocket.

As for the food, I'm not about to put it to waste, so I divide it into sections. I'm going to give some to the security guards and the rest we could eat. I'm sure we could devour it all with how hungry we are.

On top of that, we still have Ami's food to eat as well.

Our room has a mini-fridge and a microwave, so I decide to use that to my advantage. I warm up Ami's food and set it on the coffee table by the window, along with the rest of the food.

"Elena, Aaliyah— wake up!" I shake both of them.

Once they're up and sit at the table, I go out and give the security guards some food.

"This is so sweet of you. We weren't able to eat anything this morning, so thank you so much for the food," the courteous one says. The other gives me a nod of approval and I return to our room.

I feel for the security guards. Here they are, working their butts off to protect the idiot in the room who sent me the entire breakfast menu, but didn't have the decency to feed the people protecting him?

That's pretty stupid.

I have the urge to go out there and give him a piece of my mind, but I am not in the mood for being thrown out of the building.

"Why would you order all this food?" Aaliyah laughs as I take a seat.

I look away, "I was just really hungry."

Maybe telling a lie isn't doing anything, but what else am I supposed to do? I can't keep talking about him. I need to get past him. If he's moved on, so will I.

It's one o'clock as we finish up eating, and we have to get to the bookstore by two, so everyone could figure out how this was going to work.

While they do that, my job is to figure out what passages I want to read and discuss, and know how to give a proper answer to everyone's questions.

Now, predicting peoples' questions is not very easy, so the only answers I have written down are very generic. Even questions un-related to the book like: *'When are you going to come out with another book?'* and *'What genres do you write other than romance?'*

Other than that, I have to pick an outfit, and then I should be good to go. Personally, I like to have my outfits resonate with the book or at least suit the aesthetic of how the book signing would look, so I want to wear a simple, maxi dress.

I brought two dresses and a couple of separate outfits, but I'm not sure what I want to wear yet.

"Elena?"

She doesn't look up from her computer, "Yeah?"

"Which one of these looks better?" I pull one of the dresses up to me until it's brushing against my body as I look in the mirror. This dress is white and falls to the ankles. My plan is to wear it with white pumps, so the ends don't touch the floor. "Or does this look better?"

The other dress is the same as the last; falling to the ankles, but it's a little more fancy. It's an emerald green dress.

For this one, I plan to contrast it with black. I have black pencil-heels and a black hijab to match it with. I have gold-coloured earrings and a necklace that could go really well with this outfit.

Elena looks up. "Emerald, for sure."

I decide not to change yet and shower instead. Maybe I can help

Elena or Aaliyah with stuff since we still have a solid hour before we have to be there and I don't have much to do.

Typically, I'm underprepared and stressed for any event...but today, I feel fine. For once, I feel perfectly prepared even with the knowledge that I don't know what types of questions I would be receiving..

After my quick shower, I join Elena on the coffee table.

"The sun is so nice and bright. I kind of hate that we're leaving tomorrow," Elena sighs.

"Right, it's so pleasant outside today," I look around the room and catch sight of Aaliyah going through her luggage. "Are you looking for an outfit to wear? I have spares if you wanna see those."

Aaliyah stands up, eyes still focused on the luggage on the floor. She puts her hands on her hips and looks over at me with a hopeful look. "Do you have a black undershirt I can borrow?"

I smile, "It's in my luggage."

"Huma, dry your hair and get ready. We might have to leave a little early so we can start the book signing earlier," Elena says.

I nod my head and sprint to the bathroom to dry my hair. I throw on the dress, letting it descend to my ankles and put on my hijab. I keep my hijab simple, throwing it over my shoulder and stepping out of the bathroom.

"Oh good, you're ready," Elena glances over and looks back almost instantly. "Awe, you look so pretty."

I beam at her reaction, "Thank you."

After a bunch of compliments are exchanged amongst us, and rushing to get ready, we finally leave the hotel. I wave at the bodyguard next door, and he smiles in return.

As we get downstairs to the ground floor, I notice people with cameras standing by a figure wearing a suit.

Aaliyah blocks my view.

"Hurry up, Huma. Don't you wanna get to the most important part of your day already?" She grins at me.

I return the look and follow.

Aaliyah stands behind me while Elena halts a taxi. The ride to the bookstore is short, but the whole time I try to remember the passages I want to talk about.

There are a couple I have in mind, but I could always ask my reader's which passage they would like to hear about.

I find it hard to believe my own words took me this far. There are people out there who understand every nook and cranny of my story. They know the importance of the words I use, and how I chose to tell my story.

Releasing this book was very messy, but throughout all this I've gotten a lot of supportive people who have only been sweet to me. And without that, I don't think I would be anywhere with this whole book thing.

"How much longer?" Aaliyah blurts.

...

The setup of the book signing is really cute. There are a row of seats facing a small stage with a table and a chair. I'm assuming that's where I would be sitting.

A woman approaches us with a smile and briefly introduces herself.

"Hi, my name's Katie," she sticks her hand out.

I take her hand in mine. "I'm Huma."

She leads us all to meet the rest of the crew.

They tell Elena she'll be sitting right by me, but not in the audience. Just close by so she can help with any questions or anything that shouldn't be said.

As for Aaliyah, she's going to be sitting up front in the first row which helps me out a little bit since I can hopefully earn reassuring looks from her if my nerves get the best of me..

And for me, as I predicted, I'm going to be sitting on the stage, behind the table. They have a microphone for me to speak into, a water bottle, juice, and some additional snacks.

"Are you comfortable?" Katie asks while she checks my mic.

I nod my head, "Yeah, just going over everything in my head."

"Oh, I'm sure you'll do great," she says softly. "Drink some juice, it'll help with your nerves."

I take a deep breath after she leaves. I check the time, and it's only 2:45. Originally, we were supposed to start at 3:15, but with the time creeping up and us settling down earlier, we might start sooner.

I really am excited about this, but I'm starting to get those last-minute nerves. When I spoke in front of those directors, actors/actresses, I basically almost had a heart attack.

"Huma," Elena appears in front of me. "You're going to do great."

Elena knows I have done a couple of book signings already and they've gone amazing, yet she still comes to reassure me that I'll do good, and I love her for it. I talk with her a little more to calm my nerves and let her know I'm doing fine.

I place a hand on Elena's arm, "Can you check on Aaliyah, too? Just to see if she's comfortable and everything."

She leaves as Katie comes towards me again. "We're gonna start in a minute, so if any of you need to use the bathroom then maybe go now."

I don't need to. My nervous jitters have me so focused on what I'm going to say and making sure my voice doesn't shake too much.

"Thanks, I'm all good," I say, and she leaves.

Nearby, I catch a glimpse of a crowd of people. I like to believe I'm not that *popular*, but I'm likeable enough to keep writing books. What I do believe is that 'Splintered Heart' was able to connect with people, hence the attention it got.

Selling over 3000 copies overnight caught me off guard, but oh my, was I happy. I think 'Splintered Heart' gained its popularity because of how real it is. It's genuine— everything I said in that book is real. I wrote it in grade eleven and didn't publish it until recently. I'm scared of what people would think— of what *he* would think.

When I finally graduated from university, I decided I didn't care. I realized how important and accomplished I would feel if I did this. Not for Elias, not for my friends, but for myself. This was a book that was written and published selfishly by me, and quite frankly, I'm satisfied by that.

One of the people in charge of this signing goes up to the crowd, and after a couple of seconds, they come to sit down. A couple of them wave and smile. I reply with the same, welcoming them with open arms.

Okay, deep breaths.

If they ask me questions about Elias, I can't avoid them without seeming suspicious, so I have to be ready.

Just an hour or two, Huma.

Deep. Breaths.

13

"Guide us to the straight path."
- Surah Fatiha [1:6]

"What was the toughest obstacle you faced when writing this book?" A girl at the front wearing a cute pink and white floral maxi asks. She appears to be in her early twenties, like me. Her silky hair falls to her waist, brown with caramel highlights, which compliment her skin tone.

I give her a wistful smile. "I think the biggest obstacle had to be getting in touch with myself and my feelings. It was hard to do that at first, giving me a lot of sleepless nights and a lot of tears, but you get the hang of it after a while."

She nods her head understandingly.

I look around the room for any more hands in the air and see one at the back. I point, and he speaks.

"Since you mentioned the book was based on real events, I was wondering, did you ever find that guy again? Did you ever find out what he's doing now or...?"

I clear my throat.

God, why do they have to have such informative questions?

I look over at Elena, who is about to speak up, but I quickly reply.

"I'm not sure," the smile that was once on my face is now gone. "The thing is, even if I saw him or ever see him again, I think this story was more about letting him go than it was about finding him again. I will admit though, if you asked me in high school if I wanted to see him again, I would've immediately— no hesitation— said yes."

A couple of people laugh.

"And, yeah. Sometimes, even now, I wish I could see him. A small part of me refuses to let go of him, but I'm okay with that now."

Lies. Utter lies. Utter and absolute lies. I'm not okay with it. That small part of me hurts and throbs when it wants to, and I have to live through it because it's also partially my fault.

Did he talk to me first?

Yes. Yes he did.

But did I still continue the conversation?

Yes, yes I did.

Another hand raises up. "I loved the concept of your book. It really showed me the difference between being in love with someone and being in love with the idea of having a relationship. I think as humans we tend to forget that, but you really helped me and showed me it's not all that. I know for you it was being in love with the idea of a relationship and I totally resonate with that."

I fiddle with the wire of the microphone and talk for a bit longer.

After I read some storylines and explain the importance of each of them, I'm basically done. Honestly, it feels like an English class for a bit because of how we're analyzing the quotes and how people are adding to what I'm saying.

"Could you do one more line? I picked one out, and I was hoping you wouldn't mind explaining it further," an older woman smiles.

"Sure."

She takes a breath before starting, *"And, alas, even the most happiest of memories can become sad when looked from the perspective of someone whose whole life has been giving and never receiving."*

This hitches up my throat, and I no longer want to speak.

When I wrote this part, I wrote it for Elias. That's how I imagine he felt at the time.

The people who just got up sit back down.

My mind roams back to high school. Back to when he was walking me to my next class. At this point, we were having lunches together because neither of us had anyone else that we connected to.

This was the weekend before Eid, so Ramadan was coming to an end. While other girls were telling their friends what they would be wearing, or when they would be getting their mehndi done, I was telling Elias all of that.

In my head, I wanted to ask him about Eid because he hadn't told me anything. He just talked about what class he had next and how annoying senior year of high school was.

But before I could open my mouth, he spoke.

"So, what are you doing for Eid?"

I watched as he hid his hands in his pockets.

"You've asked me that already."

"I know."

For a moment, I thought he had forgotten what I had said, and that's why he was asking me again. "I need you to keep talking."

"Why—?"

"Because," he snaps. I go silent. I don't know why, but he seemed angry or just in an off-type of mood that was starting to get on my nerves, too. I moved ahead of him, about to tell him he can go to his class now and not get detention for being late for the seventh time this week. "I like that you talk a lot."

My face went from annoyed to red, so I didn't turn around to avoid his confrontation. "So what are you doing then? For Eid?" I ask after a couple of seconds.

"Right," he catches my gaze. "I'm probably just gonna hang out with friends."

After he said that, I felt bad. It wasn't the best thing for me to assume, but I thought *what if he didn't have any family to go to?* Sure, I may have been looking too much into it, but it turns out I was right. He connected to Islam through other Muslims.

Apparently, he had converted. I thought it was so cute that he found comfort in the same thing millions of other people had.

I take a breath and look at the woman, bringing myself back to this book signing. "I thought of that when he left. It was over the summer, and I just thought about how I was ready to give him my all. I was pretty immature, but I still thought about it. I realized how selfish I was being to myself and how I let impressing a guy become my top priority. I know the past is dumb, but I do believe that he came into my life for a reason. *He was a lesson to be learned.*"

"Do you really believe that, though? Sure, maybe he was a lesson, but maybe he was also put into your life so you could see not all guys are the same. In your book, you mentioned how he was so polite and sweet, unlike other guys you've had to associate and put up with."

These questions and explanations are getting a little too deep for my liking. But I don't plan on stirring up any drama, so I sit and wait for the girl to finish speaking.

Elena gives me a worried look when I turn to her. She looks like she wants to say something again, but I don't allow it.

"Yeah, I think I still do believe that. What I've learned through him is that he might've been an amazing guy and, yes, he might've treated me better, but that's the bare minimum. He probably is still an amazing guy right now, but I think if we look at the perspective of the story, it was mostly written in the past tense because I wrote this story after all of my encounters with him," I take a second to gather my thoughts before continuing. "Just to summarize, he, right now, has moved on, and I'm learning to do the same too."

I need to stop lying.

We finish up briefly after that and end up finishing on a good note.

Elena and Aaliyah cheer when all three of us gather up again.

"That was amazing! You answered all those questions so well," Elena says, giving me a hug.

"Thank you."

Aaliyah smiles, "I think this calls for a celebration."

And then for the next five hours, we stay out eating and shopping. It's probably the most fun I've had for a couple of weeks now, so it feels reviving.

When we finally decide to call it a day, we head back to the hotel. I feel like I could sleep for weeks because of how tiring today and yesterday have been.

"Oh, do you wanna check out the hotel roof? Apparently it's really pretty!" Aaliyah suggests.

I nod frantically, heading to the elevators, "Of-freaking-course!"

I know I just complained about being tired, but one, I want to believe no one is up there and it's totally quiet, so us three girls can just lounge around for a bit before heading back to our room.

And two, it's a rooftop, who wouldn't want to go there on a hot summer day?

We get to the roof and, to our luck, it's empty. I'm expecting loud music, partying— all that stuff which would have just resulted in us leaving to go back to our rooms.

And then I see a bunch of cameras and lights facing towards a couch.

"Oh, sorry, the rooftop is occupied," a guy who looks around his late 20s says. He's about to turn his head, but looks back at us. "Wait a minute."

The corners of his mouth rise up, and I get nervous.

My urge to hide behind Elena and Aaliyah grows and I almost do, but then he speaks again.

"Your outfit is perfect for the shoot I'm doing right now."

I look at Elena who's eyeing him suspiciously. She steps in front of me.

Thank the Lord.

"I'm sorry, who are you?"

He looks at Elena, annoyed. "I wasn't talking to you, sweetheart. I was talking to the girl in the dress."

Elena rolls her eyes. "She's *my* client so when you talk to her, you're also talking to me. Let me ask you again, who are you?"

Aaliyah grabs my arm and points towards a sign. This shoot was for...*Vogue!* I look at Elena and the tall man again, who are still bickering and decide to step in between them. I face my back towards the man and lean to whisper in Elena's ear. "They're shooting for *Vogue.*"

She sighs, moving me to the side and continues to argue with the guy. I look at Aaliyah, who's trying to sneak past him. Without any hesitation, I run after her. Luckily, he was too busy with Elena to notice us.

The whole setup is decorated with hanging yellow lights. It looks so dreamy, and the dark sky is only further complimenting it. Underneath the lights is a small couch— a loveseat. It's beige with rose petals scattered across the seats.

In front of the couch is a small, modern, brown coffee table. The coffee table has a vase with a single red rose, and a gorgeous, vintage teapot set.

Aaliyah's phone starts to ring, and she takes it out of her pocket. "It's my mom. I'll be right back— don't move," she winks at me and leaves the set.

I admire the setting in front of me and look at the rose again. I reach for it, but the shadow of a person catches me by surprise and I freeze, alerted.

"Unfortunately, that flower is not up for grabs," he speaks, hands in his pockets. I stand up straight and come face to face with the familiar face from the speech. I

come face to face with Elias.

I swallow hard, taking a huge step back.

Elias is wearing a black dress shirt, with black dress pants and an emerald green tie hanging from his neck loosely.

His suit contrasts perfectly with my dress.

His eyes light up, "Oh, you did that speech about your book not too long ago."

I can't even utter anything to him. At least when we met before, I was tired and was basically spitting out anything that came to mind. Now, I don't know how to find the right words without saying anything wrong or weird.

"You probably don't remember me, but I gave you the lavenders backstage, " he takes a step toward me. A small one. That probably wasn't even a step— more like one-quarter of a step— actually— that was probably one eighth of a step—

What am I doing?

"Sorry," I laugh nervously.

Seriously? That's the best I can do?

My heart is aggressively pounding against my chest. I feel as if I could faint any second. If he took another step to me, my legs are going to give out and I'm going to fall to the floor.

"Why are you sorry?"

Well, maybe because I've realized that I shouldn't be here and kind of butted into your business, but you know.

"I didn't realize you were shooting for *Vogue*."

He laughs and it sends me all the way back to grade eleven,

sharing lunches and poking fun out of every single mishap that happened to ourselves.

God, I missed that.

"Don't be sorry— I'm on a break right now anyway," he smiles, exposing his dimples.

I blink hard, thinking this might be a dream and praying that I'll wake up already.

What happened to the promises I made to myself? The promises to God? They seemed to have vanished into thin air.

You can turn around now. You can leave— in fact — *you should.* He hurt you. He left, and he didn't say anything. He doesn't even remember you. He doesn't know who you are. You're the stranger from the book talk— that is it.

"You look great, by the way. Maxi dresses are definitely your thing," he says.

I take another look at him, trying to see if there's something in his face that could tell me that it isn't Elias. He could just be someone else.

Then I remember, I'm not here to find or lose Elias. I came here by accident. Now that I know this was a mistake, I need to leave. I need to go and be happy with my single life. That's the goal. Independent woman. I don't need a guy running my life.

"I think I should go," I say as I turn around, almost bumping straight into Elena and the guy she was just arguing with.

Great.

14

"Allah loves those who repent."
- Surah al—Baqarah [2:222]

"Perfect, you've met Elias," the guy says. "I'm Jax, by the way."

"I'm Huma," I smile, trying to ignore the reluctant fear in my voice.

I look over at Elena who's biting back a smirk. She probably thinks I knew he was going to be here, which I did not. He just happens to be everywhere I go and it's getting annoying.

"So we agree on this photo shoot, right? It'll be super quick and then you guys can leave," Jax says.

My gaze returns to Elena.

"Yup. We fully agree," she says, not breaking eye contact with me for even a second.

I'll take responsibility for this one. Yes, I dragged myself into this, but I don't think I deserve it at all. I want to go home and sleep. I don't want to stand here anymore.

Heck, I'd rather leave for home right now. I don't care about the eight-hour drive.

It may sound like overkill, but it is anything but that. I'm still thinking about grade eleven and how much I miss when Elias was walking me home, hovering around just so he wouldn't have to leave.

Now here he is, unbothered and happy.

I nod my head, "Mhm."

"Oh, you're going to be a part of the shoot?" Elias asks.

I feel my cheeks heat up, "Yeah, are you uncomfortable with that? We don't have to do it if you're not okay with it—"

He interrupts, "No, I wanted to know if you were okay with this."

Why did he have to be so damn sweet?

My voice cracks as I speak, "As long as we don't have to—"

"Oh yeah, for sure. Don't worry about that. There's not gonna be any physical contact between either of us."

And then we finally get started.

The first photo is just him, holding the teacup to his lips and leaning back against the couch. He knows how to pose so well. You could've fooled me if you told me he's actually a model.

I stand beside Jax and another cameraman.

"He's good at it, isn't he?" he says, his arms crossed over his chest.

I take a second, watching as he so smoothly changes his poses. The cameraman continues with his words, praising Elias for his quick movements.

'Perfect', 'You're doing great.'

"Yeah, I didn't know he did modeling, too," I reply with a small laugh.

Jax looks at me, amused and confused. "You know him personally?"

I almost push myself off the roof. Might as well by the way I'm spitting out sentences like they don't mean anything.

"N-no. I just saw him at the book talk, so I realized he was an actor. Didn't know he did modeling too." I laugh it off, and he follows.

"Alright, can we get the girl to sit beside him?"

I plop myself onto the couch, right across from him and hear him chuckle quietly, sending chills up my spine.

"Okay, Huma, look behind the sofa," Jax instructs and waits for me to take the position before continuing. "Elias, look straight at her. Maybe face your body towards her."

I put an arm on the back pillows of the couch and look towards the roof. I fold my legs, leaving my heels dangling from the couch.

"Yes, Huma. You're doing great!"

I see Elias from my peripheral vision, gazing towards me. He holds his cheek up with the palm of his hand, his elbow resting against the back pillow.

"Perfect!"

"Now Huma, give us a smile."

Still focused on the rooftop, I raise the corners of my mouth and feel my shoulders tense up. It's the feeling of having Elias' eyes on me that's making me nervous. I shift a little in my seat when I hear him whispering to me.

"Hey."

My eyes meet his, and his face softens. He gives me an eye-smile and I feel weirdly comforted. It's just the thought of him looking at me that made me tense up, but somehow, he could have the opposite effect on me if he wanted to.

I place my cheek onto the back pillow of the sofa and continue to look at him.

"You're doing really good, Huma," his gentle voice fills my ears.

"You two were born to model!" Aaliyah shouts, catching me off guard.

I blush pink and could've sworn he does the same. I feel myself continuing to gaze at him, and it doesn't feel awkward looking at him either. He's just as comfortable.

If I could, I would sit there for hours just looking at him.

I whole-heartedly know I'm going to have so many regrets

afterwards for doing this to myself. I've had a little too much of Elias today.

Eventually, we change our position. This whole time, I'm trying to see if he's recognized me yet, or if I really have left his memory. All in all, he's enjoying himself a lot.

For our breaks, he points out parts of the sky. He seems keen to show me stuff, but that's his personality. He was always open with me in high school...this is not anything new.

This is not anything new.

He is not anything new.

"Have you ever thought about how lonely stars are?" He asks during one of our breaks.

I follow his eyes to the sky where there are multiple shining atoms.

I shake my head, tilting it to get a better view.

"They're so far apart, yet when we see it from here, they look so close together," his voice cracks. "*Stars are just lost constellations looking for a home.*"

My heart aches at that. Elias reminds me of a star, and even though he's bright just like one, he doesn't seem as bright as I remember.

It looks as if light has been sucked out of him and he let it happen.

I want to be the one to change that.

The silence between us is filled with the sound of Jax and Elena talking. They seem to have hit it off pretty quickly, talking like old friends catching up.

Elena doesn't talk about her love life with me, but I can see from the way she's looking at Jax, she's excited about whatever they're bonding over.

"So does that make you a star?" I ask, the beating in my chest becoming more frantic. I turn my gaze to him, and see he's already looking at me. "Doesn't this job make you feel lonely, Elias?"

Well, that's the first time I've said his name out loud in a while. Correction— that's the first time in a long time that I've said his name while talking to him.

His eyes relax once again, and a half smile accompanies his face.

I turn red, scared I might've insulted him and he's about to let me down slowly. He's probably disappointed deep down. Up until now, we have been having a good time and now I've ruined it.

I always ruin it.

Always.

"I'm sorry," I cross my arms over my chest.

He tilts his head to the side, examining me before speaking. "It is...lonely I mean," he laughs quietly. "I remember how confusing it was in high school. It wasn't the best at home, but it wasn't the worst at school."

I freeze.

"I remember how many people I had who were so polite and so nice to me when I told them I was a convert. They were so nice about it— inviting me to their houses, offering to take me to the Mosque. Do you know how good it feels? You just convert into a religion filled with guidance and misunderstood people who are pure and selfless, and they treat you like you've always belonged there."

I could listen to him talk for hours on end. About anything. His voice is so gentle and calm, and I've missed it so much. All the time I'm spending with him made me remember all the good memories and moments I had with him.

But this is the exact thing I was scared might happen. Seeing him makes me vulnerable. It makes me want to keep listening and talking to him until he remembers who I am.

How many hours have passed since I came up to this roof?

It's been four. For four hours we've been shooting for the magazine, and I haven't even complained once.

I'm doing it again. Going against my own morals. Going against all my promises to myself, to God. I remember telling myself I would never go against the words I said, but that's what I'm doing now.

"I do," I laugh softly. "I think people don't realize that, even if you're born Muslim, you need guidance. I did, for sure. That's how I started wearing hijab. I still need guidance, but don't we all?"

He nods his head with a beaming smile. Both dimples become prominent on his face, and I sigh.

"You have a very comforting voice. Did you know that?" He looks back towards the sky as the words leave his mouth.

I press my lips together, extremely amused by his answer.

I wish I had the courage to say the same.

He's said that to me before.

"I've heard it before," I laugh. "But thank you."

"Alright, we're done everybody! Great job Huma and Elias!" Jax claps as he approaches us. "You two were born for modeling."

Elias stands straight, and I do the same. "It seems Elena and your friend left back to your room. Do you need one of us to drop you there?" Jax asks.

"I can drop her," Elias speaks. "1317, right?"

He catches me by surprise, but I don't question it.

We start to walk to the elevator when I finally open my mouth.

"How do you know my...?"

He scoffs, satisfied by my reaction. "Are you serious? Michael, my bodyguard, told me you were staying right beside us, and he is such a big fan of your book. He insisted I give you a gift or something, so I ordered the—"

"Whole breakfast menu," I complete his sentence and we burst out laughing. "You are such a trash bag!"

He presses the button to the elevator and puts a hand on the left side of his chest, "Ouch, why am I a trash bag? I was trying to be sweet."

You are already sweet.

"You didn't give any food to your bodyguards. I came afterwards with some food and gave it to them," I say softly.

The elevator doors open, and he stands to the side, letting me in first before stepping in.

"Is that what they told you? I gave them a coupon and the company's card to go buy some breakfast for themselves after I offered them to eat with me and Jax!"

"Damn, seriously?" I look at him in shock.

He nods his head and laughs. "I can't believe they lied to you like that."

My mind is racing back and forth. I want to know what this feeling is if it's not love. I want to know why it's killing me even while I feel pumps of ecstasy coursing through me.

But if this is love, why does it hurt the way it does? Why can't it be as easy as they show in those damn movies? I want love like that. Love that is simple. I don't want whatever this is.

"You know, I would want you to act in my movie," I spit out.

Shoot. Probably shouldn't be saying that to him.

Elena would kill me if that's announced. To make matters worse, the movie deal hasn't even been confirmed.

His lips curve upwards, and the elevator doors open. He waits for me to go before him again, and we walk towards my door.

"Now that is the nicest compliment I've ever received," he walks with his hands in his pockets.

Our steps are slow as we enjoy each other's company. I want to ask him if he remembers me, but I can't do that. If he can't recall who I am at all, then both of us would be humiliated.

I stop in front of my door and spin to him. Today was a

good day. The book signing went well, and so did this unexpected photoshoot.

Although, I thought about what one of my readers said about Elias and how he might've been put in my path for a different reason then I thought. That might be true, but I don't want to believe that for the sole reason that I got to see him today or plan to see him again. That was selfish.

"Well, I had a great time," Elias says as I lean against the door.

"Same. I especially loved the part where you told me about the breakfast menu," I smirk, and receive a laugh from his end.

The elevator dings down the hallway.

"Give me one second," he runs off towards the elevator and comes back with something in his hand.

He sticks out a rose to me. The same rose from the set that I almost took. I look at him, hoping this is his idea of a joke.

"Elias, you didn't have to..." I don't reach for it at all. My mind is telling me to go into my room without even saying goodbye and learn to move on, but my heart is just...*hurt.*

His smile falls into a frown and his hands fall to his side, "Oh, I'm sorry. Is it not okay to give flowers?" He asks, disappointed.

I feel terrible. He's trying to be nice and sweet, and I'm breaking my own rules for him. I need to stop giving into everything, especially him.

"You accepted the other one before. You know, the lilies I gave you?"

That was wrong, too.

I feel my throat tighten, "I know, but that was before I realized it was *you.*"

I try to look away, but his eyes are locked on mine.

"I'm just messing with you," I smile forcefully, not wanting to see him disappointed. "I just didn't expect you to give it to me."

He narrows his eyes with a relieving smile, "Hm, I don't believe that one bit."

I laugh, taking the flower from him. "Thank you...for this flower and the bouquet from before."

I notice his ears turning pink again, and he takes a small step back, "Yeah, of course."

Still leaning against the door, I hear it unlock but I move a little too slow and almost end up falling if it isn't for Elena who catches my arm.

I see him reach out a hand for me but quickly move it away, and I blush.

What a great way to say goodbye, huh?

"God, Huma. You two talk so loudly," she turns around to return to bed as I stabilize myself on my feet, my blush deepening.

"Okay, um, I think I'll get going now...thank you for today. It was amazing."

His face softens at my reaction, "You're the one that made today better—"

"The pleasure is all ours, Huma. You can come to our photoshoots anytime." Jax interrupts, putting an arm around Elias' shoulders.

I have no clue where he came from or when he came but it couldn't have been a better time.

I nod and wave at both of them one last time before shutting the door.

Again, the dread fills me. What have I done?

I step into the bathroom and change quickly before performing wudu to get ready for prayer. The only prayer I have left for today is *Isha*.

During the photoshoot, I was able to pray *Maghrib* on the side after Elias and Jax happily led me to a more private area on the rooftop. For *Asr*, I prayed in the change room in one of the stores Elena, Aaliyah and I went to when we were shopping around.

I set down the prayer mat on the balcony. I haven't even gotten to explore this part of the hotel yet, and let me tell you, it is so nice.

Quiet.

I figured that the streets of New York would be loud, filled with music and people shouting, but tonight it's quiet.

Then I began to pray, and even though I feel so good, I start to cry after I finish with Isha. I think it's the guilt that I'm holding from tearing up all those promises that I've made. I feel bad that I can't stay away from the guy that broke and tore my heart apart, rather than breaking my promises.

I don't move from the prayer mat. I stay there and pray for hours on end.

What am I doing to myself?

I'm sacrificing my own happiness to see him smile. To see his eyes light up with joy. I can't believe I had done that. I don't even know what I'm praying for anymore after Isha. I'm in pain. Pieces of my heart fall onto the mat in front of me as I try to mend the promises I've broken.

I'm mad at myself more than I'm mad at Elias for leaving so suddenly after he graduated from high school.

Even though it was never his fault.

No.

I just needed someone to blame because it's easier if I don't accept the real problems going on here. Elias is anything but a bad person and I've never been more proud of him than right now. Even if I'm hurt, he's grown into a better person than I could've imagined.

His heart is so pure.

But maybe that's it. There's nothing more to be told about *us*. In his mind, *we* are a thing of the past. He's not one to hold onto these types of things like I assumed he might.

I switch my gaze to the rose he gave me.

This isn't right.

None of it is.

Then I make a decision.

From now on, I'll avoid Elias and anyone that associates with him. The only thing I can't do as of right now is get rid of the flowers he gave me. They're gifts, and flowers don't last forever anyway.

I'll take care of them until they die and once they do, that's the end of it.

I have to move on.

I have to.

It's the only way I can heal.

15

"And Allah would not punish them while they seek forgiveness."
- Surah Al-Anfal [8:33]

"Have you been out there all night?" Aaliyah asks.

I nod my head slowly, and she sits beside me. It's eight o'clock now and we're going to go home in an hour.

"What happened? Did something go wrong between you two?"

So Elias and I are now a *'you two.'*

That's just great.

"I don't know..." I stray my eyes away from hers and look down at the prayer mat I'm sitting on. "I kind of wish I restrained myself from talking to him, let alone agreeing to a photoshoot."

Aaliyah scoots closer and puts a hand on my back. She knows where this is coming from. This isn't exactly new territory.

"How come you guys didn't stop me?" I ask, my shoulders tensing. "I'm not blaming you, but why didn't you guys stop me?"

Elena comes onto the balcony with pancakes and maple syrup. She has the same look as Aaliyah; worry plastered all over her face.

"Because you looked happy. Like genuinely happy. Even after Aaliyah left, you two were laughing, and making jokes, and having fun," she says, handing both of us two pancakes each. "And trust me, Huma, I have never seen you happier."

My eyes begin to sting while she speaks. I have no tears to cry anymore.

All of those tears were used last night.

"It's okay. I've decided I'll avoid him. I'm just gonna get hurt again if I keep associating myself with him."

He. Was. Not. Anything. New.

I fold up the prayer mat and place it on top of my luggage inside before joining the two back in the balcony. I pick up my breakfast and pour the maple syrup all over the pancakes so it oozes down around them.

"Do you really wanna do that?" Aaliyah asks.

I shrug, "I don't want to, but if I wanna get past him then I have to."

Aaliyah nods her head approvingly...she continues nodding until her eyes steer away to the flower in a glass of water.

She looks back at me and rubs her face, frustrated, "Is this your way of getting over him? Keeping his gifts alive?"

Elena's eyes go wide out of shock from Aaliyah's reaction, and she almost spits out the water in her mouth.

"No, but it's not going to last anyway," I reply bluntly.

She rolls her eyes as my phone dings, receiving my immediate attention. I take it into my hands and notice it's a message. A message from someone that's following me on one of my public accounts.

Typically, I ignore these because most of the ones I get, which aren't many, are scams telling me to promote my story or content on a tagged account.

This one had a link to a YouTube video. Confused and curious, I press on the notification that takes me to my messages and then click on the link. Maybe this could distract me for the time being.

The title pops up first.

Elias Lee answers the internet's burning questions

Oh Lord, you had to be kidding me. Before I can click off, I hear his voice and the words '*Splintered Heart*' leave his mouth.

"*Yeah,*" he laughs nervously, "*I've been told the description matches me really well.*"

My heart stops beating and Aaliyah inches close to me to see the screen.

"*I feel like I remember everything.*"

I stare in awe at the screen. He's speaking about *my* book. How did he know...? This whole time he let me think he's the oblivious one when really it's me.

I'm too stupid, too blinded by him to realize that he really does remember me. He knows exactly who I am.

I notice a black necklace— *the* black necklace— hanging from his neck. I remember that necklace. I've never seen him take it off before, and I swear, I can spot that thing anywhere.

Although I didn't see it on him during the photo shoot, I think it's safe to assume he had it tucked into his shirt.

I try to soak in the fact that he knows, but I just can't. He remembers me. Elias remembers me. I look at the rose and then the date the video was posted. It's dated two weeks ago.

I feel my lips curving into a smile.

He gave me flowers when he knew who I was.

He gave me flowers when he knew who I was.

Elias gave me flowers when he knew who I was.

No, I can't let him get to me. I made an oath and I will stick to it. Breaking the promise from before was a mistake, but I can't afford to break this one. Nope. Not happening.

I switch my phone off and get up, "So when does the car come to pick us up?"

16

"Huma, if you wanna leave today, you have to hurry up!" Elena shouts from the door. "Traffic has already started on this street— imagine what it's like on the highway."

I sigh, throwing on a comfy outfit and calling it a day. I grab my tote bag and suitcase, and head out the door.

When I step out of the room, I see Michael, the bodyguard. He waves at me once again, and I smile. I stop to pull out a signed copy of my book, handing it over to him.

"I know you couldn't make it to my book signing so I wanted to give you a little gift," I watch as he admires it, opening up the crisp pages of the fresh copy.

"Oh, this is amazing," he flips onto the signed page and looks up at me with a smile. "Thank you, Ms.Tariq. This is so sweet of you."

"You can call me Huma," I say, not realizing this whole time he has been calling me by last name. I close up my tote bag and give him a quick goodbye before I head to the elevators where Aaliyah and Elena are waiting for me.

"Did you check to see if you have everything?" Elena asks. "Like phone, keys, bags—"

"Yeah, I triple-checked."

The elevator dings open and we all step inside.

I check my phone, unlocking it and see the video is still up on the screen. I leave the tab and go to my messages. I haven't called Ami or Abu in a couple of days now, and thought I might as well let them know how everything went.

I really need a day to relax. Perhaps going over to their house could be the perfect solution. It would be so refreshing just to have a weekend to get myself together. I think by now I deserve it.

When we get out, the car isn't there. Instead, the same big car Elias came in is annoyingly taking up all the space to the front of the hotel doors instead.

I follow Elena outside.

"Where is the car?" Aaliyah asks, whining.

I back up, trying to get a better view and bump into something hard.

"Woah."

My heart shakes at the contact and the voice that follows with it.

I don't want to turn around.

I can't.

If I do, I might as well jump onto the road right into on-coming traffic because that sounds like the best option right about now.

"Are you okay?"

I would much rather him push me out of the way than be so polite.

I spin around and smile, "Yeah. I'm so sorry."

He raises both his eyebrows in an amused expression, "Well, look who it is."

He knows who you are.

I almost jump at my own thought.

There's a possibility yesterday he figured I knew that he knew who I am and now we're mutually being silent over this.

But I wonder if it's all in my head or not. Maybe he thinks the description of my book just matches him so perfectly out of coincidence, and not because I might've written a book about him.

A security guard separates the two of us, trying to push me away.

"No, she's good," Elias says to his bodyguard, and switches his gaze back to me. "She's an...acquaintance."

Wow, I'm an acquaintance? Not even an old friend?

Not going to lie, I've never felt so offended being called an acquaintance this bad ever.

I mean, it's better that way I guess.

"Sorry about that," he says with a soft chuckle. "They have to follow protocol. I had no clue you were leaving for Toronto already."

"Yeah, I kind of need a refresher after yesterday," I laugh, but then realize that sounds bad in every sort of spectrum. "Not in the sense that I didn't enjoy myself— I had such a good time."

I see a couple of people running towards us. Well, running to him. I just happen to be here.

What I don't see are their cameras.

At that moment, so much ran through my mind.

Dating scandals.

Rumours.

Hate.

He's going to have the worst of the worst from this if people start to make assumptions. I don't know how bad it can get, but I can definitely imagine.

I've seen celebrities get attacked for the smallest rumours, and when they're a big celebrity, it's worse.

Fear climbs over me as the flashes of the camera become more frantic. I hate flashing lights. I feel myself getting dizzy from the light, wanting to crouch down onto the floor.

Yes, there are bodyguards around us, but they're only pushing us towards his car. I can't see anything. The only thing I can do is hear people's questions.

"Elias, is this your new date?"

"Isn't that the author who wrote the book about you?"

They wouldn't stop. I find myself short of breath and no matter how big of a breath I take, I'm suffocating. I cower down, the frantic noises mixing with the sound of my heart beating out of my chest. The palms of my hands cover my ears with a harsh press and I close my eyes, praying this is a dream, reciting every prayer known to man.

But just as quickly as I crouch, strong arms lift me back up onto my feet and I'm being rushed towards the car again. My arm hits something hard and I wince.

That is going to leave a bruise.

The car door opens and I'm pulled inside. I'm gently ushered onto a seat and someone kneels in front of me as I burst into tears.

I can't breathe.

"I can't breathe," I mutter, covering my face with my hands.

"Huma, drink some water," I hear, and a water bottle appears in front of me. I slap it out of his hand and let it hit the other side of the car, flinching at the sound it makes.

"I don't need water— I need to get out of here!" I shout, bawling and trying the handle to the door over and over again like it would magically open for me. "Open it, please! I don't want to be here."

In front of me I see Elias. He's grabbing stuff one by one with a worried look. He gets hold of a small blanket and sets it onto my lap.

"You're okay, Huma. Look, we're in the car now," he says softly. "It's safe here."

I shake my head, wanting to get out of here. I need to leave. "No, please. Tell him to stop driving and let me out." I gasp at the amount of breath it takes me to speak a single sentence.

Elias takes hold of the water again.

"Has this happened to you before?" He asks, lowering his voice.

"N-no." My mind is foul, not letting me understand what's happening. My body is overheating and freaking out at the way my legs are shaking the car. It doesn't help that this car is filled with people either.

"There's too many people here." I whisper.

"Okay," Elias replies.

And suddenly, the car stops. One by one, security guards are jumping out of the car. Soon, even the driver is gone and the only people left in the car are Jax, who's driving. Elias, who's still kneeling in front of me. And me.

"Is that better?"

I start to relax a little, pressing myself against the cushiony seat, trying to regulate my breath. Even with everyone gone, I still can't breathe and tears continue to fall out of my eyes when I realize nothing has changed.

"Huma, do you need anything else?" He asks and before I can stop myself, I lean close to him to hear his breath. I'm not touching him, but my head is so close to his shoulder, I might as well be. I close my eyes, trying my hardest to focus on it, but then I hear Elias starting to count. "One." He whispers as I inhale, somehow not catching me by surprise at all. "Two." I let out an exhale, listening to him count. "Three." I inhale again, a deeper breath this time. "Four." His voice comes out like he's following the same breathing pattern, and I shut my eyes tighter. "Five."

Little by little, my heart is being soothed and my breath is decelerating until I'm at my state of calm again. Even when the rhythm of our chests are basically the same, the fear that mine may start to rush again keeps me from moving.

He continues to count, and slowly, he fades his voice off, leaving the sound of our breathing my only source of serenity.

I sit up straight, exhausted. My eyes are stinging, so I press them against the front side of my hand and sigh.

"I don't wanna be here, Elias," I say through tears.

I can see the hurt in his face when I place my hands on my lap. I know this was never his intention. Who wants a crowd of people chasing after you? People who are madly obsessed with you, or will do anything to make some headlines?

He feels bad for pulling me into this, but all I can think about is how he lives with this. He from all people doesn't deserve any of this.

"I'm so sorry, Huma. I'm so, so sorry, but I'm not dropping you in the middle of the road," he replies, and I laugh a little.

He gives me a sad, but hopeful smile.

My eyes stray away from Elias to the front of the car where Jax is driving as he talks on the phone.

"Yeah, well that was never the intention! Do you think I wanted this to happen? It's not like we pay *Paparazzi* to come after us!"

"Is his voice too loud?" He asks, and I shake my head. He clearly doesn't get the memo though because he's telling Jax to shut up. Apparently *'there's nothing more annoying than hearing him shout.'*

"Is that Elena? Can I talk to her?" I speak, my throat parched.

Elias basically snatches the phone out of his hand and gives it to me, earning him a scowl.

"Elena," I feel my eyes watering again as I hold up the phone to my ear.

"Honey, are you okay? We lost you there for a second," she says quietly.

I lower my voice. "Yeah, I'm okay now. I think I might've bruised my arm a little—"

"WHAT?" Jax looks over at me with pure concern while Elena

continues. "Hon, do me a favour and give the phone back to Jax. I'll talk to you later."

I give it back, and from there, Jax and Elena go back and forth with their shouting.

"You have a bruise...?" Elias sits down beside me. I nod my head and attempt to clear my throat. Elias hands me the water bottle again, earning him a look. "If you don't want it, you can throw it at me. I won't be mad."

I give him an eye roll and take a sip, "I'm not going to throw it at you."

My legs are still bouncing, regardless of how calm I am compared to earlier. Elias catches on and finds my gaze again.

"You're going to be okay, Huma. I'm not going to leave you alone until you feel okay again." Elias taps Jax's shoulder and whispers something, before sitting back again. "By the way, we're going to get your bruise checked by a doctor."

"No, that's not necessary—"

"Yes, it is. I did bad enough not getting you out of the way before people surrounded us. It's my fault, Huma. I should've been more careful. I should've *protected you*." He flashes me a sincere look.

My heart jumps a little at his words. It feels weird to hear that from him even while he looks at me like it hurts him more than it could ever hurt me.

"It's not your fault. If anything, I should've looked around. Thankfully I bumped into you and not some crazy person."

He looks down and mutters, "I'm honestly happy you bumped into me."

His eyes sparkle when his gaze finds mine, and I curve my lips upwards into a smile despite how hard I just cried in front of him.

On a different note, my mind is dozing off to last night. I told myself I would do everything in my power to avoid him, but here I am.

In his car.

Being soothed after crying for what must've been at least thirty minutes.

Shoot. But this technically isn't my fault. I got forced into this.

Jax and Elena are still at it, arguing that it isn't Elias' fault I got stuck in this mess.

Which it isn't.

"Why would I wanna hurt my client? Only someone as indecent as you would think that!" He snaps, and Elias laughs.

Damn his smile.

"Don't you kinda ship the two together?" He asks in between snickers.

I laugh at his comment, my mind comforted to know he isn't treating me any differently after everything that just happened. "One-hundred percent."

My phone begins to ring, and I turn away from Elias.

It's Ami.

"Oh my— *Alhumdulillah* you picked up. Are you okay, *beta*? I saw the news," she says all in one breath.

My eyes grow wide.

If she is talking about the *now-news*, as in what literally happened fourty-five minutes ago, I'm definitely going to start crying again. My very own mother and father saw me being shoved into a car with probably the most gorgeous man I've ever seen in my short life.

"Give me a minute, Ami," I put her on hold.

As a desi kid, putting your own parents— let alone your own mother on hold— is never a good idea, but I'm desperate to know what this *news* Ami had seen was exactly.

Elias' eyes meet mine, "What? Is everything okay?"

I shake my head and lean over to whisper into his ear, "My mom just said there are headlines. She didn't tell me what exactly but I think we both have a couple of guesses on what they may be about."

Elias gets a hold of his phone and unlocks it. "Jax, get off the phone. We might have some headlines."

Well, I wouldn't use the word 'might' when even my mother who was not very tech-savvy knows what's going on all the way in New York, but whatever floats your boat.

Turns out, there are a handful of them.

I pick the phone back up. "Okay, Ami, I'll call you in a bit."

I quickly say bye, and she hangs up while Jax reads out some of those headlines.

"Well, these are quite intense: *'Elias Lee suspected to be dating New York Times' bestselling author',*" he scoffs. "Or get a load of this: *'Check out what fans have to say about actor Elias Lee's new girlfriend.'*"

My heart aggressively pounds against my chest. I can imagine the judgemental comments about me in there. I take a deep breath to help and only hope that the comments are not too bad.

I now have a website open on my phone for the article.

"Jax, shut up," Elias says.

BREAKING NEWS: Actor Elias Lee has been seen outside in New York with author Huma Tariq. Reporters say this might have been more of a getaway trip for the two rather than business...

I skim through it, catching only bits and pieces of what the article has to say as I reach the comments. But just as quickly as I had my phone, it's no longer in my hands. Elias shuts it off and slips it into my open bag.

"Rule number one, never look at the comment section," he says, and Jax nods his head.

I analyze him for a second. "I just wanna know what they're saying. Not everybody has bad intentions, you know."

His gaze darkens and I go quiet. He almost looks annoyed, and pretty intimidating at that. A very familiar look I would say. "You're going to get hurt."

Okay, I know I owe it to him to listen. He just helped me out with a potential panic attack so the least I can do right now is listen, but my curiosity is taking over.

What is he trying to hide from me?

I reach inside my tote bag.

"Please, Huma. I promise you, it's not worth it. People can be so brutal," he says with a twinge of sadness.

Jax has his eyes transfixed on the road as he speaks. "He's right. Take it from him. People were so rude to him about countless things...we're only trying to look out for you."

I sigh and let go of my phone, letting it drop back inside my bag. "Sorry."

His face softens and he rests against the seat, "Don't be. I get being curious and all, but some people can be super harsh and I don't want you to go through that."

I turn away to smile. Holy crap, I need an excuse to get out of here. Literally every escape plan I have is absolutely concerning.

Apparently Elena and Aaliyah are basically right behind us so if I just waited for some traffic, I could run into our car and done! Don't ever have to see Elias ever again.

But then again, what Elena said about seeing me happy...that didn't make it okay, did it? I know developing crushes is okay, but it isn't okay to be associating myself with him so much. We're not married, heck, we're not even engaged. I know this situation isn't exactly in my favour, but I should've been cautious about where I was walking. That part is my fault.

Stupid mistake.

"Do you wanna get checked, Huma? For your arm?" Jax asks, catching my gaze from the rear mirror.

I shake my head. "No, I think I'll be fine—"

"Yeah, she needs to get checked," Elias interrupts.

The fact that I was just smiling over his words and now I'm frowning. This man angers me in more ways than I can count.

"It's not Jax. Leave it." I say, annoyed.

Elias leans over and whispers something in Jax's ear. Jax's eyebrows arch and then he gives me a look I can't quite decipher before taking the next intersection off the highway.

Elias sits back down, satisfied.

"What did you say to him?"

He chuckles, "Take a wild, wild guess on what I said."

I scoot away from him. He is on my very last nerve and keeps finding ways to get under my skin even though I figured our moment not too long ago would give him a reason to, you know, not annoy me to death.

My urge to pull on the van door and open it was growing.

"It's funny you say that, 'cause I can't exactly remember why I liked you—"

Crap.

Crap.

Holy crap, did I just confess?

17

"So do not claim yourselves to be pure; He is most knowing of who fears Him."
Surah An-Najm [53:32]

I glance over and Elias is looking at me with a grin plastered on his face.

I just confessed to Elias.

Oh my Lord, I just told Elias I liked him.

Jax lets out a low laugh even though this is way beyond what I would consider funny and I look at him, flustered. I look out the window, turning my body away from both of them. I can feel all the heat in me rushing to my cheeks.

"Huma," he lowers his voice and I can hear the amusement in it.

"Whatever, Elias. It slipped out. A joke if you will."

Yes. Cover the truth with your lies.

I can hear him chuckling. How is this amusing to him? It feels like mockery to say the least. It sucks to think I like him so much and here he was laughing in my face.

...

Elias makes several attempts to try to talk to me throughout this car ride to the doctor, but I flat-out ignore him.

When we finally pull over, Elias offers to go with me. When I refuse, Jax suggests he come along, but I shut him down just as quickly. I needed Aaliyah and Elena. Not two guys who are making my life miserable.

I'm still mad at them for making fun of me, so I decide I'm not going to talk to them at all.

I get myself signed-in and take a seat. On the left side of me is a cute elderly couple who smile when they see me, and on the other side, a young mother with an infant who has most likely just learned how to walk based on the way he waddles.

I wait until basically everyone has left, and then I'm called into a room. The doctor greets me at the door with a friendly smile.

"Come on in," she says, closing the door behind us.

I hop onto the examination bed and hear the parchment paper underneath me crinkle. I try to conceal the anger I have right now for Jax and Elias by putting my focus on the pain in my arm.

It doesn't work too well.

I figured he would have at least pretended he hadn't heard me or something, but now he's in the car, laughing at my misfortune.

"So, what seems to be the problem?"

I sigh, rolling up my sleeve, "I don't know what I bumped into, but I think it was a metal pole or something. It hit my arm pretty hard."

She nods her head as I speak.

"...I wasn't gonna get it checked until someone suggested I should to be safe."

She checks my arm, and after a couple of questions and pressing on certain areas, she steps back.

"Okay, so far there is nothing super concerning here. You just have a bruise, but it's pretty big," She types away on her laptop. "I suggest you let it naturally heal. There's not much we can do about it other than let it do its thing."

"Okay," I respond as I hop off the bed. "Thank you so much."

"If you think the pain is going to get more than you can handle, I could prescribe some painkillers?" She suggests.

"Yes, that'd be great."

I open the door to leave after she tells me to go to the front desk to get my prescription, but instead, I get startled by a towering figure.

I click my tongue, "God, Elias. Why do you have to scare me like that?!"

"How's her arm?" Elias asks the doctor, ignoring my whole existence.

The audacity...

"Yeah, it's going to take a while to heal. She just has a bruise and, as long as we let it do its thing, she should be fine," the doctor nods towards me. "Is this your...husband? You two make a lovely couple."

Absolutely amazing. I love being humiliated. It's the best feeling in the world.

I smile to hide the fact I'm violently blushing, and before I can say anything, Elias stands directly in front of me, blocking the view of the doctor, "We do make a lovely couple, don't we, Huma?"

I freeze, both agitated and flustered like earlier. I turn around and leave through the door, hating every fragment of Elias as my eyes fall to the windows of the walk-in.

There I see Jax and Elena shouting at each other. I basically sprint to her and jump into her arms.

"Please get me the hell out of here," I embrace her, feeling her arms wrap around me.

"Of course, Hon. Let me finish my conversation with Jax," she pats my head, and I release her. "You get in the car."

I open the van door, hopping in next to Aaliyah. "I thought you died! I was so scared, Huma," she slaps my shoulder.

"Ow!"

Elena comes inside and sits in the passenger seat. She turns around and grabs my hand, relieved, "Thank God we got you back, sweetheart. Jax really is a psychopath."

She sends a scowl to Jax who's walking over to the car. Elias follows behind him and my lack of emotion is more than enough for Elias to know that I'm not in the mood for him to talk to me.

"Here are your painkillers," he passes them through the window. "Are you sure you don't want to drive with us? We have a discussion to finish."

"Yeah, I'm more than sure."

The car begins to move and when we're finally on the road, I lean my head back against the seat.

"What discussion?" Aaliyah asks.

"Oh, um," I audibly sigh, mentally preparing myself for pure mortification. "I told Elias I liked him."

Both of their mouths gape open. I expected this reaction. Confessing to someone even by accident is a huge deal.

I go into every single small and huge detail there is to share. I tell them how Jax ended up laughing after I humiliated myself, and I hear Elena scoff. I tell them about Elias not leaving me alone after what I said and how he was right outside the doctor's door waiting for me.

I don't want to say I'm falling into his trap again, but I am. I *really* am, and I know all these years that I've tried my absolute hardest to not think of him, to not try and recall our memories has gone down the drain. And what did this mess result in? A book. A book and finding out who he is. Not only that, but the fact that I even got to see him now.

What I'm about to say may seem like I'm ready to go against

everything I promised myself this morning, however, that is not the case at all. I'm starting to think I might be looking at this from the wrong angle. What if the reason why I keep getting pushed towards him and having all of these interactions with him means I'm looking at everything wrong?

Maybe I shouldn't distance myself from him.

"So, what happened then?" Elena asks, intrigued.

I grab the bag of chips that's sitting right next to me. "Then I just ran out and saw you, thankfully."

"Well, do you think you're gonna give him a chance?" Aaliyah takes her shoes off and brings her feet up onto the seat. "I mean, he clearly likes you back."

"Okay, now that is the stupidest thing I've heard all day." I laugh in between words.

She raises her eyebrows in a very judgy-way.

There's no way she's being serious right now. He hasn't done anything that would signify he likes me. All he's done is make fun of me for liking him now that he knows.

I don't consider that a crush. Nope, not at all. Even with him helping me after I was pushed into his car...that was purely an act of kindness.

"He does. He likes you. Why else would he pass those types of comments?" She queries. "Saying you two would look cute together—? I think he's trying to indirectly tell you something."

I roll my eyes. "*Lovely*. He said we would look *lovely* together."

Even if that is the case, I never understood the dynamic of making fun of or bullying someone when you like them. I understand not wanting to confess or feeling nervous to do so, but when it gets to the point where you're making them feel uncomfortable for confessing— or in my case— *accidentally* confessing, it hurts.

"If that's what he's trying to communicate, he needs to improve his communication skills because I'm not gonna sit around and get mocked."

18

A week passes and I've been feeling pretty good about myself. I feel refreshed and at peace. I haven't talked to Elias, and Aaliyah and Elena have avoided discussing it which is perfectly fine by me.

It feels nice to have some *me-time* for a change.

Today I have a very small list of what I have to get done: I have to go do some grocery shopping (plus, grab some iced-coffee on the way (it is a literal sauna out here)), finish signing copies of my book and send them on their way to my readers, and end it off with a nice Saturday movie night with Elena and Aaliyah.

This is even more exciting since Elena usually never stays over at the apartment. Typically, she'll stay for a couple of hours and then leave, but not tonight. She finally decided to stay over.

I decide to throw on whatever I can find in my closet as long as I can breathe in it, and end up wearing a maxi dress. It's a plain and simple pink-ish dress that has little floral prints all over it.

I set my hijab, throwing it over my shoulder, and out the door I go.

Aaliyah left this morning to go check out the bookstore. She's the manager after all and with our trip to New York, she had to take the day off. Since today is Saturday, she'll be home at around five or six, depending on how it goes and if she has to organize or take care of anything.

Elena on the other hand said she has a couple of things to finish up, which is all business related, so I didn't bother questioning it any further. I know she's having a tough time with the work she's getting and working for new clients and everything, so I don't want to push it and make her any more anxious than she already is.

I pull out of the parking lot and drive to the local grocery store. Last week was supposed to be when I got the groceries, but Aaliyah ended up taking a trip there instead. Our whole system is taking turns on every single task and errand there is to do.

Except paying for the apartment. That's split 50-50 unless the other person is saving up for something specific in which we don't mind doing favours for each other once in a while.

I step out of my car and head inside, grabbing a cart with me. I pull out my phone to look at our grocery list. Aaliyah and I have a shared note where we both write out anything we need from the store, and so whoever has to go do that errand, can easily access it.

I open up the note and there is a huge list; fruits, veggies, spices, snacks, chicken nuggets, and so much more.

I surprisingly obtain everything I need pretty quickly and set the groceries into my car.

Just as I'm about to start the car, Elena's name makes an appearance on my phone.

"Hey~!" She says in a cheerful tune, while the engine of my car roars.

I reply with a small laugh, amused, "Hi~!"

"What are you doing right now?" She asks.

I take a second to respond, driving out of the parking lot. "I just got some groceries and now I'm heading home."

It feels nice to be getting back to normal. Before it was so chaotic with the trip, book signings...*Elias* and so I've been avoiding thinking of all those topics collectively. They aren't benefiting me in any way if I decide to put my thought and time to all of that.

"What are you doing right now?" I ask, turning at the intersection.

"I've been busy with another client and she's just finished her last draft for her book, so I've been reviewing that for her and adding feedback," she sighs audibly into the phone. "And let me tell you, the book is 600 pages in total."

My mouth gapes, "Are you serious?"

We talk for almost an hour, going on about undirected things.

It isn't exactly the most productive call, but I think we both need to rant and release anything on our chests from how much has been happening lately.

While we talk, I sort through the groceries before telling her I'm going to finish up signing some books.

I sit down on the floor of my bedroom, the sun flooding inside and giving the place a glow. Typically, I would do a live while signing books, but as per Jax and Elias' requests, I've been avoiding it. They're concerned about some of the people that would be commenting. Specifically people that want to ask about Elias and I. And the thing is, that even if I didn't talk to those two anymore, we are kind of tied together right now because of this scandal.

They were even able to get Elena on board, and now, she does everything in her power to convince me not to do any lives or give any type of information that people could use against me or Elias. I hate that so much. I don't want my writing career to deteriorate because of one mistake.

I decide to stop at around the fifteenth book and just start packing them. It's only three o'clock, so if I finish up quickly, maybe I can be generous enough to try to make something for the movie night.

That is when my phone dings. I expect the dinging to stop after a second or two, but it keeps going. I place the book in my hand onto my desk gently and reach for my phone.

It's a bunch of notifications from a handful of my apps. I get notifications all the time, some tagging me, some just notifying me of what other people are up to, but each notification popping up has my name in it.

Then my phone rings.

It's Jax.

Now I don't know if Elena wants me to talk to Jax without her present since I tend to blabber and say the wrong things a lot, but I answer the call. At this point, I had quite frankly lost respect for the two so now our conversations are filled with pettiness from both ends which would end up with somebody angry.

"What do you want?" I ask, maintaining my annoyance.

"Hey, it's Elias. And save the attitude for the news. They want you to give your side of the story of this *relationship*. You're probably getting those notifications, aren't you?"

Well, we are starting off strong. All of this has to happen as soon as I say how proud I am of myself for not giving into anyone.

"I am...how do you know?"

He scoffs, "How do you think—? Anyway, avoid those posts. I'm serious. I don't even know if you've been listening to me and Jax, but you're—"

" I got it. You two need to leave me alone. It's getting annoying!" I snap, and it goes silent.

I can tell he's still on the other line, but it triggers me. I've been dealing with them for way too long.

"Huma, if this is about you liking—"

I shut him down right there. Is this why he called? So he can talk about this with me? I was over that day and I really wish I could take back everything I said to him.

"Please, Elias, I told you. It slipped out so please stop talking about it," I soften my voice to hopefully get through to him. "I'm busy right now, so I'm gonna hang up."

I don't wait for a reply. I immediately press the decline button and place my phone aside. I'm tired. I thought we all could collectively pretend it never happened if he would just stop bringing it up. If he wants to keep talking about it, he can talk to other people about it.

Just. Not. Me.

I continue to package the books until I hear the door open. Aaliyah appears at my bedroom door with a big brown bag in her hand.

"I see our kitchen has been fully stocked." She grins.

"Yeah," I reply, finding her eyes on me. I smile, not wanting to give away any sort of irritation from the call I just had. "The kitchen felt way too empty."

"Well, I brought us a lot of different things," she sits down excitedly.

Out of all of us, Aaliyah's probably the most excited for this movie night. So am I, but she wants to do so much for this movie night, and I'm all for it. For me. This movie night is really going to get us back into place. Once these scandals die down, I can start writing again and stressing about book signings instead of worrying about whether Elias is going to call me through my home phone or by text message.

"Okay, so I brought all of us masks— like face masks, eye masks, etcetera."

I nod my head as I complete packing another package.

"I also brought Ludo. Maybe we could play that later on," she continues. "...and I think that's about it. You brought snacks, right?"

"Yes, I did," I sigh. It isn't an irritated sigh, it's more like an *im-tired* sigh.

I can't wait until all of us are together watching movies and munching on some snacks.

For the next couple of hours until Elena comes over, I decide to bake cookies and set up the rest of the snacks onto the coffee table. We set it up so that it's pretty dark in the apartment. I keep the kitchen stove light on so that it isn't completely pitch-black. Mainly to be able to navigate to the bathroom if we need it during the movie.

I bring the cookies to the table and join the two on the couch.

"Are we ready for movie night?" I ask excitedly.

They both cheer and Aaliyah begins to scroll through our options.

"We can do a couple of movie marathons. Maybe we should start off with some classics," I suggest. "What do we think about *Wish Dragon—?*"

My phone begins to ring, followed by Elena's and even Aaliyah's.

Elena looks at me with confusion, but holds a finger up. "Don't answer your phones...Let me do it first," Elena says and reaches for the buzzing device on the table. She answers it and her bewildered expression becomes agitated. She gets up from the couch and walks into my bedroom, shutting the door behind her.

"Well, that was strange," Aaliyah says.

Our phones stop ringing and the screens go black.

I feel a sense of uneasiness. With everything that happened last week, I'm scared of what Elena's call might be about. I get up and head towards my bedroom.

With one hand on the knob, I press my ear against the door. I try to listen in, my eyes wandering to the wall in front of me.

However, our walls are not very thin so the only thing I'm hearing are broken sentences.

"How...? Maybe...no."

I swallow hard.

"What's wrong, Huma?" Aaliyah calls from the couch, and I hover my other hand a little bit so she knows to give me a second.

My phone starts to ring again and I give up trying to decode what was going on in my room. I look at my phone and don't recognize the number. I hesitate for a moment, staring at the accept button.

Could it be Galaxy Entertainment?

I don't have their number saved on my phone, so it might be them...? But then again, Jax and Elias work under that entertainment. Why not call me with their personal numbers?

I shake my head and answer the call.

"Is this Huma Tariq?" A sudden man's voice fills my ear.

I step into the kitchen, curiosity taking over. "Yes...Who is—"

He interrupts. "Do you mind if I ask you a couple of questions?"

I have another moment of hesitation. I should end the call now. This is stupid. This entire time, I've been listening to Elena, Aaliyah, Jax, and even Elias when it comes to looking at other peoples' takes on the news about us. I listen to them while all of them know about what is being said, but I have the right to know about what's going on.

I *need to know* what people are saying about me.

"What questions?" I query.

"Well, let me give you an example," he sounds amused, and it scares me almost. "Would you say Elias is a bit out of your league? Like maybe you two aren't fit to be together almost?"

I sigh audibly, "What do you mean by that?"

My breath is shaking now and I try to gain control of the situation, but it seems I've already messed up and there's no turning back from here.

"My apologies, that seemed a bit rude...what I'm trying to say is, don't you think you may be seen as a little *lower* than Elias?"

Okay, now I freeze.

Is that how people are viewing me? *Lower than Elias?* Is that what his so-called *'adoring fans'* refer to me as?

I fill up a cup with water and crouch down to take a sip.

He chuckles, making me even more uncomfortable than just seconds ago.

"Okay, let's forget about that one. I think we all know the answer to that."

I take a sip again.

He starts up with another question, "What about the fact that your social status compared to Elias' makes him look like he's pitying you almost."

I feel myself losing my breath again just as the doorbell rings.

God, who could it be now?

This is meant to be a relaxing day. A day for me and my two amazing, supportive friends to hang out and find enjoyment tonight after the stress we've been put through. If I had known this morning was leading up to this, I would've just taken a trip to Ami and Abu's instead.

I set a scarf over my head, "One sec," I say into the phone before placing it on mute. I open the door after throwing a hijab at Aaliyah and, low and behold, it's Elias.

I desperately want to slam the door in his face. He's letting people say all this stuff about me and then continuously telling me to avoid looking at the comments as if I would never see them.

"Why are you here?" I ask bluntly.

He answers with his own question. "Who's on the phone?"

I scoff, "Oh, you wanna know? It's a reporter asking me if I knew about the snarky comments fans— oh wait— *your* fans were making about me."

He gives me a look of guilt but I'm not done— nope— not even close.

"In fact, let me have him say it out loud for you," I unmute the phone call while keeping my eyes locked with Elias'. "Sorry, could you repeat that question again? The one you just asked?"

"Of course!" He replies with enjoyment as if this is a fun little interview. "A lot of fans were commenting under our news article and one of them mentioned something about social status and how it just about looks like Elias may be pitying you."

I end the call and drop my hand to my side. Regardless of the attitude and steam I'm releasing, my eyes begin to sting. "You let your precious fans make all these comments about me. Attacking me for being—" I make air-quotes. *"Lower than you."*

I rub the sudden tears on my cheeks, and he stands there watching me cry. He doesn't say a single thing. He just watches as I break down in front of him for the second time since we've met.

If I had confessed back in grade eleven about how much I liked him, is this the reaction he would've given me? Oh wait, no. He'd probably laugh in my face and make fun of me.

Oh wait again, he already did that.

"And this whole time—" I stop to take a breath from the crying. "You acted like you were protecting me! Like you really cared about me and I let you do that!"

"Huma—"

"No, please. If you say anything more than I might as well admit to everything they've said so far. How you're pitying me, how you never really cared about me, how you made fun of my feelings—everything!"

I feel a warm, comforting hand on my shoulder and I already know it's Aaliyah. "Huma, come sit down. You both can talk about this inside."

I shake my head and gently brush her hand off me, "N-no, I wanna talk here. Just go check on Elena or something."

To my surprise, she leaves and I face Elias again.

"Huma, you know I mean no harm. I would never do anything to hurt you and the only reason I wanted you to avoid those comments is because I know what it's like to be judged. I know how painful it can be. And even if I had said something, even if I tried to stop people from attacking you, only a small percentage would've paid attention."

"And I believe you...but you didn't even try."

Elena shows up beside me. "Where's Jax, hon?" She asks Elias.

"He's out near the elevator," he replies and Elena slips past us.

"Maybe you should go, Elias. You're wasting your time talking to me. You should be focused on your career. Do things that will benefit you. Everyone thinks so too, so maybe you should leave me alone."

The look from the car, the look of hurt.

Again, I know his intention is never to hurt me, but I don't want to be around people who see me like that. Even if it isn't him, there are way too many people who think that, and I don't need Elias repeatedly hearing that and then having doubts about whether he should've talked to me or not.

Back then, I was stupid to think there might have been something there between us. That was entirely my fault. But no one deserves to be told the things people say about me. And it doesn't surprise me one bit that basically everyone is coming to Elias' rescue as if I'm the one he should be staying away from. As if I'm not being harassed for simply bumping into him by accident.

"Don't say that," he says, softly. "That's what other people are saying, not me. Please don't go off other people's words."

I feel myself being comforted by his words. He's speaking so gently as if I'm made of glass, and I like it, but I find myself growing defensive. Defensive of myself and how I feel. I almost feel like if I give into him, he'll leave again.

He continues to speak and even though I want to do nothing but interrupt, I hold off and let him talk.

"People are going to continue to say what they please, but that doesn't mean my opinion about you will ever change. Matter of fact, Huma, I meant to tell you over the phone but you hung up on me so I couldn't..."

I feel heat on my cheeks, not ready for another moment of humiliation.

"The thing is..." He takes a breath and almost smiles. "I like—"

"Huma, get inside. This conversation can happen another day," Elena interrupts.

I look at her, utterly confused by the sudden burst of seriousness. "I think I need some time, Elias. I need some time to think."

I meet his gaze again.

He searches my eyes for a second and then nods his head slowly, "Okay. Then I'll wait for you. I don't care how long you make me wait. I'll stay here...*for you.*"

ACT 2

19

✺

"It's not the eyes that are blind, but the hearts."
- Surah Al-Hajj [22:46]

It's been a couple of days since I've left the house. It isn't because of Elias...well, partially because of him, but I'm not upset with him exactly. I'm still hurt by what his fans said about me, except I've realized I was getting mad at the wrong person.

I still wish he had said something to those people, but he's trying.

It's been two weeks since I've talked to Elias or Jax. I've been avoiding going out because of the reporters who apparently found which building I'm living in. Luckily, they don't know the exact floor or room number.

Unfortunately though, that didn't ease my conscience. It apparently bugged Elias too because he sent two bodyguards about an hour after he left. To my surprise, it was Michael with another bodyguard I had never seen before.

Michael works the morning shift and then switches with Ayaan, the other bodyguard.

I won't lie, when I saw Elias send over people to protect me, I felt my stomach tying in thick knots. Even when I feel confused about him, he makes my heart flutter.

Now I'm sitting on my bed, looking through old stuff from high school. I look at all the old assignments, my diploma, certificates— it blows my mind how far I've come. I really was able to make those *little-me* dreams come true; I published a book, I'm living with my best friend, and I found a trustworthy editor who also works as my manager. *Little-me* would be so proud.

At the bottom of this never-ending saga of old assignments, tests, and essay papers, I found a couple of diaries. Curious, I pull them out, making the pile of papers above them fall to the bottom.

I line them all up on my bed and then count them. There are seven diaries in total. I pick up the first one in the line; it has a pink exterior and a broken lock with a pen I'm surprised I didn't end up losing.

I open it up and immediately see words. This was the start of my diary phase and it lasted until I graduated from high school. I started writing in freshman year, so I whole-heartedly know these entries are about to be so humiliating.

I roll my eyes at the papers and set aside the first diary.

The next one is grey and has a tiny coffee cup at the front. No pen, no lock. Just a diary.

Diaries are like unboxing memories. Typically, people who write entries would write daily— I however— wrote when I needed to rant or when Elias did so much as look in my direction.

I try to organize the placement of my diaries by year, but realize the one in my hand is from grade eleven.

I open it up and see a blank page. I turn it again and find a bundle of letters. I start to read it and slowly pick up on who this is about.

I saw him today. He talked to me and was even here after the bell rang. My math teacher picked on him for being late to his next class and he laughed it off. He has a very, very, very contagious laugh. It's those types of laughs where he can make everybody in the room smile. Not to mention, his dimples. He looked so sweet and innocent and like an absolute ball of sunshine. He even had me smiling and when he looked back at me, he smiled back. The cutest most contagious smile ever.

Yup, I should probably burn this. That is the cringiest thing I have ever written and seen. I need to cleanse my eyes, soul, heart, mind, and body. This needs to be taken to the gates of hell.

I toss the book, landing it straight into my laundry basket.

Huh, I guess even the jinns want to get rid of that.

I look at the other journals and pick up a random one. This one is probably the only simple and 'to-the-point' diary I've ever owned. It's a plain diary coloured by the sky.

I flip to a random page and start to read again.

I can't believe I wasted my time on someone who couldn't even take the chance to get to know me. Was all of this for nothing? He graduates, he has fun, he leaves? Is that the whole story?

Ah, yes. The worst era I have ever gone through. This was the summer before grade twelve where I did not do anything but write about him in my diaries. I hated the idea of him and that's when I started making promises to myself, to God that I would never fall for anyone ever again. I was shattered and hurt and I needed myself to find peace, but I never did.

I still haven't.

The thing is, it worked. I didn't ever end up liking someone as much as I liked Elias. Never. I had crushes here and there, but I became protective of my feelings in the fear that if I ever gave any-one a part of me again, they would step on it and break it apart in front of me. I was scared to let myself fall into that hole again so I shut myself down. I disconnected myself from people because

I realized if I didn't, if I decided to keep associating myself with others, there was a small chance that I was going to get hurt.

And I continue to live by that.

Elias is everything I have ever wanted in a person. He's confident and sweet and considerate, and I find myself thinking about him often. I never thought once that he would ever go as far as hurting me. I gave him my all and he gave me ten months of happiness and heartbreak that lasts for all of eternity in return.

Of course, I never expected him to ask me out, but I hated him because he talked to me as if he never wanted to leave my side. He invited me to sit with him when I had no one else to talk to. He let me rant and go on about stupid things that didn't even make sense.

He listened to me, and I did the same thing in return.

He needed people in his life that would bring him closer to his deen, and I wanted to be that person. I wanted to be there for him because I couldn't fathom how hard it must've been for him ever since he converted.

I knew it was wrong, but I did it anyway and, for a while, it felt good. But things like these— *like us*— only last so long...I never thought he would leave and not want to keep contact with me. It hurt, but it helped me realize how bad this was. Even though we were each other's best friends, it was wrong. He needed me and then he didn't, and when I finally started accepting that, he showed up.

I still don't know whether he knows it's me or not. It's a fifty-fifty chance he thinks the story is by coincidence and I don't want to change that. He looks like he's in a better place now, and if he's happy, I don't want to ruin that for him by exposing myself. But even so, what he said at the door the other day about waiting for me...

What did he mean by that...?

The Adhan goes off and I blink back into reality.

It's been an hour since I started to read these.

My phone lights up, Aaliyah's name appearing in small text at the bottom of my phone screen.

Aaliyah 😳
Need anything from the store?

The only stuff I need from the store is a lot of snacks because I'm going to sit here and read every single diary entry in all seven of my diaries. Every single one of them. Maybe I can replay the memories that made me fall in love with him.

It's possible I may have to work alongside him, so I want to have control over my feelings and reassure myself that I won't end up making uncalled for and reluctant decisions.

2 0

I'm on my way to the cafe after a couple of days of being perched up in the apartment, so it feels refreshing when I finally leave home.

I walk in through the doors and see Elena sitting by our usual spot. I sit across from her with a sigh.

Elena has papers, files, and her bag scattered on the table.

"So, how are we doing?" She shuts her laptop, giving me her undivided attention.

I smile at that.

"Mostly tired. I was just reading the third diary out of the seven," I dig through my bag and pull out the diary I'm halfway through. "What about you?"

She motions towards the mess interspersed in front of her. "Annoying, but I signed up for this, so I'm sure we'll progress eventually."

I nod my head reassuringly, "Is there anything I could help you with or is this more of a different type of situation...?"

She puts a hand over mine, her features relaxing.

"No, hon. You focus on taking care of yourself," her eyes light up suddenly. "I almost forgot, Jax called me this morning and said we got the movie deal!"

My leg starts to shake underneath the table uncontrollably. I feel a burst of emotions inside of me: Ecstasy, anger, and sadness all at the same time. I feel tense and am no longer sure whether I could handle arranging my book for a movie in this condition.

I blink a couple of times and Elena's face softens from the excitement. She gives me a sad-smile and leans back against the chair.

"It's a lot, huh?"

I swallow and close my eyes, nodding my head.

It is a lot. All of this is. There is so much on my mind, so much I had to deal with at the current moment that I don't think having this here would be such a great idea...just not yet. I still want to make a movie, but maybe I could hold it off for a little while. Of course, I'm eternally grateful for this opportunity, but if I'm not in the right place and mindset, how am I meant to give my all when I direct this movie?

Elena leans forward, "You know, Huma, I think you should do the movie now."

I take a second to reply. Forming words is getting difficult again.

Just like after Elias left to pursue a new life.

"I don't think I'm ready for that," I say, startled by my own shaking breath.

"I get that, but don't you want this? It's possible you'll never get this opportunity ever again...isn't it better you risk it all and take advantage of what you have?"

My breath hitches, and the beating of my heart starts to get louder.

"I don't think I'm ready—" I stop myself, realizing I'm repeating my words.

What is wrong with me?

"Sorry," I laugh, agitated out of my mind. "Today is just not my day."

This whole week has not been my week. Everything seems to be going wrong other than finding the diaries, and even that is a roller coaster of emotions.

"First off, it's okay if you're not ready. I'm only suggesting it. I would and will never force you to do anything against your will. Second off, it's okay if you're having an off-day, or an off-week, or an off-month— all of that is perfectly normal. And third, the only reason I'm suggesting such an idea is because when you first came to me and told me you had a book you needed help editing, we joked about you getting a movie. We joked you would do the craziest things and one day you would land a movie deal. That's why."

My eyes well up and I turn away for a second to catch my breath. I'm starting to realize how much every little thing has been affecting me and how I've been reacting to it. I don't like how tense and irritated I've been acting recently. I don't want to complain to anyone in the fear that they will be just as annoyed as me as I am with myself.

"It's probably something in the air."

We both laugh quietly at my remark.

"Do you want me to call Elias?" She asks suddenly.

"What—? N-no, don't call him!"

Her hand reaches for her phone, "Let me call him—"

I grab onto her phone and pull it away from her. "I don't need him here—"

She interrupts, reaching over and taking the phone from my hands. She settles back onto the seat and puts her phone facedown on her lap.

"Look, Jax told me everything. He filled me in on how Elias was taking care of you when those reporters showed up in New York. The fact that he was able to calm you down when you had that sudden burst of panic...does that not make you feel different about him? Or what about when he showed up at your door to see if you were okay?" She asks rhetorically. "Do you remember what he said to you before he left? About waiting for you? What do you think he meant by that?"

This is becoming a therapy session and I am not here for it. I am here to get work done, not share my feelings and, as much as it frustrates me, I have to admit, having Elias there helped. He's the biggest ball of sunshine I've ever met.

I hold my head in my hands.

This is pissing me off. Every little thing about it. Everything I've been doing ever since I met him has always taken me through a path back to him. *Everything.* And as much as I appreciate him for helping me countless times just because he wanted to, I *need* to move on. If I don't, I'll find myself in a painfully familiar place again.

"Please don't call him," I say. "I don't want to see him right now, or tomorrow, or anytime after that. I don't want to see him. If we do the movie, we do it without him. He doesn't have to be the love interest in the movie. We can find someone else."

Elias is an amazing person. He is. But he can't be the right one for me in any sort of way. Everything messes up when the two of us are together.

"Okay," she responds with an exhale. "But I think you should still talk to him. You need to tell him everything to get it off your chest, or the dread you're feeling right now is never going to leave."

That is a valid reason, but not right now. I'll talk to him when I'm ready. First, I need to find a replacement for Elias. I need to know who my cast is going to be and then I'll try to contact him.

"Let's meet up here tomorrow, okay?" Elena places her elbows on the table.

"We just got here. Where are you heading off to in such a rush?"

There's a slight pause and I notice her cheeks reddening at what is simply a genuine question.

"I'm..." She clears her throat. "Meeting up with a client today, actually."

I frown, disappointed. "Oh, alright then. I'm going to get going. I need to finish reading this—"

"Oh, you brought a friend to our date?"

My eyes follow Elena's startled ones to behind me where I see Jax standing, leaning against the wall.

I press my lips hard together to hold back the grin that wants to desperately make itself known as I look back at her. "...A client, huh?"

"Not a date, Parker," she seethes.

He steps towards us, satisfied by the annoyance on Elena's face and pulls up a chair from a nearby table to sit down.

"See? She calls me by my last name because she wishes it was hers," Jax looks over at me, amused. "Wanna know what she said to me the other day?"

I raise a brow and glance at Elena. I was going to leave, but remembering she just lied to me about meeting up with a client...*why not hear what she said to Jax that's making him so excited to see her?*

"Oh, do tell."

"Jax, don't you dare," Elena glares and he looks at her for a second, but goes back to finding my gaze just as quickly.

"She said I look cute when I wear glasses," he chuckles. "I don't even have a prescription, but that's why I'm wearing unprescribed glasses now."

"Did she now?"

He turns to her and brings her hand up to his lips, "I wear them just for you."

Elena rips her hand away before he can kiss it, and I take that as my cue to leave.

As much as I would like to stay and see how this unpacks, these two weren't meant to meet up with me in the middle of everything.

On a different note, I plan to sleep when I get home. I can't bear to do anymore work, and a long nap could probably help with that.

I audibly sigh, unlocking my car and preparing myself to relax for the next couple of hours.

...

I wake up to a painful, throbbing headache and Aaliyah who must've just gotten home. She's standing at my bedroom door with her work clothes on, raising a brow at me.

"Are you okay? You didn't answer your phone," she moves further into my room while I take in the fact that I can see two of her. "You're literally sweating— are you sick?"

I do feel really hot right now.

I sit up and feel the stickiness of my skin ripping off the mattress. My throat feels foul as if I've been screaming for hours and my chest is burning.

Ugh, this feels absolutely nasty.

"Let me bring you a thermometer," she says after placing her hand on my forehead.

I check the time and it's 5:30.

My stomach grumbles out of hunger.

The second I got home, I went straight to bed so now I'm starving. With all the strength left in me, I get up to see what's in the fridge to eat.

"Here," she hands me the thermometer as I open the fridge, and I slip it into my mouth. We both wait for the beep before I take it out.

"105." I rasp.

My own voice surprises me and it hurts to speak. I groan,

annoyed and walk back towards my bed. I throw my blanket on the floor and lie face-down.

"Do you want me to call your parents?"

I shake my head, my words muffled by the pillow in my face. "No, I'm good. I don't wanna worry them."

"Okay, I'll warm up some food for you and then I'll go out to buy you some medicine."

She leaves for the kitchen.

I turn over and reach for my diary.

Even though I found my old entries cringe-worthy and quite humiliating at that, it's fun to recall all those memories from a handful of years ago. It's like my very own biography about events that mattered so much to me at the time.

I find the little bookmark I placed in between the papers and flip back onto my stomach, resting the book onto my pillow.

I start to read, getting lost in my own words.

He was ranting to me today. About how annoying Advanced Functions was. Did I know what he was talking about? No. I knew that was a math course but that's about it. He told me how annoying his teacher was and how she wasn't providing any help to the class. I cheered him up by halving a shawarma with him. He kept smiling and laughing while we ate even though I hadn't said anything. I knew I was blushing everytime he looked over, and everytime he did, I would turn away until the heat in my cheeks would leave. When I looked back, his ears would be red and he would be biting back another smile. I don't think he realized how much I liked him. I don't think he could ever realize how much I like him. I think he's the type of person you can never forget. Even if you catch a quick glimpse of—

"Here, Huma," Aaliyah comes inside with a tray.

I'm not one to eat on my bed so having Aaliyah bring my food into my room made me scrunch my nose.

"It's okay, I can come out to the living room and eat," I reply. "But thank you."

She narrows her eyes with a grin as she spins back around and out the door as I follow.

"What you reading there?"

I sit down on the couch and her eyes find mine. She takes a seat next to me as I close up the diary, tucking it underneath my knee.

"Nothing," I try not to smile.

"Hm, that beaming look on your face is telling me otherwise," she turns to me. "Oh, by the way, Elena said she'll pick up the medicine and come over. We get a sleepover redo!"

I cheer with her, nearly choking at the act.

I'm hoping tonight won't be as intense as the last time we tried to do this.

She hands me the plate of *chana chawal* Ami sent over a couple of days ago after she saw the news along with a billion other stuff in the hopes that we would feel better.

It did in fact help me a lot.

Nothing's better than Ami's cooking.

To pass some time, Aaliyah and I settle down on watching the rest of *Haikyuu!!* until Elena gets here. As much as I love this show, I want to continue reading.

I have the urge to remember where everything went wrong between us. Even if Elias doesn't remember me, I need to know how he could forget me, how he could forget us when I've been cherishing the idea of us ever since we've met.

I pick up the diary just as it's quickly snatched out of my hands, "Give it back, Aaliyah!"

She closes it up, "No. I know what these diaries are about. You told me before, and I am not about to let my friend spiral into a never-ending game of '*he loves me, he loves me not.*'"

I roll my eyes and throw myself at her. I grab the diary and lean away from her so it's out of her reach. "My diary, my rules. He gave me the time to think about him and that's what I'm doing. Plus, this has become an investigation for I have a billion questions and this—" I hold up the diary. "Has become key evidence along with the other six books."

She shakes her head, disappointed, "What? Are you planning to date him?"

I smack her with a pillow, "No, you idiot!"

The doorbell rings and we both flash each other a suspicious look. Last time this happened, Elias was at the door with nothing but concern.

Aaliyah stands up while I adjust a nearby scarf onto my head. She hurriedly grabs her own and covers her head before opening the door.

The bodyguard covers her field of vision and questions her.

"Do you know this woman?" He asks, his voice stern and cold.

Elena appears being almost completely blocked by the bodyguard and seems a bit startled. I let out a sigh of relief, happy to see it isn't Elias.

Elena's let in and she has medicine in one hand, and another holds a grocery bag. She sets both items down on the coffee table in front of me.

"One of you has spare clothes, right? I packed a bag to stay over with you guys, but I forgot to bring it," she sighs audibly.

"Yeah, let me grab something from my room for you," Aaliyah responds and disappears into the darkness of her bedroom.

"How did you get sick, honey? You were perfectly fine when you met with me earlier."

I unpack the blanket, drowning myself underneath it, "I have no clue."

She places a hand on my forehead, "You are way too warm. Did you eat?"

The thing that stuck out to me about Elena the most is how much she represents a mother figure. She has her friend traits, but her motherly characteristics continue to shine through.

She's like a third parent to Aaliyah and I.

"Yeah, Aaliyah warmed up some food for me," I reply, shuffling through the medicine bag.

"Okay, take some medicine and then we can watch something."

She stands up when Aaliyah comes back with clothes in her hands and gives them to Elena. Aaliyah replaces Elena's spot and I scoot over a little to make more room.

When Elena returns, she's wearing a *salwar kameez* with the biggest smile plastered on her face, "Did you mean to give this to me?"

I grin at her, "You look so cute in that."

She blushes, "Thank you."

Aaliyah smirks, amused by the way she's satisfied with the outfit. "Yes, I meant to give that to you."

She sits in between Aaliyah and I, and switches the TV on, joining us underneath the blanket. I lean against her, setting my head against her arm. The medicine seems to play its effects pretty briskly because my eyelids grow heavy.

Before I know it, I'm out cold.

...

"Huma."

I open my eyes slowly, letting them adjust to the light. My throat is worse than before, making it painful to swallow and my nose is completely blocked off.

"You're really gonna fall asleep during a movie, Huma?" Aaliyah teases.

"She's sick. Show some sympathy," Elena scolds as I force myself to sit up straight. "You still have that fever. Do you want me to put a wet towel on your head?"

I blink hard and look around. Elena and Aaliyah are watching a movie I've never seen before, and there's a huge mess of chips and food everywhere on the table.

I rub my eyes, "No."

Even with how bad this fever is, I'm way too cold for Elena to be putting a wet, freezing towel on my forehead.

"Are you sure? You're warmer than before."

"I'll bring the ice water," Aaliyah goes to the kitchen.

I scrunch my legs up to my chest and place my head down. I'm so tired and drained, I feel like I could faint at any given moment.

I feel a vibration from beneath me and come to register it's coming from Elena.

It stops.

"Hey, Jax. What's up?"

Of course. Why am I not surprised?

I wonder if they're going out secretly...maybe even dating?

"No, I'm not busy," she laughs. "I'm over at Huma's...she has a fever."

I look up and shoot her a look. She puts a finger to her lips and silences me, making me grin. If that laugh and that smile plastered on her face doesn't say she likes him, I don't know what does. I open my mouth but she covers my lips with her hand. She words *'Shut up'* and goes back to talking as if she didn't give me a death threat with her eyes.

I roll my eyes and look through the bags of snacks. Digging through, I pull out a packet of lozenges.

Perfect.

"Okay, I don't mind. Let me just run it through them real quick," she takes the phone away from her ear and I watch as she presses the mute button. "Are you guys okay if Jax runs by here quickly tomorrow morning?"

I look over at Aaliyah who comes back with a bowl of ice and sink water. She has a towel thrown over her shoulder and grins at me.

I return the look.

"May we ask why?" I query, crossing my arms over my chest.

She gives us an annoyed glance and sighs, "Can you tell me yes or no? I'll tell you why afterwards."

"Sure, as long as everything remains *PG-13*." Aaliyah says, and we both laugh.

Elena ignores us, unmuting her phone, "Yeah, they said it's all good...I say come around twelve."

I switch my gaze to my phone. It keeps lighting up, and just as it's about to turn off, another notification brightens the screen. When I finally take a look, I see Elias' name pop up on the screen a couple of times.

I reach for it but then hold back.

No.

Nope.

I won't lie, I'm tempted to pick up the phone and reply. I want to know what he's saying, but if I see the texts then I would want to reply, and this is a break from him. I still need the time to figure out what these feelings towards him mean.

Tomorrow, Huma. You look at those texts tomorrow.

I swipe left on the texts so they disappear off my lock screen, and switch my phone off.

"Huma, look at me," Elena says, holding the towel. She immediately sets it onto my forehead.

I lay down with it on my head. I'm about to argue with Elena for not listening to my request, but I no longer have enough energy to spark up a fight. "Now you can go to sleep."

"You have never said anything better," I mutter as she adjusts the blanket onto my shoulders.

21

The sound of a melodic alarm is what wakes me from my slumber. I extend out my arm towards the music and feel the vibration of a phone.

I pull it to me and turn it off.

"Elena."

She's lying on my legs, and Aaliyah's lying on hers.

We really need a bigger couch.

"Elena, wake up," I shake her gently, and instead of her waking up, Aaliyah does instead. Still half-asleep, she helps me until Elena's eyes are open...well, halfway open.

"Is everything okay...?" She asks, confused.

I nod my head while Aaliyah gets up to use the bathroom. I hand Elena her phone as she stretches her arms and legs before taking it from my hands. She sits up, slapping her forehead and sprinting off the couch, straight into my room.

Aaliyah appears with a toothbrush in her mouth and a raised brow, "What was that all about?"

I shrug, "I think it's because of Jax. He's supposed to be here soon."

She scoffs, walking back into the washroom. I'm not in the mood to get up, so I stay put until they both return.

My mind is continuously going back to the journals and how badly I want to finish reading them already, but that's pretty hard to do when you're living with your best friend who thinks you're torturing yourself. So, while Aaliyah's gone, I grab the diary and lean against the back pillow, picking up where I last left off. I was able to get a little bit of the reading done early morning after *Fajr*, but quickly got tired and fell back asleep.

I take a deep breath and ignore the fact that Aaliyah's already back.

I'm going to get through more than a couple of pages today.

I want to finish this diary today.

This morning was tiring. Our history teacher gave us a project to complete by the end of the week and I was not in the mood to do everything on my own. She gave us the option to do it with other classmates if we wished to and I chose to do it alone because I hate relying on people to finish up work. But anyway, today was so weird. I was waiting for Elias outside of his classroom door since the lunch bell had already rung and he waved me over with a smile and I walked inside.

"Do you have lunch?" I asked.

He frowned. He hated when I asked him that because he always knew I would share if the answer was no.

"No," he muttered.

Even with his upsetting look, I kept my smile and waited for him to finish packing up before leading him to the school benches. I placed all my snacks and my lunch in between us. I told him to either take my lunch or pick all the snacks but he turned away.

I remember convincing Elias to take my lunch so he wouldn't be hungry during the day. He never met with me outside of school so

I never knew if he was hungry then, or if he had food for the night. I wasn't too worried about that, though, because his physique was pretty strong for a guy that only ate once or twice a day.

I moved to the other side of the bench and forced his eyes on mine. I slid my lunch over even though it was a spicy chicken sandwich and I was hoping to eat it today. I basically begged him to eat it and when I finally saw him put it in his bag, I felt relief in my body. I snuck sliced apples into his backpack when he wasn't looking and forced him to take some chocolate chip cookies from me. I normally don't pack this much. Elias doesn't know it but I do it for him and I don't regret it at all. If that's what it takes to make sure he's okay then that's what I'll do.

Wow. Some heavy stuff in the morning.

I close up the book.

I wish I could give him a hug. Just to say thank you. I talk a lot about how much I hate him for how he left, but that could never in a million years amount to how much I loved him back then. He taught me how to be a better person, to be grateful for everything that I had, and he was very successful in that. I don't know if my words would matter to him if I told him I was proud of who he's become but I want to tell him that.

"Oh, by the way, I did the laundry while you were asleep yesterday. We just need to fold up the clothes now," Aaliyah brings the clothes over and dumps it onto the couch on top of me.

Elena sits down on the carpet and helps us fold. Most of the so-called clothes are actually hijabs, so we get through the laundry pretty quickly.

"Do you mind if I...?" Elena hesitates to speak. In her hand, she holds a maroon coloured hijab and I tilt my head to the side, wondering what she's trying to say. "Could I try it on?"

My face softens, "Of course you can. Do you want me to help?"

She nods her head and I flash a smile at Aaliyah who looks like she could scream. I slip my head cap past her head and she pulls her hair out from under the cap. I pull it back up so it's covering up the hair on her head and she hands me the maroon hijab. I smile wider, placing it on her head and throwing one side over her shoulder.

"Oh my God— you look so adorable!" I squeal and she laughs.

"Wait, stand up. I need to see this whole outfit with the hijab," Aaliyah instructs.

She stands up and twirls around for us as we both excitedly squeal. She looks stunning. It makes me beyond happy that she finds the hijab so beautiful like us Muslims do.

The doorbell rings and Elena waits for us to cover up before walking to the door. Forgetting Jax is coming, I head into my bedroom and sit down, surrounding myself with the blanket. My fever is better but it's still there a little bit.

Thankfully it isn't too bad anymore. I just can't breathe and my throat hurts and I'm overheating...

Okay, maybe it's still pretty bad.

"Oh wow...you look—" Jax's voice is cut off.

"I was just trying it on."

"Pretty. You look *pretty."*

I smile at that. I may not know what's going on between them, but at least I know they would make for a good couple.

"Oh, Elias, I didn't know you were coming!"

Elena says that loudly I'm assuming so I can hear too.

I hide the diary under my pillow, leaning against the bed frame as I scramble for my phone and pretending as if I wasn't just reading diary entries fully written about him.

"Is Huma here?"

I press my lips together and continue pressing random stuff to make myself look busy and distracted.

"She's in her room."

Seconds later, there's a knock at my bedroom door.

My stomach ties into a billion separate knots. I want to see him, but I'm wondering if what I feel towards him are the feelings I felt towards the *grade-twelve* him and not the *twenty-five-year-old-actor* him.

One shallow breath later, I creak open the door. I check to see if my hijab is still intact and not floating away off into the abyss by patting my head.

Yup, still there.

"Hi," he smiles, holding a deep steel bowl in his hands covered with a lid. "I brought you some soup."

"Thanks," I adjust my hijab again and, without thinking, take the bowl without noticing how it's almost flooding with soup. Not to mention the steam coming out of it. The liquid falls through an opening in the lid and right onto my hand as I wince.

I turn around and shut the door. I set the bowl down on my nightstand and suck in my teeth, cringing at the pain. I stand there for a second and my eyes widen when it comes to me that I just shut the door in his face.

"Huma..." The door opens a little bit. "Are you okay...?"

"Y-yeah, I just spilt a little on my hand. That's all," I hide my hand behind my back like a little kid hiding candy, and force a smile. "You can come in."

He walks inside slowly and stops when he's in front of me, "Can I see your hand?"

There's no longer a dimple or eye-smile on his face, both disintegrating at the sight of me.

I step back, shaking my head, "It's nothing. I was just being clumsy. My bad— sorry."

He leaves the room and I can't even blame him. I was so much better back in high school. At least I never embarrassed myself as much as I do now.

I sit down on my bed and sigh. I'm not going to leave this room until they're both gone. He could probably entertain himself on his own anyway.

Me, still feeling like crap from my fever, I decide to tuck myself in while I lean against the headboard. I reach for my diary safely tucked underneath my pillow just as the door opens.

To my surprise, he returns and has a towel on his hand. The same one Elena put on my head last night.

"Here you go. This might help a bit," he says with a mollifying voice.

I welcome him to sit down on my desk chair, not wanting to leave him standing and apologize for the billionth time.

"Huma, if you use that word again for things that aren't your fault, I promise you I'll read everything in that diary you're trying to hide from me," his gaze locks onto mine. "Don't think I haven't noticed it."

My lungs stop expanding and my breath delays.

I can't seem to take my eyes away from his as I become flustered.

"Stupid."

He chuckles, taking the soup from my nightstand and holding out his arms for me to take it from him. I'm about to, but he pulls it away from my reach, "Put a pillow on your lap first."

He sets the bowl down in front of me after I place the flat cookie plush toy onto my thighs. "You must've not gotten my messages yesterday. I hope you weren't too surprised to see me."

I let out the nervous laughter I have been trying to conceal since he has arrived, diverting my attention to the soup. He catches on and interrupts the sudden awkwardness in between us.

"If you don't want me here, I can go—"

"No!" I blush at how loud that comes out of my mouth. "I mean, I want you to *stay.*"

My eyes catch his when I raise my head, and he's guaranteed to be holding back a laugh. Not even a laugh— a cackle.

"You haven't changed a bit."

22

"W-what?"

I have thought about the fact that Elias might realize it's me, but I didn't think it would be now— nonetheless— in my bedroom.

He looks at me, his dimples appearing as he arches a brow, "Are you serious?"

I pray somebody will interrupt us. I hate confrontation and he is not helping the anxiety building up in my head. My heart is aggressively pumping to the point where the mattress is shaking with every beat.

"I need to go," I get up from the bed and walk out of the room fast. I sprint past the others and open the apartment door, slipping through.

The door opens back up almost immediately while I head towards the sketchy staircases.

"Huma, wait!"

I stop walking to his command.

Forget about me calling him stupid when I'm the dumb one.

How could I be so foolish, so gullible? He has us both fooled. I should've stayed away from him like I was supposed to.

"Do you know the lengths I went through to convince Jax to let me go to your speech just so I could see you again?" He asks, his voice no longer gentle.

"I—"

"No. This time you listen to me."

I swallow hard.

"I don't know what you're doing, but you need to cut it out. This *'I don't know you'* BS— cut it out. It's so humiliating having you act like you don't know a thing about me and I—" His voice cracks. "I thought you forgot me—"

"I could never forget you, Elias. Never," the words leave my mouth like a whisper.

I watch as he lowers his head, his eyes welling up.

I wish I could reach up to him and rub his tears away for him, but I hold back.

"Then why did you act like I was a stranger?"

I hate that this is the second time we are put in a position like this. As if no matter how much time passes, we are no longer compatible. Everything that happened then is so much different than now. We don't have the same type of connection we used to have.

I shake my head frantically and find his eyes again. *"Because you hurt me just as bad."*

He looks at me with guilt and regret, "I never meant to hurt you. You know that, Huma. I wanted to keep talking to you but you know better than me that it's not okay."

I found my face to be wet from my own tears, "I know, but you didn't even say anything! You just left me alone."

When he left me, I was surrounded by darkness. Everything I thought I knew was a lie and he so quickly became a memory. I fell into a deep, dark hole with Elias and he was my light. He was *supposed to be my light,* but he climbed out without me.

"I'm sorry, Huma. I know I should've, but I didn't have a choice. I was struggling to live, and you made it so much easier, and I left you when I knew I shouldn't have. That's completely my fault. I'm sorry."

The urge to pull him towards me and embrace him is growing.

But, of course, I hold back.

"I want you to leave, Elias," I spit out.

He searches my eyes, concern growing in his own as he realizes I'm not messing around.

"No, Huma, please. I'm done with giving you time. You've had all week to think about me— about *us. I need my best friend back.*"

I swallow, my throat hurting more, "Please, Elias."

"You don't even know how much I think of you."

"Elias, stop. This is so wrong," I shake my head, mad at him. "You can't just say things like that. We're not in high school anymore where you need more Muslim friends or I need help finding the prayer room. We're way past that, Elias."

He looks hurt as I presumed he would be. The thing is, I have to set my boundaries. We are Muslim after all, he shouldn't be saying things like that to me. And now I'm so much more mature now. I've had time to get closer to my deen and learn right from wrong.

This, without a doubt, is anything but right

"Huma, please," his voice breaks again. "You know I don't mean it like that. I didn't mean to make you uncomfortable. I'm sorry. I just...*have really missed you.*"

I have too. God, I've missed you way too much.

"Don't apologize," I whisper. "But this isn't okay. I think you need to rethink how you feel about me. Maybe you should focus on yourself, Elias."

There are tears in his eyes as Jax approaches us. I don't know when he got here, but he couldn't have come at a better time. I watch as his eyes move back and forth from Elias to me. I don't mean to be so cruel. I know it hurts him just as much as it hurts me. I know his intentions are innocent, but how am I meant to get past my feelings when it comes to him?

I love him a little too much.

Jax must've heard us talking because he puts a hand on Elias's shoulder, "We should head back, Elias."

Elias's gaze continues to pierce through me. "Huma..."

"Please, Elias. Move on," I say, looking anywhere but him.

I sit down on the stairs and continue to cry for a solid fifteen minutes after they leave. My mind is in a spiral as I try to understand where all of this became a mess.

Soon, Aaliyah comes, approaching me with caution.

"What happened?" She asks, taking a seat next to me.

"He remembers me."

She pulls me into her arms and embraces me.

...

The next couple of days are stressful.

I spent a lot of my time trying to get better from this stupid fever by doing nothing but sleeping and eating. I even tasted some of Elias' soup, and I have to admit, it was delicious.

Fast forward to the start of the week, I'm getting ready to go to the cafe as per usual. I need a breather since I haven't left the apartment in a hot second

Today was the day Elena and I were meant to meet and discuss who Elias could be replaced with. However, Elena said she had something important to discuss with another client so the meeting was cancelled.

Instead, I'm going to spend some time doing promotions and planning new potential story ideas.

Ami and Abu have been worried about me since I haven't been calling or texting for the past couple of days. They want to know about Elias and he isn't someone I want to talk to my parents about. I wouldn't call this ignoring; I'm just avoiding the questions I don't want to answer.

When I arrive at the cafe, I order a french vanilla, and get comfortable in my usual seat. I unlock my phone and go to a folder in my notes app labeled *Story Ideas*.

I take out my laptop, setting it down on the table. Although all these ideas are already in my phone for me to reach easily, I want to have all of them on my laptop as well so I don't have to be dependent on a handful of devices when I finally start writing my next book.

I open up a new document and start to make jot-notes on each story individually. I fill in different gaps and extend on certain parts. These ideas are the types that I get at the dead of night. Some influenced by dreams, others by random scenarios I create in my head.

'Splintered Heart' was my debut novel. It wasn't supposed to lead to a writing career, but I don't mind it.

Originally, my plan wasn't to become a disappointment to my *rishtedaro* in Pakistan. I was planning on becoming something along the lines of an English teacher. I still hear the judgemental aunties telling me writing isn't the way to go— *nope— computer science exists, too—!*

My eyes dart up, thinking Elias is there for a second but it's only an employee bringing my coffee.

I thank him and set the coffee down onto the table.

I continue to work, trying to think of more possible story plots. The more outlines I have, the more I can send to Elena for approval.

I just need a stable base for my plots in order for me to start these outlines.

As I go back and forth from my phone to my laptop, I'm able to create three new ideas with a very, very rough outline of the next book I could potentially write.

And as I sip my coffee, my gaze finds Elias barely standing in front of me.

Except he hasn't seen me yet.

I hide my face with my hood and continue working, but it's hard to focus when the guy you were just telling to go away is standing right there—

Oh my God, he's looking over now.

Pretend to work, pretend to work.

I type away, slapping at the keyboard and making up all sorts of new words along with the rough chapter outlines displayed on the screen.

"Huma," he sits down across from me and slides something I don't care to see over.

It's my book.

"We need to talk about this."

His eyes are staring daggers at me and I sigh, sitting up straight.

"The story's fictional."

"I haven't said anything about it yet."

I feel something scratching at my throat and take a sip of my coffee, careful not to burn my mouth as he speaks.

There's not a speck of a smile on his face and it frightens me a little. In high school he would get mad over things like me giving him my lunch and sneaking snacks into his bags, but I never took it seriously.

This is definitely something else because he looks exasperated.

I look over at the bodyguard who's standing a couple feet away, and then stray my eyes back to Elias.

"This book, first off, is not fictional at all and you know that. You must really think I'm that dumb if you're gonna try and pull that again," he shakes his head at me. "Second off, I asked you not to act like you don't know me and you're doing it again."

I scoff at him, "Yeah, because I asked you to leave me alone."

He raises both eyebrows, "I was going to, but while I was reading your book—"

"You read it...?"

He nods his head slowly.

My stomach drops, "Listen, the things I said—"

"I felt the same way."

He said 'felt.'

It's electric shock after electric shock. He's constantly hitting me with new information and I'm convinced if he keeps this up, I'll be in the ER pretty soon.

I rub my thighs back and forth, my hands sweating like crazy while I take deep breaths, regulating my heart rate as much as I can.

"You didn't ever act like you liked me. I mean, I made it obvious— I gave you so much because you needed it— but I was also falling in love with you."

I can't believe I'm confessing my love for this man in the middle of a cafe. There are people staring. I'm sure it's because a crazy big celebrity is sitting across from someone who looks like she's nervous because she's his biggest fan, but it's quite the opposite; he's here to meet me. If it were up to me, I would give up.

If he didn't bother reaching out before, he shouldn't do it now.

His face softens, "I was just as much in love with you as you were with me. It hurt me to leave you, but I already told you—"

"I know. It's not your fault."

I swear, he comes back each time because he enjoys the sight of me crying. Even as I sit here across from him, I refuse to believe he only comes here because he misses me and because he's *loved* me. He doesn't even know that those feelings are still lurking in the present as well.

He lets out a sigh of relief, "Is it possible for us to get past this?"

I press my lips together, thinking hard. I think realistically we could. We could see how things go and see how it works from here. We could pretend like high school never happened and start with a fresh palate, but I don't think it's even a good idea.

"Let's have a do-over.".

He gets up, taking the book with him and leaves the cafe as a whole, leaving me bewildered. He comes back through the other door and approaches me.

"Oh my God. You're the author of 'Splintered Heart.' I love that book," he says, all with the most delightful dimple and eye-smile on his face.

And because I think it's not even a good idea, I take the chance.

"My name's Elias."

I look at him, biting back a smile, "My name's Huma."

"Do you mind if I sit?"

I shake my head, "Be my guest."

We talk for hours. Catching up, playing back memories, everything. And, I swear, I've never felt this way before. I can see his hand pulling me out of this abyss of my reluctant feelings.

"Now guess what I get to say to the press?" He asks cheerfully. *"My best friend is a best-selling author."*

His words take me aback.

My best friend is a best-selling author.

"Does that mean I get to say my best friend is an actor?"

He grins at me, resting his chin on the palm of his hand, "You really haven't changed."

I laugh, blushing at his foolish words, "You're one to talk, *lover boy.*"

His ears turn pink and he looks away for a moment.

I *do* want him to be the lead love interest in my film. I would love that.

Obviously, I'm going to talk to Elena and Aaliyah before I make any more actions, so I make a mental note to bring it up tonight.

"Do you remember the stuff you used to put into my bag? All the food and everything?" He asks, a new sweetness to his voice.

I nod my head with a confident smile.

"I remember one time where," he laughs before continuing. "You packed a whole entire meal— and I think it was butter chicken? It was way too good. You have to give me that recipe. I wanna try it so bad."

"I'll ask my mom first. She's the one that makes these dishes."

"No, but seriously, thank you for everything. I never told you this back then because I had a fear you would give me your house—"

We both burst out laughing, "But I never had anything to look forward to until you came. You were the literal definition of generous."

It's like he's touching my soul when he says that. It's like I'm giving him my heart to break again.

"You really are a star, Elias. I hope you find your home soon."

His gaze becomes relaxed, "I think I already found my home."

I break into a smile that hurts my cheeks the longer I hold it.

"Unfortunately, I have to go. Jax is probably calling my phone like crazy," he smirks at me, standing from his seat. "You don't need me to walk you home, do you?"

I scoff, "No, I can take myself home. It's so much more peaceful to walk alone, anyway."

He rolls his eyes, gently placing my stuff in my tote bag before lifting it onto his shoulder, "C'mon, I'll drop you."

He really is the same as before, and I love it. Still such a gentle-man, such a tease, and *so perfect for me.*

I'm happy the fame hasn't changed him. I think that was one of my biggest fears when I realized who he was. He turned me into a grateful person, so I hoped he became one himself and here he is; the most finest and sweetest person to ever walk this earth.

"Elias, why did you talk to me?"

His eyes focus on the street ahead of us.

"Because I was taking up your seat...it seemed rude and awkward for me to completely ignore you."

I nod my head, a little disappointed by his answer as we cross the street towards a crowd of people standing in front of my apartment building.

They haven't seen us yet, but my eyes can't seem to leave them. There's a bodyguard trailing behind us, though it brings me limited comfort.

Elias blocks my view, concern in his eyes, "You have headphones, right?"

I nod, not caring what he needs with my headphones as I continue to stare at them past his shoulder. He catches my attention almost immediately by handing me the headphones as one of the reporters points over at us.

"There's a new nasheed that you just have to listen to," the corners of his mouth curving into a breathtaking smile. "Stand in front of me and don't stop walking until you're inside the building, okay?"

His voice sends shivers up and down my spine. I nod my head and position myself in front of him, slowly making my way past the crowd with the help of Elias and his bodyguard.

The feeling of suffocation overwhelms me again. The flashes of the cameras overtaking us blind me and I lose sight of direction. Everytime my vision comes back to me, another flash of a camera messes it up. But the sound of the nasheed is overtaking, drowning out the reporters and camera people.

I focus back on reaching the door, and when I finally do, I turn around to see Elias an inch away from me, his head turned to look at the reporters. The bodyguard keeps the door open for him as I slip off the headphones so they slide to my neck.

"You did so well," Elias says proudly.

My voice shakes as I speak and I inhale a huge breath, "Good Nasheed."

"I thought you'd like it," he smiles. His gaze switches to the cameras outside, still flashing at us. "I'm sure they're satisfied with their pictures."

We walk away from them and to the elevators. The lift arrives right away and we step in. I have no clue what just happened, but I'm baffled by how quickly everything unfolded.

I blush, waiting for my cheeks to settle before I look back at him. My eyes wander to his neck and then to his collarbone as I try to spot the necklace I can't seem to forget.

"I'm sorry, Elias," I say, watching as he frowns..

"This better be a good reason, or I'm not kidding, I *will* read that diary."

I hold back a laugh and keep a subtle face, "I mean for blaming you about the press making those comments. I know you have no control over that."

I should be apologizing for much more than that. There's definitely a lot of things we have silently agreed to leave unsaid. Like the fact that there is so much more in the book besides the confession and food I gave away. That the years after that were hell trying to move past something that was completely my fault. Or the fact that there was a period of time where I blamed Elias for ever making me feel the way he does. I know that's on me. I know I shouldn't let my feelings get in the way of what was so special.

Until it wasn't.

"Was something in that coffee you drank—? All of a sudden you're so understanding," he narrows his eyes.

The elevator doors open, and we walk towards my apartment. We don't say anything as we walk, but I can feel his eyes on me.

"Hey, Michael," Elias shakes his hand. "How's the wife? Is she doing any better?"

Michael smiles, "Yup. She's supposed to go into labour in two weeks."

I cheer, "Congrats! I had no clue she was pregnant."

I had no clue he's married.

"Thank you, Ms.Tariq. Oh, she read your book by the way and she loved it."

I laugh with amusement, "I'm flattered! Tell her I say hi."

He nods his head, and I turn back to Elias to say goodbye. Today was an amazing day. Who knew all I needed was to have him confront me for us to start talking again.

"Today was fun," Elias leans down to my level with a mischievous grin. I notice the necklace I was looking for earlier fall out of his shirt. "We should totally do it again."

I raise an eyebrow, "We'll see, *lover boy.*"

He gives me a look, "Why am I *'lover boy?'* Why aren't you *lover girl?*"

"Because you're love-struck, I'm not."

"Well, isn't that just a lie?" He scoffs. "Your book says otherwise."

"Oh, and you read every single page probably twice, for all I know," I roll my eyes.

"Three."

"What?"

"I read every single page *three times.*"

My breath halts.

He read my book three times...?

"I'm extremely flattered," I lean against the wall next to my door and cross my arms over my chest, acting as if I'm not having an internal heart attack.

His phone starts to ring, and he pulls it out. "This conversation was great, *lover girl*, but I've gotta run."

He hands me my tote bag that I hadn't even realized was still set on his shoulder, and sends me a quick wink before he leaves.

I enter my apartment, extremely satisfied by today. I don't close the door right away as I look back to see Elias standing by the elevators.

If I wasn't satisfied enough already, I am now because he's waving at me before disappearing into the elevator.

Adorable. Absolutely adorable.

"So, you two made up, huh? I should let him know his place, shouldn't I?" Aaliyah threatens. "He should remember I'm your best friend. Not him."

I look at her, pleasantly surprised by her reaction.

"Of course," I look at her, pleasantly surprised by her reaction. "You're my best friend before him."

"Good," she says sternly. "On a different note, tell me everything."

We talk and talk, while I tell her everything he said to me. I break down even the most minuscule details, and she only adds to my excitement with her squeals.

"And he remembers everything, Aaliyah," I say, all giddy.

The door opens, and in comes Elena.

These past couple of days, Elena has been staying over with us. She claims it's because she wants to make sure I'm okay, but I'm not quite buying that.

She lives alone in a studio apartment not too far from here, so she must feel lonely not having any company besides herself. Meanwhile, Aaliyah and I are more excited than ever to let her stay with us because of how natural it feels having her here.

"Guess who's in love~" Aaliyah teases with a smile.

"That's not true!" I protest. "I was just...catching up with an old friend."

"That's not what you told me."

Elena joins us on the couch and turns to me, "Does this mean you two are okay?"

My cheeks heat up as I nod subtly, "I want him to be the love interest."

"I think he's already the love interest in the story that is known as your life," Aaliyah blurts out, and I blink hard, glaring at her.

The audacity this girl has.

"Are you sure?" Elena tilts her head to the side.

I have other options. I can always resort to holding auditions, but why would I do that when I have the real thing with me?

"Yeah. Why—? Is it not possible anymore?"

"No, no," she responds, waving her hands in the air. "I could arrange that with a single phone call. I just want to make sure."

I stand from the couch, "Great, I'm gonna go to my room and see if I can find the lead actress."

That is a flat-out lie.

I want to finish reading my diary.

While I remember everything from grade eleven and twelve so clearly, there's this urge in me to want to replay everything day by day, letter by letter, entry by entry. I need to know the little details that I might've forgotten.

But first, I need a shower.

"If you are grateful, I will surely increase you in favour."
- Surah Ibrahim [14:7]

"So that takes away this week's schedule," Elena sighs, moving her laptop so it's facing her.

I was able to read a little more of my diary before Elena called me out into the living room to discuss the schedule.

Monday, which is tomorrow, is when we meet up with Jax and Elias to confirm this whole ordeal. I'm not going to lie, I'm quite excited about the part where we get to see each other.

Tuesday is dedicated to finding the female lead for the film, but that's not going too well to begin with. Every celebrity that was offered the job, blankly refused, claiming the story was *'not suitable to their liking'* which I can't help but feel disappointed in hearing.

Wednesday is when we finally hit the filming set which has been arranged to be at a storage house with multiple different sets of my childhood bedroom, my old school, and basically any other set that's described in the book. At first, I thought we may have to cast younger people but we want to avoid casting child actors, and Elias looked pretty young so he fit perfectly.

Thursday and Friday are going to be spent on set. So far, the plan sounds great. I have no objections other than my only worry, which is finding a female lead for the movie.

"Works for me," I reply, biting into a cookie.

Aaliyah squeals, "This is so exciting! You're filming a movie, Huma! Let alone the fact that this is *your book* that's becoming a movie!"

I match her energy with a laugh, "I think this calls for a pizza party."

...

The others are out-cold. They fell asleep after a couple of playful arguments over silly debates.

I would say tonight was a successful girl's night; we ordered in, talked a whole lot, watched an entire movie, and all without any interruptions.

Now, I lie in bed with the diary in my hands. I'm not sure if I should be ending the night like this considering I have no clue how each diary entry ends, but maybe I can keep reading until I reach a satisfying conclusion.

I adjust into my bed just as my phone dings beside me.
It's Elias.

Elias
Looks like lover girl finally figured im
worth the acting job

I scoff to myself.
Idiot.

Me
You must be thrilled

Elias
Thrilled is an understatement
Im ◇enthralled◇

Me
Mhm…go back to sleep elias.
You have a big day tmrw

Elias
Wtvr you say maam

The corners of my mouth threaten to create a smile, but I keep myself from doing so.

Who am I kidding? He's anything but an idiot. He's just ruining me. Again. And I'm letting him.

I place my phone on my side table and pick up the diary that's patiently waiting on my lap.

What are you doing to me, Elias?

Could ask the same thing right now.

I spent a whole hour yesterday thinking about Elias. I think it was finally hitting me how much I liked him. He is so much in one person and it's hard for me to see myself without him. Like today, he told me he would take me to Umrah with him one day. He wants to take me to Madina. If that's not a marriage proposal, then I don't know what is.

I remember the day he promised that. He gave me his word that no matter what, even if we drifted away from each other, he would take me there with him. Granted, we were young and naive, making promises we would most likely never keep.

I might've believed it back then, but I for sure do not believe it now.

But yeah. It makes me excited. I don't know if he feels the same way, but sometimes it does. It's not what he says, it's what he does that makes me think that I have a one in a billion chance that he likes me back. Like the fact that he walks me home. Every day, after school, without fail, he will walk me home. He doesn't let me carry anything extra like a textbook I can't seem to fit into my bag, or even a single permission slip for a trip that I need to keep in my hands to remember I have to get my parents to sign it when I get home. I'm very capable of carrying a paper, but I don't argue with him. Mainly because it makes my heart warm to think that he does not like the idea of me carrying anything extra.

I call it cringey, but in reality, I love it so much. I find him so admiring and sweet, and all of this makes me want to protect him.

On a different note, he caught me sneaking snacks into his bag and he was not very happy with it. He told me to stop in probably the most serious tone I've ever seen him in, but I didn't. He kept taking the snacks out of his bag, annoyed by my stubbornness and I responded with how he needed it and if he refused to take it I would force it down his throat. He laughed at my remark but I was dead serious.

"You would never dare to do that. You're too sweet to do anything so inhumane."

I rolled my eyes at him and reached for the sandwich he took out of his bag. I threw it back into his open backpack and looked at him, "I dare you to take this out and see for yourself."

He didn't and I was very satisfied with myself. Did I scare him? Yes, very much indeed but he should've seen it coming.

I smile to myself. I sometimes forget how petty I was back then. I think I'm less of that now, but it comes out when it pleases. However, I had to force him to take my food and eat for a great amount of time that we spent together.

I know I made it sound funny or somewhat laughable in the diary entries, but it was sad. He didn't eat at all when I first met him. He would have a single snack to last him the whole day, so I took the initiative of packing him lunches and sharing my snacks. I was worried about him.

Thank God, he looks healthy now.

And besides, it was important for his health. I wanted him to gain some weight and continue whatever workout he was doing in the weight room.

Lucky for me, he started giving in whenever I gave him something to eat. Sometimes he would lash out and tell me to stop giving him food but I wouldn't listen because I wanted to see him okay. Even if he started hating me, I would continue to do so to see him healthy and okay.

I shut the book and lie down after marking the page I leave off on.

I'm still a little hurt. There are parts of me that need to heal from liking him.

The stuff he said this morning about liking me back was said in the past tense, so I highly doubt he thinks like that anymore. He thinks of me as a friend.

Emphasis on *'best friend'* from what he said earlier.

I close my eyes. I should be sleeping right now.

Tomorrow is another day.

...

"We meet at the cafe in fifteen minutes," Elena says, making her hair in front of the bathroom mirror.

"Okay," I sigh.

I stand in the kitchen, searching for something to eat.

I'm planning on buying some coffee at the cafe. The thing with getting food from the cafe is that it's ten times more expensive than the plain old french-vanilla coffee or I would've resorted to their piquant pastries and double-toasted bagels.

Digging through the cabinets, I'm able to find a single granola bar. It's those delicious chocolate-dipped ones that could make for a perfect snack.

I throw it into my tote bag to eat with my coffee.

"Let's go," Elena unlocks the front door, as we're immediately greeted by Elias, Jax, and Michael.

Michael's on duty, so it makes sense to see him here at our front step, but Elias and Jax...what are they doing here?

"Fancy seeing you here," I narrow my eyes at Elias.

"*Paparazzi* are right outside your building, so we decided to come and escort you out ourselves," Jax says, a hint of humour in his tone.

Elena rolls her eyes, giving him a sarcastic smile, "Jax, didn't you think by coming here, you would also be bringing more reporters? Or were we not using all those brain cells?"

I step out, stepping closer to Elias in the process.

"I know you're happy to see me here," he grins.

We start to walk towards the elevators with Elena and Jax close by behind us.

I face away from him, trying my hardest not to blush at what he just said. He does not know the power he holds over me. Everything he does that's directed to me makes my heart sink in my chest.

I don't think this is a '*she fell first, but he fell harder*' scenario. This is a '*she fell first, he didn't fall at all.*'

Sure, he fell back then when we both were so young, but that was *how many years ago…?* Seven?

It's been seven years and I'm still not over him.

I don't know if it's love anymore, though. I don't know what it is that I feel towards him. Maybe I don't love him at all. Maybe this is something entirely different.

"Watch there be no reporters or press waiting outside," I shoot back, earning a laugh.

"It's funny you say that because people got quite the photo yesterday," he pulls his phone out, beginning to type.

I switch my gaze away to be respectful, but I hear him chuckle as he turns his phone to me again.

"Do you remember this photo?"

My jaw drops.

It was a photo of us in high school. It was Eid that day, and we both had salwar kameez on. The only difference was mine was embroidered with different designs all traced in a gold colour, while his was more on the simpler side with subtle white outlines around the sleeves and breast pocket.

"Oh my God, how do you still have this?" I ask as he hands me his phone.

I zoom into myself, a beaming smile on my face as I remember how much fun we had that day.

"I never deleted it," he replies.

My eyes go back and forth from the Elias and Huma on the screen before I return his phone to him.

"You have to send this to me."

He smiles, "I'm doing it right now."

The elevator arrives with two bodyguards standing inside. I don't question it. Knowing how the press and fans can be, it's probably best for us to have maximum security as much as possible.

"You two take this lift. We'll come in the next one," Jax instructs, standing right by Elena. "Wait downstairs."

We both give him a nod, hopping inside.

The photo is adorable.

Well first, Elias looked adorable; eye smile, dimples, and everything. Not to mention how I was smitten over how he looked in a kurta. It makes it even better to know I gave the suit to him as a gift. I have no siblings, but I bought it with my own money after school so he would have something to wear for Eid. I know I didn't have to, but I really wanted to. It felt wrong for me to dress up without my best friend having the chance to do so, too.

I was feeling great wearing my own cultural clothes that morning. I remember waking up and having the most fun I've ever had getting ready for school. I put on jewelry, arranged my hijab nicely, and enjoyed the entire walk to school.

"We look so cute," I say, stepping out of the elevator.

He smiles sweetly, "You, especially. Last I recall, you were telling me weeks ahead about how excited you were."

I notice coruscating lights appearing on Elias and turn around to see people outside of the complex.

Just great...

"Right, let me show you the photo I was gonna show you earlier."

He shows me a picture of him leaning down to reach my height, almost like he was about to give me a hug. As I hark back to yesterday, this was him telling me to not stop walking until I reached the front door, but it looked so much worse in the photo.

I don't give a response— can't. My mind is too focused on the fact that there are people outside who want a reaction worth making headlines about.

It seems Elias has noticed too because he's asking me where my headphones are again. I get them on like a little kid being instructed as he connects them to his bluetooth.

"It's a shared playlist of only the most comforting nasheeds you will ever hear," he winks, lightening the mood a bit.

"Okay you two lovebirds, we have to get going," Jax's voice booms into my ears right as the nasheed begins.

We escort ourselves out the door as the security guards clear away the crowd, screaming things I'm grateful I cannot hear. I follow Elias closely as we reach the car, but he stops in front of it. He moves to the side, imitating the security guards, and lets me in before himself. I climb in, sitting on the far end of the car to be away from the flashing lights.

As soon as everyone is in, we're off to the cafe.

"What if they follow us to the cafe?" I ask, slipping my head-phones off to mold my neck.

"They *will*, but they're not allowed inside," Elias replies noncha-lantly.

So the second we get to the cafe, I sprint through the doors, and straight inside where the cameras can't follow as I catch Elias laughing at me.

Soon, all of them join me in a booth where the sun is peeking through the vast windows. Elena sits beside me, and Jax and Elias sit across from us. After we all receive our orders, Elena and Jax get straight down to business. "First things first, we are signing some contracts," Jax says, pulling out an abundance of papers.

I send Elias a look, but he appears just as startled as me. I thought by the amount of movies he's been a part of, this is something he's used to, but I'm wrong.

"Since Huma's book is copyright-claimed and it's fully protected by the law, we have to get you to sign a contract agreeing to make your book into a movie. This protects the cast of your book, the entertainment, you, Elena, and the list goes on," Jax goes on to say. "Plus, it makes it official."

He slides it over to us. I look at the pages of random words, acting as if I know exactly what's going on.

"I'm gonna have to do a deep search on this one, Parker, and I swear to God, if you put anything that is equivalent to dumb in here, you'll never hear the end of it," Elena says, clicking her pen.

There's definitely something going on between the two based on the way Jax looks like he can laugh right now. He almost looks flattered by Elena's reaction to the handful of papers.

If they're not somehow acquaintances, I would say they're trying to get under each other's skin for the thrill of it.

"If you two want to sit separately, you can," Jax says, his voice laced with mischief.

I shoot another look towards Elias, who's already standing.

"Shall we, Huma," his expression is telling me to get the hell up and scoot myself to another seat.

"What was that move you just pulled there?" I ask, eyeing Jax and Elena suspiciously as we sit down at another table.

He bites back a smile, "Apparently our suspicions were true. Jax is catching feelings faster than I thought he would."

The same way I caught feelings for you?

I chuckle, "So it seems."

"Anyways," he turns back to me with a smile. "How was your morning?"

Sweet old Elias.

I purse my lips, "It was pretty good. Couldn't find a snack to go with the coffee— which reminds me— do you wanna half a granola bar?"

I pull it out of my bag as his smile becomes softer, his dimples becoming lighter. "You don't have to share your food with me any-more, Huma. I have my own."

I widen my eyes, afraid he might have misunderstood, "No, no. I meant if you'd like to share. I know you're perfectly capable of affording your own snacks. I just wanted to be polite— I mean you could probably buy this cafe if you wanted to— but—"

He laughs, resting his chin on his hand, "I know what you mean, Huma, but only if you share my snacks too."

My cheeks burn up.

Why is communication so hard for me? God, I majored in English, and I can barely speak the language.

It starts to dawn on me just how much Elias says my name when he talks to me. Everytime, instinctively, I shiver a little when that word leaves his mouth.

I know by realizing this, I'm going to catch onto every time he says it just because my mind has made a decision to give me mini heart attacks.

He surprises me when he pulls out a bag of a well known desi snack.

No way he's actually got taste.

"Mr. Lee, what is this? When did you develop such quality taste?" I ask teasingly.

He bursts out with laughter and I tune in, "Wow, I love the reaction."

"No, seriously. Did you one day decide you wanted to impress me? Because, let me tell you, it's working pretty well."

He pops open the package and faces the open side towards me.

"I remember someone in high school telling me these snacks were the best, so I kind of had to go try them out."

"You are so cheesy," I roll my eyes.

He sighs, "It happens to the best of us."

I feel a burning in my heart. An intense feeling similar to years ago. It feels familiar, reminding me of the way I would feel great at first, almost like I had an epiphany, and then it would ground me to the floor. It would crowd me and mess with me, playing mind games, and making me think I was the foolish one for thinking Elias liked me.

Turns out he does, but does that change our situation now? *No, it doesn't.*

So why am I wasting my time then? If this didn't lead anywhere, what am I doing? What happened to those morals, those promises? I must've soaked the energy out of them because they're entirely empty now.

We're not best friends. He thinks we are, but we're not. This is one-sided love. This story won't have the happy ending I keep hoping it will.

I keep hurting myself for him because that's what I believe is love. If it doesn't hurt, is it really love? But is it love when I'm the only one hurting?

The worst part is that I didn't learn the first time. Repeating mistakes is okay, but repeating mistakes that took years to heal from makes me rethink everything.

I don't know why this is hitting me now. I think this came from all the built up anger and regret I held in me. Not to mention, how this is religiously wrong for us to be doing. Being friends with the opposite sex is prohibited, and I understand that. This is not to defend our take on being "friends" in high school, but we were so lost, and when we found each other, we also found peace.

While I hadn't realized at the time how wrong this was, Elias and I ended up guiding each other towards Islam. Yes, it was wrong in certain ways, and I know I shouldn't have done this as the more knowledgeable one at the time, but I was tired of not having anyone to turn to.

Back in high school, I had no one, but he consoled me. I had someone to rest against when no one was there for me. I had my parents, but not everything you experience you can easily tell to a parent no matter how good they are to you. He was hurting just like me, and so we found comfort in each other. But I couldn't see that comfort in him anymore. Seeing him now is just to show me he's okay now. He's safe. He only needs me here because he still needs that comfort. I want to give it to him, but it's taking everything in me to keep him happy, and any more of this and I'll give out. The ground beneath me is going to end up sucking me in deep, and not even he could pull me out. If I had known we were a losing game, maybe I wouldn't have put this much time and effort into us.

"Elias, why do you still talk to me?" I ask.

He sits back, "You already asked me that."

"No. I asked you why you talked to me in high school— now I'm asking you why you're talking to me now."

"I don't know," he tilts his head to the side, confused. *"I missed my friend."*

"We're not friends, Elias. We're far from that."

He scoffs, "Why are you acting like that, Huma? What are we if we're not friends?"

All my built up feelings are begging to come out, but I swallow them back in.

"I don't know what we are...don't you feel this is wrong, Elias?" I query. "Calling each other *friends?* Acting as if those seven years never happened?"

His shoulders tense. I feel bad making him overthink, making him upset, but what am I meant to do? I need serious answers.

"Did I do something? Did I say something wrong?" He asks. "Because if I did, please tell me so I can make it up to you. Please don't fight with me."

I notice the sudden intensity in his eyes.

"I just don't understand this relationship we have. You're not a friend, Elias," I breathe out.

Right after we make up, I have to go and ruin this again.

"Then what am I, Huma? *Who am I to you?*"

There is a pained expression plastered on his face, screaming for me to shut up and act like everything I said never happened.

"Elias, are you that blinded by whatever's in front of you to not be able to see that *I still love you?*"

My own words surprise me, but when I think about it, it makes sense.

He doesn't say anything. He just stares at me blankly.

I don't know what else to say to him. I've said everything I needed to.

"Can we talk somewhere private?" He asks softly.

I push back my chair, creating enough space for me to stand. My eyes search for a secretive area we could go to before I notice a column at the corner of the cafe.

I walk over, standing behind it where the sunlight doesn't hit, and cross my arms over my chest.

"Go on, Elias. Tell me what a pity party this has been."

"Huma, please don't be like this. It took so much from me to be forgiven. Please don't get mad again."

He's giving me unlimited reasons to keep going, and right now, he's my biggest one.

But I'm not going to stand here and let him rip me into shreds.

We're not friends.

"I'm just confused, Elias. If you could somehow make me *unlove you*, then I'll be okay."

His voice cracks, "Are you stupid, Huma?"

My eyes sting even more, making me step back and away from him.

"I just told you that I loved you, and that's your response? Forget about being friends, Elias. I don't want anything to do with you—"

"You must be just as blinded as I am because I've been in love with you for almost eight years now, and I haven't fallen out since."

"That's not funny."

"It really isn't," he replies. "And I've been really lonely for the past seven years. I find friends back and forth, but rarely. I wish I could explain the excitement I had after seeing you. *I finally found you.* Do you know how good that made me feel? You were the only one who would listen to me. To every negative I had, you would find the light in it. The part of it that made it positive. Do you think I liked living with those people at home who acted as if I was a stranger and not having you to look forward to anymore? They wanted me out of the house, so I left. I never wanted to leave, Huma. Never. I would never leave you without a valid reason."

I take a breath, except it's only reaching my throat. "What are you saying?"

"I don't know if you're willing to, but," he shifts a little. *"I want you to marry me."*

24

"So race to [all that is] good."
- Surah Al-Ma'idah [5:48]

"Elias—"

"Say yes or no, Huma. Don't extend it. Be straightforward," he interrupts.

How do you reply to something like that? He just proposed to me. I would have to talk to my parents, talk to Elena and Jax to see what they said. I mean, would this really fix everything we were going through right now?

"Huma, it was a mistake to leave, and I don't want us to be distant again. This isn't the type of love that you can move on from," he speaks with a spark of sadness in his voice.

He's right. This type of love hurt and stung, and could break anyone. Now I have the chance to make it right. This is my chance to heal my open wounds, and help Elias heal from his own.

"I have to ask my parents first," I mutter. "And it's a fifty-fifty chance with them, so be prepared."

He stares at me for a second, "Is that a yes...?"

Without any hesitation, I reply, "Yes. I want to marry you, too."

His whole body relaxes at my words as I feel myself being comforted.

Maybe I don't see the comfort in him anymore because he gave it all away to me.

"Are you serious?"

I nod my head as it starts to sink in.

Elias loves me.

Realizing that, my eyes start to water. I have been longing for him to love me, and now he's professing all the feelings he has kept hidden.

All those seven years, I believed it was one-sided, but it wasn't all along.

"I can't believe I didn't see this coming," I laugh through my tears.

He laughs with me, a smile appearing on his face, "I didn't either."

This man loves me.

"I'll be back— I need to clean this mess up," I motion to my face, excusing myself to the bathroom.

I splash my face with water in the stall.

Oh my God, Elias loves me.

I can't stop smiling at my own reflection.

I cannot believe he said that.

He wants to get married, and he wants to get married to me.

I take a deep breath to calm myself down, knowing it won't do much. After a couple more minutes, I step out and walk back to our table.

"I'm scared of what my parents might say about this. I don't want them to be upset, you know?" I say nervously.

He chuckles, "My parents never cared about that stuff."

My heart aches for everything he's had to go through. His parents were so good to him before he converted. He told me about how converting made his parents upset. They weren't religious people, so I never understood why they couldn't just accept him.

"Did you talk to your parents after high school?" I ask, munching on my granola bar.

"No," he chuckles.

"I'm sorry, Elias. You don't deserve that type of treatment."

"I'm gonna need that diary of yours, Huma. This was your last strike and you used it up," he says. "Your apologies are getting on my nerves."

...

Later in the night, I spend a lot of time thinking about how I'm going to bring this up in conversation with my parents. I wonder how I'm going to tell them everything without getting in a huge amount of trouble.

I know I told Elias it was a fifty-fifty chance, but I doubt it is. I have a weird sixth sense telling me they're going to say no.

"Okay Huma, what did he say that's making you pace like a maniac?" Aaliyah rolls her eyes. "For the love of God, sit down."

I stop and look at Aaliyah, "I don't even know where to start from— everything became so overwhelming for a second, and then he said *that*, and I was completely speechless!"

"How about you start with what he said?" Aaliyah suggests.

I close my eyes for a second, and then blurt it out, "He asked me to marry him."

Aaliyah blinks hard and her eyes go wide, "ARE YOU SERIOUS?"

I see Elena in my peripheral vision with a similar expression on her face as I spin towards her, her jaw hitting the floor.

"Huma, you absolute idiot, what did you say to him?!" Aaliyah asks, grabbing my shoulders and violently shaking me back and forth.

"I told him I wanted to talk to my parents first."

I swallow all the grins and smiles that are desperate to make themselves known. Unfortunately, I would have to wait for a couple of days until I could go over to my parent's place since they're staying over at a family friend's.

Four days of absolute torture.

"Do you think you could still do the casting for tomorrow? We still have to find someone to cast the MC in your book," Elena states.

"Yeah, for sure."

I sit down with a thud. Today was a pretty eventful day, and my body is starting to give out because of it.

I am exhausted.

"I might call it a night," I announce. "I'll see you two in the morning."

I get myself cleaned up in the bathroom before changing into some comfortable clothes. I adjust myself in my bed as I lean against the headboard.

My overthinking mind is at it again; I wonder if Elias is having doubts about this. I know everything happened all of a sudden, but I feel so sure about him. He understands me in a way no one can, and the more time I spend with him, the deeper I fall in love with him.

I can only hope he isn't regretting everything he says now.

With my phone still in my hand, I decide to send him a text.

Me

I hope youre not having doubts

Elias

Im the one who proposed to you rmbr

I smile. At least he's being reassuring. I still need that part of him in this whole ordeal.

Elias
I wanna talk to ur parents
myself huma

While I'm scared to see what my parents are going to say about him, he's over here ready to ask himself. Bold of him to assume they would willingly talk to him.

Me
Let me talk to them myself

Elias
Your parents still live in the
same house right

Me
Yes

Elias
Perfect
Thx
Ill be talking to them

Me
They arent home

Elias
The lights are on
Ok bye future wife

My cheeks heat up, hurting from the smile that's forming on my face. I place a pillow on my face and scream.

I hate and love this guy so much, it hurts.

Even when I try to call his phone, he doesn't reply.

Me
Answer ur phone elias

Elias
No can do
Im abt to ring their doorbell
so sleep tight

How did he get there so fast?

Stupid, stupid boy.

It's one o'clock, so even if they are home, they're probably going to sleep, but it makes my heart flutter to know he wants an answer so badly.

I call him again, and this time he answers.

"Huma, go to sleep. I'm going to talk to your parents—"

"Elias, wait for me. I'll talk to them with you."

"No, you won't me."

This demanding brat. I am not about to let him boss me around.

I get up, and set a hijab on my head.

"I'm coming, Elias. Don't go inside without me."

He sighs into the phone, "Fine. Try it out to see what happens."

I walk out of my room, and walk over to the front door. I open it to see Ayaan, the overnight bodyguard, standing there. I'm about to walk past him, but he steps in front of me.

"Mr. Lee has instructed me to keep you indoors," he says bluntly.

"Elias, you idiot. Tell him to let me go," I demand, annoyed.

"No. Now close that door and go to sleep."

"Goodnight, Ms. Tariq," Ayaan says as I shut the door.

"When I see you tomorrow, I'll kill you," I threaten through gritted teeth.

He scoffs, "Well see you tomorrow then."

He ends the call while I stomp back to my room. If he's going to act like this, fine then. He's going to mess it all up, and that'll be all his fault.

25

"Okay, can you read a passage from the book?" I ask, looking at the young girl holding a paper in her hand.

She is the first out of the thousands of people who want to be a part of the cast in the movie. I quickly came to realize there are more people than expected because everyone wants to act with Elias.

I wouldn't say it's jealousy, but I don't like the idea of these girls reenacting scenes from *mine* and Elias' past.

They should stay in their place.

We're basically married.

On one side of me sits Elena, and on the other was supposed to be Elias, but he didn't show up. I'm afraid something might've gone wrong, and my parents had told him no. I tried to call him this morning, but he didn't reply. I left him multiple text messages just in case he got busy with something else. Even Elena contributed to helping me by ringing Jax who said he'd be on his way. When asked about Elias, he said he told him he might be resting for the day because the rest of the week was filming.

I shake my head to bring my attention back to the girl.

"I'm going to read the passage from page one-hundred-sixty-five," she says.

I nod my head as a cue for her to begin.

"When you hear the words 'I love you,' you expect it to be a story of love. A story that bonds relationships and brings people closer. Whether it be between mothers and daughters, or the love of your life. You think when you hear those three words, it'll be a fulfilling and adorable thing to hear and see. But that's not how it worked for me."

She makes a dramatic pause, and I have to admit, I'm impressed by the way she expresses emotions because there's none on her face, and that's how I want it.

When I wrote the book, I wrote it to emulate a monotone voice. This is meant to show how people shut off their emotions when it becomes too much. When the amount a person can hold surpasses, and instinctively, our feelings shut off because we become protective of ourselves. We don't want to be damaged the same way again, so we learn to turn off our emotions and become expression-less people.

"I don't know if this is love, but I think it may be. One-sided love. I think he didn't like me the way I liked him He didn't view me in the same way I viewed him. And every part of me thinks about him every day. It feels like a weight is being lifted off my chest when I say those words. Those words break hearts, but they also mould back the broken souls shattered from the hurt caused by past events. I feel cold writing this. I need the heat from love. It hurts. It does. I don't know how much more healing I need before I'll get over him. Or maybe I never will. But God— I can't with this. I can't with the way he makes me feel. When I saw him, he made me want to do only good things. Drop all my bad habits and focus on him. It scares me, though. I need to get my mind off of him. I need to learn to forget him."

I make a note as she finishes and smile at her, "I loved how expression-less you were. You really brought out the importance of the passage, and I truly appreciate that."

"Thank you," she replies.

"Any other comments?" I look at Elena and Jax.

She shakes her head, "No, I think you did great."

She leaves through the exit, and in comes the shadow of a guy. Before he can completely walk in, I speak, "I'm sorry, we're only casting for girls at the moment—"

It's...*Abu...?*

I hop out of my seat with a huge smile on my face. I greet him with a hug, "*Assalamu'alaikum*, Abu. What are you doing here?"

He kisses the top of my head with a soft chuckle, "*Walaikum Assalam, beta.* I just wanted to see how you were doing. Look at you, casting people for your movie."

He waves at Elena and Jax.

"That's Jax. He's Elias' manager," I pull away from his warmth. "And you already know Elena."

Elena raises her hand to wave back.

"I need you to come over to our house tonight, okay? There's something we need to talk about," his tone grows serious.

I shiver.

What did Elias do?

"Okay."

I don't want to break into an interview right now. If this really is about Elias, then I cannot talk about it right now. We're in the middle of casting and I'm scared of what my father possibly has to say about him.

"Okay, *meri jaan,* I'll see you soon," he kisses my forehead again before finding his way out.

Elena's eyes dart towards mine, "Is everything okay?"

"I have no clue...he said to go over to their house after I'm done with this," I shiver again.

They both nod their heads.

"I'm sure it's not anything too bad. Don't worry about it," Jax reassures me, though I wish Elias was here to do it instead.

I walk back to my seat, "Yeah, it's probably nothing."

Jax has no clue what Elias did last night. I thought it may be a possibility Elias told Jax, but it appears not. Either way, my mind needs to be focused on this. He told me he'd let me know everything once it's solved.

"Next," I say loudly.

A woman who's probably a couple of years older than me walks in.

"Can we get your name?" Jax picks up his pen, ready to make notes.

"Aamina."

...

"So, do we have anyone in particular we liked?" I ask after hours of trying to find the right girl.

It is nine now, and no sign of Elias at all. No texts, no calls— my worry from earlier can't even compare to this very moment.

"The twentieth girl— Aiza— did really well," Elena sits back, satisfied.

I hum in agreement.

"Really? She was very pitchy to me," Jax comments.

Elena rolls her eyes, "Jax, this wasn't a music audition you fool. Getting a voice crack is not a problem."

What if something happened to Elias?

I text him again.

Me

Please call me elias

How did the talk go

My leg starts to shake as I wait for his reply.

Could it be that he's ignoring me?

It must've gone pretty bad if he's avoiding a text message.

"I think number four did great. She just flowed with everything she said," I say, trying to distract myself. "Like her voice was calming to listen to."

"See, Jax. That's partially how you analyze someone when it comes to acting. Even Huma is more knowledgeable than you, and this is her first time."

My leg shakes a little faster. I try to stop the shaking by putting my hands on my knee, but it doesn't do anything.

All this anxiety isn't just the worry about Elias and his lack of response to me. I'm truly worried about what was said in my absence.

I know Elias is the most respectful person ever, and he would never say anything rude or offensive, especially to my parents. I'm more worried about what my parents might've said to him. My parents are extremely respectful as well, but a random famous guy showing up at your doorstep at the dead of night and asking for your daughter's hand in marriage is probably not the ideal way they would like to be greeted by someone their daughter wants to marry. I'm scared for if they unintentionally might've insulted him.

"Okay, it's getting late," Elena says. "How about we assess this when we get home. We have to get into the warehouse to start filming by tomorrow, but if we stay up a little late, we could probably find a conclusion, or pull a couple of girls to come back early tomorrow morning and give us a bit of a show...? How does that sound?"

"Yeah, I think that's great, but I have to go to my parents' house today," I sigh.

"It's okay, I'm sure Elena and I could figure something out. Then we'll run it by you tomorrow."

"Okay. Well, I have to get going. I'll see you two tomorrow," I get up, throwing my bag over my shoulder. "Bye."

Once I'm out of there, I sprint to my car, desperate to see whether Elias could be hanging around waiting for me. And then it dawns on me that I can check online to see if there's any news on Elias.

I unlock my car, hopping in, placing my bag on the passenger seat. I search Elias' name on my phone and...*nothing*. I assumed *Paparazzi* might've had a run-in with Elias wherever he might be, but it seems even they can't find him.

I startup my car, placing my phone on my lap.

Elias, please answer.

The drive to my old home is making me more jumpy as I get closer. It is fortunately not far from my apartment, which makes it easy for me to get to Ami and Abu quickly if I ever have to.

When I moved out, I made sure to live closeby, and the apartment complex I live at now worked for Aaliyah too. We kind of were right in the middle of both our parents' places.

A text message pops on my screen just as I stop at a red light.

Oh thank God, it's Elias.

Elias
Im fine

That's it? Just an *'I'm fine'*?

I pull into their driveway, and see them standing at the doorstep. My mind is ablaze, my body tensing up at the sight of my parents.

As I pull the key out of the ignition, I take a breath, deciding to leave my bag in the car. I step out, hugging both of them as I approach the two.

"We need to talk about Elias," Ami says when I pull away.

26

"Take care of your own souls."
- Surah Ma'idah [5:105]

"He told us everything, Huma, and I have to say, I'm so proud of you," Ami says, surprising me with her words.

Ami and Abu are sitting on the three-seater sofa, and I'm on the single chair. It smells of *chana chawal* in the house which gives me a rush of nostalgia.

I have come to a conclusion that if I don't hear from Elias at all, or my parents tell me that they somehow were the reason behind his absence, I will stay here tonight. I will stay here because at this point, the only way to get over Elias would be to sleep it off, and give up on life as a whole.

"Why would you say that?" I ask, confused.

"Because he was finding himself when you two met. He explained it to us. He told us that all he ever wanted was someone to rely on, and you gave him that and so much more," she continues. "But that doesn't mean that we're okay with this entirely."

There it is. The *no* I've been waiting for. The disapproval that he is not fit for me.

"Look, I know this is sudden, and I know what I did in high

school was stupid, but I was also struggling. You guys know how hard it was for me then, and he made me feel important. He actually found importance in me when I started to believe I had no purpose," my voice breaks. "You don't understand how hard it was for me because I didn't have anyone to talk to at school."

Elias crumpled up all of my pain and threw it away.

"You really wanna marry him?" Abu asks, his face sympathetic.

I nod my head slowly, "Yes. I want to marry him."

My heart is racing, scared of what they might say. I can't tell if they're okay with this, or not. I just wish Elias had let me come with him last night, so I could've backed him up with everything he said.

The doorbell rings, but their eyes stay trained on me.

"Then go check to see who's at the door."

I search them both for humour, for some sort of a punchline that's going to hit me right in the gut, but there's none.

Then there's a subtle knock that pushes me to finally hop back onto my feet, and force myself to the door.

My eyes meet Elias' who's looking at me with the softest smile I've ever seen.

"I was getting our *Nikkah* papers."

This is a setup.

"Elias, you idiot," I burst into tears. "You could've called me or warned me! I was so worried about you!"

He laughs sweetly, "The rest of them are meeting us at the Masjid in five minutes. You're coming with me in my car, and your parents will come themselv—"

"Get out of here, you two! If the imam calls it a day, it's going to be your fault, and you'll have to get married tomorrow," Ami shouts from the living room. "We'll see you there in a couple of minutes!"

"Come before your mom kicks us out herself," he says, laughing.

We settle into his car, and as we're arriving at the Masjid, the car comes to a halt.

"What happened?" Elias asks the driver, but he seems just as confused.

A couple of minutes later, there's an incoming call from Jax.

"So it seems *Paparazzi* has found you again," Jax says humorously as Elias puts the phone on speaker. "They know where you're going, and they know what you're going for."

"If they already have their story, why are they following us?" I ask, my nerves on edge.

"To get footage," they both say at once.

"You weren't very smart in high school, were you?" Elias bites back a smile.

"Shut up."

"Okay, Jax. I'll see you there then. Just hold back the imam until we get there."

He ends the call.

My leg starts shaking again. I'm basically vibrating the whole car because of my anxiety.

"Hey, don't worry," Elias lowers his voice, his eyes glancing down to my leg. "Watch. The car will start moving...now!"

To our surprise, it really does as I applaud him.

"Wow. I didn't know I was marrying a wizard."

"I think you're just jealous that you're a regular human," he raises an eyebrow.

"We've arrived," the driver says, and we both exit.

I stop when we're at the front doors and turn to him, one hand gripping the handle, the other hanging loosely, "Elias, I can't marry you wearing this. I look like I just woke up."

I'm wearing sweats. My favourite pair of sweats, but they are still sweats, and last time I checked, I like to dress up. Not to mention, the fact that I'm going in there without any make-up at all.

Since my schedule today was only castings, I dressed up like a homeless person to be comfortable. This will be marked down as one of the dumbest mistakes made in history, that's for sure.

"I don't care. I would marry you in rags if I had to, *Cinderella*." He says sternly as I blush.

I open the door to the Masjid, and we walk in. Somebody grabs my arm, pulling me into the lady's section.

"I brought your lilac suit you wore when you two met," Aaliyah appears in front of me, shoving the clothes towards me. She pushes me into the bathroom and sighs.

Everything is happening so quickly that it's starting to overwhelm me.

I'm getting married.

This is a lot for something that was arranged yesterday, and that makes me nervous. A lot has happened since yesterday; Elias not listening to my requests, the auditions, Ami and Abu wanting to talk...and all of it led to this.

I start to change my clothes.

"Huma, I can't believe you're getting married," her voice cracks a little. "You fool, you're leaving me for a guy."

I open the door with my undershirt and dress pants on to give her a hug.

It hurt me to know that eventually I would move out of the apartment to live with Elias. I don't plan to do that now, but eventually I think I would have to in order for us to become a family. I don't like the idea of leaving Aaliyah alone, but this might work well for Elena. She would have someone to live with and there couldn't have been a more perfect time for me to be moving out.

Not now. Eventually.

"I'm not leaving you, you idiot," I choke up.

She looks at me, "I know, I know. I'm just happy that you found someone."

My gaze softens, and I smile, "You'll find someone, too. I promise. He's probably waiting for you to notice him."

I put on the blazer before dashing out of there to where I see Elias sitting in front of the imam on the floor.

As I approach them, Elias rubs his face, his eyes not leaving mine.

"You look...so beautiful," he says.

"Calm down, brother. She's not your wife yet," the imam says, making everyone laugh while Elias' ears turn red.

I lower my head, heating up from his compliment.

The imam starts, and we sign the papers.

I look up to see him smiling so much it makes my heart flutter.

"Let's stand for this part," Elias says.

"Why?" I ask.

"Just do it, please."

I oblige, confused as he faces me. His hands are tucked behind his back like he's just barely resisting the urge to hug me.

Or maybe that's just me.

I can't tell.

"*Qabool hai?*" the imam asks.

"What does that mean?" Elias asks quietly.

"He's asking you if you accept," I reply, amused.

"*Qabool hai.*"

His words make me shiver. He just agreed to marry me. *Elias* agreed to marry me. He says it two times after that, bringing my tears on edge, but I'm able to hold off.

"*Qabool hai?*" the imam asks again.

I nod my head, feeling my eyes stinging. "*Qabool hai.*"

And then I say it two times after that, further confirming the marriage.

My eyes dart to the clock right behind Elias on the wall.

At 10:26 p.m., Elias and I got married to each other officially.

"Go on and give each other a hug," the imam says, and before I can argue why I would rather do that in a more private setting, Elias has his arms around me.

His head rests in the crook of my neck as I feel his whole body relax. I swallow hard, comforted by the way he's holding me, and place my arms around him. I wish I could describe how bad we both needed this hug from each other. To finally have him in my arms where I could protect him and feel protected makes me melt, and I didn't want to let go.

His embrace is warm, but I feel myself shiver at his touch.

I tighten my grip on him, feeling him reciprocate the contact.

His body starts to shake and I hear him sniffle, making me pull him closer. I rub his back gently, listening to him cry into my neck.

If anything, he needs this more than anyone in the world. After all these years of loneliness, he needs this. After all of the pain of his own family rejecting him, he needs this. After needing someone to tell him how important he is, he needs this. After finally finding someone that cares so much for him, having to move on to become an amazing person, and falling in love, *he needs this.*

"I love you, Elias," I whisper. "I always have."

I can feel his heart racing against me as I break away from his strong hold. Ami and Abu come over, and I wrap my mother tightly into my embrace. As I pull away to hug Abu, I see he's busy hugging Elias.

I myself start to cry right as Elena and Aaliyah give me a hug.

"Oh my God, you're married!" Elena says through tears.

I laugh, and slowly one by one, everyone says bye to us until it's only the two of us left. Elias stands in front of me, a rush of his emotions displayed on his beautiful face.

When I lift the corners of my mouth, he starts to cry again.

"Awe, Elias," I cup his cheeks.

"I probably look so stupid— I don't even know why I'm crying," he sniffles.

"You look far from stupid, Elias. You deserve this," I stroke my thumb over his face.

"God, Huma," he places his head on my shoulder, forcing my hands off his cheeks. "I love you more than anything in this world."

It's ironic to think Elias was just teasing and making jokes right before we got here, and now he's completely breaking down in front of me.

He lifts his head up as I slip my hands into his, earning a smile from him.

"I'll be your home, Elias. *I'll be the star that makes you a constellation.*"

And I truly mean that with every crevice of my being.

His eyes fill up with tears again, "Stop making me cry!"

I laugh quietly, wiping his tears away. "I love you, Elias."

He drops one of my hands from his.

We take the back door of the Masjid to avoid reporters since they're still circulating the area. His car is waiting for us as we exit out the building, and we get in.

"Do you want to come home with me?" He asks, letting me into the car first. "I can drop you home, but if you're okay with it, then I'd like to take you to my house."

I lean over to him, and with one hand resting on his shoulder, I kiss his cheek. "Sure, I'll stay with you tonight."

...

27

⚭

Huma

"And do good as Allah has done good to you."
- Surah Al-Qasas [28:77]

"You have a very big house," I breathe out in awe.

Elias chuckles, "Please, you're making me blush."

"No, I'm serious. Look at these and—" my eyes drift to the huge bookshelf in the corner, making me gasp. I run to it after taking my shoes off. "Oh. My. Lord. I didn't know you were a reader! You used to make fun of me for this!"

He has all sorts of books on the shelves, and all of them are sorted by size. Elias comes next to me, reaching for a book at the top shelf.

"Here's yours."

I gasp even louder when I see he has fully annotated it, too.

I don't think it's possible to over-annotate a book, but *mine* has so many markings.

So many markings.

"Elias, I'm going to steal this just to look at everything you annotated," I say, absolutely mesmerized by him.

"How about you get settled? I'll warm up some food for you," he says, taking the book from my hands.

I meet his eyes to see he's blushing.

Hm.

I'm much more curious now.

Unfortunately, I didn't think of packing some comfy clothes in my bag this morning— maybe because I had no clue I would be getting married today, and not going home, but you know.

I know for sure I'm not about to sleep in a suit, let alone this pretty one, so I'm either going to have to take a trip home or I'm going to have to thrift my own clothes out of some old bedsheets.

"I didn't bring any clothes," I say blankly, and he grabs my hand.

I don't know what was making me redder; the fact that he took me home, or the fact that he's holding my cold hand with his warm one.

"Well lucky for you, I happen to live here, and have a closet filled with clothes," he says, pulling me into another room.

I thought this was a second living room...that is until I see the king-sized bed with a dresser and nightstands. There's a painting of The Ka'aba hanging right above a prayer mat laid out on the floor. As my eyes scan the area, I catch sight of a bathroom. The door is closed, but I could only imagine how big it is.

 I think I might've underestimated how rich Elias really is.

I don't mean to be unprofessional with this, but it's all so new to me. I'm used to living in your standard Scarborough apartment, not whatever this qualifies to be.

"Elias, how rich are you...?" I ask. .

He raises an eyebrow, "More richer than you think, clearly."

He releases my hand, and searches for something in his walk-in closet. Meanwhile, I drift away, walking out to seat myself down on his bed. I take out my phone and text Aaliyah to let her know I would be staying with Elias tonight.

I expect a bland reply, but she sends me the winking emoji.

I swear to God, this kid....

28

Elias

"And they will say, "Praise to Allah, who has removed from us [all] sorrow. Indeed our Lord is Forgiving and Appreciative."
- Surah Fatir [35:34]

"Okay, Huma. I found you something, but it probably won't fit. All of my clothes are going to be a little baggy—"

When I lift my head to look at her, I see her out-cold on my bed. I can't help but smile a little at how cute she is. So peaceful, so calm.

This whole day went perfectly, just as I planned it to go...except the emotional part. That was not meant to happen, but I couldn't control it. I never thought I would have the chance to see her again, and I always had this fear that she had changed. I'm glad I was able to shut down that fear so quickly because she is the exact same. The only thing that's changed is her maturity, but that's only by a little bit. She still has a little bit of those childish features in her, but I love every part of them.

I walk over to the bed and set the clothes down next to her before gently shaking her.

"Huma, I know my bed is comfy but that suit isn't," I say quietly. "C'mon, get up."

She hums back a response and forces herself up, disappearing into the bathroom with the clothes.

I take myself back into the closet to get changed as well.

I'm still in a bit of shock that I finally married her. It feels so surreal and euphoric all at once because this is something I have wanted since we have met.

This house is so empty that sometimes the silence echoes. Sometimes the silence is so loud that I can hear it bouncing back from the walls. I don't like being alone in this house. I've even asked Jax to move in with me countless times, which each time I've asked, he's always said that he wouldn't be able to afford to pay the rent that came with it. I've even offered to pay for his half as well, and in exchange, he could be the one to do things like buy groceries and small errands involving the house, but he argued that it felt wrong, that he would feel selfish doing so little.

I step out of the closet and sit at the foot of the bed.

Now I have Huma. Although I'm not sure if she's willing to live with me yet or anytime soon. I think eventually that will have to change for the both of us, but as of right now, I'm unsure and I don't want to bring that up right before sleeping.

She comes out of the bathroom with baggy clothes and messy hair which steals a laugh from my throat. She's blushing, turning a darker shade of red as the seconds pass. It's really cute seeing her blush at my words or my actions, and it's quite flattering to me to think that I can have such a huge impact on her.

She sits down next to me as I lean over to give her a forehead kiss.

"You look very pretty," I say, making myself tingle from my own words.

I can't believe I just said that to her.

"Liar," she mutters, facing her body to me with a tired smile.

"If I was lying, My Star, you would be able to tell. I suck at lying," I say, cupping her face.

Her smile becomes giddy. "What do I call you?"

"What do you mean?"

"You just called me *"My Star,"* I think it's only appropriate that I refer to you with a pet name," she places her hand on my knee. "So, what do I call you?"

Anything. Anything and everything.

"My Love?" She suggests, and I feel my heart almost beating out of my chest. I've never been more grateful to be sitting right now or my knees would've given out. "Or— oh— this is a good one...*Ellie.*"

Ellie, My Love.

I soften at her words, pulling her close into my hold. "You're going to drive me insane."

Huma doesn't understand how soothing her energy is. She has this thing about her that makes me want to protect her and keep her away from all the bad things in this world. Even in high school, I had this feeling that nudged me to be close to her and connect with her, and so I did exactly that. I fell for a girl who just magically happened to be in love with me, too.

The best part of finally being able to hold Huma is how she would never be the first to pull away. She would wait for me to finally let go before she even moved, and I could fall in love all over again just by that.

"I love you, My Star," I say, my lips against her hair.

"I love you, too," she mutters.

We stay like that for a couple of minutes, and she lets me hold her. I reciprocate when Huma fully releases all the tension in her body and melts into my arms.

Everyone needs someone to rely on. Someone they can turn to

when they need to be heard and listened to. Huma is my person. She was the one that was there for me when no one else was. When I felt like I had fallen deep into a tight, narrow ditch, Huma was the star that would guide me out. She was the star that followed me around everywhere I went and reassured me even in my darkest nights. When my family started to reject my beliefs, Huma stood there with a reassuring smile, telling me that I'll be okay.

That's who Huma is to me. This sweet little ball of happiness who deserves the world, and I as her husband, make an oath to myself and her, to give her all of that and so much more.

I match my breathing with hers as I rest back against the headboard of the bed, pulling her further into my arms. She hugs me, resting her head against my chest.

"No, wait," she looks at me with a sly, yet tired smile. *"Meri Jaan."*

I tilt my head to the side, raising an eyebrow, "And what does that mean...?"

She closes her eyes, letting me take in her face. Her features are soft and calm, and friendly at that. Like anybody in the world could approach her and she would become their best friend in an instance.

"Search it up," she murmurs under her breath, snuggling up against me.

Meri jaan.

I've definitely heard it before somewhere, but I don't know where.

I press my hand on her back, reaching for the blanket that's folded at the edge of the bed.

"My Star, could you move a little for a second?" I ask.

I don't receive an answer.

She's sleeping.

At least one of us will be able to sleep tonight.

I put an arm around her and reach for the blanket. Thankfully, it's more on my side to begin with. I open it up and place it on her and myself.

This does feel strange to some extent. It feels great to have her here, but I don't want her to leave me the next day. I would be back to living alone in this house and I don't want to do that anymore. My communication skills suck, though, and I have this fear she won't understand what I mean if I try to explain exactly that to her.

These past few days, I've been looking back at these letters I wrote for Huma. They're love letters that I keep in a folder. I wrote them when I fell in love with her back in senior year of high school.

A dreadful feeling passes over me.

I'm overwhelmed by how I got here. My whole childhood was great up until high school where I started connecting and researching Islam. I felt great and I invited my parents to come to the Masjid to see me convert, but they were not as thrilled as I hoped they would be. Growing up as an Atheist made me feel incomplete, and being able to comfort in this beautiful religion made me feel like I was finding myself. I expected a loving reply from them when I told them, but my father was the first to flip. He was throwing the dishes, picking up anything to stop me. So instead of having the beautiful night I wanted, one that I *needed,* I ran to the Masjid in tears.

In my head I had it planned out so perfectly so that one day, maybe, they would convert, too, and we could celebrate Eid, have fun making iftar during Ramadan, *but instead* they hated it so much, they didn't want me there anymore.

They didn't even consider me their child anymore.

I came home and saw them at the door, awaiting my return. I was hanging onto any type of hope at that point, praying that maybe this was them apologizing for their actions, but I didn't realize people like them only had bad intentions. I came home with a Quran and a prayer mat that the imam was nice enough to give to me.

I squeezed past them, not uttering a word, and headed to my room. I hid the Quran and prayer mat in the fear that they might do something vile to the two Holy Objects.

My mother came in first, sitting on my bed next to me. She listened to my cries, and even held me before letting me down. She started talking about faith and how she wasn't mad that I found guidance— she was mad that I found guidance in Islam.

I started shouting, getting mad at how she could even say that. But everything I said after that triggered her.

And everything. And I mean *everything* became horrible from there. I dodged them and had to start hiding from my father's belt. Our house was tiny too so most of the time he would find me and I wouldn't be able to lie down for days after the both of them were done. Sometimes it wasn't a belt, sometimes he would just throw things at me as if I was an intruder in their house.

I had to start barricading my door with my desk chair, having to leave the house hours before school started just so I wouldn't see them. It hurt my soul because they were such good people before. They were these caring and loving parents, and I loved them so much.

But all of that changed overnight.

Three years I faced them alone. Three full years of pure torture, and then I met this stunning, sweet ball of sunshine.

Her name was Huma.

29

Huma

"And that it is He who makes [one] laugh and weep."
- Surah Najm [53:43]

The sun floods in through the curtains, which I quickly come to realize do not belong to me. I look around the room as it all begins to click again.

Right, I'm married now.

I bite back a smile, remembering how magical yesterday was and notice there's no sign of Elias anywhere. I check the time to see it's ten in the morning.

I wonder if we're still going to start the shoot.

Oh my God, the castings!

I send a text to Elena to see if she's figured it out, receiving a call from her instead.

"Hey, Elena, did you find a better solution? I know I was sup-posed to help you guys out with —"

"It's okay, Huma," she interrupts, amusement in her voice. "We may have found a solution, but how about we meet up in a couple of hours to discuss it? How does that sound?"

"Yeah, I can do that. At the cafe, right?"

Before she ends the call, I ask about Aaliyah, and Elena says she's doing pretty well. My only issue is she is also under the impression I'm coming home tonight. Right now, I'm unsure because I don't want one of them to think I don't one of them as much as the other person and then create a problem.

I stretch, walking over to the bathroom to get myself cleaned up.

After how Elias cried yesterday, even if it was out of pure joy, he made me worry if he'd be okay without me tonight.

As I enter the bathroom, I see a toothbrush, toothpaste, face wash, face cream, and sunscreen on the vanity counter with a note on the mirror.

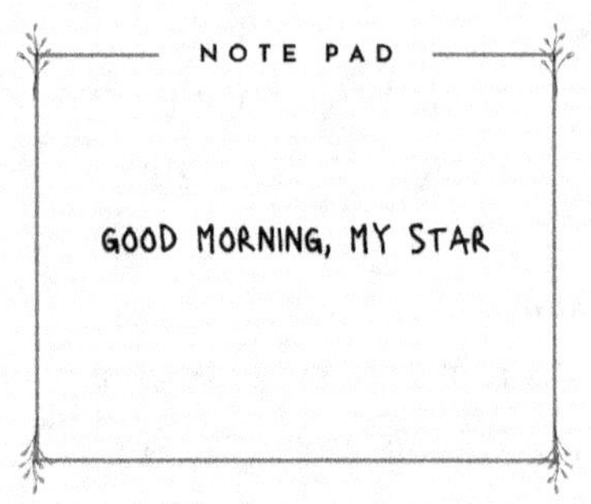

I smile, picking up the brush and applying some paste onto it.

If this is what I'm greeted with every morning, I'll happily live with Elias, but leaving Aaliyah hurts me and her a lot. We grew up together and we've been living together since university, so this is going to be a huge change for both of us if I leave.

I perform wudu before leaving the bathroom.

My eyes scan for a prayer mat which I see has already been set in the corner of the bedroom right by the painting of the Ka'aba I saw last night. I use my hijab from yesterday and pray before leaving the room to search for Elias.

The only places I've been in his house so far are his living, bed, bath, and closet, and I've seen his kitchen since it's one of those fancy ones that molds into the living room.

My eyes catch sight of Elias who's back is turned to me. I walk over and stand behind him, wondering whether I'm safe to hug him or not. Last night we were embracing each other like it was nothing, but being wide awake is a bit different. I was tired yesterday, and now, I'm fully energized.

My eyes are burning through him.

He has a very huggable back.

I don't even think he knows I'm here.

"Huma," he says slowly.

Nevermind.

"Yeah?"

He turns enough to catch my gaze, "I wouldn't mind."

"Wouldn't mind what?"

He looks back at the stove, "If you hugged me."

Shoot. Am I thinking out loud?

I step forward, hearing him chuckle, which takes me through a whirlwind of emotions, and suddenly, my arms are embracing his scent. He hums out of approval, which for some reason, reassures me. But even with my nerves on edge, I relax against him, feeling myself comforted by his warmth.

"What are you making, *Meri Jaan?*" I ask, peeking over and past his arm.

"I'm making french toast for us," he turns on his heels to me, forcing me to release him. He gives me a mischievous smile, and I feel his lips press against my forehead, my cheeks heating up at the sweet gesture. "Also, are you gonna tell me what that means?"

I tilt my head to the side in confusion.

I know exactly what he's talking about, but I need to hear it from him.

He blushes, "You know what I'm talking about."

I stare at him blankly in the hopes that he'll say it, but he turns back around and starts to place the remaining french toast with the rest of them on a plate.

"No, what are you talking about?" I ask.

He shifts, trying not to show the smile on his face, *"Meri jaan."*

I melt. I can feel him chipping through every remaining piece of my soul in the best way possible when the words leave his mouth.

I cover my face by looking the other way, blocking the view of my tinted cheeks.

"Do you want coffee—? You want coffee, right?" He clears his throat, walking out of the kitchen, and sets down the breakfast onto a huge coffee table in front of the very gorgeous white fabric couch. I love white couches, or just light coloured couches in general, but it gives me anxiety thinking if I spilt anything on it, there would be a permanent stain.

"Why do you keep looking at me like that?" I laugh between my sentences.

"Like what?" He asks, relieved that I'm not talking about what just happened.

I can see the smile wanting to show on his face, and in an attempt to force it away, Elias presses his lips together which makes his dimples known.

I pick up the coffee cup, "Like you're planning something— you're not tryna get rid of me...are you?"

He laughs, his eye smile appearing.

Cute.

"Yes and no. I *am* planning something, but it's not to get rid of you," he replies, scooting close to me. "It has to do with a date and you, though, if you're up for it."

My breath stops.

A date—?

I put my head down, reddening. This guy can't be serious.

Hearing all of this stuff is so new. Elias is basically used to seeing me melt in front of him, especially at his words, but *wow*. A *real date.*

He tips my chin up so our eyes meet, and if I'm not red enough already—

"Are you blushing?" He smiles, raising an eyebrow at my misfortune.

"Where do you want to take me?" I query, entirely ignoring his question.

"Well," he drops his hand, his eyes narrowing. "Since you discovered my reading secret— you might not like the idea and it kind of was a last-minute thing since I was just thinking of it this morning so I understand if you don't want to go—"

"Just say it," I laugh.

"Well, I was thinking..." He rubs his neck nervously, his ears pink. "Maybe a bookstore date?"

Oh my God.

Oh my God, Elias is so blessed.

"Seriously?" I ask excitedly.

He looks at me with doubt, "Yeah...do you not like the idea?"

"Elias, are you kidding me," my eyes sparkle. *"I would love that."*

He looks at me and raises an eyebrow. "And you actually think that? You wanna go to a bookstore for our first date?"

I nod my head frantically and his face softens into a smile as he leans down, kissing my cheek.

"You're so cute," he says, his voice echoing in my ears, and I shiver.

"Says the guy with the dimples and eye-smile," I shoot back teasingly, earning a scoff.

"I'm far from cute. I'm quite the opposite." .

"Oh?"

"Yes," he replies, hiding a smile. "I would say I'm more on the handsome side."

"No," I mutter, looking up at him as I try to conceal a smile of my own.

"What do you mean, 'no'?"

I laugh softly, "Nevermind."

"Say it," he insists.

"It's nothing."

"It's definitely something. You wouldn't laugh like that if you weren't hiding anything from me."

I sigh, and he takes the opportunity to slip his hands onto my face, "Say it. I want to know what you think of me."

I've never seen Elias like this before, though I must admit, it's pretty entertaining. I never thought for a second that he would act like that based on a single opinion. Of course, Elias does have his handsome aspects and everything, but his sweet side is much more overpowering.

"I just see you as more on the sweeter side than...intimidating," I say as he looks at me blankly. "Which is a great thing— I love that a lot about you."

He narrows his eyes and smiles slyly, letting go of my face, "What can I say to change that?"

So cute.

So damn cute.

"Oh, I know," his smile gets wider. "I have to become those book men, don't I? I'll become *morally grey.*"

We both burst out in laughter.

Honestly, I don't think I can ever picture Elias as an extremely intimidating and serious person. That's just not who he is at all, and to see him think my opinion would change is amusing, to say the least.

"So, you tell me how you want me to be. Which book man is your favourite?" He asks, his tone a little more serious.

"No, My Love. I prefer you this way," I argue as he turns away for a moment. I laugh when I see his ears turning red.

I pick up my coffee cup to take a sip, surprised to see it's still hot.

It feels so weird to have Elias here. Him being my husband is one thing, but the fact that we even somehow were brought back together after all these years is something I will never be able to get behind.

"What about one of the Aaron's?" He asks, nearly making me spit out the drink. "Blackford? Warner?"

"I think I'm gonna go get ready now," I say, placing the mug down as I stand.

"No, come back! I'll stop, I promise!" He snickers.

I walk to his bedroom to pick up my clothes from his closet before heading to the bathroom.

Morally grey? This sweet, cute, adorable man wants to become morally grey?

Elias is handsome— don't get me wrong. But he has such a bubbly personality most of the time, it's hard to take him seriously when he blurts out something like that.

On a different note, I'm planning to meet with Elena first and discuss the castings for 'Splintered Heart'. This is already taking way too long, and I was hoping by tomorrow we would get on set. Elena did sound pretty confident on the phone, so maybe their solution is better than I'm making it out to be.

I change into my clothes from yesterday, crossing the long side of the hijab around the back of my neck and adjusting it onto my head. I open the door to see the closet light on. Figuring Elias' changing, I head back to the living room with my bag and finish up breakfast.

I send Elena a text to meet me at the cafe in fifteen minutes, and pull out my laptop. I need to start arranging proper manuscripts for Elias and whoever would be acting as the main character. I'm nearly done, but there are some specific parts that still have yet to be edited.

I'm still in awe that a book I wrote years ago has struck a movie deal. It baffles me to think about how lucky I am to have such an opportunity. There are billions of other stories that deserve way more attention and this kind of popularity more than I do, and to be that person that gets to do all of this makes me feel so special and appreciative of those who have helped me achieve this much.

I hear the closet door open and turn to see Elias beaming as he looks at something in his hands. I shut my laptop and place it back into my tote bag. He walks over and sits beside me as I see that *something* in his hands is a felt box.

"I meant to give this to you last night, but I was in such a rush, I forgot it at home," he opens the tiny box and the most beautiful diamond ring comes into view.

"Is that real diamond...?" I ask, stunned by how shiny it is.

"Yup."

"Awe, Ellie. You did not have to get me this," I say, my eyes stinging.

It is bad how much I cry at the smallest things Elias does. All these years of crying over the need to get over Elias all led me back to him. Little did I know, it would result in this.

This whole time he has been kept in my mind as both a lesson, and so I never forgot him when the time came. The way past-me is disappointed by how much of a joke I've made out of myself is astounding, but at least he's mine now.

"Yes, I did," he takes the ring out of its box and places the box on the coffee table. He takes my left hand in his right and gently slips the ring on my ring finger.

I feel myself tearing up as I pull him into my embrace.

"I hate you so much," I say, a little part of me mad at him for spending money on me over something that must've cost hundreds, maybe thousands of dollars.

"I love you so much, too," he chuckles. "Please never take it off."

I pull away, dropping my gaze to the ring, "I don't think I ever want to."

"Don't cry, My Star," his laugh is laced with sweetness as he wipes the tears from my face and gives me a gentle kiss on my forehead.

This is what I mean. I can't see Elias being a cold person at all. He's too much of a sweetheart to ever appear as such.

"Ellie, promise you will never fall out of love with me," I say, my hands on his arms.

"I don't think I could, Star. *You complete me.*"

...

I turn around to say bye to Elias for the time being. Unfortunately, Elias can't stay for the meeting at the cafe. He has some errands to run right before our date, so he's a tad bit busy.

"Okay, I'll see you in a bit," I say, going on my tiptoes to give him a kiss on the cheek.

"Goodbye, wife. Just call me whenever you're done and I'll come pick you up," he says, and leans down to my ear. "I feel like that's the type of husband I'm meant to be, am I not?"

His eyes meet mine again, making me smile, "Yes, for sure."

"Okay, no, but seriously, Huma. If you need anything, you let me know. I'll basically be right around the corner," he says, flashing his dimples at me.

I laugh quietly, "Okay, husband."

His smile grows and he kisses my forehead, squeezing me into a hug before leaving.

"Bye, My Star."

I wave at him before opening the door to the cafe, and find Elena, Aaliyah and Jax waiting for me at the table. Elena and Aaliyah both get up to hug me excitedly while I send a quick smile to Jax, sitting across from him and sliding in the booth next to Aaliyah. Elena takes a seat next to Jax, opening up her files.

I notice a new file named *'movie folder'* as she sets it down.

"So, are we not gonna get any inside details on what happened last night?" She asks, a pleasant look on her face.

I hesitate, "I mean, it was mostly just getting used to each other's company."

Jax gives me a look that's both judgemental and nudging me to spill, but it really is all that. We were getting used to each other—minus the pet names...and the cute notes. That's all that happened.

"What about that diamond on your ring finger? Where did that come from?" Jax raises an eyebrow, smirking.

"I—"

"Oh my God, it's so pretty!" Aaliyah grabs my hand.

Elena locks her eyes with mine and gasps, "I bet it's real diamond, too!"

I stare daggers at Jax, hoping the message is getting through to his unicellular brain.

"Are you gonna sleep at the apartment tonight?" Aaliyah asks as I soften.

Again, I don't want to leave Elias alone anymore, but the same goes for her. I'm sure in her head she's expecting me to be at the apartment while I'm completely confused and on edge on where to stay.

"Of course," I smile.

I'm not sure what life is going to be like now. So much has

changed in such a small time frame, that there's so many things left to figure out. Logically, I should be staying with Elias...he's my husband. But how am I meant to leave my friend behind? Even if she's only living fifteen minutes away, *how do I just move out?*

We're roomies.

"Okay, so, all of us decided on the perfect girl to play the part of the protagonist. She was actually at the castings yesterday which works perfectly," Elena starts. "We just wanted to run it by you, just to make sure you're all good with it."

I nod my head, recovering my thoughts. "Yeah, I'm sure she's—"

"You should be the main lead," she interrupts, bringing me to a full stop.

I stare at them blankly, wondering what kind of a joke this is. I look at them with confusion written all over my face, switching gazes frantically.

"I can't act, guys. Elias can, but I am very much incapable."

Jax leans forward, "You're gonna have to. We told all the other girls we chose someone already."

I scoff. The audacity. I know I gave Elena and Jax the responsibility on who to pick, but if I had known they were going to throw this at me, I would've done everything on my own.

"No you didn't," I say, hoping he would take back his words. "Guys, seriously. I can't do this. I cannot act to save my life! This is why I stick to writing, and now, making scripts. You have to call up one of the girls again and ask them to come in."

Aaliyah's sitting awfully quietly beside me, scrolling through her phone. She doesn't want to be a part of this at all, but I have a feeling she might've been the one to start this discussion in the first place.

I dart my eyes towards her and snatch her phone, "You were the one with the idea, weren't you?" I quire.

She looks scared, almost.

"No— I swear— Jax said so. I only encouraged it."

Wow.

I check the time to see that only five minutes have passed by and I'm already disappointed with this arrangement. I hand the phone back to Aaliyah, placing my elbows onto the table and leaning forward.

"Are you in your senses, Jax? Who on earth told you I could act?!"

Now I'm really freaking out. I don't mean to snap at anyone, but I wouldn't have to be this hysterical if there was still at least one of the girls from yesterday on standby. I don't understand the sudden need for me to become...*me*.

"C'mon, Huma. You're acting with *your husband.* Do you know the wonders this could do for you guys?"

"Hm, that is a great way to put it and maybe could've been better if it weren't for the fact that I. Cannot. Act." I shoot back as he scowls.

"You're quite the drama queen right now," he mutters, making me pick up my tote bag and nearly chuck it into his face if it isn't for Elena who stops me.

"Okay, how about we all calm down," Elena gives us both a look. "Maybe give it a try and if it really doesn't work out, then we'll reach out for another casting. Okay, Huma?"

I have never in my whole twenty-four years of life ever taken an acting class or anything related to that. What overwhelms me is that this isn't some random practice run; this is supposed to be a movie. This is not a small thing, and it costs a lot of money for all the sets, paying the cast, etcetera, so to see all of them calm and relaxed as if this is nothing new isn't quite settling in my stomach.

"This isn't free. I'm paying for the sets—"

"We're covering everything for you," Jax interrupts.

Why?

"Why?"

He arches a brow, "You don't know?"

I shake my head.

"Elias requested us to do so."

30

Elias

"It is He who created you from one soul and created from it its mate that he might dwell in security with her."
- Surah Al-A'raf [7:189]

I'm cleaning up the bedroom, folding the blanket and clearing up dust when my eyes fall over the letters. They're all placed in my drawer under a bunch of scrap objects. One of them falls underneath the bed, and I get down on my knees, crouching to reach for it. After a bit of struggle, I get it in my grasp. I'm about to set it back in its respective place, just as I see a single word catch my eye; *Mom.*

I sit against the bed, on the floor.

July 2
I don't know how to start writing this without mentioning how much you've changed my life. I don't know where I would be without you.

I know this sounds extremely sentimental, but it's only because everything in this family that I thought was meant to be my solitary has betrayed me. Mom and Dad are ignoring me. I've cried multiple times in front of them— begging them to talk to me. They've been avoiding me ever since I told them I converted. At first it was the beatings, the pain that they put me through because they were so mad and now they were torturing me with their silence. In a way, I would much rather endure the beatings than have them completely ignore my existence. It sounds bad— I know, but it's not. Mom and Dad are far from bad people. They're really good and I think they may need more time to adjust to the new normal. I just wish they would cope in a different way.

But with you it's so much more different. You just have layers of uniqueness and I can see in your eyes that you're not a judgemental person...well, even if you are, you are extremely good at hiding it because everytime we speak— everytime we talk— I can't stop admiring you. I never want to stop talking to you. Everything about you is so comforting.

The Adhan goes off and I snap out of the past, placing the letter back with the others. There is a lot that I hold in my heart about my parents, and at a time like this, it feels wrong to be thinking about any of it. I just got married to someone I've loved for almost a decade, and to be thinking about my parents...it feels inconsiderate. It feels *selfish.*

I quickly do my wudu and pray.

As I finish up, I sit on the prayer mat and cover my face with my hands. There are countless things on my mind that I want to make duaa for, but the only one that comes to mind who's worth thinking of is Huma. I have this fear of losing her, that if I become any more comfortable with her, I would give in and tell her everything. Huma knows about how neglectful my parents became, but she doesn't know about the scars on my body that hold secrets. I know eventually she'll find out, but I'm not ready for that. I don't want her to see this part of me. I don't want this to be her reason for leaving me.

...

I turn at the intersection. It's very rare that I get to drive myself around places, but when I get the chance to, I take it. It feels peaceful to drive alone with no one in the car, even if there's a security car behind me, but that's just for extra precautions. At this point, I'm okay with having a car patrolling me. Especially with Huma now. It's reassuring to have a van there just in case something happens. I like to know that she's safe.

I pull into the parking lot, killing the engine in front of the cafe. Through the window, I see Huma frowning as she speaks.

Hm.

I walk inside and make eye contact with Huma, who smiles at my arrival. She scoots over towards Aaliyah as I sit beside her, greeting her with a kiss on the cheek.

"God, I want what you two have," Aaliyah says, earning a hand pat from Huma.

"Thank God you're here," Jax sighs. "Your wife has been driving us all nuts."

Your wife.

Sounds perfect.

Huma rolls her eyes at his words while I send Jax a humorous look as I watch Huma move her hand closer to mine.

"Oh?"

Elena probably looks the most exhausted, tired of being in between what I suppose was a pretty heated argument.

"No, she hasn't. Jax just doesn't know how to be professional," she says.

"Somebody fill me in on what's going on because I am utterly confused," I say, slipping my hand into Huma's.

"Basically—"

Jax interrupts Huma as she clicks her tongue in frustration, which, I have to admit, is quite adorable.

"Basically what happened was she gave us the responsibility of choosing who would be casted with you as the lead. You're with me so far, right?" He asks.

I nod my head, and he continues.

"We decided since you two are married, and you and her both know best about what happened in high school, you two could act together," he sighs as he switches his now hardened gaze to Huma. "She got mad at us because she thinks that's dumb. She thinks she can't act, and she wants us to call one of the girls from yesterday to take her spot."

I catch Huma's eyes, "You don't want to?"

She shakes her head, "I mean, it would be fun, but I've never acted in my life. I don't know the first thing about it."

"I can teach you," I reply softly. "If you still don't want to then we'll cast someone else."

She hesitates for a moment before audibly sighing, "Okay."

Jax scoffs, "I said the same damn thing!"

I laugh, stroking the back of her hand with my thumb.

"Do you wanna go to the bookstore now?" I lower my voice.

She smiles, "Yes, please."

I scoot out of the booth, my hand still intact with hers. She follows, not letting go.

"We have plans, so we'll get going, but it was an absolutely productive meeting today."

Jax grins at me, "Have fun then."

"Okay, bye."

Huma waves at them as we walk out of the building. To my surprise, there are more reporters than I anticipated there would be. About a dozen surrounded us, and they're quickly shoved back by security.

Huma's grip on my hand tightens and I take that as an indication to pull her in front of me. I open the passenger door for her, allowing her to comfortably sit before I shut it. I walk around the car to the drivers' seat, and lock the car as soon as I get in.

"Are you ready for this date?"

...

We walk into the bookstore, but she stops me, turning me to face her.

"So, I have a plan."

A plan, huh?

I raise a brow, "Which is?"

With a beaming smile, she looks around the store. I imitate her expression, taking in her sweet face. My gaze follows hers, scanning my eyes throughout the bookstore. I mostly catch the eyes of people blocking the view of all the bookshelves and setups, but I kind of expected this to happen.

"Okay so, the plan is that we have to individually pick a book we think we would wanna read together," she picks up a small book. "Like for example, if I wanna take this book, and I think you would wanna read it too, then I'll choose it."

I look at her, impressed she thought of all of this. "And what happens if I find multiple?"

"Then you can pick up all of them," she laughs softly. "Any questions?"

"No. Oh, by the way, no cheating and trying to see what the other person will pick," I add, receiving a nod of approval.

"Alright, shoo, Ellie. I have a list to go through," she says, making me chuckle.

I get lost in the bookshelves, finding myself in the romance section. There are a multitude of books to choose from— all in which I think I have already purchased.

I unlock my phone, going to my notes app where I have a note filled with book titles and authors to buy from. I look through the shelves, my eyes lighting up when I see the *Shadow and Bone* Trilogy.

I have the money to buy it, and honestly, I need more series in my house anyway. I kneel down and grab two copies of each book. I peek over the shelves to try to find Huma, and see her selecting a handful.

She has a full basket of them.

Where did she even get that from—?

"Would you like me to hold the books for you, Mr.Lee?" one of the bodyguards ask.

"If you could find me a basket similar to Huma's, I would really appreciate that," I say, continuing to eye Huma suspiciously.

He leaves, returning soon after as I slip the books into the basket gently to not create creases on them, "Thank you."

I find a couple of other books before sneaking up on Huma, "BOO!" I shout, and she actually jumps, making me burst out laughing.

 She slaps my shoulder.

I grab the basket from her hands, "So, what did you choose?"

"A lot— not to buy though. We can just see what we each got and then vote on which ones to keep," she says with a smile.

Or I buy all of them.

"Yes, to buy, Star. I'll get all of them if you want me to," I reply. "Matter of fact, I'll buy the whole damn bookstore if that's what you want."

She freezes as a shade of pink fades onto her face. "That's not necessary, Ellie."

"Oh, it is."

I take both baskets of books into my hands and walk to the

register, but she comes in front of me, "Elias, stop. You're not buying all of these books and that's final," she argues.

"Fine, the bookstore it is," I say, flashing a mischievous smile at her. My eyes meet with the cashier. "Excuse me, do you happen to know the price of this store—?"

She slaps a hand over my mouth, "Fine! But the books only— no more than that."

I place the two baskets down on the counter, watching as the cashier starts scanning the books, "Could you put it on my card?" I ask, taking my wallet out of my pocket. I almost get it into his hands, but Huma grabs my card and replaces it with hers.

"Here, his card is actually not working properly so I'll save you the time," she says.

"Huma, stop talking and let me pay for it," I pull her behind me by her wrist and ask to get her card back, putting mine in its place.

She deserves the best treatment she can receive, and if no one will give it to her, *I will.*

I let go of her when he finally scans my card.

"You did not have to do that," she looks at me with guilt.

I smile, "*'What's yours is yours and what's mine is also yours.'* So technically, I'm using *our* money."

Her gaze relaxes, the corners of her mouth curving upwards.

And you are mine, and I am yours.

"Don't—" she starts.

"Don't you want a husband who will spoil you rotten, Star?" I ask quietly, interlocking my fingers with hers.

"Here's your bag and your card," the cashier says, and Huma takes both into her hold. She hands me the card and we exit the store.

"Do you, or do you not?"

She doesn't meet my eyes. Instead, she avoids me completely.

"Of course I do, but I feel like that's a bit different with you."

I press my lips together. I think I know where this one is going and, to be brutally honest, it hurts a bit.

"Why is it different?"

Now I don't want to look at her either, not because I'm mad, but I don't think I want to look at her while she tells me she still pity's me.

"Because..." She trails off.

"Because why?"

This date was not going as I planned anymore. We're supposed to be having fun and going to the mall, shopping around and everything that newlyweds do. It's not a *friendship* anymore...it's a whole damn marriage, and if we want to start resolving issues, we have to start somewhere.

I just wish it wasn't right now.

She stops walking, "Because I don't want you to do that, Ellie. I don't want you to spoil me because you think you owe me. What I did for you in high school was solely because I cared about you. I never did it because I wanted something in return."

As someone who is going to be the closest person to her from now on forth, I think it's only right to spoil her. And granted, I do partially want to do it because of senior year, but mainly because I love her. I can't help but feel like she's saying this because she still pity's me.

"It's not *only* because of that, Huma. I also do it because you're my wife and I love you," I reply. "Do you really think I'm doing this because I feel like I owe you? Because if that's the case, you've never been more wrong about me."

She finds my other hand and steps close, "That's not how I see you. I have so much respect for you. I know you have your own reasons for why you do this."

"Huma—"

"No, I'm serious. I need you to get that," she says softly. "And about the money, you don't have to buy every single thing for me—"

"Lemme stop you right there. Islamically, I should be," I smile, at ease that this didn't become a fight. She returns the look, and hops into the car when she notices people approaching. I join her, but on the drivers' side, pulling out of the parking lot quickly.

Throughout the ride, my hand entangles with hers. She doesn't look at me when it happens, but I notice we share a blush when it does.

As we get home, Huma unbuckles her belt and looks at me with eyes that look nervous and hesitant, "Are your windows tinted?"

I find her fidgeting with her hands, and nod slowly, "Why—?

Her lips interlock with mine, her cheeks fully pink when she pulls away. My eyes are wide open, shocked by what she's just done to me.

She kissed me.

Huma kissed me.

I grab her wrist and pull her back into me. When I finally release her out of my hold, she's red, too, and we're smiling like idiots. Flushed idiots.

Her hands slide down to my chest, to my heart where it is aggressively skipping beats. My breath hitches, knowing well she's going to feel my heart imploding underneath her touch.

I clear my throat, "Should we make cookies?"

...

31

Huma

"Don't lose hope, nor be sad."
- Surah Al-Imran [3:139]

I watch as Elias talks on the phone. He looks anxious, continuously running his hands through his hair as he sits down on the couch, his legs bouncing up and down.

It's been a month of going back and forth from the apartment to here, and most nights, I stay with Elias since it doesn't really make sense for me to go to sleep in my bed alone when I can be here with him.

Right now, I'm making us sandwiches, *spicy* chicken sandwiches. It's pretty early in the night. I bring our plate to the couch with a bottle of soda and sit down.

"Okay, I've gotta go. Okay, bye," he switches the phone off, taking a deep breath.

I grab the plate and stick out my arms for him to take his part, but he takes the whole plate out of my hands and places it back on the table.

He shuts me up before I can speak by hugging me. His hands rest on my lower back and his head on my shoulder.

"Is everything okay?" I ask, blushing subtly.

He grunts, "No. I'm tired."

I shudder a bit, my heart screaming at how warm and chilling Elias' touch is against me.

"Do you wanna go to bed then?"

"No, I don't wanna sleep there tonight."

"I can bring the blanket outside, if you'd like," I suggest.

He relaxes a little more against me, "Mhm, that sounds good."

In the moment, I black out. I can't focus when Elias is so close to me, and I can't focus when Elias is holding me. He makes me weak in more ways than one, and I wonder if I ever have the same effect on him as he does on me. It's like when he's close, time freezes and everything around me ceases to exist. The only ones there are Elias and I. Even in my most vulnerable moments, I tend to forget this isn't high school. I let myself go to places I never knew I could go.

I spent year after year thinking about if he was really worth it, and I went as far as to ask in the name of God if he was worth this pain and suffering, or if I was hurting myself in the process. I asked for years, but I guess I didn't realize how near the answer really was. That the reason why I couldn't forget him was because I was never meant to leave him in the past.

I used to be so mad at how much I thought of him on a daily basis, and how he would be so amused if he ever learned that. At the end of the night, he was who I was thinking of. When I woke up, he was the one at the front of my mind. The books, the journaling— everything— somehow connected to Elias, and it made me hate myself. It made me think of myself as a fool. A love-struck fool that was driven by anger. But when I consoled myself, when I learned how to shut my feelings down and become protected by Islam and God, I was safe. I found my safe haven in my faith. And then I was protected and concealed. It was like there were guards of angels surrounding me, protecting me from myself and my feelings—

"What are you thinking about, Star?" He asks, straightening himself up.

I can hear the tiredness in his voice. This whole day was supposed to be dedicated to us having a day off, and here he is, tiring himself out.

"Nothing," I reply. "Kind of just zoning out."

He smiles, taking half of a sandwich into his hands, "You're very—" The sound of his phone ringing interrupts him as he sighs, annoyed. "I'm sorry, My Star. I'll be back."

He kisses my forehead, taking the sandwich with him and leaving the room.

I turn the TV on.

We started shooting for the movie a couple of weeks ago, but that was also when the press decided to release photos of Elias and I at the Masjid getting married. It caused quite a stir and people went bonkers over it. A majority of them were people congratulating us, but we definitely had our fair share of judgemental comments. Most of them were targeting me, except I was taking Elias and Jax's advice to ignore them.

They're jealous they didn't steal his heart before me.

But anyway, the movie shoot is going pretty well. I'm playing as…well, I'm playing as *me*. And let me tell you, I did not know acting could be so fun. For the most part, we're following the book, but sometimes Elias would remember certain things which would result in me remembering certain things, and then it would become a whole mess of beautiful memories again.

We have a new director— actually— new *directors*; Elena and Jax.

I asked Aaliyah if she wanted to help, but she refused. She's more interested in watching Elias and I act together, than instructing.

"Alright, I say we have some fun," Elias emerges from the room with the blanket in his arms. He sets the blanket down onto the couch and crashes down. "Oh, by the way, I have to tell you something."

Oh God.

"So, Jax and Elena are going to confirm our marriage to the press."

Right.

So apparently, although there is literal video evidence of us from the Masjid, Galaxy Entertainment has to release something confirming almost every rumour that comes about every one of their stars if they want to avoid scandals and excessive rumours. Jax asked Elias, and Elias asked me, and I told him I was fine with it.

"The thing is, it means we can't go out for a couple of days, or maybe a week or two just until the media calms down about the news," he says. "You're okay with that, right?"

That's the annoying part. I have already given my part and so had Elias, so there really isn't any going back in this situation.

"Yeah," I say, nodding my head.

He meets my eyes and raises a brow, "Are you *really* okay with that?"

I feel intimidated by his question and lean back as I feel his hand grasp my own.

"I can make it worthwhile, My Star. Just tell me what you want me to do to make these days special. Consider this our *getaway.*"

I smile at that.

Elias and I had a discussion about having a honeymoon which we both agreed to have after we're done with the movie. Not to mention, it will feel like a reward for all our hard work as well so it's perfect. We've talked about going to Madina, Pakistan, and Korea. I told him I didn't mind where we went. I just hope wherever we go, it's going to be memorable.

He chuckles, "You like that, don't you?"

"What?" I narrow my eyes, my smile not leaving.

"The idea of *a getaway.*"

I adjust the blanket behind Elias, setting it on his shoulders and surrounding him with warmth.

"It does, honestly." I beam, bringing my hands to his face. "And I don't care what we do— you just can't keep leaving."

He dips his head just as my hands slip onto his chest. He rests his hands at the back of my head, tangling his fingers into my hair before pressing a kiss to my forehead. "I,"

Another kiss, "Will,"

Another one, "Never,

Again, "Leave,"

Twice more, "You,"

Last one, "Again."

With his strong arms, he moves me completely into his chest and secures me by bringing the blanket tightly around me. He leans against me, making me press against the armrest as he lays his head on my collarbone.

"Mine. You are all mine, My Star."

His words boom in my ears, causing the butterflies in my stomach to hitch up to my throat.

I look at him, "I mean, you can't keep leaving, as in don't take your phone calls unless they're absolutely urgent."

He flashes me a dimple-smile, curving his mouth upwards, "And I meant it exactly as you imagined."

Our chicken sandwiches are getting cold, but I don't care anymore. It feels safe and comfortable to be in his presence. To be so close to him makes my heart flutter up to the seven skies and into heaven because that's what it feels like to be with Elias.

Elias reminds me of a teddy bear. That's what his hugs feel like; like you're hugging a very big, cozy teddy bear that hugs back, and I love every single second of it.

I'm sure he can feel the frantic beats of my heart because he chuckles quietly.

I get hold of the remote and start to scroll through a variety of programs. I didn't know it was possible to even have these many services available to you, but what am I expecting by marrying a whole celebrity?

...

I feel my body violently shaking as I wake up suddenly. It takes me a couple of seconds to realize it's Elias who's actually the one shaking.

He's still in my arms as I place a hand on his back, "Ellie?"

No reply.

I can hear him murmuring something under his breath.

I used to talk in my sleep when I was little, but it wasn't anything like this. There's this distressful tension luring around him.

He's still asleep.

"Ellie, My Love, are you okay?" I ask, both of my hands rubbing his back in an attempt to soothe him. I sit up and he slides down to my lap. I try to wake him, but he doesn't budge, and I start to freak out. "Elias, wake up!"

Could he be having a nightmare...?

I continue to try to get him to respond to me until he shoots up, gasping. I look at him, startled by the sudden reaction before I get on my knees, cupping his face gently.

"What's wrong, Ellie?" I ask, worry in my eyes.

I've never seen him like this before. The fear in his face makes me frown, gently stroking my thumb over his cheek.

"I..." He scans the room, looking around as if he doesn't know where he is. "I don't know what happened."

I let go of him and give him a glass of water.

"That's okay." I say soothingly.

He takes it from my hands, but the shaking doesn't stop. The water in the glass is at the brink of spilling.

"I was in a— in a room and I— I saw my Dad," his voice breaks.

"Drink some water, My Love," I usher him, and he obliges. He tries to set the glass down, but it drops to the floor. The sound of it shattering makes us both jump, and he leans down to pick it up, but I grab his hand in a hurry in the fear he'll cut himself. "It's okay, I'll clean it up."

"Sorry," he says, burying his face into my neck. "I'm sorry, I don't know what happened."

He keeps repeating that over and over again. '*Sorry, I don't know what happened.*'

I wrap my arms around him, and with every repetition of his sentence, I would reassure him that everything is okay.

"Shhh, you're okay," I repeat. "It can happen sometimes."

"There was a rod— I couldn't breathe," he let out.

I slowly make him lie his head down on my lap.

"It was a nightmare, My Love. You're okay now," I brush his hair back and kiss his forehead.

I don't move, I don't stop holding his hands, and more importantly, I don't stop repeating my words until he's out cold. Even when he is, in the fear that he might wake up scared again, I don't stop doing anything at all. I can't fathom what's going on, but what he said about his father— a rod—? I can't even bring myself to imagine what he must've seen.

When the shaking stops, I sigh, almost relieved, but still disturbed. I gently move his head underneath a pillow and get up to clean the glass and water.

I pick up my phone from the table to ring Jax.

Maybe Jax knows. Maybe he knows how to make sure he's okay.

Jax answers after the fifth ring, "What do you need, mate. Make it fast 'cause I have a lot to do for—"

"Jax, Elias was panicking," I say, picking up the pieces of glass and placing them into a plastic bag padded with flyers.

"Huma—? What do you mean he was panicking?" He asks, utter confusion in his voice.

I lower my voice, "He was shaking and he woke up all of a sudden like— like he was having a nightmare. He kept muttering the same thing over and over—"

"Woah, slow down, Huma," he says calmly. "Did he tell you what happened in the nightmare?"

I nod as if he can see me, "Y-yes. He was talking about his Dad like he was—"

"Like he was *scared?*"

There's a brief pause from my end.

Is this normal for him...?

"Yes," I rasp. "Jax, what do I do? He looked like he was in pain and— oh my God— the way he was shaking— I can't. I can't."

I put a hand on my forehead and face Elias who's sound asleep, and thankfully, looks peaceful. There's no sense of fright or anything.

"Okay, Huma. Take a breath. You can't react like that in front of him when that happens. It's going to make things worse for the both of you, okay?" He says softly.

"No, I didn't. I— I made sure he was asleep first."

Jax's words help bring me to ease. Even though he typically annoys the crap out of me, I'm happy I called him first.

"Okay, good. Good. Where is he now? What's he doing?"

Still looking at him, I shiver and look away, "He's sleeping. He just fell asleep."

"Huma?"

It takes me a second to realize that Elias is the one who said my name and not Jax.

"Was that him?" Jax asks.

"Y-yes." I tie up the bag of glass, placing it to the side. I kneel on the floor, my hand on his knee. "Are you okay, My Love?"

"Let me talk to him," Jax says.

Elias looks at me blankly, staring away, as I wait patiently for an answer.

"Huma, let me talk to him, *please.*"

I hesitate, but then hand him the phone.

"It's Jax," I say, and he continues to look at me with that pained stare.

"I don't know what happened," Elias repeats into the phone, standing up. "It was my Dad— he was holding a rod..."

He walks away from the couch and goes away into his room. The part that throws me off the most is when he shuts the door.

I don't know why, but I'm hurt.

And he doesn't come out of the room.

The whole night.

He's in that room.

He doesn't invite me in, he doesn't come back out.

He shuts me out.

32

Elias

"If Allah knows [any] good in your hearts, He will give you better than what was taken from you."
- Al-Anfal [8:70]

"Well look who finally decided to wake up," I say, looking down at Huma who is still waking from her slumber. I lean down and place a kiss on her cheek. "Good morning, Star."

Last night was something, and it didn't help that I decided to freak Huma out, too. I should've left the room sooner instead of waiting it out for me to explode, but I couldn't control it at the moment. Of course I didn't expect it either, but I still feel bad for scaring Huma like that, although she looks pretty calm right now.

She sits up, ushering me closer, "Come here."

I scoot over, her palms moving to my cheeks.

"Are you okay, *meri jaan?*"

I still have to find out what that means. It's a simple search away, but I don't know if Loogle would give me the exact answer I'm looking for.

I overlap my hands onto hers and pull them off my face, "Yes, I'm okay. Like you said, it was a nightmare."

She frowns, searching my eyes, "I wish you had talked to me, though. You left the room and didn't come out the whole night, Ellie. *I was so worried about you.*"

I'll admit, for someone who didn't want to scare her, I probably caused a worse reaction by completely denying her a sign of comfort. That wasn't my intention at any level. The nightmare felt...so real, I thought it was actually happening, and waking up and seeing Huma, while bringing me comfort, also confused me. But it was my father and the way he was looking at me. Like all he could see was disappointment in front of him. Like he had failed as a father, and it was true, he had, but not in the ways he believes.

And the rod in his hand gave me wild flashbacks of what I figured was something I had left in the past. I could see him clear as day just heating up the rod over the gas stove before coming over to me with the heated metal. *I felt it* and I can still feel it; nothing at first, but then sudden pain that shot through my nerves and made that noise spark up from my throat.

I shiver out of the thought.

"I'm sorry, Star. I think I was so lost in thought that I forgot to come back out," I stroke my thumb over the back of her hand. "I won't let it happen again. You can hold me on that, okay?"

She smiles softly, "Okay. I just wanted you to tell me that you're fine."

I move close to her, "Well, I'm very much fine."

She grins, leaning in further and kissing me.

When she pulls away, I keep my eyes shut with a smile, "Please do that again."

She laughs, making my heart drop. This time her index and thumb grip my chin as she presses my lips against hers.

"You sit there and look pretty. I'm gonna go pray."

"I'll join you."

As soon as we're done performing wudu, I adjust the prayer mat and move to the side, giving her room to pray first. She smiles at me, all cheeky and everything.

"You can go first," I step off the mat.

"Can't I pray next to you?" She asks, her face tinting pink.

Her expression makes me blush, "I only have one prayer mat."

She grabs my hand and pulls me in next to her, "Even better. We can share."

God, this woman is gonna be the death of me.

I give her a sweet and tender kiss on her temple, earning a soft laugh from her end.

After prayer, we sit there for a while, making duaa and smiling at each other like fools. Honestly, there is no better place to be right now than here. With her. With nothing but the silence we share as we pray together.

I glance over at Huma who crashes down on the bed. "Oh, yeah, *Ami* called and she wants us to come over for lunch."

"I—"

"And I know you said that we can't leave the house 'cause of our marriage being confirmed, but it's only for a couple of hours and then we'll come back home," she interrupts. "They really wanna get to know you, Ellie, and I think this is the perfect way for you to form a bond with them."

"I was going to say, Jax said he would announce it early morning tomorrow instead of today due to some complications with the video," I join her on the bed. "So, yes, I would love to see your parents, My Star."

Even though, in the span of a month, I've seen Huma's parents at least once every two weeks, I wish I could put it into words how grateful I am to them for trusting me with their daughter. I do wonder sometimes how they could put so much trust into me since Huma never told them about me when we were in school. Regardless, they treat me like their son and that has warmed my soul. It reminded me of my parents and how they used to be towards me. All the love and sweetness they provided.

That was all gone now, though.

"Great. I'll get ready then—"

I pull her back down by her wrist, "However, we might have to go over for dinner. We still have to finish filming that scene."

The shoot for Huma's movie is going extremely well. Within a couple of days into filming, Huma's completely fine with acting and, I've got to say, she's pretty good at it. Her expressions, her tone; she learned quicker than I did, and I don't know if this just came to her naturally, or it's because she already has experienced these events before. Either way, I praise her for it.

"Well, I guess that means I should dress for the occasion, huh?" She pats my cheek, walking into the closet.

With Huma almost living with me, I gave her a separate area to place her clothes and other belongings. Just about a week ago, it was empty, but with all the shopping trips and her staying over, it's slowly starting to fill up, and it's so adorable how much she likes it.

I follow her inside as she spins around to look at me, holding one of her dresses.

"How is this for tonight?" She asks. "Or is it too fancy?"

I quickly caught on to what Huma likes to wear in terms of clothing. She has quite the obsession with maxis and jewelry and, *wow*, I could fall in love all over again.

The dress she holds right now is a dark, mystic purple that has a band going around where her waistline would be, but it's loose enough so the features of her person won't be defined.

"It's perfect," I breathe out. "But I would like to pick out the jewelry."

She looks at me lovingly, "You wanna pick out my jewelry?"

I look through my options, finding a gold necklace I got for her just the other day and shift her around so her back faces me, "Yes." I place the necklace around her neck and clasp the ends together before twisting her around again. Along with it, I pair a couple of rings and a bracelet. "Now go change, Star."

...

When we finally arrive at the set, everyone's already waiting for us there. Huma and I are pulled away from each other for wardrobe change, and hair and makeup; hair for me, makeup for Huma.

I sit down and the hairstylists get straight to work.

"You feeling okay?" Jax asks, appearing out of thin air with a hint of concern in his voice.

Even though Jax wasn't the one there when I was living with my parents, he knew about the marks on my body. He knew about the detrimental experiences I had to undergo, and that's why I consoled in him instead of Huma.

While I want Huma to know me best, I don't think it's necessary for her to know *this* part. It's a part of the past. It holds no importance to the present.

"Yeah," I reply. "But Jax, seriously, don't tell her a thing."

He audibly sighs, pulling up a chair, "I don't intend to get in between you two and you're making that really hard."

"You're not getting in between us— you're simply not telling her for her own well being."

He hesitates, "She called me yesterday telling me she was worried about you—"

"And that is exactly why I can't have her knowing that. I don't need her *worrying* about something so dumb."

He pats my shoulder, a sudden calmness in his voice as he speaks, "It's not stupid, Elias. I know you're still—"

"Stop, Jax. I don't need a pity party," I say bluntly. "Just please try to understand. She doesn't need to know this info. It's not gonna benefit her at all."

He stands up from his chair, "Then think about it this way. Her voice was shaking last night. Shaking, Elias. What if I hadn't answered? What if she had a panic attack? If you both were in a state of shock, what would've happened? I doubt you could've calmed her down then." He sighs. "If she calls me again freaking out because she doesn't know what's going on with her husband, then don't expect me to keep my mouth shut."

And he leaves to the set.

Well that's great— he's mad at me now. What I don't understand is why he's so worried about telling her. It doesn't matter if she doesn't know because it's not something that matters to me anymore.

The truth is, it *is* stupid no matter how many times Jax tries to convince me otherwise. It's not worth thinking about when I have my whole life ahead of me with the only girl I've ever wanted.

The only thing that freaks me out is the part where she gets a panic attack. He is, without a doubt, right about that.

What if she had a panic attack?

"You're good to go, Mr.Lee," the hairdresser says.

I flash a quick thank-you-smile at the hairdresser and make my way to the set right around the corner. On set, I see Elena and Huma talking both with amused expressions on their faces as I approach them.

"Are we ready to shoot?" I ask.

I thought it was very sweet of Huma to let Elena and Jax do the directing. The only expectation is to follow by the book, keeping all parties equally happy.

"Yeah, we're just about to start. You two can get into position, though. I'm just waiting for Jax to come back," Elena says.

Huma walks into the set that's supposed to be imitating our school and our sitting spot. And I have to say, it's spot on.

This is probably my fourth time seeing it ever since we started shooting, and every time, I notice something new about the attention to detail.

There are posters behind us with some type of anti-bullying awareness, the wooden bench we would sit on, the weirdly tiled floors, and when Huma sits down on one end of the bench, it brings back a rush of unforgettable memories.

I take a seat beside her, two feet away, and one of the film crew workers comes over to me with the same backpack from then.

"Is this the actual thing...?" I ask in awe.

She nods, "I believe Mr.Parker found it somewhere."

I turn to Huma, holding up the bag "Look."

She holds up hers, and just like mine, it's the exact same bags we had from high school.

Her jaw drops and a smile forms, "Is it the real thing?"

I nod my head and go to open it. Inside is a binder that they must've gone out and bought. Whoever was in charge of props went down to every last detail with random homework pages to lined paper, which is a disaster of mixed memories from the past.

In Huma's, there are your usual school supplies and a lunch box. The lunch box has a bundle of snacks arranged into sandwich bags.

Just like back then.

This scene is when Huma begins to sneak snacks into my bag, and the first couple of times, I don't notice. That's accurate, though I don't know how I was unable to catch Huma being all sneaky, but I did have a couple of theories. One of them being that she was a very talkative person which at first glance, I found very hard to believe.

"You wouldn't notice if I snuck them in your bag right now, would you?" Huma teases with a cheeky smile.

I narrow my eyes at her, "I'd like to see you try."

Elena and Jax walk over, both holding a clipboard in one hand and a pen in the other. I glance at Jax, but he avoids my eyes.

"Alright!" Elena tucks in the clipboard under her arm. "So we know what we're doing for this scene, right?"

We both give a nod.

It isn't hard memorizing my lines. In fact, it's quite easy since these book chapters and scripts are a reflection of what really happened. I remember what I've said to Huma, but I noticed some scenes in her book that I recollected differently. Like how she thought I could never have written her a letter because I just didn't seem like the type that would journal out my feelings...more of a straight-forward, expressive person which is and isn't true. The moments I remember differently are only nooks and crannies, but for the most part, Huma is accurate. She somehow tattooed literal stuff I would say into her brain. Word for word to the point where sometimes I don't even remember exactly what I said.

"Ellie, where are you looking?" Huma waves her hands in front of my face. "We're about to start."

I smile at her, pressing my lips up against her forehead.

"Can you two hurry up and get set? We have to finish shooting this scene, plus a couple more by tonight!" Jax announces, using the megaphone, and still undeniably resenting me silently.

...

33

Huma

"My Lord, put my heart at ease for me, and ease my tasks for me."
- Surah Taha [20:25]

I don't know what it is about today, but something feels off. I'm already concerned about everything that has happened with Elias last night and, while it worries me where his state of mind is, his argument this morning was convincing.

We just finished up on set and now we're on our way to my parents' house. Just for Elias, I especially made sure Ami would make butter chicken which she quickly obliged to when I requested for it.

"Do you ever want kids?" Elias asks, his hand intertwining with mine.

My eyes widen, mouth agape.

Well that's sudden.

"R-right now?" I stutter.

He turns his head to look at me and then looks back at the road ahead of us, humour on his face. "Not at the second, Star. I mean, eventually," he laughs.

"Yes."

"How many?"

I want three kids, but I wouldn't want one out of the three little ones to feel left out all the time so two might be the one I stick with. Four kids feels like too many and I don't think I'll have the energy to take care of four little scoundrels, let alone any more than that.

"I want two kids. One boy, one girl, but can't really pick and choose, so…" I shrug.

He scoffs, amused by how quickly I delivered my answer.

"What about you?" I ask.

"I think the same, but maybe four kids instead of two. I would say three, but then one would be left out and then I'd feel bad."

He really does think like me.

"That's why I want two," I laugh between my sentences.

He pulls up to the driveway before turning himself to me, "That's how you know we were always meant to be, My Star," he leans over, using one hand to cup my cheek. "Soulmates think alike."

He presses his lips against mine, and I smile.

As we leave the car, I bring the little gifts of chocolate and flowers that Elias and I made a pit-stop for. It's those chocolates that have a variety of shapes with some that have those disgusting jelly filling that Ami loves. The flowers are tulips for Abu. He loves gardening, so I thought I might add to his collection.

We walk over to the door and ring the bell.

"Assalamu'alaikum," Elias says in a cheery tune when Abu pops into view. He greets him with a hug, followed by me.

"Wa'alaikum as-salam, come in beta," he steps to the side to let us in.

It's funny to think Ami and Abu call Elias '*beta*' too because, as far as I know, Elias has no clue what that means, and he's never questioned it either.

We quickly take our shoes off as Ami comes into view. I leave Elias on the couch, talking with Abu while I go into the kitchen.

"Assalamu'alaikum, Ami," I wrap my arms over her shoulders and squeeze her, not too tight because she's fragile as glass and skinny to the core.

I let her go as she turns on her feet to look at me.

"Wa'alaikum as-salam. You don't need to help me. I can bring the dishes, beta."

I open the cupboards, feeling nostalgia from when I used to live here. I take out the deep plates with the floral borders, glad to see they're still in the same spot. "It's okay. I'll help."

I take the plates that every brown person and their mother has, and place them onto the dining table. I return to the kitchen to find Elias giving Ami a hug, and grow soft at the sight.

To see Elias becoming close with my parents, to see him making an effort...it touches my heart. It's the little things he does. The first time we came over for lunch, he insisted on washing the dishes, and I assisted. The second time, he made a whole meal of his own and brought it over. And this time, he brought both my parents a gift. To see him forming a bond and trying his very best to create a relationship with them makes me love him more.

"You can go sit down, Huma. I'll help your mom set the table," he says, winking at me.

"You can call me Ami, beta. *I'm your mother as well.*"

And there goes my heart.

He chuckles, flashing me the sweetest smile ever, his dimples creasing his cheeks. He's glowing with happiness and it's the most pleasant thing to witness.

"Alright then. I'll help *Ami* set up the table. You can sit down," he says, softening his voice further.

I make my way back to Abu who's peacefully sitting on the couch, watching the news. He watches as I sit down, the corners of his mouth creating a smile.

"He's a really good guy, Huma," he nods approvingly, and I return the expression.

"I know."

To hear that from my father is refreshing.

"You know, I was worried at first," he says, amusement in his voice. "I thought maybe he wasn't a good fit. I thought it was possible he was leading you on, but when he came to talk to us for the first time, I could tell the love was real."

I look at the hallway, childhood memories flooding back to me one by one like I'm unlocking forgotten moments from when I was younger.

"What did he say?"

Abu clears his throat, "He said a lot. He said you saved him from his family, that you became the person to console him, and when I asked him what he meant, he started to cry. Huma, I know his parents are terrible people, and it was so painful to see because of his choice, that's why his parents resented him. I kept thinking to myself that if you ever left Islam—"

"No, I would never," I say, shaking my head.

"I know, *meri jaan*. I just mean if you were to ever— which I know you wouldn't— I would never do that to you. I would never hurt you like that. Whatever you choose to do is not something I can be in control of. Whatever you do is something you face with *Him* and no one else."

I rub my eyes.

No one in this world has the right to treat you like nothing. Elias is so much, *so much* in a single person, and he, like anybody, should've been able to make choices without the verbal abuse he had to undergo.

He continues, "But you guided him, Huma. You know everything that happens, it happens for a reason. And even if what you did in high school was wrong, you still managed to twist it into a good thing. You both guided each other."

I swallow hard, swallowing back all the emotions stirring up in my gut, "I just wanted to take care of him, Abu. *He didn't have a home. He needed a place to feel safe and I wanted to be the one to become his home.* That's all. *Kasam se,* I never meant it to be wrong."

I feel his hand on my head, "You can't be perfect, Huma. No one, including Muslims, can ever be completely perfect, and you know that. The important thing is that you repented. You're Iman is strong and that's what matters."

"What he had to go through...I can't believe he had to—"

"And the scars...*tauba, tauba.* Thankfully, he's out of that home."

I look back at him, confusion taking over, "Scars—? What do you mean *scars?*"

My breath is brought to a halt when the words leave my father's mouth.

"You know, on his body. *From his parents.*"

I rub my face, trying my hardest to digest this information. Elias' abuse— I thought it was fully verbal— not physical, too.

I try to grasp what I hear as my ears ring. This news doesn't only shock me. It freaks me out. My distasteful mind starts to create pictures in my head of what I imagine his scars to look like, but I push it away.

"Did you see them? The scars on his body...?" I say, breathless.

He shakes his head, "No. I didn't think it was the right time to ask about it."

I never thought to question him when he told me then. I should've asked to see if he would tell me the truth, but maybe if I ask now, he'll give me a truthful answer.

"The food is ready!" Elias shouts.

I look back at Abu.

"I'm just happy you married him," he says, standing up. "Are you coming?"

"Yeah, just give me a second."

Abu leaves, and I stay.

He told my parents before he told me.

Correction, he told my parents, but didn't tell me.

Ouch.

34

Elias

"Say, "Surely My Lord hurls the truth [against falsehood]. [He is] the Knower of all unseen."
- Surah Saba [34:48]

"Where's Huma?" I ask as her father takes a seat.

"She's coming, beta," he says. "Go grab her, though, or the food is going to get cold."

I walk into the living room to see Huma sitting on the couch with her head in her hands and her elbows resting against her knees.

"Are you okay, Star?" I ask, inching to her step by step.

She lifts her head and smiles, "Yeah, I'm just...a bit tired."

I kneel in front of her, checking her forehead, "Do you feel sick?"

"No," she says. "Today was just a very long day."

It was. We were non-stop acting through every scene, and our breaks were only five minutes. Since the rest of this week we won't be able to do anything but be at home, Jax and Elena pushed us to get way more done than we were prepared for.

I lock my hand into hers, "How about we eat, spend some time with your parents for a bit, and then go home? How does that sound?"

"Okay," she replies.

"Good, now let's go eat."

I stand, helping her onto her feet as I drop her hand to let her walk in front of me.

She sits down next to me at the table.

"You can go first," I insist, and after a bit of arguing, Huma's parents have their plates full. I take some of the butter chicken myself before I start eating. It reminds me of back then, but in the best way possible.

I notice Huma barely eating anything. She keeps a smile plastered on her face, but she must really be tired if she can barely eat anything either. I wait for her parents to excuse themselves from the table before taking a piece of roti and scooping up some chicken.

"Open," I say, hovering my hand underneath the food.

"Ellie—"

"Just open your mouth."

She caves in.

"It tastes really good, doesn't it?" I take a bite myself. "Your mom really is a chef."

"No, you call her Ami now. She's your mother as well. Just like how you're gonna have to get used to calling my father, Abu," she says, shifting to face me.

The corners of my lips rise and I kiss her cheek. But just as I do that, *Ami* comes in, causing Huma to nearly cough out the food in her mouth.

I try not to laugh as Ami smiles at the sight of us before picking up the rest of the dishes and leaving.

"Here," I give her another bite, dragging her chair close to me. "Do you wanna try the other dish?"

She nods, "Yes."

I take her empty plate and pour some of the *chana* before setting it in front of her. I hand her a piece of roti, but she rejects it, keeping her hands neatly on her lap.

I frown, "You don't want it anymore...?"

She turns pink, gently pushing the roti in my hands away from her. "I want you to feed me."

I look at her with a smug expression, "Whatever you say, Love."

...

"By the way, Jax said it might take a couple of days until the news dies down about us. See how popular we are?" I ask rhetorically as Huma climbs onto the bed on her knees. She comes over to me and wraps me in her embrace.

She sighs, "That's great, *Meri Jaan.*"

We just got home and it's twelve at the dead of night. Both of us are exhausted from today since the shooting took the entire day-time hours, and then staying with Ami and Abu took its own time. Granted, there's much less stress being with Huma's parents, but the fatigue from this morning is enough to take us out for the rest of the week.

"That sounds sarcastic, Star." I comment as I'm about to pull away, but she tightens her grip before I can.

"Thirty seconds, Ellie. That's how long a hug is supposed to last, and it hasn't even been ten," she says, moving closer.

I beam, "Where did you learn that?"

"Loogle."

"You know, that's not even close to how many hugs you should be getting in a day, right?"

"Oh?" Her voice grows tired.

"You should be getting twelve."

I rub her back gently, soaking in her scent.

"Where did you learn that?"

I chuckle, *"Loogle."*

"I'll make sure to start counting our hugs then."

She's cute.

She's about to sit back, but I don't let go, "Give me another second."

I lean my back against the headboard.

"Have you thought about what we should do together this week? We won't be able to leave the house, even for food and stuff."

She sits down in front of me, "Right, and, I have."

To my surprise, she reaches for her phone from the nightstand and grins all giddy as she unlocks it, swiping her finger across the screen.

Personally, I thought we could have a bit of a date night, but at home. We can make something and then eat it out on the balcony upstairs, or maybe I can create a fortress for us to lay under and watch movies all day.

"Okay, so I have a list of what we should do," she says, handing me her phone.

I catch on to how organized her notes are, noticing how for every day of the week, she has a plan for everything. I notice how reading is a Monday to Friday thing as I bring her phone down from my hands to look at her.

"It takes you a week to finish a book?" I ask, squinting my eyes.

"Usually two or three weeks, but I think if we—"

I burst out laughing, "It takes you almost a month to finish *one* book?"

She crosses her brows, slapping my shoulder, which only pushes me to laugh harder.

"Nah, I'm just messing with you, Star." I kiss her temple.

Still funny, though.

"And let me guess, you take a couple of hours?" She rolls her eyes, pointing a judgemental finger at me.

"Definitely not a month," I tease.

"Okay, I'm going to sleep! good night!" She says before lying down, drowning herself underneath the blanket.

"No, I'll stop," I put a hand on the blob that is my wife. She quickly turns on her side, facing her small exterior away from me. "Huma, you tiny human, don't you still have to pray?" I ask, thinking of any reason for her to look at me again.

To my luck, she lays flat on her back and peeks from underneath the fabric, "I can't."

Oh?

"You feeling okay?" I ask, putting a hand on her head.

I entirely forget about what we were just talking about, my concern going completely to her.

I'm afraid she might be coming down with something. With the exhaust she felt when we were over at Ami and Abu's house, I slightly expected this. But even with that, this is the perfect time to get sick since we have the week off.

"I got my period."

Luckily, my reading addiction pays off in moments like these. I've seen multiple encounters of the proper way to take care of a girl going through her week, and I'm prepared for the most part. I mean, that is how you're meant to take care of your significant other, and whatever Huma needs, that's what I'll provide.

"Is it really bad?"

I know the pain differs for certain people, scaling from no cramps at all to pain as severe as a heart stroke, so I want Huma to be as comfortable as she can be.

"Not that bad. It probably will be in the morning, though," she murmurs. "We'll get all the pazazz tomorrow."

Her eyes are closing slowly, giving into her fatigue. I watch as she dozes off, and as much as I want to stay here with her, I still need to pray.

"I'm gonna pray Isha, My Star. I'll be back soon, so don't doze off too far into dreamland without me."

She hums a response.

You know what? Let me do something first.

With Huma's phone still in my hand, I search up the meaning of that word she keeps calling me, and the results...well, they're pretty gratifying to say the least. There are so many different meanings, but the exact translation from Urdu to English means, *'my life'.*

I press my lips together, hard.

Other meanings say things like, *'sweetheart'*, *'love'*, *'dear'*, *'angel'*, *'treasure'*, *'beloved'*...it keeps going on and on, and I wonder how a word can have so much meaning.

It makes my heart flutter knowing she calls me all of this, all at once.

I shut her phone down, setting it on the nightstand quietly as I dip my head to her forehead to give her a kiss.

She is my life.

...

35

Huma

"And that is not difficult for Allah [at all]."
- Surah Ibrahim [14:20]

A lot is swirling in my mind from Elias to his scars, and how much I want to see how bad they are. I decided to wait for him to tell me about them, rather than trying to force it out of him.

I'll wait until he's ready.

I watch as the blinds deluge with the light from the sun, casting shadows all around the room. Elias is fast asleep next to me, a secure hand on my lower back.

I wonder if our souls knew each other before we were brought to this world. Before we were born, maybe our souls were attracted to each other, and we were close then. That's why there's a sense of comfort and a sense of security we find in each other because we may have known each other from the start. I did my fair share of research on soulmates, but seen through an Islamic perspective, and as far as I know, that isn't a thing. But to know so many attachments and attractions we feel towards certain people could have a deeper meaning behind it makes me curious.

I hope Elias and I were close to each other, but he also wasn't Muslim since birth. He was an Atheist, so it may not apply to him the way it applies to me. Even then, I don't see that as a negative. Quite the opposite actually. To be born outside of Islam and find your guiding light towards it shows how special you are.

I switch my gaze to Elias and let my hand roam on his face, tucking his hair away and out of his eyes. His mouth curves upwards into a breath-taking smile just as I do that, and I return the look, happy to see him in a better state.

All I need from him now is for him to be open with me. I need him to realize that I'm here to listen to whatever he has to say. Those scars that he has on his back— I'll wait for him to come to me and tell me. I'll just wait.

I get out of bed, planning to make breakfast.

Elias tends to be the one to make food in this house, but by choice. There have been countless times where I've offered to help or make something for us myself, and in spite of that, he insists he'll do it. It's pretty rare I make anything, so I try my best to take advantage when I can.

As much as I love Elias and how he basically does everything for us, he needs a break sometimes, too.

Scratch that— I'm going to order something instead.

Specifically, *halwa puri with chana*.

The way I've been craving this for so long is just unacceptable. Everyone has to try it at least once in their life, and although we might've already eaten chana yesterday, I need him to try it with the puri and halwa. It's just too good not to.

I order it over the phone just as Elias submerges from the bedroom.

"Yeah, I think one will be enough."

By ordering this, not only will I be quenching my hunger, but I'm also making Elias become a husband that even my extended family in Pakistan will fall in love with. Not that I need him to be any way to impress them, he is already everything I need and more.

"Hello, *gorgeous girl*," he says, kissing my cheek, and taking me by surprise. He wraps his arms around me loosely, his chin resting on my head.

"Your order should be there in twenty minutes."

I end the call, my eyes meeting with the complacent face he's got on.

"Aren't you in a good mood this morning?" I tease, patting his cheek.

Lately, I haven't been doing any promotions, so I think it's time I be productive today. Elias and I don't exactly have much planned besides the stuff I suggested, which he didn't confirm either, so I have no clue if we're going to follow up with my ideas.

I was able to move in a couple of boxes filled with my books that still need to be signed from last week, and I think that's when it started to sink in how my transition to living with Elias is finally happening.

Sometimes I miss living with Aaliyah and Elena, but that doesn't mean I regret living with Elias. This was meant to happen eventually whether it would be me or her first. We both wanted to get married sometime in the future anyway...I guess we didn't expect it to be so soon and so suddenly.

"Yes, I am. Very much," he says confidently. "Wanna know why?"

"Why?" I pass by him, walking into the bedroom and dragging one of the boxes of books out into the living room. I drag it to the couch and sit down on the fluffy carpet, my legs criss-crossed.

"Because I found out what the word means. The one you keep calling me."

I smile almost instantly, amused by the adorable, pink tint of his ears.

"And I mean every single word you saw, *meri jaan,*" I say, smiling from ear to ear as I pick up one of the books, grabbing a pen from the little utensil holder that sits underneath the coffee table.

"Stop flirting with me, Star. You're making me blush," he says, and I laugh. He rubs his eyes, still a bit tired from last night before picking up a book from the pile. "Look at you, all popular and everything."

I take one in my own hand, flipping to the first page and stamping my signature on it.

"Look who's talking, Mr.Lee," I say, taking the book from his hand.

He grins, "I'm not even *that* popular. I don't have thousands of people reading the pages that I wrote."

"Yeah, because you have millions paying to see your face on a screen, Love. There's a very huge difference between us," I shoot back, a bit of an edge in my voice.

He frowns, "Don't say it like that."

I continue to sign each book, placing it to the side as I create a complete pile next to me for all the copies the ink has touched.

I switch my gaze to Elias who still has an unpleasant expression on his face.

"What—? How do you want me to say it then? People are buying this book because they know now. *They know it's about you.*"

It isn't a lie. This book got more popular because of Elias. Because of the movie. Because we got married. Because the book revolves around him. And I'm happy that it's selling like hotcakes, but it seems as if my work only gained this much appreciation because Elias came around.

If this book was a made-up story, I wouldn't care that much.

But that's the thing.

It isn't.

He grows silent, breaking it not even a minute later.

"Huma," he lifts my chin up. "That is not why people post reviews, and tag you, and compliment everything you do...that isn't because of me. That is solely because of you."

A smile creeps up on my face, and I kiss him gently.

He has a point there.

God, this man has my whole heart.

"Are these methods of shutting me up—? Because they work really well," he raises a brow.

I nod my head, "For sure— mhm."

He stands from the couch and walks over to the bookshelf, grabbing something as he comes back to sit next to me. At first, I thought he selected a book for us to read together, but he only has a single book in hand.

"Star, I need you to do something for me," he says, the book submerging from his hands.

I look at him, "Anything."

"Sign my copy, please."

I could've sworn he was joking, but then I see my book with the cute annotations in his hands. I wait for him to start laughing or make a joke, instead, he opens the first page, exposing his colour-coded book marks.

"Seriously?" I ask, genuine confusion in my voice.

"Yes," he replies. "Please."

I place it on my lap, flattered by how willing he is to get my name scribbled on the front page of his copy.

He is the cutest man I've ever met.

"Did you ever watch *Pocoyo* growing up? You know, the cute boy with the blue outfit?" I ask, biting back a smile.

"Yes— I lived off of that show," he chuckles.

"Do you remember the name of the pink elephant?"

I close up the book and look at him, my lips pressed tightly together as he scoffs, his mouth gaping.

"You did not get that nickname, of what I thought was a *custom* name just for me, from a kids cartoon!"

I shake with laughter at his reaction, "No, I didn't get it from there, but I just remembered the name."

He shakes his head disapprovingly with a smile.

"I can't wait till one of our kids is going to be running around this house, and they'll overhear me calling you *Ellie*. Do you know how cute it would be if they repeated it? If they called you *Ellie* just to tease?" I flood with excitement.

"*Our* kids," he beams, resting his cheek on his hand.

He opens the book up again, and I go back to signing copies.

"No, you know who we are?" He stretches. "Pocoyo and Nina. They were such a cute duo."

I grow worried as I notice his shirt lifts up a little, exposing a pink-ish patch on his skin. Without thinking, I lift his shirt up further as I feel him tense up. The blood drains from my face to the sight in front of me, the pieces finally start to click.

There are multiple, thick, uneven patches of skin going from one side of his body to the other that have been damaged, leaving a unique pattern on his body.

These are scars...scars Abu told me he had.

They're...so big.

"Ellie," I look at him, horrified.

He swiftly moves my hands away from his body. He swallows hard, at a loss for words.

"Is that what your parents did to you?"

Another piece clicks; the rod he talked about when he had that nightmare...was that what he was hit with? But that wouldn't ex-plain why— *no. No, that is disgusting.*

My stomach turns, making me nauseous.

"How...?" I try to form sentences. "How did I not see them?"

"Because I didn't want you to," his gaze becomes stone-cold, eyes darkening as he speaks. "This is not something you should be worried about."

So I'm right, then. That *was* what his parents did to him.

As disgusted as I am with his parents, something in me lights up. It fills my insides with rage and anger. How a parent could hurt a child, let alone their own, is beyond me. But what angers me the most is the ignorant and mindless excuse behind it. The excuse that made them believe their child was to be completely rid of because he had no purpose anymore except to be hurt and tortured. How inhumane did you have to be to the point where you're continuously hitting your child?

"This is my worry as much as it is yours," I say, moving my hands back to the hem of his shirt, and he again, pulls my hands away.

"Don't touch me," he says with not even a shrivel of emotion on his face.

I know I said I'd wait for him to come to me, I'd find the patience and just stay put, but how do you do that when the thing being hidden from you is so big, it's left multiple marks as a result.

He fixes his shirt, pulling it down like it's somehow going to go back up and expose him.

"You don't get to tell me what to do, Elias!" I shout, tears streaming down my face. "You don't get to say that when you've been doing anything but communicating to me! "

Shock takes over both of us, but I'm containing mine.

"It's been two weeks since that nightmare you had and you haven't uttered a word! You haven't said anything about it! I respect you taking your time to digest it, and then come to me to tell me—"

"I was never gonna tell you," he mutters.

Wow.

So not only was he so open with my parents and with Jax, and

God knows who else, but I just found out my husband was planning to hide these from me forever.

Which is ironic to say the least.

My husband wants to hide his scars from me.

"You're kidding..."

I wait. I wait several minutes for him to debunk everything he just said but, *surprise, surprise,* it doesn't come.

"Do you think by marrying me, you could hide that from me? It has been a month of just back and forth, and back and forth, and I haven't said anything to you about that nightmare either because I know it goes back to your parents, and I know how you feel about that," I take a breath. "So I thought I would wait, and now you're telling me you were never gonna tell me?"

He stares blankly, his eyes piercing through me and straight into my soul.

I don't even know him.

I get up and rush into the bathroom, locking the door behind me. I sit there by the tub, wondering what just happened and how I even got in this position.

I understand his situation. I understand how he's gone through so much trouble, but ever since that one breakout, that one panic attack he had with his father appearing in his sleep, he has talked to everyone but me. I saw him talk to Elena and Jax, and I saw him talk to my parents. Not to mention when he shut me out of the room, so he could talk to Jax alone. He doesn't discuss anything with me, while I tell him all my problems, all my internal issues.

Everything. He knows everything about me, and now I'm starting to think I'm living with a stranger.

"Huma!" he knocks on the door. "Huma, open the door, please."

I bring my knees to my chest, watching the door as if it will break open any minute.

I have never in my whole life felt this hurt by someone. Even

Elias leaving can't compare to this. At least then it was only a matter of saying goodbye.

Or am I in the wrong for this? It is *his* body. *His* right to tell me or not, but I can't wrap my head around it. If he wanted to keep this a secret, why become so close with me?

I miss the old Elias.

He didn't hide anything from me. Even though I never knew about how physical his parents were then either, I fully understand why he never told me in high school. It was actively happening to him over and over again. He must've been scared to death.

I don't care if he was waiting to tell me now, that's okay...but he just admitted to never wanting to tell me.

"Please, Star. Open the door," he begs.

I want to. I do. But if I do, then what will become of us?

The doorbell rings.

Great, there's the food that I wanted him to try. Just great.

I hear his footsteps fade away as I bury my head into my knees, sobbing. My body is overheated, my face wet, and my whole person is aching.

Why did he marry me if he wanted to keep this stuff to himself? Why not ignore me and forget about me. That couldn't be too hard, could it? His idea of love must be separate from mine. His morals and his truths must be incompatible with mine.

"The food you got just came, My Star. Please come out," he whispers, knocking on the door again.

I stay silent, muffling my crying as much as I can.

I'm hungry, but my appetite has been completely ruined after this discovery. It's astonishing how he thought he could become my husband and go on to hide such huge secrets.

36

Elias

"He brings them out of darkness into the light."
- Surah Al-Baqarah [2:257]

June 5

"Stop, Huma! Stop putting these lunches in my bag!" I shout. "Your mother packs these for you, not for me." I take out all the food she's throwing into my backpack and slide it over the bench to her.

"You're hungry," she mumbles.

I roll my eyes, pushing them closer to her. I pick up my bag as people start to leave the school, and see her swinging her legs at the edge of the bench. I sigh, clearing her things up and placing them neatly into her backpack.

Unlike me, Huma actually uses all the pockets in her backpack for something; her binder in the biggest pocket, her snacks and lunches in the medium-sized one, her cringey little rom-coms in her small one, and her headphones in the smallest one.

I kneel down onto the floor and unzip her lunch/snack compartment as she kneels down with me.

"I can do it, Elias. Leave it."

I ignore her, already irritated by last night when I tried to complete my homework, and instead, found an entire meal placed inside my bag.

I throw her bag over my shoulder as I stand up, and she follows.

I start to walk away from her, towards the exit. Her backpack is much heavier than I anticipated it to be, but I pretend as if it's not adding to the pain on my body.

She walks faster until she's in front of me, coming to a halt.

She faces me.

"Please, take something. I packed a lot. It's going to go bad if someone doesn't eat it."

I click my tongue, "I'm not going to argue with you right now."

I continue to walk, opening the door for her, but this stubborn brat won't let me do anything.

"Please."

I slip my hands into my pockets, watching as she goes on to make excuses. It's almost as if I'm the one that's pitying her.

"Huma, shut up," I lower my voice. "I— I have food at home."

That's a half lie. I do have food at home, I'm just not allowed to eat very much of it. My parents have started replacing all the fruits and veggies with food they know I can't eat.

Like *pork.*

The rest of the walk to her home is silent.

"Sorry," she says, her pace slowing as we finally reach her house. "I'm only insisting because you need it."

"I told you, I have food—"

"That's bullshit!" she explodes.

Oh? An attitude?

"You and I both know that you're lying. I'm only asking you to take a couple of snacks so you don't starve to death, you idiot," she comes behind me, unzipping her bag, and taking some of the weight off my back. She appears again, holding out a total of six snacks placed in sandwich bags.

"Choose at least three. If you don't, I'll shove them all down your throat. *Wallahi, I will.*"

I'm a bit scared, not going to lie. She's quite intimidating when she's serious.

More of a reason to like her, though.

I don't take my eyes off her, not letting them drift off her face as she goes on to tell me how I should take at least two healthy snacks and one unhealthy one to balance it out.

When she looks up at me, my ears heat up.

"Do you want me to pick them for you?" She raises an eyebrow.

I give her a small nod, not realizing what she's asking as she disappears behind me again.

I'm not happy that I have to return to that hellhole that is my home. I wish I could just be here with Huma. Maybe we could find one of those buildings that have a rooftop and star gaze all night.

That would be a dream.

"Alright, you're all good to go."

I give her the backpack, adjusting mine properly onto my shoulders. I wish I could just pull her into a tight hug and thank her for being the way she is, but I don't.

"Thanks, Huma," I say, and she smiles humorously at me.

She's pretty. Very pretty.

Stunning.

"No, actually, Huma. Thank you...for everything."

Her eyes open again, and I feel like I could drown. I really hope whatever this feeling is will leave soon. I've never felt so good with someone before, but I don't want to get too attached to her.

"You're welcome," the humour on her face is replaced with a genuine curve of happiness.

In'Sha'Allah. In'Sha'Allah one day, I'll make her mine.

"Okay, I have to go. Be safe, Elias," she says. "If you ever need anything, come running here and I'll help you."

I'm happy that she has come to terms with the idea that there's not anything she can do with my situation. She knows that if she reports my parents, they won't be able to do anything because I'm eighteen and can't be put into foster care.

She told me that once. That she wanted to get me out of there, and would've a couple of months before I was of legal age, but she got really scared of what might happen in those facilities and homes if she did, so she didn't.

Yes, I could move out, but I don't have the resources like money or a place to live if I leave. I'm sure they would love to see me disappear.

Not everyone can be saved after all. And it isn't about not wanting to be saved— I want to get out of here so bad— I need someone to save me, and I've found that person. Even if she isn't physically consoling my burns, she's giving me hope.

Not false hope, *genuine* hope. Like if I pull out of here, if I just keep my faith strong, I can make it.

"Bye, Huma."

She turns around to look at me one last time, "You should smile more, *it's sunnah.*"

I bite back a smile, pushing her by her backpack, and she laughs.

When she's finally inside, I start to walk home. My house isn't too far from Huma's, but I kind of wish it was. It means I would have more of a reason to get there later.

I try to sneak through my bedroom window, except it's locked.

Front door it is.

I pull out my keys and jumble the lock a bit before carefully opening the door. I walk in silently, the floorboards beneath me creaking like they're going to give out any minute as I meet eye to eye with my mother.

"Why are you so late?! I told you to come straight here after school!"

I pass by her and walk into my bedroom, shutting the door. I throw my bag on the floor, about to bolt the door behind me with my dresser, but it's open as she stands there.

"You're not welcome here. Please let me have at least one space in this house where I don't have to worry about whether you want to hit me this time, or have a respectful talk about how I'm doing."

She comes inside, sitting down on my bed.

I don't get it. I don't get why she's like this. Why she acts like she cares one day, and then the next she watches as I'm basically beaten till I pass out. Is this her idea of making it up to me?

"Get out."

She pats the space beside her, crinkling the bed sheet. "Come here. I want to see how bad the burns are."

I scoff, astonished by her.

Now she wants to take care of me? Now she wants to see if I'm okay?

My eyes are stinging, my throat becoming lumpy. If my dad was here right now, he would've stricken me for not answering her. He would've given me a bruise for not speaking.

And she would simply watch.

"No, you don't get to see them. Now get out, or I swear to God—"

"What? What will you do if I don't leave your room?" She queries.

I would never hurt a woman. Ever. But my urge to throw her out of this room is growing briskly.

Even so, I stay still.

"You need to understand that as your mother—"

"You are *not* my mother."

No mother on this earth acts like she does. I thought maybe

she was just scared of my father and she was only following orders requested of him, but she *watches* as he hits me over and over again, burning the flesh off of my body. She doesn't care. She doesn't even look away— not once. I hear them at night, laughing and watching movies, so I don't want to hear her crap. Everything she says is going through one ear and out through the other.

There are tears rolling down my cheeks now. "If you were my mother, you would ask me how my day was and whether I ate lunch or not, but you don't even give me anything anymore. You would help me with my homework and applaud me when I do well on a test, but you don't notice those things anymore. And if you really were truly my mother, *you would never ever let him treat me like that.*"

I expect her to show me the little amount of sympathy she has left as she turns me around so I face her. And for a couple of minutes, I see her again. I see Mom again. She holds my face in her hands and strokes my tears away with her thumbs.

"I'm trying, baby. I really am."

I start to cry harder, feeling her embrace me with her warmth.

"But you have to try, too."

I pull away, nodding my head frantically, "I'll do anything— you name it."

At that second I feel something spark inside of me. Maybe she's changing. Maybe her motherly instincts are overpowering her selfish ones. Maybe all hasn't been lost after all.

"*I want you to convert out of Islam.*"

Statement retracted.

If I wasn't already hurt by them, they've definitely done it now. It's like she reached into my chest and squeezed my heart until it stopped. Until it turned grey. Until the colour from it drained it out. I feel like I can hear her laughing in my head at how gullible I've become for just an ounce of their affection.

I pull her hands off my face roughly.

"Get the hell out of here."

"This is why your father does what he does. This is why he hits you."

I swallow, stepping away from her. I don't know this woman. I don't know her at all.

"I don't get it!" I shout. "What's so wrong about what I believe in?!"

She raises her hand, and before I can react, she slaps me hard. "BECAUSE WHAT YOU BELIEVE IN IS UTTER SHIT! YOU REALLY THINK THERE'S SOMEONE UP THERE WHO'S PROTECTING YOU?!"

I do.

Every shrivel of hope drains away from me. I can't believe this is happening.

"If it's true, then why do you have those marks on your back?! Why isn't *He* protecting you?!"

I'm silent.

"Your father didn't raise you to become a failure, Elias. You're a complete disappointment. *You are nothing to me.*"

Ouch.

My eyes widen a little at those words. That hurt more than the burns on my body, and she doesn't even know it.

She stomps off and out of my room. I rush to barricade it before laying on the carpet that substitutes as a prayer mat. I cover my eyes with my palms and press hard.

"Oh my Allah," I whisper, my voice breaking into a million pieces. *"Please save me."*

37

Huma

"Allah wishes to lessen your burdens."
- Surah An-Nisa [4:28]

I spend a lot of time sitting on the tiled floor that you can probably eat off of for how clean it is. I have no sense of what time it is because my phone isn't here with me.

As for Elias, he has no plan of stopping and leaving me alone.

I'm crying anymore, I'm just hurt.

I play with the wedding ring on my finger.

I shouldn't be doing this to him. It's rude and dumb of me to isolate myself away from him. He doesn't say it, but I think this house makes him feel lonely. This house is supposed to give him safety, and it clearly isn't doing its job.

I hear something slide underneath the door. It's an old paper that has a couple of creases all across the writing.

It's Elias' handwriting.

I hold back from touching it, and give in not even a second later.

It'...a letter?
It's dated, too.

June 5
I think I'm falling in love with you. I know, great opening, right? I should become a writer.

I smile a little. Pretty ironic if you ask me.

But it's true, though. Listening to you talk, hearing your voice...it's so comforting and peaceful even in the state that I am. I only didn't come to school yesterday because the burns on my back are stinging. I had to sleep on my stomach because it hurt so bad, and I would keep waking up because I would end up rolling onto my back. I tried to apply toothpaste, but I couldn't reach the area that needed it.

I get up, about to open the door when another letter slides underneath.

This one is dated to June second, so just a couple of days back to the letter I'm reading.

I pick up the letter, sitting back down.

June 2
I don't know how to start writing this without mentioning how much you've changed my life. I don't know where I would be without you.

I know this sounds extremely sentimental, but it's only because every-thing in this family that I thought was meant to be my solitary has betrayed me. Mom and Dad are ignoring me. I've cried multiple times in front of them, begging them to talk to me.

My eyes start tearing up again, the pages in my hands shaking.

They've been avoiding me ever since I told them I converted. At first it was the beatings, the pain that they put me through because they were so mad, and now they were torturing me with their silence. In a way, I would much rather endure the beatings than have them completely ignore my existence. It sounds bad, I know, but it's not. Mom and Dad are far from bad people. They're really good. I think all they need is more time to adjust to the new normal. I just wish they would cope in a different way.

Does he still believe that? That his parents are good people? Because what type of a parent would mindlessly beat and torture their kid while having them wrapped around their finger? I surely hope he doesn't think that anymore. Elias is worth so much more than what his parents made him out to be.

But with you it's so much more different. You just have layers of uniqueness, and I can see in your eyes that you're not a judgemental person...well, even if you are, you are extremely good at hiding it because everytime we speak, everytime we talk, I can't stop admiring you. I never want to stop talking to you. Everything about you is so...comforting.
I cried a lot last night. Not about my parents...but about you. I asked God who you were. A blessing He sent, perhaps? Maybe even an angel sent to protect me? And each time, the answer was the same; a fallen star. Because everytime I asked, I looked out the window and there would be a star perfectly in my view. I think that star was you, darling.

I'm up on my feet in a matter of seconds again as I throw the door open.
Elias isn't there, though. He's on the floor beside his side of the bed, and I rush to him, crying my eyes out.
I wish I had known sooner.
He so quickly pulls me down onto his lap as I'm encircled by his

arms. I expect to see him crying, too, but he looks empty when I get a flash of his face.

"I'm sorry, *Meri Jaan*. You didn't deserve that. I'm so, so sorry," I say, my hand tangling into his hair.

I used to pray for him. In my duaas, I would pray for his protection. That he was safe from his parents' insults, but I didn't even know the half of it. I thought they just hurt him with words, not their hands, too.

I remember repeating the same words over and over, five times on the prayer mat and over one-hundred times before I fell asleep, *"Oh my Allah, protect him from his parents. Let this world be gentle with him."* Because even though he told me just a speck of what was going on at his house, I wanted God to see that there was another soul that wanted to protect him, too.

"It's okay—"

I push back a bit, my eyes meeting his, "It's not okay. You can't do that again, Ellie. Promise you will never keep a secret as big as that again."

He picks me up and sets me down on the bed, kissing the tip of my nose. "I won't do it again." He sits next to me and sandwiches my hand in his. "I'll show you my scars, but please don't get scared. I know they look disoriented, but *please.*"

I nod my head, eyes focused on his in a serious tone.

Even if it does frighten me how painful they might look, I'll try for him.

"Okay."

And without any more pleading or questions, he lifts his shirt up.

38

Elias

"And whoever does evil, it is to their own loss."
- Surah Fussilat [41:46]

I can see the intensity in her eyes as they stray away to my body.

"Why are they so prominent?" She asks. "What did they do when they beat you?"

I swallow hard.

Do I really want her to know? Do I want to give her something that will keep her up at night?

But then again, do I really want to keep secrets?

"My father beat me. He would..." I take a shallow breath. "He would heat up an old curtain rod over the gas stove and then press it against me."

I hear a quiet gasp leave her mouth.

It's becoming harder for me to talk as I start to remember significant pieces to the story I don't want to leave out. "...But before that, he *experimented*. Used different objects. Like his belt, or throwing things at me. Anything. *Just anything* to conflict some type of pain onto me."

Hearing myself say that out loud makes it feel so real.

Barricading the door, locking myself, and not eating for days became its own lifestyle. I was scared they would be waiting for me on the other side of the door, so I made it a habit to sneak through my bedroom window and get to school that way, or else I would have to wake up extra early in order to sneak past them. I lived in a bungalow, so it wasn't hard at all.

"And weekends...they were the worst. My escape was school but I couldn't go there during the weekends, so I would just stay in my room for those two days."

She looks at me, but doesn't say anything.

Like all she's doing is listening.

Just what I need.

"My skin can't grow back anymore in these areas." I turn around. "There are more on my back."

I'm not going to hide anything from her anymore. She's going to get everything, all the truths.

My shirt is no longer being lifted by my hands, instead, she does it herself. I don't say anything more. There's dread in my heart, so much stinging in my soul that only Huma can heal. I don't know what I would've done if it weren't for Islam bringing her to me. How lost, how lonely I would be.

I feel her finger on my back and flinch.

"Did I hurt you?" She asks, startled.

With how gentle she's being, I don't think I would even be able to feel it if it wasn't for how focused I am.

"No," I say.

I feel her finger again, tracing one of my father's markings from one side to the other.

Acknowledging what he did was the hardest part. Making myself realize that those people who were supposed to protect me from evil turned and showed me their devilish faces were not my parents. Parents and guardians make sure their family is okay and protected, but I didn't receive that. I had to become my own guardian and rescue myself.

I freeze when I feel her lips against my back. I fall silent. She gently kisses my back right on one of the biggest burns I was given. It doesn't inflict pain, but it does remind me of how much it hurt back then.

Huma could've done anything. She could've left the room, she could've been disgusted— scared even— but *she's kissing them instead.*

I shiver a little, my eyes welling up a bit.

Huma's kissing my scars.

As it starts to sink in deeper what she's doing, I burst into tears. It's a bit unexpected, but I've never been taken care of the same way that Huma takes care of me.

She puts my shirt down, and I face her to see an uneasy look.

"Stop worrying. They don't hurt anymore," I say, trying to keep myself together.

Guilt peeks through her eyes and her gaze stirs away from mine, "I could've protected you. I should've made sure you were okay."

I stroke her cheek with my thumb, tilting her chin up to me. "You did. You gave me a reason to live."

"Which is?" She looks at me again.

"You." I can feel the tears working up to fill my eyes. I'm not crying over my parents, I don't think I ever could, but what I'm really having trouble controlling my emotions over is Huma.

She comes to ease.

"I don't consider these flaws, Ellie," she says, her soft hands resting on my forearms. "I consider them *imperfections.*"

"But aren't those the same thing?"

She scoots close to me, "People define flaws as if they were faults. As if having these so-called flaws are immoral, but they are so beautiful to me," she lowers her voice before continuing. "Plus, it sounds so much more cooler to say imperfections."

My throat is tightening at her words like everytime she talks, another clog would stop me from holding back emotions.

"Then tell me, why do you love me for these *imperfections?*" I ask, curious for her answer.

"Because there is nothing more beautiful than your imperfections."

I look at her for a long minute, feeling my eyes stinging until the smallest, yet most gorgeous smile accompanies her face.

Just like when we got married.

I start to tear up, followed by sniffles, followed by water streaming out of my eyes like a river. Huma wipes the tears from my face away.

She kisses away the pain over and over again, bringing relief to me. I don't know how long I've needed this cry for now, but I know I won't be stopping anytime soon.

"Huma," I say.

"Yes, Meri Jaan?"

She continues to clear my cheeks before they stain from my tears.

"Please don't do that again."

Huma is my home.

"Never again. You have my word, My Love."

And the only one I need at that.

"And I promise, if either of them ever try and hurt you again—"

I laugh a little, "I should be the one saying that."

"No, seriously," she says. "If they even so much as take that adorable smile off your face, I will give them hell to live through, and they'll never hear the end of it."

I plant a kiss on her forehead, pushing her down until she's laying flat on her back as I hover over her.

"You are everything I could've asked for." I kiss her forehead, lying down beside her.

She turns to me, holding her head up with her palm.

"What do you want, Meri Jaan? Is there anything you want me to do for you?" She strokes my hair. "Anything at all?"

Alhamdulillah for this life.

"Hold me."

I doubt this would ever get easier. Our relationship and my past with her is being put to the test to see how strong we really are. And I have to say, I think it couldn't have been any better. Yes, we have these imperfections that define us, and yes, there are a lot of ups and downs for a couple that got married a month ago, but overall, I'm happy. Even if it doesn't seem so at times, I would never want my life any other way.

Huma leans against the pillows that are against the headboard and motions me to come over to her. I move myself until my head is on her lap, my body in between her legs.

My eyes grow heavy almost immediately. It's only eight o'clock, but I'm tired regardless.

God, to be safe in her arms.

I'm not exactly playing the role of the *protective husband* I'm meant to be playing. In fact, I'm playing quite the opposite. Shriveled up in Huma's embrace isn't exactly how I planned to be sleeping every night with her, but I guess you can't pick and choose. Either way, I refuse to move. It's safe here.

I close my eyes.

So comfortably safe here.

39

Huma

"My mercy encompasses all things."
- Surah Al-A'raf [7:156]

I'm awoken by a pain in my lower abdomen. Remembering the leakage that is my period, I swiftly sit up.

These cramps just get worse and worse. I press on my stomach in an attempt to decrease the pain which ends up, *big shocker*, doing nothing at all.

I fiddle with my phone, nearly dropping it and waking the whole house just to check the time.

4:34 a.m.

Great.

The cramps couldn't wait till there was actual daylight outside to make an appearance.

I look over to my left and see Elias who's peacefully in his slumber still. *Thankfully.* He must've rolled over halfway through our sleep.

I'm happy he opened up to me. What I do regret, though, is

locking myself in the bathroom with all the *jinns* who probably watched me bawl my eyes out on the floor.

I fix the blanket on Elias before creaking the bed as I struggle to make no noise. As much as I would love to stay tangled in these sheets, I need to use the bathroom and possibly find a snack to munch on.

"Huma?"

Absolutely, tremendously amazing. He's awake now, when he probably could have slept a couple hours more if it weren't for how loud I was being.

"Yes, Love?" I dart my eyes in his direction.

His hand reaches for mine, squeezing it, "Where are you going?"

Now, I could lie and simply jump back under the sheets to cozy up next to him, or I could be a big girl and excuse myself out of there.

"I was just about to use the bathroom," I say, patting his hand with my other. "Now go back to sleep."

To my surprise, he does exactly that, giving me the chance to slip away.

Unfortunately for me, there is none but a single pad left in the cabinet. I make a mental-note to get some tomorrow, or at least have Aaliyah or Elena bring me some.

As I step out, the lights still off give me the signal to continue forth into the living room. Just as I reach the door, the lights switch on, scaring me straight out of my skin.

I think I might've peed a little.

"Well, if it isn't the liar herself," Elias crosses his arms and furrows his brows in a condescending way. "I know you weren't about to sneak out of here looking like a hobo."

I am deeply offended. Considering that the clothes I'm wearing are entirely his, so if anything, he's insulting his own wardrobe.

"Hobo?!" I squeak. "I will let you know that I haven't eaten since

this morning, my cramps are at their peak prime, and my period contraband is finished!"

I'm happy to see Elias making jokes even after the intensity of last night. It just means he's getting more comfortable with me. Plus, it fills me with joy to know there isn't any awkward tension between us or this unspoken need to be sensitive and sentimental, although I wouldn't have minded that either.

"Awe," he, with his tired face, walks over to me and cups my cheeks. "I'm just kidding, Star, but why didn't you wake me up?"

I roll my eyes, "It seems you've already done that on your own."

He looks around the room, dropping my face from his hands and opening up the nightstand drawer to find a heating pad. While he does that, I notice the captivating stain on the bed. Where I was sleeping. Right on his white sheets.

"Ugh," I audibly sigh, pulling at the sheets as Elias stands.

"What?" His gaze follows mine back to the bed.

In the bathroom, I didn't see any stains on the clothes because both of my bottom pieces of dressing are black.

"I'm sorry, Ellie. I knew my period was bad, but not this bad."

I'm not the type to apologize over something like this because I know better than anyone that periods are painful and just overall frustrating, but these are new bed covers.

He's standing in front of me now, giving me an annoyed look, and I just know he's either going to kick me out of his house right at this second or he's about to make me sleep on the floor, which I wouldn't be mad at him for.

"Huma, I know this may be news to you, but I do not give a single crap about whether you stained the bed or not, got it? Matter of fact, I wouldn't have cared if you stained my clothes—"

"Oh God," I look down at the black sweats I have on and desperately want to scream out of pure rage.

He slaps his face with his hand and sighs, walking to the closet.

I follow him as he hands me a new pair of sweats and my under-garments.

"Go change. I'll take care of the sheets."

"Seriously, leave it. I'll wash the sheets when I get out," I argue, blocking his way back to the bed.

"Huma," he darkens his gaze. "Go. Change."

I don't bother speaking further and proceed myself back to the bathroom. When I come out, the sheets have been replaced with new darker ones.

Elias is fixing the pillows back onto the bed as I walk over. Without warning, he heaves me up in his arms and carries me out of the room.

"You know, as dandy as I am to be in your arms, it's not necessarily taking away the pain in my body," I joke as I descend down onto the couch.

He hovers above me with nothing but a mischievous smile, "I plan to take that pain away with this—" he shakes a heating pad in my face. "I'm just going to heat up some water on the stove and I'll be back. Don't. Move."

He kisses the bridge of my nose, and away into the kitchen he goes.

I switch the TV on, my eyes adjusting to the light. There's an episode airing of *Beat Bobby Flay,* and my hunger is starting to get the best of me, so that's what I'll watch until Elias comes back. I take a quick trip back to our room to grab my phone and the blanket before comfortably crashing down onto the couch again.

I see a message from Elena pop up on my screen, sent at 10:26 p.m. last night. It's not like Elena to text so late, so I check it while my mind overthinks every terrible scenario possible.

Oh.

OH.

OH MY.

There are multiple different screenshots of a news article, and then photos. The photos we took for Vogue way back when have finally been released.

How were we not informed prior to this?

I send an excited text back as Elias comes into sight.

He gently moves the blanket out of the way and sets the heating pad on my lower abdomen.

"Did you know they released our Vogue photos," I ask, coming to the conclusion that if he told me he had known this whole time, I would swallow him whole.

His face lights up, "Did they really?"

I nod my head and show him the photos.

"Oh my, are you sure this was your very first shoot? " He says in a dramatic gasp.

He sits at the corner of the couch as I adjust myself to make more room for him.

"You know, if I hadn't already been in love with you, that probably would've been the moment I fell for you because I could not stop thinking about you that night."

Exactly what I'm thinking.

"Alright," he sighs. "Give me a bit. I'll make you some soup."

I shake my head, checking the time to pin it against him, "No, you won't. It's almost five in the morning! Let's go back to bed."

Now, just to be clear, I'm used to Elias' touch; holding my hand, touching my face— all that great stuff— but it still gets me. Like right now as he tucks a piece of hair away from my face. My cheeks heat up with I-don't-even-know-what, and there's this look on his face that sends me straight to heaven.

"It's the least I can do for everything you've done for me," he argues before a smirk creeps up on his face. "Or we could always go back to that bookstore and have me purchase it for you."

"Shut up, you wouldn't," I smile impishly.

"I would." His face moves close to mine, "And I will."

He kisses me, making my already fired-up cheeks burn to the highest degree. I probably have a fever at this point.

Then I remember what he said, and grab his arm tightly before he can run off into the kitchen, "You're not buying it for me. I'm serious, Ellie. Use your money on something that is useful."

He stops and looks at me, narrowing his brown eyes. I can feel how strong the judgement is.

I would love a bookstore, though I have no clue how I would maintain one. And anyway, if I want a job in one, I can ask Aaliyah if I could join her. I don't want my bestie-boo feeling like we're suddenly store-rivals because my sweet, sunshine of a husband went out of his way to, well, buy me a whole gosh-dang bookstore.

"Will it make you happy?" He asks.

I shake my head because I know what he's trying to do and it's not going to work on me.

"Will you smile more?"

Another shake.

"Don't you lie to me, crazy girl," he uses his index finger to push my forehead back. "I would take you to Madina a billion times and bring you back every single time if that's what your heart desires, so something as small as a bookstore could never compare."

I smile, "Yeah, but you pledged to take me to Madina years ago, so I would hope you would keep your promise."

It takes him a second, a rush of confusion before the realization strikes him, and the corners of his eyes crinkle.

"I did say that, didn't I?" He dozes off into what I assume are his memories, and he lights up, his face glowing. "I still will, though."

"Elias—!"

I get a hold of his hand and pull him towards me, leaving barely a centimeter between us. "Yes?"

"I was going to suggest we eat the halwa puri I got this morning," I breathe out, flustered.

I think he's starting to see just how much I tense up near him because he's smirking now.

"Fine then," he replies, and heads back into the kitchen to heat up the cold food.

I turn back to the TV, smiling to myself.

I'm so happy.

Who knew I would end up with someone like Elias? So kind-hearted, sweet, not to mention, so fine and gorgeous. I understand his popularity and why people are so madly in love with him.

Not as much as me, though.

As the minutes pass by, Elias comes back with warmed-up food. And the smell, *oh Lord*, it smells delicious.

He sets it in front of me, and I smile, "You're going to love this."

"Am I?"

I rip a piece of the puri, scooping the chana and halwa into one fold before bringing it to Elias' mouth. I hear the smile right through the breath he releases as he parts his lips to taste it.

"Good, right?" I ask, containing the excitement of sharing my culture with him.

His smile grows as a chuckle escapes his throat, "That is pretty good."

"I must ask, where did you learn to cook?" I bite into the food.

He raises his eyebrows, satisfied by my question. "A couple of culinary classes and online recipes go a long way, Star. I'm sure you learned a different way, though, huh?"

He isn't wrong. All the dishes I know were because Ami shoved them down my throat when I was a teenager, which did end up working out when it came to Elias. Most of the dishes Ami made, but when my parents were sick, I was the one who cooked in the house.

"Yeah, Ami kind of made me learn." I smile teasingly. "But I'm glad you know how to cook, too. It *is* a survival skill, Love. Everyone needs it."

As we finish up the food, I start to doze a little. He continues to talk, but it's only making me more tired. That's a compliment, though. His voice is so soft, loud enough that I can hear, but quiet enough that no one else can.

"Mhm," I nod my head, my eyes closing as I desperately try to keep them open.

He chuckles, "Don't fall asleep yet. You should let that food digest first, Star."

"I'm not sleeping," I grunt. "I'm simply resting my eyes."

"Oh, my bad," he rolls his eyes.

I scoot close to him, getting comfortable before he tries to stand up again for what seems like the billionth time. Luckily, I pull him right back down and latch onto his arm. "Oh please, don't go again. You just got here. Read me a bedtime story or something. Help me fall asleep."

"I don't think you need me to fall asleep, Star. You look like you could pass out at any moment," he says, sarcasm in his tone. "And I was just going to drop the dishes off in the kitchen."

I push him away, annoyed, and shoot off the couch. I make my way to his gorgeously-sorted bookshelf and try to find something that can temporarily entertain me. I see The Holy Quran sitting separately with a couple of other copies. There are two original Quran's, and then two next to it. One of them is translated into English, while the other is translated to...*Urdu?*

I hear Elias' soft footsteps approaching, and he kisses my cheek, my back gently brushing against his chest.

"That one is for you. I wasn't sure if you preferred the English one or the Urdu one, so I got both of them," he informs me. "I *do* want to hear you recite it another time, though."

I beam at that, and I contemplate rolling into a ball and scream-ing into a pillow on how amazing this man is when his hand inter-twines in mine and he takes the original Quran out.

"But until you can do that, *I'll read to you.*"

Read to me...?

My heart starts to pound hard against my chest as he tugs on my hand, leading me away from the shelf. He walks with me behind him towards the staircases upstairs.

"Why don't we just read here?" I ask softly. "On the couch?"

He chuckles, not answering my question at all. Instead, he con-tinues to lead me up the stairs, one hand wrapped around mine, and another securely cradling The Quran. As we get there, I notice a speck of the dark, blue sky becoming lighter at the horizon line.

There is a pool table in the middle of the room that Elias has yet to teach me how to play. I know the basics, but I still need to perfect my movements in order for us to play a proper game competitively.

"I can read it out there to you," he says, his voice gentle and sweet.

I automatically nod my head, and he finds a thin blanket in the billions of rooms in this house, leading me out into the summer haziness. There's a slight breeze as I spot his beautiful, nude, lounge chair in the corner of his balcony.

He walks past me and settles down, wrapping the blanket around himself before ushering me over and pulling me into his warm embrace. I fall right into his arms, hugging his chest as he clears his throat.

"*A'oodhu Billahi Minash-shaitannir Rajeem,*" he inhales. "*Bismillah-irahmanir-rahim.*"

His chest vibrates as he starts to recite the first Surah in The Quran; *Surah-Al-Fatiha.* I wish I had heard him recite sooner be-cause, *wow, his voice is beautiful.*

I listen to him as he takes breaks, as he pulls me a little closer. I hear as he blissfully reads out the translations to me. How it touches his soul as much as it touches mine.

Soon, the sun is peeking through, falling in love with the words of God just like us.

It's at this moment I start to realize that I've been forgiven. That all the repenting and duaas have paid off. All this hatred I've had for myself for letting my guard down and becoming soft-hearted just for him has finally been put to ease.

My stresses and frights have all ceased themselves and my mind has finally found its peace.

Elias comes to a halt, "Can I ask you something?"

I look up at him in response.

"What is your favourite verse in The Quran?"

Every verse.

But I actually mean that. Even as Elias reads, it is so, *so perfect.*

If I had to choose, it would take me longer than a lifetime to settle on only one.

But I want to hear what Elias' answer is because I know by the giddiness on his face, he has something he desperately wants to say.

I smile, a lightbulb going off in my head, "*Indeed what is to come will be better for you than what had gone by*', and I saw that right before meeting you after almost eight years."

He brushes his lips against my head, keeping his mouth there, "And you called me the cute one."

I laugh softly, "What about you?"

His hand lingers on my face for a moment.

"Oh, okay. This just resonated with me so hard, but," there's a hint of nervousness in his voice that makes my heart feel warm. "The one that goes, *'And He found you lost and guided you.'*"

Before I can utter a single sound, he clears his throat and opens The Quran up again.

"Anyway, shall we continue?"

"Why did your dad hit you?" I ask, my mouth moving faster than my brain can process. I hesitate, but the way Elias is looking at me makes me relax. "I just mean, *why?*"

Elias doesn't move or speak. He just looks at me. His lips part, letting out a quiet sigh as if he's preparing himself for what he's about to say.

"My father was Muslim once."

Something in me freezes. I don't know why, but that is the last place I would've gone.

He chuckles, his fingers brushing out my hair. "Big shocker, I know. My dad was Muslim before I was born. My parents met after he converted out of Islam."

Oh.

"My dad was beaten when he was little. Even though he was brought up in a Muslim family, religion never really mattered to them, but my dad changed that. He became very loyal to Islam. His whole entire life revolved around praying and reading The Quran. And I wasn't lying when I said he was a good man. He got a job at the Masjid, and then opened up a program for children and adults for Quran lessons," Elias stops, taking a deep breath. "But he was starting to struggle. He moved out of the house, leaving his younger sisters with their parents and moving into a small studio apartment."

"Was he still working at the Masjid?" I ask curiously.

"Yes. He hated that he left his sisters in that house, but if he cared so much why didn't he go back for them?"

The question is rhetorical, but there's a hint of anger in his voice. I sit up, scooting close to him. His hands are on his face, rubbing back and forth, The Quran set on the table next to him. There is so much hurt written all over his face, even though he isn't talking about himself. Somehow this hurt him just as bad.

"He never went back for them, Huma."

I pull his hands off his face, holding them in mine as he sighs.

"His sisters— *oh my Allah.* They must've felt helpless."

I squeeze his hands, my eyes never leaving his.

"Everything was going south for him, regardless of how much hope he tried to hold on to. He was in debt, and he kept praying to God to give him the money to get out of it. That same night, he was robbed. And he held it against Him. Every bad thing after that, he held it against God as he began inching himself closer to the idea that there might not be anyone up there after all."

"*Astaghfirullah,*" I whisper, and Elias' eyes find mine.

He relaxes, pressing a kiss to my forehead. His arm wraps around my shoulders to hold me in place as his other hand holds mine.

"Huma, he hurt me because he thought he could get it into my head that there was nobody protecting me up there. He wanted to put me through the pain to show me that if there really was a God, there was no reason for Him to not stop my father from hitting me. *He thought he could beat it out of me.*"

That makes me shiver.

"He met my mother a while after converting out of Islam. My mother was raised in a Christian household, not very practicing either, but after my father told her everything that happened, he made her think of Islam as this terrible religion."

I push back from Elias' hold, noticing a tear sliding down his cheek. I reach up, stroking it away with my thumb.

"You surely proved them wrong, My Love."

If I had known, I would've offered up my basement for him to sleep in while he tried to find jobs back then. I would've done anything to make sure he didn't have to return back there.

I can't imagine what it was like to walk home, to a place that should've been his protection.

"Huma, I don't want you to think I'm any less of a person because of my *imperfections.*"

I place my hand at the back of his neck, bringing him down to my level so I can hug him. My body molds into his as I embrace his everything. His burns, his sweet smell, his pain, and his everything-in-betweens.

"Your imperfections add to your character, Ellie. It only makes you better," I kiss his temple.

The back of my shirt— *his shirt*— is scrunched up in his hand as he plants sweet kisses on the top of my head.

He takes a deep breath after a few minutes and smiles, sitting back. "We should keep reading."

I listen to him go on for a while before my eyes are closing to his tranquil voice. Regardless of our fight and how upset I was, I still found a sense of appeasement in him, and I think that is all I need in order to see how these little things matter so much. His effort to make it up to me shows me how sorry he is, and that is all I need from him.

ACT 3

40

Elias

"And your Lord does injustice to no one."
- Surah Al-Kahf [18:49]

I place The Holy Book on the table.

Huma is curled up in my arms, sleeping away to the sound of birds chirping.

I had to fight the feeling of staying here and holding Huma, before finally giving in to my deen, and leaving her on the chair with the blanket keeping her warm.

The morning air is warm but breezy enough for a blanket, exactly how I like it.

I use the upstairs bathroom to do wudu and come back out onto the balcony to pray. The sun has almost fully risen, with its bright orange radiance falling onto the prayer mat in front of me.

I have plans on what I want to do for the next couple of days, which includes telling Huma everything. I don't even want her to think I'm going to give her little by little anymore, but I'm not dumping all my trauma on her either. I want her to know everything now because if I keep barricading these *secrets*, she might leave me

And I can't lose her again.

I've never felt more relief leaving my body than when I started to talk about how bad it was. And while Jax was such a good listener when I told him, there was something special about how Huma stayed silent. She waited for me to finish, and instead of pitying me, she comforted me. She quietly held me, something I didn't realize I needed so badly.

Before high school, when I had no clue where I was going, I was in a bad place. I was lost and hurt, but I didn't know why. Even with all that, my parents were so good to me. We really were the picture-perfect family— and it was all real— I know it was.

But the second my dad started shouting at me, the moment he started threatening my life and continuously hitting me, it was like I was in another world. It was like I woke up, and suddenly, I was in a parallel universe where everything was not so amazing anymore. No more bonding. No more family movie nights. Those memories that I lived for disappeared. I thought the relationship between me and my parents was unbreakable, and nothing I could ever say or do would change that, but *wow. Was I wrong, or what?* Everything was gone. Everything and *everyone.*

At that point, I didn't even have Huma anymore. I only had myself and my beliefs to protect me. So every day, during the summer after work, I would go to the Masjid and just look at the words on the pages of The Quran, hoping that eventually the Arabic language would all of a sudden make sense, and I would just start reading. I knew this was getting me nowhere, but I didn't stop. It wasn't until a very nice man, who looked to be around in his mid-forties approached me. He offered to teach me how to read, and from that day on, I would meet up with him during the weekends so he could help me out.

There was something so familiar about how soft-hearted he was. He became the father figure I missed in my dad. The sweet, friendly dad who used to take me out for bike rides after school. I missed that dad.

But he wasn't there anymore.

My dad was far from my dad anymore. He was undoubtedly someone I used to know.

I started talking to the nice man from the Masjid regularly, which, I know, *stranger danger*, but I knew how to protect myself, and everyone knows that any soul that goes to the Masjid are only of the kindest of people.

He asked me about my life.

About if I had a family.

I told him no.

He took me out for a treat one day when he heard my stomach growling like a freaking lion. Like I hadn't eaten in days, which wasn't true, *I had a granola bar.* But he was one of the most generous people I had ever met. That is when I got a flash of his phone, showing me a photo of a young girl. It scared me to death when I realized who it was. This selfless soul was Huma's father.

At that point, I could read The Quran, and of course, for a while I played it off like everything was okay, like I wasn't panicking that if he ever found out the things Huma did for me, how he would probably snap.

I remember going home and all I could think about was Huma, Huma, Huma. How I had just left her behind like she was there just for my entertainment until I could get a grasp on myself. *Like I was using her.* But I knew truly that if I wanted her to be happy, I had to leave her behind. That if I really did care about her and wanted the best for her, I wouldn't put my number in her backpack before lunch was over, which I didn't, for the record. I loved her too much to make this into something haram.

She doesn't know it, but I would try to remember her voice when I was in my room, while I attempted to shut down the noise of my parents shouting and banging on the door, telling me to come out. Her voice is the type that's hard to forget because it's so unique and soothing to the extent where you don't want her to stop talking. You want her to keep going on and on— *she could make politics sound interesting if she wanted to.*

I kiss Huma's cheek right as I set the mat down onto the floor and begin to pray. I take my sweet time, my heart filled with whatever Huma is giving to me.

It isn't even love...*it's so much better than that.*

I clean the house a bit after praying, deciding on a shower as well. All the fun stuff.

I say this with the greatest amount of sarcasm there is to offer.

Before I do all that, though, I need to get Huma some of those period products— *or as she calls it— 'period contraband.'*

I grab her phone and dial Aaliyah. She probably knows exactly which products she needs, and I don't want to wake sleeping beauty, so I'll wake her friend instead.

"It is almost seven in the morning—! Why are you ringing me at this time?" She asks groggily.

"Well first off, lower your voice. My wife is sleeping."

It's silent for a second.

"Well if it isn't the roommate-stealer himself! What do you want, old man?"

Old man...?

"Do you know what pads Huma uses? She ran out and I wanted to get her some, but I don't know which ones—"

She laughs, "Are you trying to impress her?"

"What—? *No.* I'm trying to be nice—" I click my tongue, not understanding why I'm explaining this to her. "Just tell me, please."

"I'll just drop it off," she says, her voice returning to monotone. "I need to run some errands anyway."

"Alright, I'll see you—"

"Wait, I wanted to ask you something."

My brows crease, "Go on."

"Okay, so I know you and Huma already got married, but when is the wedding?" She asks, excitement hidden in her voice. "Like the *official* wedding—? 'Cause Huma always talked about a big Pakistani wedding."

Oh, did she?

"Soon."

"How soon? Give me an actual date."

"*Very* soon. Now go run those errands. I'll see you in a bit."

She ends the call just like that, but I am not about to waste any more time. I have plans to put into action, and now, I can't forget this wedding that Huma wants, apparently.

My phone comes to life with Jax's name plastered across the screen. I pick it up as my body tenses, "Hello?"

"Well you sound dandy!" Jax jokes.

It feels way too early for whatever Jax has to say and I don't think my brain will be able to process whatever he's about to tell me. Honestly, I'm a bit surprised Jax isn't mad. He doesn't know Huma knows now and maybe he doesn't care if she *does* know...but I need to get this off my chest.

"Huma knows," I say, feeling the heaviness in my chest slowly dwindling away. I go down the stairs and into the walk-in closet to get ready for a shower.

I know he's not going to say anything now.

"She was mad that I didn't want to tell her." I grab my towel, along with some sweats. "She didn't talk to me for a bit, and locked herself in the washroom."

"*Didn't*, so this happened, but you guys are okay now...right?" I could hear the worry and hope at the same time in his voice as he spoke.

"Yeah. I told her. *I showed her.*"

She read the letters.

"And do you feel better?" He asks as if I'm a patient in his office, telling him about all the ways I could've possibly messed up my relationship.

I nod my head like he can see me. "I still wanna tell her more, though."

"See? Elias, if you can't tell already, this woman is so madly in love with you that she wrote a whole book about you two," he chuckles. *"Two cuties together."*

I smile at the last part.

"Fine, I'll give you that. Huma and I are pretty cute together."

He laughs, and I interrupt before he can start asking more questions.

"But anyway, tell me something about you. Anything new with you?"

Jax is a pretty lonely person himself. He has tried everything from dating apps, to trying to find something meaningful through friends. So far nothing has worked for him. He's thirty-one years old, and reminds me of it every single day because he's convinced himself he's too old for anyone to end up falling in love with him.

"Well, funny story actually," he laughs nervously.

I drop my clothes onto my bed and raise an eyebrow, "What happened?"

There's an uncertainty in his voice that I can't recognize...almost as if he's questioning whether he should tell me or not.

"I think I'm catching feelings."

My eyes widen, "Who—?"

"Like she's out of this world gorgeous, and even though she loves to talk about how annoying I am, she has this thing about her that has me twisting."

"I mean—"

"And the way she laughed when we met for coffee— oh. My. God."

"Jax!"

He goes silent. I'm a bit scared for him because I can hear the smile in his voice. As lovely as it sounds, I don't know who this girl is. She could be someone he met at the bar—

Wait...*Is he drunk?*

"Jax, were you drinking?" I ask, concerned.

There's a slight pause before he continues.

"No."

I click my tongue.

Jax doesn't drink very often, but when he's overwhelmed, he goes straight for the bottle. Sometimes I think that's the reason why he didn't want to move in with me. He knows I don't like seeing him torture his insides with alcohol, but I don't know what else to do to stop him.

"Where are you?"

"Hmm," he murmurs. "A very safe place."

I slap my forehead, losing my patience with him. I've asked him to quit multiple times, and each time he says that he will. I even tried talking to him about all the after effects he's going to have to face if he keeps this up, but I can't get through to him. He doesn't seem to care.

He chuckles as I hear a girl's voice in the background.

"Jax, you idiot!"

With such kind words, it doesn't require much effort for me to put two and two together.

"Elena, you're *soooo* dumb."

There's a bit of shuffling, and then Jax's voice sounds distant.

"How does it take you this long to figure out I'm not with you?"

Elena's voice sounds closer now as she scolds him. She sighs, "Does he usually malfunction like this?"

I scoff out of amusement, "Not all the time."

"Malfunction?!" Jax shouts. "Now that's just mean."

There's more shuffling.

"No, no. Don't leave," Elena's voice is softer now. "I'm just teasing, hon."

Even though Elena calls everyone and their mother 'honey,' my delusions are telling me she says it with so much more sweetness when she speaks to Jax. It's cute since I know Elena would never hurt him, and Jax is too soft to do anything bad to her without feeling guilty about it afterwards.

They would be an adorable couple.

"Should I end the call?" I ask, smiling to myself. "It seems you two are a bit busy."

"Hush, Elias. The poor thing called you to tell you..." She lets out a sigh. "...what did you wanna tell him, Jax?"

"It's a secret," he says, his voice quiet and gentle.

I press my lips tight, careful not to release the laugh that desperately wants to make itself known.

How adorable, he doesn't want Elena to know.

"Either way, he came to my door at five in the morning in tears...he kept crying and crying that *I* was the reason he was like this," she releases a breath again. "Now he's telling me he doesn't remember saying any of that."

I talk a little longer with Elena as she continues to ask me questions about Jax. It's quite an informative conversation, though I start to feel bad for him. Jax doesn't talk to me about his problems as much as I wish he would, but he seems to be comfortable and safe with Elena.

Just like how I am with Huma.

Before I end the call, Elena mentions interviews and how sooner or later, Huma and I are going to have to come in and talk about us with show hosts. Just so people don't go and create rumours about me leaving the industry due to my inactivity and this new chapter of my life. The media works in strange ways, but I get the whole gist of it.

My only problem with this is that I want to keep Huma away from the toxicity the entertainment industry can be. I can't protect her from every single thing that crosses either of our paths and lock her up in this house like she's Rapunzel.

Of course I know she's aware of what people have to say about me and her, and as much as I hate it, it's something she has to get used to.

I've also held off interviews and visiting places just so we could adjust, which I don't regret at all. I'm having great fun, actually, but maybe these interviews could be the perfect thing to transition back to work for me, and a bit of an introduction for Huma. It may not be the most ideal way, since an interview isn't anything small, but we have to eventually settle somewhere.

The one thing I'll promise is to do my part as her husband to defend her and our marriage. I'm not going to let the media affect our relationship.

Not now, not ever.

41

❧

Huma

"Show forgiveness, enjoin kindness, and turn away from ignorance."
- Surah Al-A'raf [7:199]

"Ellie?"

I look all over the place for him, hoping to see him just around the corner, but then I hear the shower turn on. Just as I'm about to go into our bedroom, the doorbell rings.

I throw on one of Elias' hoodies, pulling it over my head to cover my hair before opening the door.

To my surprise, it's Aaliyah.

"Oh— you didn't tell me you were coming over," I pull her into a hug and invite her in.

She smiles, taking her shoes off before handing me a shopper that I hadn't noticed she was holding.

"Here," she says, and I peek inside.

"What a strange housewarming present, but I needed these,

so thank you," I say humorously, setting them to the side of the staircase.

She laughs, "Elias actually asked me if I knew what pads you used, so I thought this was my opportunity to take a look at this drop-dead gorgeous house."

Sweet Elias.

"By the way," she shuffles through her handbag as I take her towards the couch to sit down. "It came in the mail."

I know exactly what she's talking about, and I beam with excitement when I see the grin on her face.

"Oh. My. God. Show me!" I squeal.

Just the other day, I ordered a ring for Elias. It's sterling silver, matching the diamond ring that he bought for me. Since he doesn't have a wedding ring, I thought this might make it feel more official.

She hands me a felt box with a beautifully-set ribbon to tie it all together, similar to the one my ring was in, and I look at it in delight, opening it immediately.

"It's so pretty!"

I show her, and she jumps with joy.

After giving the security guards a heart attack with our squealing, we finally dial down to a more *indoorsy* voice.

"Okay, but tell me everything."

"About what?"

"About everything! About your dates, your cute, little affirmations— I wanna know everything."

I bite back a smile. "He is so adorable, Aaliyah. God, I can't believe I married him."

She scoffs, amused.

"And he has the cutest dimples! Aaliyah, save me. My heart can't take this." I squeal.

"You're the one that ditched me for him, so suffer the consequences."

"Who has the 'cutest dimples'?" Elias grins, walking towards us as he dries his hair with a towel. "You're not looking at pictures of me, are you?"

Aaliyah and I simultaneously give each other a look that's screaming *'he-doesn't-know.'*

I hide the box in my sleeve as his eyes divert to my hands and his grin widens as I shake my head.

"Aaliyah was just telling me about her crush on your bodyguard."

I can feel Aaliyah's glare burning through my head, but I keep the poker face on. She slaps my shoulder as Elias laughs.

"Who—? Oh, don't tell me it's Michael. He's a married man!" He teases with a twinge of genuine concern.

I look at Aaliyah who's blushing profusely.

Huh, is it true, then?

"No, not Michael," I blurt out. "She likes—"

She slaps a hand over my mouth, "I don't like anybody!"

I give her a look that only she can interpret, and she gets up in a rush, leaning down to hug me.

"It was great seeing you two, but I've gotta go," she stops, and I see a speck of a smirk making it's way on her face. "By the way, Elias, Huma has a surprise for you."

And then she's gone, leaving me and Elias...and this *surprise.*

"Hm," he gives me a smug look. *"A surprise?"*

I take the chance to go to the kitchen to find something to eat.

This ring also came at such a perfect time since this was pre-planned and I've been waiting for it to be delivered to set up a cute date for us at home. The date is a bonus in this, and the ring is the gift that I'm about to make a very big deal about once I give it to him.

I open up the fridge as a familiar scent accompanies the air behind me. I drop the box into the big sweater pocket when I feel Elias turn me around. His hand shuts the door with a cocky smile.

"So, I have the 'cutest dimples,' huh?"

I don't know what to focus on; the fact that his dimples are so prominent at this very second, or the fact that his eyes are sparkling like he's never been more attracted to me than right now.

"I thought you didn't like being called 'cute,'" I shift, but his hand finds my wrist and grips it tightly.

"Is this like a guessing game? I wanna know what you got me."

He's quite the impatient man if you ask me, and I found it pretty amusing to see how eager he is to know what I'm hiding from him.

I smile, patting his cheek, "Well, you're gonna have to wait. I need to plan out exactly how I want this to go, and then I'll give you your gift."

Note to self: strangle Aaliyah the next time you see her.

His brows furrow up, "What are you planning to do?"

It's question after question, and it doesn't stop. He follows me everywhere I go in the house with a new curiosity and refuses to leave me alone until I give him an answer. On top of that, we happen to have no butter, which I needed in order to make chocolate chip cookies.

But how am I supposed to get anything done when I have an adult man following me everywhere I go, who also happens to have an almost-empty fridge?

"...because whatever it is, I want you to clear up your schedule," he ruffles my hair. "I want to take you somewhere."

This man really needs to take a break. He needs to let me do something for him for a change.

"How about you go do some grocery," I suggest as he asks yet another question. "I'll send you a list of what we need, and you simply go get it."

He tilts his head, eyes filled with debation. I imagine his brain is going, *'should I or should I not bother Huma?'*

If he goes, this means I can actually set it up and it will turn out to be an even better surprise than I initially planned it to be.

He has on a decent outfit— white shirt, black sweats— perfect outfit to go grocery shopping in as I twirl him around and push him to the door.

"Alright, My Love. I'll see you in thirty minutes," I quickly grab his wallet and face his hand, palm-out, before setting it in. "It shouldn't take you too long, and if you need anything, you can call me."

On my toes, I kiss his cheek and reach for the door, opening it, and pushing him a little further until he's outside.

"Okay, bye Ellie."

From there, I close the door and get straight to work. I know Elias and I are on a bit of a ban of leaving the house for the week, but he'll be fine as long as he has one of his security guards around. He could even have one of them fetch the groceries while he sits in the car, so I don't see the problem with any of this.

My phone beeps in my hand, and I see it's Elias.

Well, that was quick.

"Yes, Love?"

"Can you open the door, please?"

The phone still pressed against my ear, I do as he asks, and he's standing there like he's ready to send me out to do the groceries myself.

I smile, "Forgot something?" He nods his head, his hand wrapping around my wrist, pulling me out of the house. He pulls me behind him and locks the door.

"What are you doing?" I ask, frowning.

"I forgot you. My apologies, Star. I meant to pick you up and throw you into my car because we both know I suck at doing groceries."

I sigh, agitation coursing through my veins. All I've been trying to do is set up something for him, but he's ruining his own surprise without even knowing it.

"I'm not even wearing a proper hijab!"

He hides away the little pieces of my hair into the hoodie I'm wearing and proudly beams. Cute, but not cute enough that I want to waste time on this mini assignment.

"There."

"Elias—"

"Plus, let's not forget you're wearing my favourite sweater right now."

The bodyguards are standing still, their gazes focused ahead, but it still makes this a bit embarrassing as Elias continues to adjust the hood on my head.

"Don't do that in front of everyone," I try to pull his hands away, but he resists.

"Don't stop me. They should know just how much I love you."

I sigh in defeat, "At least let me get my hijab."

...

We arrive in the parking lot of what I can for sure tell you is not a grocery store. There's none in sight.

"What are we doing here?" I ask.

He hops out of the car, but I stay put, planning my escape. If I run towards the crosswalk and successfully convince the woman driving the silver van at the intersection to give me groceries and drop me home, I might be able to set this up on time. I just need a way to distract Elias long enough to do that. Would it work? Probably not. But am I curious to see how—

"Huma!" Elias' hand is tugging on mine, the door to the passenger seat wide open. "Can you daydream later?"

I step out, and he locks the car. "This is not a grocery store."

He rolls his eyes, "Are you sure you're not the descendant of Sherlock? You're quite the detective."

I let go of his hand, crossing my brows. "You're not funny."

A chuckle escapes his throat, and he throws an arm over my shoulder, pulling me back to him as we stumble walking towards the unlabeled building.

"I *know* I'm funny, love."

42

Elias

I rented out the rink.

As a thank you gift for how sweet Huma was last night to me, I wanted to bring her here. I learned roller skating a while ago just for fun. There was no deep or crazy reason behind why. I just thought it would be fun to learn something new, and now I was going to push Huma to learn this with me.

"Shut up," Huma smiles. "This is so nice."

I pull her hood further until her eyes are out of view, her tiny face still twinkling.

The corners of my mouth rise up and I push Huma's shoulders down until she's sitting on the bench. I kneel down on one knee and help her put on the skates, tying her laces for her. I do the same for myself before I help her to the rink.

"What about our helmets?" She asks, looking behind us. I pull her in front of me so her back is facing me, hands on her waist for support.

"You don't need a helmet, My Star."

"Why not?"

We carefully step down the three sets of stairs to the actual rink where the floor is smoother and I let go of her, linking hands with her instead.

"Do you trust me?" I ask.

"Neither of us have a helmet—"

"Do. You. Trust. Me?"

She exhales, "Of course I trust you."

"Then don't worry about it."

I glide a little ahead, turning around to Huma who's standing like a deer learning to walk for the first time. I slide my other hand into hers and pull her a little ahead as her eyes drop to her feet. I smile a small smile, skating backwards little by little everytime she moves closer.

"Stop moving so fast!" She complains, her hold on me tightening.

I try not to laugh at how scared she is, all the past wholesome excitement gone. Her hands move up to my forearms, her nails digging into my sleeves. Thankfully, I decided to wear a long sleeve today in the scorching heat, or God knows that I'd be bleeding thanks to Huma.

"We're not even a quarter into the rink," I say and her eyes meet mine. This is when I basically burst out laughing at the fear in her eyes. Honestly, I don't mean to, but by the way she looks like we were going to get eaten by a bear, I couldn't help it. "I'm sorry."

"You can keep your apologies, loser—"

"Loser!?" I scoff, humourously.

"Yes," her face softens a little. "You're so inconsiderate.""

I slow down, grinning, "Am I?"

She confidently nods, "No doubt about it."

"Hm."

And just like that, just to piss her off and push her buttons, I rip her hands off of me and skate away from her. When I finally reach the other end of the rink, I lean against the wall, watching as she stares at me in utter hatred making my grin grow in size.

"I'll turn around and go home, Ellie," she threatens. "And I'll take the car with me."

"Go for it. Let's see how far you get before you fall," I challenge, entertained by her frustration.

I'm surprised when I see her spin around and move a— *is that a millimeter?* A millimeter towards the steps. She nearly loses balance and, still facing away from me, she gasps.

"Elias?"

"Yes?"

"If I die, will you give my life-savings to my parents?"

I chuckle, "Of course, My Star."

I hear her let out a determined sigh as I glide towards her just so I'm close enough that I can help her if needed, but far enough that she can't exactly reach me.

She moves a couple more steps, lifting her skates off the ground and attempting to walk, which is only making it harder for her.

Just as I expected, she trips over her own foot and falls. Luckily, she falls right into my arms, which only pushes me slightly backwards. I help her straighten up, and instead of an aggravated, death glare, I'm surprised to see her smiling.

"You are so moody, you know that?"

"Well, clearly you didn't want me to leave," she teases. "Don't worry, Love. I was just kidding."

If Huma's a star, I'm an astrophile because I completely lose my mind when it comes to her. She drives me insane in all the ways you can drive a man insane and it messes with my soul.

Getting a bit heated at the tips of my ears, I pull her hood down again and with a hand still gripping me, she laughs as she lifts it back up.

"Stop doing that!" I tilt her chin up to me, inching close.

"Wait, wait, pause this magical moment. I have something for you," she interrupts.

I tilt my head slightly, narrowing my eyes. "Is this the gift from this morning?"

She digs through the pockets of her sweater— wait— *my sweater.* "Yes."

"Oh?"

"Okay," she watches as my eyes fall to her hands, hiding whatever this tiny object was in her sleeve with a sweet laugh. "Stop looking there! Look at me instead."

Gladly.

I switch my gaze back onto her face and can't help but imitate the pleasant look on her. "Okay, so. It's nothing too big. In fact— it's much more smaller compared to anything you've ever given me— but I thought it was adorable so I bought it for you," she smiles a little wider at that part. The part where she says '*I bought it for you*' and it scares me a bit. "But you know the best part—? It matches so perfectly with one of the things you got—"

"Huma— tell me what it is!" I shake her by her arms.

"I'm getting to it!"

"Then be quick 'cause you already ruined our perfect moment," I peck her forehead gently.

She takes a deep breath, a bit red. "Well, I actually had this whole thing planned where I'd send you off to do groceries and I could set up the house for you while you were gone. Almost like a date at home. But then I realized that some of the ingredients I needed for the meal I planned to make—"

"Wait— wait. Roll back a bit," I keep my smile hidden for the time being because my lips are already hurting by how much I've been doing this mouth exercise. "You were making a homemade date? And you planned to do everything on your own?"

She looks flustered by my question, but I don't mean it in a rude way. I'm genuinely curious to know what she had to say.

"Yeah..."

I blush, "Okay. Go on."

"A-anyway, it was all set so that by the time you came home, I would have everything ready. And then after dinner..." She shifts her hands, opening a very, very familiar felt box. "...I would give this to you."

A ring a size too big for her appears into view. There must be something blocking my voice box because all of a sudden, I can't speak.

"I know, it's nothing compared to the gorgeous diamond ring you got me, but you know," she shrugs, her smile getting softer, more delicate.

"You are just..." I try to create words by how in awe and how touched I am by her. My hands find their way to her face. "...*So matchless.*" I give her lips a kiss. "So exquisite." *Kiss.* "So sublime." *Kiss.* "Beyond compare." *Kiss.* "And just so..." *Kiss.* "...*Heavenly.*"

To say the least.

Her mouth is agape, stunned by the words that left my breath.

"Just so...*perfectly imperfect.*"

"Ellie, it's just a ring," she laughs, cheeks completely red.

"No, no. It's not *just* a ring, My Star." I wrap her into my embrace like a blanket. "And I don't need the amount of money to define the value of what you give me. Everything you give me, I'll cherish."

She slides the ring onto my finger. My heart feels so full. Like suddenly the feeling of emptiness in me is being filled with whatever this addictive dosage of Huma is.

Her arms come around my lower back and I hold her a little tighter, loving every moment of this. "Got it, cheaper is better."

"Alright, shall I teach you how to skate?" I hold out my hand.

Huma Tariq, I will love you forever.

"Yes, please."

Without the sense of time, she takes my hand.

...

43

Elias

"And rely upon Allah."
- Surah Al-Anfal [8:61]

As the night makes an appearance, we exit the building and into the cool air. I let out a dramatic sigh, catching Huma's waist.

Even under this dim streetlight, she still fails to disappoint me with her beauty.

Her head is facing towards the sky, hands resting on my chest, "There are so many stars, Ellie."

So gorgeous.

"And somehow your smile is outshining every single one of them."

Her eyes lower to my gaze and I catch a glimpse of her rosy cheeks. She turns away, looking back at the sky and I push her until we're directly underneath the streetlight with the widest of grins on my lips.

"Is that red on your face, I see?" She struggles to escape from my arms only making me tighten them. I bring a hand up to her chin to test my theory and just like I suspected, she's blushing.

She slips out of my hold and sprints towards a plaza. I follow.

"Elias, stop!" She whines, a twinge of laughter in her voice.

She comes to a halt when she reaches a store I haven't ever seen before. It's an ice cream store.

With the cheekiest of smiles, she spins around, "Have you ever tried the ice cream from here before?"

I shake my head which quickly earns me a frown and an eyeroll. "Oh, right. You eat ice cream with gold flakes on it, am I right?"

Offended, I grab her hand and open the door, letting her in front of me before proceeding, "Fine then— let's try your adult—on—a—budget—ice—cream."

"Wait," she stops on the spot and brings my hood to cover my head. *"You're a celebrity, remember?"*

I adjust it, "What about you? *You're the wife of this celebrity.*"

She smiles, "No one knows who I am, trust me."

We go inside where there's barely anyone, except a select few couples who were probably thinking the exact same thing as us.

She forces me to sit down on a chair assisting for two people and kneels down, lowering her voice.

"I'll order for us—"

"With my credit card."

She lowers my hand and pulls out a five dollar bill, "No. With *my* money."

I inch myself closer to her, "Then you can say goodbye to this store."

"Oh yeah?"

"Yeah, and I have no problem carrying you out of here if you wanna try something with me right now."

"It's one time! And it's for two dollar ice cream!" She argues, letting out an exasperated sigh.

"I. Don't. Care. You don't get to pay for anything," I say, pushing her buttons. "And if you don't want me to go order it myself and let them know who I am, I suggest you take my card."

In defeat, she snatches the plastic out of my hand but I grab her again.

"M-m, give me yours so I know you won't use it behind my back."

Her glare is probably one of the most frightening things about her.

She places her money down on the table and lazily turns towards the counter. I smile tenderly, absolutely drowning in the love I have for this girl.

When she comes back, she's holding two cups and two spoons with my card between them.

"You still like french vanilla, right?"

My face lights up, settling as the corners of my mouth curve upwards. "You remember."

She plops herself on the chair across from me and slides over my belongings with the ice cream.

"Of course I do."

Kill me.

I see her looking around and— *God*— if she could just know how beautiful she is, it would ruin me. She's humble, and while I love that, I know the way she sees herself is nothing compared to how I see her. If she just knew how her smile makes me feel, she would remember those butterflies forever.

"Do you want this store too, Gorgeous?" I ask, resting my face in my palm.

She scoops up a spoonful of the chocolate ice cream and slips it into her mouth, biting back another one of her killer smiles.

"You know what I've realized—? Your love language is gift-giving."

I shake my head, "You're wrong there."

She takes another bite.

"Oh?"

"My love language is doing anything to make you happy."

"Anything?"

"Anything."

"Can you give me a bite of your ice cream?"

I chuckle, moving my tiny container to the center of the table.

"Here," she holds out a spoonful of her ice cream, pointing it to me. "It's only fair."

"It's okay, I'm good."

"No, take it or I'm gonna feel bad."

Side note: I hate chocolate ice cream.

I forcefully open my mouth and try to ignore the strong taste of cocoa that accompanies my tongue within seconds.

Side side note: She doesn't know I hate chocolate ice cream.

"It's good," I rasp as I try to hold in a gag.

"Really?" she asks excitedly. "Take some more— I'm full anyway."

"Huma—"

"Oh, c'mon. You paid for this, you paid for my books, you let me move into your mansion of a house, just take it."

I hesitantly take the container from her hands, and she gives me a satisfied look.

"Well I know I wasn't about to move in with you. That would just be rude."

I'm not about to tell her I don't like chocolate, especially now. If I go back, I'm going to end up embarrassing her and myself.

This, I can keep a secret.

This, *I will not be telling her.*

When we're done, we step outside hand-in-hand. We walk back towards the car, but take a hike around the plaza.

I'm wondering whether it's the right time for me to mention the huge wedding Huma apparently wants, but I don't know how to bring it up. She clearly didn't tell me for a reason.

Or maybe she wants me to break the ice.

"Huma?"

"Yes, Love?" She says softly.

I'm not typically shy or hesitant when it comes to what Huma wants, but this is harder to bring up since she has never uttered a word about a wedding to me at all.

"I...I didn't know you wanted a big Pakistani wedding."

Just as I say that, she looks at me with an embarrassed expression and stops walking. I take advantage of the situation as I realize I have the upper hand right now. I give her hand a little, reassuring squeeze.

"Aren't you gonna say anything?"

She blushes, continuing to head towards the car with her hand still in mine.

"You weren't supposed to know that."

When we're only a step away from the car, I stop moving and pull her to me, caressing her cheeks.

Huma blushing is a beautiful sight to witness. Not because I like to make her nervous, though I won't lie, teasing her is its own sport, but because her face gets all soft and tender like she's finally relaxing from the tension.

"Why wasn't I supposed to know that, Star?"

Her eyes drift away to the ground as her hands cup mine. "Well, we were in such a rush to get married that I figured you probably didn't want one."

She looks back at me, guilty.

"I'm sorry, Ellie."

I tuck in the baby hairs escaping her head cap, smiling tenderly, "Don't apologize, *meri jaan*. I've kept bigger secrets from you."

She sighs deeply. It's not a relieved sigh, but a more frantic one, "I'm going to actually kill Aaliyah when I see her again."

I laugh quietly, amused by her cute aggression.

"But just so you know, I would love to get married to you again, Star."

She looks back at me, her hands falling to her sides again as she steps closer, "Do you really mean that, or are you saying it for my benefit?"

"I really mean that," I kiss her forehead, before embracing her into a warm hug. "Don't forget what I told you before, *I'll do anything just to make you happy.*"

44

Huma

"And your Lord says, "Call upon Me; I will respond to you."
- Surah Ghafir [40:60]

"No Elias, I'm not going to a talk show."

I shut the door before he can even try to convince me why I should. I have had it with trying to reason why *me* and a *talk show* could ever possibly go hand-in-hand. I stutter and stress so much during public appearances, and I cannot imagine how much will go down when we have to talk about our relationship.

The car ride home was probably the best ten-minute drive I've had in my whole life. Elias and I were planning out how the wedding would go; what types of dishes would be served, who we would invite, and the list goes on and on.

But then we got home and Elias sat me down on the bed with *quite* the news. To be more specific, he talked about the possible chances of having to attend one of those late night shows they show on TV.

Sure, eventually I would, but I plan to hold that off for as long as possible. I know people have warmed up to the idea that Elias and I are one now, but I haven't exactly warmed up to them. If they were just haters that would've been a completely different tale.

But they aren't.

They're fans of Elias who said all those things about me. Who said he could have done better.

Elias can handle it, I can't.

Yeah, probably not the best blend.

But anyway, I have more important things to focus on. Like this shower. I can worry about this afterwards.

"Huma, open the door for a sec," I hear and blatantly ignore.

I unbraid my hair and brush it out with my fingers.

"I promise it's not about the talk show."

I move the towel from the counter to the circular towel holder near the bath and take out a black charcoal mask.

Because of this period, I have been breaking out and I'm in desperate need of these atrocious pimples to be gone—

"I will rip the door off its hinges, My Star. I need to go pray and you're using up my time," he says, startling me.

The door is still intact, *thank God*. However, I don't think my neck is after I so quickly shot my gaze to the door to confirm it's still there.

"Ow," I grunt, rubbing my neck back and forth.

"Are you okay, Huma?" Elias knocks quietly.

I close the lid of the toilet and sit down. The pain lessens slowly, but I stay seated, soothing it with my hand.

"Huma? You okay, Star?"

Without thinking, I start spitting out random words.

"No, I think I broke my neck." I laugh humorously.

"YOU WHAT?"

"Yeah—"

In a matter of seconds, the door is open.

Well, actually, *it's broken.*

It falls with a loud thud against the bathroom tiles and nearly takes my feet underneath it. Luckily I jump onto my feet, moving to the side enough that it misses me as Elias hops past it, tilting my head up with caution.

"Does it hurt a lot?"

I stare at where the door's supposed to be before looking at him in utter shock.

"YOU JUST BROKE DOWN A DOOR!"

His hands fall to my shoulders, "YOU TOLD ME YOU BROKE YOUR NECK!"

"I was laughing when I said that!" I sigh, drifting my eyes back and forth from the door and back to Elias. "How are we gonna fix this?"

He leaves for a second, leaving me in absolute dismay as I take in my surroundings. There is debris on the floor surrounding the frame that I lean down to look at as if I'm investigating the scene of a crime. The edges of the wood are rigid. I touch it and feel the sharpness of the thin strips of wood peeling off. I sigh again.

"Elias!" I call out.

"I'm right here," he appears, startling me for the second time today, causing me to scratch my finger against the loose pieces of wood.

"Ow!" I suck in my teeth, standing straight. There's a piece of it piercing through my skin, stinging even more than it already is.

He drops what I figure to be a toolbox on the floor and comes to my aid.

"Show me," he backs me up against the vanity, and I cringe at the way it feels when I try to pull it out. He gently grabs my wrist, nudging me to let go as I grip onto the counter behind me. The way he's so calm like this is just a normal occurrence in his daily routine is what ends up distracting me from the pain.

He reaches to the cabinet that stands right above the toilet and takes out a tweezer. Instinctively, I pull my hand away and shake my head.

"Oh, hell no. I'm not doing that, Ellie. It hurts enough as it is."

"Huma—" he tips towards me, somehow making my legs wobble a bit.

I don't fight him when he finally gets his hands on the fresh splinter lying in my skin.

"You need to be more careful," he yanks out the piece, earning him a wince. "This isn't a joke, Star. Splinters can become infections."

I shift, feeling a twinge of irritation, "I'm not the one who pushed down the door now and nearly crushed his wife, am I?"

His eyes catch mine which quickly replaces the annoyance with guilt. Suddenly, he's closer, pressing a kiss to my shoulder, and making my heart vibrate a little.

"I'm so, so sorry, My Star. I should've been more careful."

Stupid Huma.

I swallow, quietly hearing his muffled apologies.

"I would never purposely hurt you, My Star. Never."

My comment wasn't blaming him, just challenging his statement. I guess I didn't realize what I was saying to him until I had said it, and maybe he took it differently than I intended him to.

I cup his cheeks, pulling him to eye view, "I'm not blaming you, Ellie."

I see him swallow hard, "You're not?"

"Of course not."

"Oh."

I hear a low sniffle as he steps back. He turns away towards the bedroom as I watch as he starts to pray.

What did I do?

45

Elias

"O you who have believed, remember Allah with such remembrance."
- Surah Al-Ahzab [33:41]

Huma didn't do anything. This is completely my fault. I should've listened to her properly. I really could've hurt her just now.

Sitting down on the prayer mat, I crouch forward, placing my elbows on the carpet, and covering my face with my hands.

I don't get it though. I don't get how I was able to protect myself back then, yet when it came to Huma, I'm soft. The overprotective-ness leaks out of me like I'm made out of jelly, which sounds stupid. Of course I'm overprotective of Huma, but when it's just us, she makes me feel less like a flawed human. She makes me feel like the freaking luckiest person in the world.

Even when she comes over to sit down next to me, I don't want to look at her. I know what she said meant nothing, but it's true.

I could've hurt her.

"I'm sorry. That was so inconsiderate of me to say," she says, rubbing my back gently. "I understand if you're mad at me."

I lift my head up, straightening myself out, "Don't do that to yourself, Huma. You know it's not your fault so stop apologizing."

"It *is* my fault," she argues. "Tell me, do I remind you of back then? Do I remind you of when you would hide away in your room and pray just to hear the door break down? Does taking out the splinter from my skin remind you of yourself when you had all yours fixing your broken bedroom door?"

My heart shatters.

"Is that how you think I see you?" I ask, noticing there are tears filling her eyes.

Why is it that when we finally figured things out, something comes to ruin it all over again?

"No," she rubs her eyes. "I don't want to remind you of all that you went through, but I can't help but feel like I'm a walking reminder of what happened."

The irony is uncanny. Huma was one of the only things that was my escape then. The only person I could rely on to create a barrier that divided me from reality. I feel as if my whole body is aching from her words because I'm starting to realize how clueless I have been.

"Don't say that, Huma," my voice breaks.

"Is it true, though? Because if it's true, I don't want to hurt you."

I shake my head, my soul hurting so badly by the way she's looking at me.

Of course it's not true.

Of course she's my saviour.

No one else could be.

"No, sweetheart."

"I'm sorry, Ellie. I don't mean to hurt you like this."

I pull her onto my lap, holding her like her heart is going to break in front of her, too. I listen to her quiet sobs, giving her a place to hide as I press my lips hard against the top of her head.

I can't help but feel confusion.

"I just don't want you to think I would ever intentionally hurt you," I swallow, slipping my hands into her hair. *"I'm nothing like my father,* I promise."

She frantically searches my eyes, cupping my cheeks in the process. "Of course you're not. *You're my Elias."*

I break like glass in front of her, letting the tears stream down my face.

I'm hers.

"And whenever we have kids—" I breathe. "I would never, ever lay a hand—"

She brings me closer to her, pressing my head against her shoulder, "I have never doubted you, My Love. You are nothing like your father."

I don't want to create a wall between us because of our feelings. I want our feelings to be one of the things that pulls us together.

The only thing I can't stand right now is seeing how much Huma is hurting on her own.

Are we in a broken relationship, or are we just broken people?

"Promise me one thing," I say, swallowing the tightness in my chest.

"Anything."

"No matter how bad this gets, neither of us can walk away from each other."

I've been so caught up in myself and my problems, I forgot to check up on Huma. I forgot to take care of my only support system. It could've been that I would never know how she really felt about all this if she didn't tell me now.

I hold her a little tighter, swiping her hair back to kiss her forehead.

She cries harder, and I feel as if the sky just fell on us. My throat hurts with every swallow, seeing her in this state.

"I don't know what *this* is. I don't understand what between us is getting so hard to get around."

She's looking up at me, her honey eyes watering as my thumb strokes away a tear on her face.

"We're not always gonna be happy, *Meri Jaan*," I say, surprised by my own words. "I mean, aren't you proud of how far we've come?"

It's something I haven't given much thought to; how effective our prayers really are. How I had a one in a billion chance to see this beautiful girl again. How we were able to change that if us meeting again wasn't meant to happen on its own already.

This world isn't small like everyone says it is. Sometimes if we think hard enough, if we put enough thought into someone, anything can happen. Even if you aren't thinking about anyone, sometimes our soul longs for that someone that brings us comfort when we need it the most.

"Yes," she mutters. *"And I promise."*

This is the part where I wait for her to fall asleep, but I don't want her to sleep this off. If she does, it'll feel like this never happened, and I don't want it to be like that. I want her to understand that I'm here for her, too. That she can run to me when everything becomes too much.

I can protect her, too.

She sniffles, "You have to promise, too."

I open and then close my mouth.

After what she just said, I don't know if I can keep any promises. If I make her feel like a reminder of then, how do I fix that?

"Elias," her eyes are looking up at me now and she's smiling through her tears, soaking me in with her beauty as usual. *"Promise?"*

I don't flinch for even a second, my silence shutting down the remaining amount of hope left in her.

She straightens herself, keeping her gaze transfixed on me, "*Say it. Promise that you'll never walk away from me.*"

No matter how much I try to get myself to say it, I can't seem to let those words leave my mouth. I know that if I do, I'll be lying right to her face.

Her smile is disintegrating until it's gone, her shoulders drooping. She places her hands on my shirt and pulls at it gently, moving me back and forth.

"*Why won't you say it?*"

It breaks my heart to think I'm making this worse, but I myself don't understand why it's so hard to slip out two simple words; *I promise.*

It's that easy.

I love her, I do. And I wish nothing but the best...except if it's her that's being affected by my own problems. I don't want her to feel pained by my traumas, my past. She's my girl, the one I wish to protect from everything in this world that can ever inflict any kind of pain on her.

I guess I didn't realize that maybe the person she needs to be away from is me.

Those tears that were once in her eyes are now streaming down her face again.

I cup her cheek, "Huma—"

"No, shut up."

She's up on her feet in a matter of seconds, and before I know it, she's leaving through the bedroom door. I run after her, thinking she's about to leave the house, but then I see her sitting on the couch, bawling her eyes out.

I get on my knees in front of her, regret seeping into my heart as she turns away from me.

"Please, baby—"

"Leave me alone!" She shouts, making my heart shatter.

Quietly, I get up and walk back to our room. I fall onto the bed, lying in the dark as I stupidly regret everything. I bury myself underneath the blanket, listening to Huma crying out in the living room. I want to go there and apologize over and over until my voice gives out, but I don't want to make her feel any worse, so I stay put.

Throughout the night, I listen to her cry until it's completely silent. I consider going now just to give her a pillow and tuck her under some sheets, until I hear footsteps getting closer.

Her figure stands at the doorway, and I can tell even through the darkness that she's looking at me.

"Please come to bed, Huma," I plead. *"I'm so sorry, My Love."*

"That's the last thing I'll do," her voice breaks as she walks away again.

I never thought this would happen. I always thought after we got married that it's entirely impossible that I'll ever be unhappy again, but here I am.

As the minutes become hours, I go over to her, holding the blanket from our bed and two pillows. I lift her head to set the cushions underneath and then tuck her underneath the blanket.

I sit at the corner of the sofa, gently brushing my lips against her cheek, "I'm so, so sorry." I kiss her again. "It's all my fault, I'm sorry."

I keep going until my eyes are watering, the feeling of dread overtaking.

I want to stay here *so bad.* I want to pick her up and place her next to me in bed so when I wake up it's her face I see, and not an empty mattress next to me.

"Huma," I press my lips onto her temple. "Please forgive me. *I promise.*"

A part of me feels she may be awake and she's waiting for me to leave, but I don't want to.

"Over my heart, I'll never leave you no matter how bad anything gets. Just please, *please* come back to bed."

I know I'm the one who hurt her, but I wish I could explain how hard it is to keep all these promises. To promise anything when I didn't get that treatment at all from my parents.

And I wouldn't consider something like that, something that does not even involve her, as a reason for me to treat her this way. I love her to death, but I don't think she believes that after what just happened.

The most faintest of whispers leaves her mouth, and suddenly, the blanket is lifted up as she scoots over to make room for me.

"Come."

Without hesitation, I lay next to her, burying my face into her neck.

What is happening to us?

46

Huma

I didn't sleep.

All night I've been questioning everything that happened a couple of hours ago. If *we* mean anything to Elias, or maybe this is all just a test and I'm failing it all over again.

It broke me hearing him last night when he came over apologizing, and it started to remind me of when I found out about the scars on his body. The amount of guilt he held for not telling me.

Except this scenario had quite the difference. This scenario he hesitated to promise something *so simple*. Something I expected he would be able to do without hesitation.

I know he's in pain, and I know he's going through a lot right now. And all night, I've been thinking about us. About whether all of this is worth it, or if our problems are only getting worse.

"Please tell me you forgive me," he said. "I love you so much."

He made promises before falling asleep, but it felt forced so I just covered his back with the blanket, "Go to sleep, Ellie. We can talk about this tomorrow."

Now it's early in the morning.

I carefully slip out of the covers and start to dress myself to go out for a walk.

But just as I'm about to leave, Elias is standing at the bedroom door, looking at me with pure betrayal. Kind of like how I looked after he couldn't complete the other half of the promise.

His voice breaks, "Are you leaving me?"

I want to stay here.

I do.

But then where would my sense of self-respect be if I do that? If I let this breeze over me like it didn't shatter my soul, I'll just be broken.

"I just need some time alone."

He's nodding his head as he walks over to me. "Okay, I can send you with a bodyguard."

No.

"No, Elias. I want to be alone," I say, a fury of anger rising in me.

But how do I shout at someone who's been so vulnerable with me? How do I express my anger when all I want to do is hold him?

"It's not like you care anyway," I mumble, walking past him.

To my unluckiness, he grabs my wrist and brings me against the wall. His gaze has darkened in mere seconds of us talking.

"*'I don't care?'*" his sadness has switched to frustration. "When did I say, "*I don't care?*""

My eyes search his, freaked by the sudden burst of energy. His hand is still wrapped around my wrist, as he steps a centimeter closer. And even though we're not very happy with each other right now, his touch is warm.

"I might've messed up, but I *do* care. Matter of fact, I have never cared more for someone than I do for you—"

Arguing coming from outside interrupts him as we both go completely silent. He's about to brush it off, parting his lips and finishing off what he was about to say when the doorbell rings.

Elias gives me a confused look, a moment of hesitation as he squeezes my wrist gently before leaving the room and, as I assume, heading towards the door.

I continue dressing myself when my selective hearing catches a single word coming from outside.

"Dad?"

Me, being scared but also protective, places hood over my head, making sure no hairs can escape before proceeding towards where the voices were coming from. My eyes quickly notice a slightly-taller-than-Elias figure standing before him.

When I approach them, all I can see is fright in Elias' face.

I switch my gaze back and forth between the two men just as my hand is pulled.

"Huma, I need you to go to our room." Elias' voice shakes. "I want you to lock the door and—"

"What—? No— I'm not leaving you here."

I try to keep my voice low, but that's pretty hard to do when there's a strange man being held back by bodyguards staring back at us.

Obviously by the singular word that left Elias' mouth, this is his father.

"Mr.Lee, do you want us to take him away?" one of the body-guards ask.

"No, please. Elias, let me talk to you for just a second," his father interjects. "It's about your mother."

When I look at Elias, he's still. In a state of shock at the sight of the same man that hurt him all those years ago.

His hand tightens its hold on mine.

Though it's not my place to decide what Elias wants, he doesn't look like he's going to speak up anytime soon.

"Take him away, please." I give a subtle look to the bodyguards.

"No, please. You don't understand," his father continues, struggling to escape the hold of these men. "His mother is in the hospital."

"*What?*" Elias looks at him.

The guards hold him back again.

"Your mother is in the hospital. The doctor's say she doesn't look like she'll be recovering anytime soon. She wants to see you before she goes, Elias," he says. "I know I'm the last person you wanna see, but she's not going to be here for very long. She wants to see you one last time."

I watch the exchange of looks in between them. Elias can't speak. He's reached his limit of words because, even as I give his hand a squeeze, he doesn't respond in any sort of way. I'm scared he's going to pass out or something so I speak again.

"What hospital?"

His father gives me the details, and then he's taken away.

Just as the door shuts, Elias falls onto his knees. I fall next, afraid I was right about him fainting, but he's crying instead.

"Why does it never stop?" He asks, weaker than I've ever seen before. "All of this— why doesn't it just end already?"

His past emotions have been completely consumed by fear and tears. I don't know what to tell him anymore. I don't want to tell him everything will be okay because I don't know if it ever will.

But I'd be an idiot to tell him it won't.

So I don't say either.

I pull him to my arms.

He cries all day, and when he's quiet, I've realized he's too tired to keep weeping.

When it's around eight, he gets up from the floor as I follow. "Will you sleep with me tonight?" He asks, tugging on my hand.

I nod, "Of course I will, My Love."

An hour passes by, and I've finally got him to relax. He's staring at the ceiling, his head resting on my lap. One of my hands is clasped with his, while the other is busy massaging his hair.

There's not much left for me to do. I've been trying to think about how I can make this better— easier— for him, but I really don't know how to do that.

I don't expect him to just go on and forgive them, but I don't want him to regret his decisions later on. Forgiveness is a process of healing as much as anything else, so truthfully, I think he should go see her, but whether he chooses to forgive her is a decision he has to make on his own.

"You think I should forgive them, right?" He asks as my lips press against his knuckles. "You're thinking I should accept their apology."

"They didn't apologize to you."

"But you think I should anyway."

He's saying it as if that's what I'm thinking.

There is some truth to what he says, but barely. I refuse to let my opinion interfere with something that has nothing to do with me.

He sits up, his glass eyes streaming tears out.

I didn't realize he was crying again.

"How do I do that without betraying myself?"

My heart aches for the state he's in. I want to take all his pain and crumple it away the same way he did for me, but I know I can't.

All I can do is comfort him.

"You start by forgiving yourself," I cup one of his cheeks. "And I mean it, Ellie. It's not your fault. Everything that has happened since you converted— none of it is your fault. Say it."

"*It is my fault,*" he moves away, about to leave the bed.

"No," I grab his arm. "Elias, look at me."

His eyes refuse to meet mine after I reposition myself in front of him.

"It's not your fault, Elias. Admit it."

"I can't! My mother is dying because I left them!" He's sobbing, gasping as he speaks. "She might've not been as good of a mother as yours, but she's still my mom!"

My eyes are stinging now.

This is what goes through Elias' head. Regret and guilt for leaving his family behind. But it wasn't even something he got to decide. His life was miserable back then. If he hadn't left, God knows what could've happened to him.

"What am I supposed to do with myself, Huma?" He tucks his head away into the crook of my neck. "The second everything is finally okay, my life falls apart again."

I swallow. My heart is racing against his, scared for him.

This only shows how different we both are from each other.

"I'm sorry," he whispers. "You're one of the only people that hasn't turned on me."

Hearing that brings me some sort of ease, knowing he has a different level of trust with me brings me to another level of love with him.

"Let's pray. It's Maghrib," I say, and he finds my hand, leading me to the bathroom to do wudu.

While we pray, I hear him crying.

When we finish, he's still crying.

I face my body to him, brushing back the hair that falls on his face, "What if I'm not ready to forgive them?"

The corners of my mouth form a comforting smile, "That's okay."

He takes my hand into his, pulling it away from his hair to kiss it.

"I. Don't. Deserve. You."

He holds my face in his palms and joins his lips with mine.

"You are one of the only stable things in my life, my gorgeous star."

My gorgeous star. I'm adding that to the list of things that make me blush.

His father was here just a couple of hours ago. He was here for several minutes, but caused my Elias so much damage that it took hours for him to finally show me some type of comfort.

He unclips the black necklace I've never seen him take off, clasping the ends together around my neck, "Abu gave this to me when I met him."

"But—"

He's had that since high school.

"He taught me how to read Arabic," Elias smiles, dropping his hands to mine.

Shock overcomes me.

"I didn't know he was your father at the time, but the second I realized I ran off."

My father would stay at the Masjid late most times, but he didn't work there. He would go to the Masjid everyday and grew accustomed to coming home later at night.

My father knew Elias before he really knew who he was. I'm not surprised he did such a thing. Abu has always had a kind soul when it came to helping people. I'm more surprised by the fact that it could've been anyone, but somehow he ended up teaching Elias.

"Oh my God, Ellie." I take off the necklace. "I'm not keeping this, sweetheart. Abu gave this to *you* for a reason."

I get on my knees, my arms resting on his shoulders as I join the ends together. Elias wraps his arms around my waist tightly, falling onto his back and earning himself a gasp. He laughs. It's a quiet laugh, but it's progress.

I plant my lips on his temple as I sit back up, getting off of him.

The next couple of days, I keep my tabs on Elias. I make sure that he's eating well and that he's getting enough sleep. I'm not sure if I should be worried about the lack of emotion he's been show-ing...specifically how upset he was compared to now.

"I want to give you something,"

I search his eyes, waiting for a response.

He smiles and takes my hands into his, "Come with me."

Before I know it, we're leaving the room. He continues to guide me, stopping right in front of the bookshelf.

He reaches to the highest shelf, my book coming into view.

My book that he annotated.

I stare at it as my mind imagines all his notes in there.

"Go ahead, My Star. Take a look inside."

I take the book into my hands, my eyes darting back and forth from the papers to Elias. He's pretty protective about this specific copy, so whatever's inside must be important to him.

"Any page?" I ask, grazing the book tabs peeking out of the pages.

"Any page."

I flip to a random part in the book where I see a burst of his writing on the border of the papers. There are arrows and under-linings on my words, highlighting random events or things I've said to him. I start to read the things he's written, blushing at how sweet his writing is.

I look back at him, softening. "You predicted our marriage?"

"I didn't predict it. I knew it was gonna happen, by any means," he replies, shyly looking away.

I bite back my smile, placing a kiss on his cheek as I continue to reread everything he wrote.

"I think my favourite is *'I'm so in love with you, it hurts.'*"

He reddens when I capture his gaze, "Good to know."

That's a lie. All of them are my favourite.

'I promise I'll marry you.'

'I love you.'

'You have my whole heart.'

'*Love of my life.*'

'*Can't wait to see you again.*'

'*You're so pretty.*'

All. Of. Them. Are. My. Favourite.

All of them remind me of how lucky I am to have Elias here with me. The fight we had a couple of days ago doesn't matter anymore. All that matters is keeping Elias and his feelings safe. He deserves all the protection in this world, and I can give that to him.

"I want to show you something too." I say, setting the book against the others on the shelf. "Wait here."

He nods his head as I basically sprint to the bedroom, smiling sheepishly to myself. I find my diaries in my nightstand drawer neatly stacked on each other. I take out the one from eleventh grade, about to rush back to Elias, when I see him leaning against the door frame looking at me.

"Is that the diary? The one I saw in your room back in the apartment?" He asks, a frown on his face.

I stand before him, holding the book out for him to take, "Yes. Entries of you."

"Huma," his voice cracks. He steps back, walking to his side of the bed and pulling his drawer open.

He stops, and I have to squint my eyes to understand what's happening.

"Ellie," I rush over, dropping my diary onto the bed. "What's wrong, My Love?"

His tears are hitting a mess of papers...a mess of...*letters?*

"I wrote about you, too." he swallows hard. "The letters I showed you before weren't even close to half of it."

I place my hand on his.

Based on what I've already read, these pages of writing are not only about me. They're about his own experiences. They're about his parents and what they did to him.

When he lifts his head, his bottom lip is quivering, "I feel so selfish."

"Sit down," I say, nudging him towards the bed.

He obliges, and I sit right next to him, my body facing his. He squeezes my hand, moving it onto his lap.

"Why do you feel selfish, Love?"

His sudden sobs make sense as I piece together everything. His inability to show me how he's been feeling for the past two days has only resulted in a build-up of emotions. But I want him to tell me that himself.

"I can't keep pretending that I didn't just find out my mother is dying," he gasps, gaining his breath again. "Sh-she could be dead already, and I'm sitting here, acting as if none of that happened."

I run a hand through his hair, trying to rid him of his sorrow, "You wanna go see her?"

My arm drops when he leans close, placing his head against my shoulder. I leave gentle strokes on his back as he cries.

"No," he whispers. "No, I can't."

Everything came crashing down on him, and I can see in his eyes that he doesn't know where to go from here. Confusion and guilt merging in his broken heart.

He lifts his head after a couple of minutes as I reach my hand up to remove his tears.

"I'm sorry, My Star. I'm sorry you have to see me like this."

"Don't apologize for being in touch with your emotions, *my imperfect star*," I say, realizing what I just called him.

He finds my eyes, tucking away a piece of my hair as I turn pink. "You have a very comforting voice, did you know that?"

"You've said to me..." I hold back a smile. "...*two times before*."

He leans down to kiss my temple and then my cheek, "I know, sweetheart."

For a second I think I've gained him back since there's a sad smile perched up on his lips, but it drops almost immediately. I see his throat bob as he swallows, gaining his composure before he speaks.

"I want you to know something, Huma."

My hand slides to the back of his neck, rubbing it back and forth in an attempt to soothe him while he speaks.

"I will never hurt you or our children—"

"You don't need to tell me that. Your heart is pure, Ellie. I know I can trust you."

He closes his eyes, a single tear falling as he cups my cheeks, "No, I need to say it. I promise, I will never even raise a single finger at our children and— and I'll hurt anyone who does."

"I know, baby." I pull him to me, tightly wrapping him into my arms like a gift. I count the seconds. *Thirty seconds is how long a hug is supposed to last. No less— only more.*

Minutes pass and I still haven't let go of him. He's only relaxed further into my arms, like he's melting into them. I don't mind. I like how comfortable he is with me.

He lifts himself out of my hold, "You wanted to show me something? A diary?"

He's attempting a smile, which I imitate, pleased.

"Are you sure you wanna look at it?" I ask, aware that right now may not be the best time.

"Yes, My Star." For a second there, his eyes look into mine, capturing them in his essence. He dips his head and kisses me gently. It's short and sweet, making me smile against his lips, which seems to have a contagious touch to it. "Of course I want to see it."

I reach for it, holding it out in front of him, "Don't mind the writing. I was a bit choppy back then."

He chuckles, taking it into his hands. "And you read those letters...they're a mess but they're in order."

I kiss his cheek, happy to see the subtle smile forming on his lips.

He rests against the headboard and begins to read.

Meanwhile, I take a couple of papers and sit across from him, cross-legged on the bed.

"Wait," he says, standing from the bed. "Come with me."

I look at him curiously, but follow closely behind. He takes my hand, starting to walk up the stairs, just like the time when he read The Quran for me.

This feels slightly different but similar all at the same time.

"Are we going to the balcony?" I ask, smiling softly.

He stops when we reach the top, glancing at a different door before looking back at me.

It almost looks hidden.

"How about something new instead?"

He opens the door, more stairs coming into view. I head up, and a locked door appears. He gently tucks my hair into my hood, taking my free hand once more, unlocking the door with keys I hadn't noticed he had.

In front of me is a beautiful rooftop. I'll admit, not as pretty as the photoshoot rooftop, but it's still gorgeous.

There are a couple of lounge chairs close to the edge of the roof. How I didn't know he had a whole roof—? I have no clue.

"We're actually not supposed to be here, but if you keep it a secret, we can sneak here late at night all the time," he whispers.

He doesn't hesitate, lifting me off my feet and carrying me to one of the lounge chairs. He sits across from me on a different chair, opening up the diary, and not hesitating to start reading.

I do the same, taking only minutes to start tearing up as I read his beautiful words. His letters are a mix of love and pain, and when I look over the pages, I see him crying, too.

The dichotomy of me thinking he didn't love me, while in reality he was busy writing such moony letters for me. How does one even recover from love like this? I sure as heck didn't.

Neither did he.

And then here we were; each other's safe haven.

How am I supposed to love again, Huma? You were the only one meant for me, and it'll stay that way forever. Even once I enter Jannah, my first request will be to have you by my side. You are a beautiful sight, My Dear Star, and I would hate to not be able to see such an enticing girl like you again.

"*Fii dunya wal akhirah.*"

I lower the papers and look at him, bawling. "You thought of that nickname before we saw each other again—"

He opens up an arm for me as I quickly crawl into his hold.

"You are a sight for sore eyes, *My Dear Star. Just looking at you made it worth living.*"

I leave the papers on the side of the chair crying harder as I get onto my knees and hide into his chest. He's crying, but he lets out a soft chuckle, rubbing my back *oh-so* gently. His lips caress the side of my head as he pulls me in tighter.

And all night, we stay like that. Neither of us fall asleep.

There were moments when he would start shaking as he asked me rhetorical questions.

Why didn't you just tell me how you felt?

Why didn't you tell me I hurt you this bad?

And for every question, I cried with him. A sad, yet comforting sight to witness. A couple finally giving everything left in themselves just to heal each other.

By Fajr, we're both back on the prayer mat in our bedroom. We're both silently telling God all of our problems, and He listens. I wipe away the tears on Elias' face as he makes duaa.

"I think you should see her," I say as he finishes up.

"Do you really think so?"

I give a small nod, earning a smile from him. He leans towards me, pressing a kiss to my temple that lasts longer than a lifetime.

"I promise, *meri jaan*. I will never, ever leave you no matter how bad this gets. I need you here with me forever."

It makes my cheeks hurt by those two words that leave his mouth. *Meri jaan*. His voice is a literal blessing in disguise.

"But I want you to come with me."

I caress his hand, "Are you sure?"

I don't want him to be alone with his dad even if his mother is present. I don't trust his father alone with Elias, especially seeing how he reacted.

"Yes. I want you to come, my sweet star. I need you to be there."

"Okay."

We don't bother changing.

Elias puts the hospital into his GPS, and we get there within fifteen minutes.

To think I was going to leave Elias for a ten-minute walk just the other day. If I had left a second sooner than I did, he would've had no one in this house with him. He would be left to make all these decisions by himself with his abuser standing in front of him.

I fix the hoodie over Elias' head, making it harder for him to be recognized as we head inside.

"What's the name of the patient, dear?" The receptionist asks.

"Maya Lee," Elias says, his voice rushed.

She types away on her keyboard, looking at us with a smile, "Follow me."

We're led into the intensive care unit, giving both Elias and I a rush of anxiety as we both tighten our hold on each others' hand.

"She's just in this room."

"Okay," Elias says, tugging on my hand when I don't move.

I don't think it's right for me to be in the room with him. I'll stand outside so if he needs me, he can get me, but this is his family.

This *was* his family.

"Aren't you coming inside?" He asks, looking at me.

"No. I'll wait for you here."

Surprisingly, he lets go, kissing my forehead before opening the door to the room.

47

Elias

"And that it is He who causes death and gives life."
- Surah Al-A'raf [7:158]

"You came," my father looks at me, forcing a smile.

Even with all the abuse, there's no denying that he loves my mother a lot.

Or maybe he really has changed.

I wouldn't know.

"I came for her," I reply bluntly.

My eyes divert towards the woman on the hospital bed. She's lying on the white sheets, eyes closed with an oxygen mask over her face. Beside her is a machine, monitoring her blood pressure and heart rate.

"Mom," I settle down onto a chair next to her bedside. "Is she asleep?"

"Elias," my father catches my eyes. "She has lung cancer."

My heart drops.

"We found out way too late. Just a couple of months ago," his eyes stray away, avoiding mine.

"She's sleeping, right?" I panic.

With an exhausted sigh, he walks over and gently strokes her arm.

"Maya, Elias is here. He came to see you."

Her eyes start to open.

Thank. God.

"Elias?"

"Yes, Mom. I'm right here," I say, sandwiching her weak hand in between both of mine.

Even though I haven't seen her in years, my heart is aching at the thought that I could lose her at any second. Even though she was terrible to me, I'm not ready to see her leave me just yet.

"Hi baby," she cups one side of my cheek, smiling.

My eyes are stinging, tears falling already, "I wanna forgive you."

Her face relaxes, letting out a peaceful sigh, "Thank you, sweetheart. It means the world to me."

I'm bawling now, weakened at the sight of my mother.

"Don't cry because of me. I promise, it's not worth it."

I stand from my seat, "I want to show you someone."

She looks at me, waiting for me to continue.

"I think you'll like her a lot. She takes care of me," I open the door to the room, seeing a startled Huma.

"Is everything okay?" She asks as I grab her hand and pull her inside.

"Yes," I smile, turning my attention back to my mother. "This is my wife."

Both of them blink while Huma's arm wraps around mine.

I feel a surprising amount of comfort right now. Even though Mom wasn't the best person to me, I can see the guilt in her eyes. And even though I know there will always be a sense of hurt and pain because of those four years of trauma, my heart is at peace.

"Ellie... I don't think she wants to see me," she whispers, just as Mom ushers her closer.

"Come here, darling."

She pats the area on her bed, letting it crinkle underneath her hand. Huma looks at me, and then back at her before sitting down.

"You'll take care of my baby boy, won't you? Take care of him the way I wasn't able to?"

Huma grips the sheet into a fist, her leg shaking, "Y-yes. Of course."

I place a hand onto her knee to soothe her.

"Thank you," Mom whispers.

Her voice is getting quieter as the seconds pass. Then it dawns on me what's happening and my gut stirs. Even Dad is on his feet, watching as the machine starts to beep louder and more frantically. He calls for a nurse while I sit still in my seat.

Huma hops off the bed and moves a little to the side.

"Mom," I whisper, her eyes fluttering closed. *"Eomma,* please don't."

I move her into my arms, fitting myself onto the bed as I hear the high pitched noise of the machine monitor going off. My mind is a mess of emotions, but somehow in between all of this, there is a rush of relief as well.

I have forgiven her.

In barely a minute, I'm pushed off the bed and away from her. Nurses and doctors crowd the area around her, shouting things my mind cannot perceive.

I find Huma outside of the hospital waiting for me. I stop just a step away from her, lowering my head. Something on my shoulders has been lifted. An unspoken amount of anger in me that's finally leaving in gentle waves.

Huma bumps her head against my chest, wrapping her arms tightly around me. Her hug holds force that pushes me back a bit.

"You're the strongest person I know," she muffles against my shirt.

When she pulls back a bit to look at me, I notice there's tears in her eyes.

One thing I've learned from knowing Huma is that she's very emotional. And I can tell by the looks of it, she was trying to hold those cries in.

My heart feels lighter than anything else right now. Like there is nothing else left to do except move on from the past, and put my focus on the present. On Huma.

I muster up a smile, stroking her tears away with my thumb, "I would really like a thirty-second hug right now, my beautiful star."

Huma has taught me so much, but in between these lines of teaching and our relationship, not once has she lost hope in us. She hasn't fixed me. She's given a new meaning to those pieces of me, meanings that I would not be able to form by myself.

She pulls my hands off her face and places them onto her waist before wrapping her arms around my neck. She presses a kiss against my cheek and then my temple.

"You call me a star but you're the one that glows, Ellie."

I tighten my grip on her, sighing into her shoulder.

"God, you're such a blessing," she whispers, her voice shaking.

I hold her in place while she cries, and she grips onto me like if she loosens her hold, I'll slip away.

I can understand why she's crying. Everything right now is purely overwhelming.

I feel...okay, though. For once, there's no lingering sadness hovering over me. I finally feel like I've found my peace by forgiving my mother after all this time.

She lets go when her arms get tired, and takes hold of my arm, "Let's go home."

My eyes are directed towards the sky.

"What a pretty star."

"Where?" she asks, squinting her eyes and trying to find the non-existent dot in the sky. I tilt her chin until she's looking at me, softening, as she realizes what I'm doing. I open my mouth, but she covers it with her hand. "Don't— don't say it. Not only will I start crying again, but I'll shudder from your cringiness."

I'm glad I found my home in a person and not a place. Because no matter where I go and no matter how many times I break down, she will always be there. She'll remain as mine for the rest of my life and I don't plan on changing that. Ever.

I laugh quietly before pulling her hand down.

"Right here in front of me, the most prettiest star I have ever laid eyes on."

And just like she promised, she begins to bawl. I don't hesitate to pull her back into me. "Oh, My Star is so emotional," I smile, my eyes stinging as I kiss the top of her head. "It's okay, Love. I won't move until you've let it all out."

Her grip on me tightens as I feel a single tear slide down my cheek.

"Thank you," I say softly, knowing He's listening. "Thank you for letting our paths collide."

The End.

Epilogue

I quietly unlock the door as I enter inside.

It's pitch black in the house. All the lights have been turned off as I pull my luggage into the house, gently closing the door and hearing it lock automatically.

With the limited amount of availability in my hands, I turn on my phone to guide myself through the room until I enter a new one.

I leave my luggage to the side of the room, smiling as I make out the figure on the bed. Huma's fast asleep on *my* side of the bed with a soft look on her face. I want to wake her so badly just so I have an excuse for seeing that adorable reaction she gives me when I come home from work.

This time around it's the longest I've been gone. I haven't seen her in a full two weeks; fourteen days of pure torture without being able to hold her close to me.

I quickly change into a t-shirt and sweatpants before climbing into bed next to her. She shifts as I try to soundlessly get beneath the covers.

"Ellie?"

"Ssh, go back to sleep." I whisper softly, moving swiftly to lie next to her.

I see her faintly smile through the darkness, slowly waking up as she fits herself into my arms. I kiss her cheek, pulling her closer into my chest and soaking in the feeling of being this close to her again.

"You weren't supposed to come until tomorrow," she whispers, her quiet voice a mix of worry and excitement. "Is everything okay?"

I chuckle, pressing my lips against the top of her head as I close my eyes, "Yes, My Star. Everything's okay."

There's a long moment of silence as we adjust to each other. My heart is still racing from the moment I entered this house to the second I heard Huma's voice.

It's been an entire month since my mother has passed away, and I've been visiting her grave every week. I've been coping well with her passing, though it sometimes hits me that I wasn't there for when she found out about her illness.

I regret it deeply, but it must be like this for a reason.

"Ellie?"

"Yes, my sweet star?"

"Are you hungry?"

I look at her as I feel her shift. Her eyes are on me, though the darkness makes it hard to tell.

"If you're about to get out of bed, then my answer is no."

I hear her laugh softly, "What time is it?"

I grab my phone from the side table, a hand on her lower back as I do. It's pretty late into the night when I catch sight of the time; 4:30 to be exact.

"It's almost five," I go back to holding her close with a content sigh.

She breaks our hold on each other, sitting up and stretching, "Perfect. Fajr is in an hour so we might as well stay up and eat, hm?"

I smile with pure satisfaction, agreeing to her proposal.

She heads to the kitchen before me as I lie in bed for a moment longer.

It's nice to not feel so alone anymore. Having Huma here and knowing I can be vulnerable with her makes me feel a little lighter on my feet. She has become both a protector of mine and the one I protect.

As I finally go into the living room, Huma's humming softly as she sets the coffee table with breakfast menu items. There are two cups of chai, halwa puri, and the sound of the air fryer lets me know there's more.

"I'm gonna go brush my teeth," Huma kisses the top of my head before leaving for the bathroom. "Start without me."

When she leaves, I open my luggage to pull out the *'just because'* gift I got her. It's a box of chocolates and another special surprise that I'm sure she'll be thrilled to see.

My heart brightens thinking about the way she'll react when she opens this envelope.

I place both the gifts behind me on the couch as I set the luggage back on its wheels, and wait for her to return.

I decide to set the scene a bit as I grab the blanket and bring it to the couch. In the kitchen are four vanilla-scented candles that I light and place onto the coffee table. I dim the light of the living room just enough so she can navigate back and hopefully straight into my arms. On the TV, I turn on a movie that we both have probably watched a billion times together just as I hear the bathroom door open.

"Ellie, could you check on the..." Her voice fades off.

I watch as her eyes scan the area in which I stand; the candles, the blanket, *everything.*

"Happy three-month anniversary, My Star," I hold out the chocolates and envelope with a new tranquility to my voice.

She walks over, drying her hands with her shirt. There's a beautiful smile on her face as a blush forms on her already rosy cheeks.

"You didn't have to do this, sweetheart."

"Oh please, and let you forget we got married three months

ago today?" I tease, planting my lips against her cheek. "Never, gorgeous."

Her gaze on me becomes one of excitement as she takes the envelope from my hand first. She peeks inside, her jaw dropping when she realizes what it is. I can already see the tears forming in her eyes while she pulls out the two pieces of paper.

She covers her face, starting to cry.

I chuckle, pulling her close into my chest, "You truly are the most emotional person I have ever met."

The plane tickets to Madinah have fallen onto the couch.

She sniffles, wiping her tears as she looks up at me. I stroke my thumb on her cheek, amused.

"You have the exact habits of our prophet," she says, her eyes glimmering.

"Do I? Didn't notice."

With a soft laugh, she places the tickets back into the envelope and onto the table before making me fall backwards onto the couch with a hug. I chuckle, cuddling her close.

"My pretty star," I stroke her hair. "I'm gonna make you the happiest woman on this earth."

Acknowledgements

First things first, I would like to apologize for how terribly worded this thank you note is going to be, but I have no clue how to put into words how grateful I am to everyone that has only been nothing but supportive to me. And so I want to start by thanking my parents. My mom and my dad who have been so sweet and didn't even stop me for a second from writing a book. They have really been an asset to my writing. I love them so much for their overall need to just be there for me instead of being critical. I will never not need them in my life.

I would also like to thank the guy that gave me this idea in the first place. Yes, I switched up a lot of the story because I could only wish these things would happen (crying right now), but he made this story possible. Nonetheless, he would probably think I'm an idiot for writing this (and I would agree in a heartbeat), but he helped in ways I could not ever be able to explain. He showed me Islam through a different lens. One that made me understand every aspect and every angle of this beautiful religion. I understood things I used to wonder about a lot. And I'm happy my questions have been answered. So, thank you.

My followers. My followers are the sweetest and the kindest people ever. I really do not know where I would be without them. They have shown and added so much to this book. They have made key decisions and helped me through tough moments without even knowing it. This book is dedicated to them. I really, truly appreciate these people.

My editor, Saf. Girl, you already know how much I love you. She not only has crazy editing skills, but has also helped my book become what it is now. She's provided such a huge amount of love and encouragement whenever she was going through it.

And last, but my favourite, my best friend. She is just amazing. Just absolutely amazing. She has been my number one freaking fan and I love her so much for how she is. She's helped me with the plot, listened to my annoyingly stupid complaints, and all in all, provided a great amount of support. I doubt I would even know half of what I know right now if it wasn't for her...heck, I didn't even know what a draft was until she brought it up.

But thank you to all of you that have been rooting for me. It means more than anything that I was able to publish this book and make connections with other people through my own experiences.

sz.laiba <3

9 781738 302543